Rise

Of the

Fallen

*For the readers who read book one and came back for
more. You're the best!*

The Silver Castle
High Stone
The Black Wood
Lord Thribil Estate
LUSTRAYA
IMERIA
Trading Outpost
Sapphire City
Dani Manor
Sapphire Isle

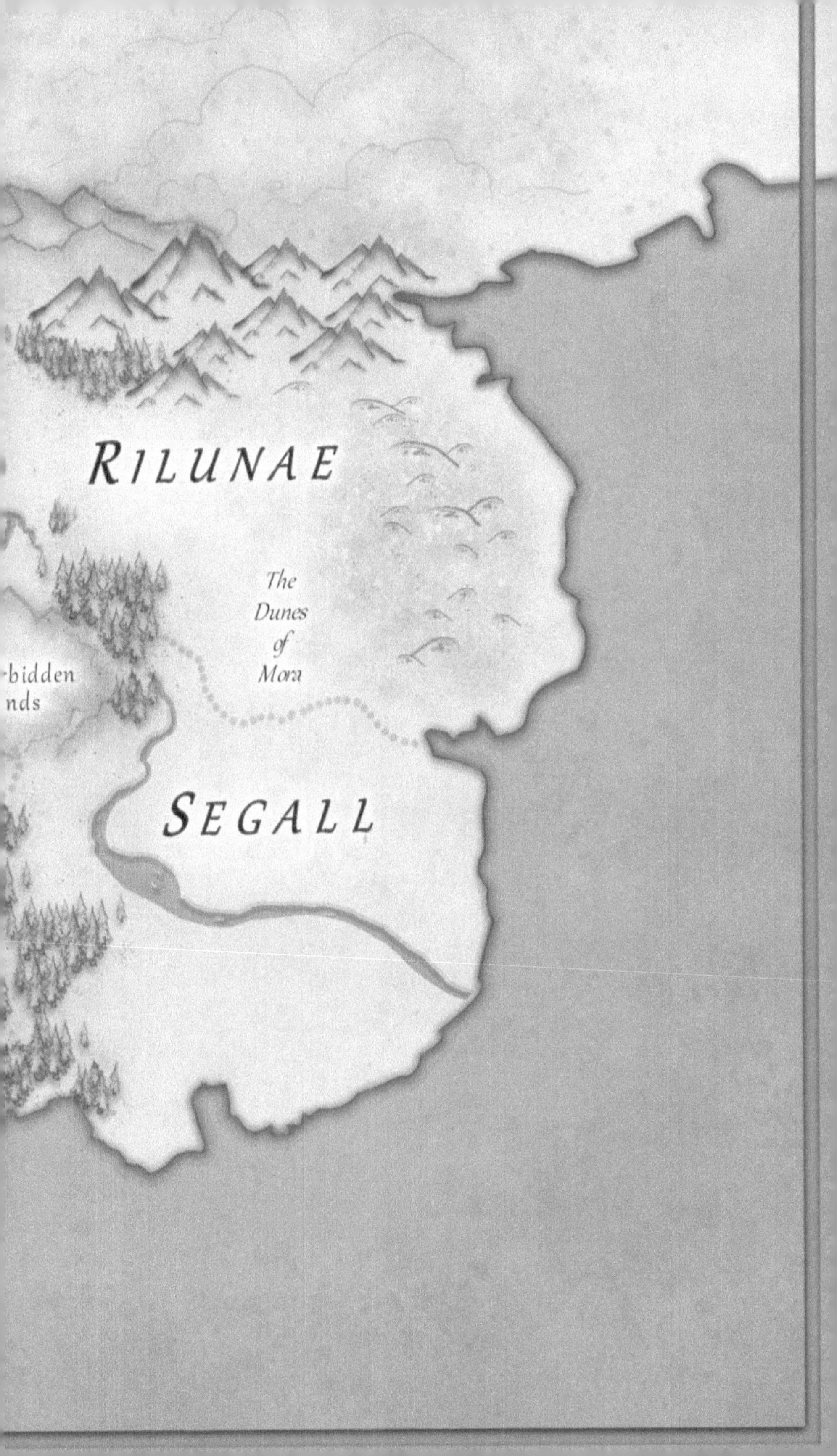

RILUNAE
The
Dunes
of
Mora
bidden
nds
SEGALL

CONTENTS

Rise
of the
Fallen

Book II

LAUREN AGUIAR

Prologue

Damien

"It's time," the whispery voice of the Oracle said.

"It can't be," I replied sternly. "She has only just arrived."

"Your enemy waits no longer. They intend to strike and strike hard. You have no choice but to make her ready now."

I looked at the woman next to me, her half-shaved head reflecting the cool glow of the green and blue flame in front of us.

"What do you suggest we do?" she asked.

Her faith in the Oracle was unwavering, something that made me uneasy. She trusted him too much. It was a relationship I let grow under the circumstances, but once it had run its course, I would terminate it as fast as it started.

"She is going to want to do something to feel needed. She is not the type of person to sit by and let others do the work. Give her something. Feed into this sense of duty and honor she has."

I squinted my eyes into the flame, knowing that the person behind it could feel my uncertainty.

I had never married, never fathered a child. The woman next to me was as close to a daughter as I had been able to have in my less than happy existence. I lived for my kingdom and my kingdom only. Whatever I had to do to protect it, I would.

But the new princess that slept in the room just a few levels above us challenged this feeling in me.

The night I had gone to claim Princess Arabella per the addendum in the Kingdom Accords, I felt the air shift the moment I was over the Imerian border. I felt this pull grow from the pit of my being and felt it grow stronger as we closed in on the palace.

Clara was throwing her lavish party to celebrate her lavish competition between her best soldiers. Based off the reports from the Oracle, it was a blood bath, and everything Clara needed to see, for the winners were now at her personal disposal. Her own cabal of assassins.

To hear of such life and potential being wasted made my skin crawl. Lustraya was in dire need of soldiers of that caliber, and she pitted them against one another for sport, instead of sending them to me as the aid I had been begging her for nearly two years. She had to know I would come eventually; that I meant every word I had ever written her.

I was not the type of man that looked at someone as young and hopeful as Arabella and immediately thought to marry her. On the contrary, she was much too young for me. But a daughter raised by the scheming Clara and merciless Raddison was someone I could use at my side. The young princess may present as a lighthearted soul, but deep down, I knew she could rage a war as cruel and vindictive as anyone else in our history.

That's what I was prepared to take when another option was presented to me that night.

Clad in a black ball gown, her hair wild from fighting, and blood spattered across her neck; Clara's ward. I had heard rumors about her over the years. Knew she was not well liked in Imeria because she was not born of its soil yet reaped its benefits. The Oracle had informed me that she was one of the greatest soldiers he had ever laid his eyes on. She was sharp, disciplined, and angry. Angry at a world that didn't seem fair. And when she held that sword to my throat, proclaiming to take her sister's place, I knew that this was what the Fates had planned.

So, I accepted. I took her in place of Arabella because she was the true strength and might Lustraya would need to pull themselves out of the deep, dark hole we lived in.

But the woman I had taken the night of the ball and the one who lived upstairs now were two different people. She was more melancholy and tight-lipped than I knew her to be. She retained her anger like it was second nature, but there was something very different about her now. And for some reason, I wanted to protect her from the horrors that pervaded my kingdom.

I wanted to make sure she stayed safe and blindfolded, that she never know the true scope of what persisted in these borders. Our enemy was cruel and unyielding, and the thought of her being caught up in that fray made me sick to my stomach.

I know she hated me. Hated her new life. But I did what had to be done. Maybe now Clara would see the true fear and desperation I felt and would send people to help us. If she did that, I would give her adopted daughter back, but until that day, Daniella was the best bargaining chip I had in my pocket.

"We can't risk it," I finally spoke. "The threat is too great."

"Your Majesty," the Oracle argued. "She is your last hope. If you do not use her and her skill set, more lives will be lost until the only thing remaining of this once mighty kingdom is this mountain and the few that remain."

"If she dies, there is no future for Lustraya ever."

A harsh truth. I intended to die on the battlefield as my fathers and mothers had done before me. I had no intention to marry, but every intention to leave my kingdom in the hands of the most capable people I could.

"Your Majesty," the woman next to me said hesitantly. "I believe the Oracle is right in this matter. I know you want to protect this girl, but if what you two have told me about her is true, then we have to take the chance."

I had known the woman since she was a child. She was as equally strongheaded and determined as Daniella was, and if there was anyone I could trust to keep an eye out and protect Lustraya's newest weapon, it would be her.

"If I agree to this," I said, crossing my arms against my chest, the fight leaving my voice. "Then she will need someone by her side to show her the way."

"Of course," she replied readily. "Gunnar and Kristian—"

"No." I raised my hand to stop her. "You, Poppi. You will be the one to guide her."

"What?" she asked incredulously.

The Oracle hummed his approval.

"This seems a wise course of action," he agreed. "I sense something in her that is similar to you, Poppi. You could offer her great guidance through all this. And if she starts presenting, she will need you."

Poppi remained wordless and wide-eyed.

"This is for the good of Lustraya," I reminded her.

This snapped her focus back to the real mission and she acknowledged me with a curt head nod.

"Then it is settled," I said to them both, dropping my arms. "Daniella will be gradually entered into this court. Start small and work your way up."

"And what if she doesn't want to start small," Poppi interjected. "She is already giving Gunnar and Kristian enough trouble as it is. Now with her handmaid off to the Fort, she is becoming even more insufferable."

"Her loyalty to those she deems worthy is astonishing," the Oracle commented. "Maybe she sees something in the girl that reminds her of herself."

"Either way," I pressed on. "She is to be given more. I don't care how it happens, just as long as she is safe and introduced to . . . her potential, when the time is right."

The last part was meant more for the man that lay beyond the blue flame. He watched her carefully while he was in Imeria. He now watches the ones she left behind even closer.

"Yes, Your Majesty," they both agreed.

"Oracle," I said. "You may go."

The flame sparked high for just a second and then extinguished itself to embers. Poppi looked at it for a moment before turning to me, her shoulders slumped and fatigue weighing heavy in her eyes.

"I want you at the Fort tomorrow," I told her. "The new recruits are going to need all the help they can get." She nodded in agreement.

Recruits. If we could even call them that. But I was left with no other options. Villages were being ransacked and burned with a fierce determination by our enemy. I had no choice but to mobilize every healthy body I could. This batch of recruits would be lucky to survive one of those raids.

"You can go," I finally said, dismissing the woman with sadness weighing heavy on my chest. She left with a quick bow and on silent feet, the click of the door being opened and closed echoing through the air. When I was sure I was alone, I sat down in my chair and let a lone tear fall down my face. The war's ugly head was rearing its final blow, and I couldn't help but think that if Dani didn't come into who she was supposed to be, then we were all doomed.

1

ON SHAKY GROUND

Y
ou know, you should smile more."

The ultimate words to get under any woman's skin. I turned my stare from the window to the haughty male seated in front of me. Long gone was his finery from the disastrous ball and in its place were black pants, and a white and blue tunic and vest. An otherwise very understated wardrobe for a King, if I didn't recognize the silk from the southlands and riding boots from the east.

"I will smile when I have reason to," I hissed back at the man I promised my life to. The thought still made my stomach swirl the more

I thought about it. It swirled even harder when I replayed Aeddan's looks of anguish in my head. The agony he showed, my heart breaking second by second . . .it was too much to comprehend. Five days on the road have done nothing to erase the pain of what could have been.

Emphasis on 'could have been' because let's face it; we were doomed from the start. A tale of would-be lovers forced to face a reality that was as subtle as an arrow notched in a bow.

I turn my head away from the King once more and out to the rolling hills that were now leading into the foothills of the mountains. The sun is high in the afternoon sky, displaying the radiance of the river we ride past. Snow covers the ground, and I huddle further into the fur lined cloak I have been given.

While Damien had enough clothes for himself, I was still in the same black dress from the ball. A once stunning piece of art, now ruined and tattered because I had nothing else to change into while we rode back into Lustraya.

I wanted—no, needed—a bath and a pair of pants so that I might actually be able to sleep warmly.

"How much longer do we have?" I asked, not hiding the ire in my tone.

"We should be there sometime tomorrow morning," he replied nonchalantly. "We'll make camp a final time just before we reach the forest line."

Great. Camp again. More like a lumpy bed roll next to a fire that did nothing to cut out the growing cold that ensued the further we traveled north. In all my life, I swear I had never been so cold. And that was saying something because I traveled a lot, especially in my early life.

"You're more than welcome to sleep in the tent," Damien offered for the twentieth time.

"Yes, but you sleep in there." I countered.

The proximity to my captor was even more unappealing than the cold, hard ground that awaited me come nightfall. I was a seasoned warrior. I could handle one more night on the ground, even with this damn dress.

"Suit yourself," he replied, reading through a stack of messages. "But you would be a lot warmer if you did."

I didn't respond, instead turning to watch as the river disappeared and the tree canopy above us began to grow thicker the further along we moved. Not for the first time since I left, I wondered what Ary was doing. What Aeddan, Maddox, and Harrison were doing. Their absence left a gaping hole in my chest, right next to the one from my mother.

As much as I wanted to feel pity for myself and my circumstance, I couldn't. I couldn't make the tears form, nor the anger that usually would be behind them. Instead, I felt numb in acceptance. This was my life now. And no matter what, I had chosen it, and I would have to bear the burden of it.

I snuggled further into the cloak around my shoulders. The soft, white fur was my only comfort to the sad thoughts dancing in my head. Damien eyed me suspiciously but let our silence continue. It wasn't until the carriage halted and a set of knuckles rapt on the door that either of us broke the quiet between us.

"After you," Damien offered, gesturing with a hand to the door.

I nodded solemnly at him, stepping out into the crisp winter air. All around us, soldiers scrambled to unpack their horses and made camp as quickly as they could. Multiple heads were bent down as fires began to spring up, their heat essential against the chill. I felt Damien's presence just behind me, his broad figure one I was hardly able to miss.

"Daniella," he said. "I can already tell you are a stubborn woman, but I implore you to please refrain from sleeping out in the cold. The tent is big enough for us both and I can assure you, you will have privacy in it, if that is what you need."

I turned my head to stare up into his grey eyes. I knew his offer was sincere, that he would give me the privacy I needed, but I couldn't do it. I didn't know what it was, but something in me refused to allow such a comfort. Was it self-inflicted punishment? Or was it the fact that I knew if I accepted his offer, my looming status as future Queen to Lustraya was sealed?

"No. But thank you," I replied, pulling the cloak closer to my body and walking away from the King. As I had done every time we made camp, I sought out the spot closest to the outskirts of everyone. I remained in sight for those who were assigned as my guards but rejected their help when it came to making my own fire and setting up myself for the night.

I ate alone, the crackling of the small fire in front of me the only company I kept until it was time for me to hunker into my meager blankets and go to sleep.

I awoke the next morning to my muscles violently shaking and my teeth chattering against each other painfully. I blinked a few times, noticing that there was something clinging to my lashes. Snowflakes. If I had the ability to move my body faster than a trudge, I would have. But since I couldn't, I slowly drug my body into a sitting position, noticing a thin slush covering the ground.

"Princess Daniella," a soldier said, coming into view. "The King requests you in his tent. Immediately."

"D-Dani," I chided through frozen lips. "It's Dani and t-t-tell His Majesty that I will join him when I can f-f-feel my toes again."

Swiftly and without warning, I was swept up into a pair of arms and off the ground.

"Who the hell do you think—"

"Apologies, Your Highness, but the King mentioned you would be reluctant and gave clear orders for me to carry you in if I had to."

I did not argue with the man, mostly because I could not muster the energy to do so. I was frozen to my core. So instead, I grunted my disapproval and let the man carry me across the encampment and into the large white tent.

Instantly, I felt the warmth of a large fire lick against my cheeks. A small whimper escaped my lips at its decadence, the soldier still holding me smiling because he knew his King had won this battle. He dropped me onto a couch in front of the fire, disappearing as Damien walked around a partition and into the main space.

"Here," he said gruffly. "You look like you need this."

He reached out a mug, the top of it steaming as it was placed into my cold hands. I sniffed it carefully, noticing notes of chamomile and something . . . other.

"It's not poisoned," Damien clarified as he snapped his fingers toward another soldier. "It's firewater and tea. It'll wake you up and keep you warm." To the soldier he said, "Please fetch Princess Daniella a new cloak and a blanket. We will need to leave here shortly."

"Dani," I ground out. "My name is Dani."

"Fine. Dani." Damien sat down across from me, crossing an ankle over his knee as he looked me over. "Though, you need to get used to your new title. While admirable what you did for your sister, you now must fill her shoes. Princess is part of that agreement, whether you like it or not."

All things I knew, and all things I thought I had begun to come to terms with on this journey, but evidently not. I brought the tea to my lips and sipped carefully, not wanting to burn my tongue. The concoction was sweet with a bite and did just as Damien hoped it would. The burn of the firewater left a trail of warmth after it as it hit my stomach.

Just as I was about to take another sip, the soldier returned with a new cloak and blanket.

"Thank y-you," I said as I exchanged my cold and soggy cloak for the new and warm one in his hands. He nodded once to me, disappearing out the tent moments later. Damien sat watching me the whole time. I could see the gears behind his eyes spinning along as he studied me.

"When we get to Lustraya," he began. "The people will want to welcome their new princess with open arms. I expect you to do this willingly and cheerfully."

"How else would I do it?" I asked, sipping at my tea again.

"Without the snark, for starters." He stood from his spot, giving me a pointed look. "Lustraya has faced more adversity than I care to admit these last few years. With your arrival, there will be reason for them to celebrate again. To be distracted. No matter what you feel, I expect you to put on the happy, shining face of a princess who is excited to meet her new people."

Of course he did. He wasn't the one who was expected to upend his entire life for some stupid agreement that may or may not actually exist. But I did know this; whatever it was that was threatening Lustraya was also a threat to Imeria. And Clara would do anything to protect her people.

"Your wish is my command," I said, draining the rest of the tea and standing. "Should we be on our way then? I'm sure you want to greet *our* people before sundown."

The word felt like sand against my tongue, foreign and wrong. Damien took note of the inflection I put on it, huffing out his annoyance as he followed me back out into the cold. He nodded to one of the soldiers standing guard and immediately a team of them descended out of nowhere to begin disassembling everything to get ready for the journey ahead.

Damien walked me to the carriage, his hand light against my back as he guided me through the slush and frost of the morning. Any evidence that a traveling band of soldiers had been here was gone. Small flurries descended to the ground, their tracks covering ours up. The door to the carriage swung open, the inside offering very little warmth in the face of the frozen morning.

I climbed in as quickly as I could, pulling at the new and dry cloak around my shoulders. Damien watched every movement I made as he climbed in after. A short moment later, the carriage jolted forward, and we were on our way.

My new life was beginning at last.

2

A GILDED CAGE

Based off all the stories I had read or heard about the other kingdoms, Lustraya always seemed to be the worst of them. Tales of a shiny castle that was always surrounded by unseasonably cold weather and shrouded by the mountains; it was also known as the one of the most ill-tempered towns across the realm. It was once the pinnacle of Taelle. It was because of these stories that I expected the absolute worst when our road forked and began curving around one of the smaller foothills.

The trees had begun to lose their green hues, cloaking the landscape in nothing but a white and grey blanket.

How I longed for the blue of the Sapphire Isle water, or the smell of citrus and flowers in the gardens.

Home. I missed home.

Damien watched me from his spot on his bench, his eyes taking quiet notes on everything I did. His head cocked to the side slightly as I felt a quiver cross my chin.

"Are you crying?" he asked, almost surprised.

I tried my best to force down the wave of emotion that had suddenly sprung up in my chest as I turned from the window to face him directly.

"No."

Damien scoffed but let the topic drop as the carriage began to descend further down the road. He peered out his own window, muttering under his breath as he did.

"Shouldn't be long now. We're about to pass through the gates," he said.

I nodded once, quickly wiping the lone tear that had escaped my eye.

"When we—" I began to say but stopped to clear the crack in my voice. "When we arrive, I would like to be shown to my quarters. As quickly as possible."

Damien turned his gaze to mine, an eyebrow lifting lightly at the corner.

"Please," I added to be polite.

He chuckled, wiping a hand down his face. "Of course."

Damien went back to that calculating silence I was beginning to learn was normal for him. I noticed it the first time we made camp during this journey. He watched and studied every man and woman under his command like they were each a piece of a puzzle. Damien watched me with the same fervor, sometimes more.

I could tell he thought I was strange—at least for an Imerian princess. I shied away from the pomp and circumstance of our court. I took comfort in getting dirty and sweaty, the physicality of working hard the solution to my problems. Most problems, anyway.

When he invaded Imeria, I'm sure he thought he was getting the perfect, demur princess that was Arabella. Someone who would fight battles with her words and a stroke of her pen. A princess who was adequately equipped to run a kingdom. Damien has already pointed out my penchant for being stubborn. I wonder how much else he realized he was foregoing in getting me as a bride instead of Ary.

Not for the first time over the last six days, I found myself wondering just what my sister and my friends were doing, and how it would compare to my new life.

One step forward . . . six back.

This was not the life change I expected, but I tried to look at it in the lens my mother would—a new adventure. The carriage jostled as the wheels left the dirt road and switched onto stone. Voices carried around us as someone gave the command to lift the gates and let us through. Anticipation for what was going to come began to build in my chest. The feeling like when the waves swept me under during the first trial and I struggled to breathe. But just like then, I knew the anxiety would pass and soon this day would be over. All I had to do was take each day one at a time.

I inhaled deeply, holding the breath for three heartbeats before releasing it. I repeated this three more times till I felt my nerves settle and my mind calm. Damien watched me through the whole process. Never once taking his eyes away from me, not even when the carriage came to its final stop and the door was torn open.

"After you," he said, gesturing to the cold outside waiting for me. I smiled half-heartedly, gathering up the skirts of my dress and cloak, and stepping out onto the white stones.

Everything I had thought I'd known about Lustraya emptied out of my mind the moment I laid eyes on the exterior of the castle. White and grey marbling and stone stretched into tall towers and spires. Large oak exterior doors sat in the middle of the stone; their arms open for the King's arrival.

Damien came up next to me, noticing the look of amazement as I took in my surroundings.

"Not what you were expecting, was it?" he asked.

I was rendered speechless, so I just nodded in response because in truth . . . this was the furthest thing I had ever thought Lustraya would look like. I had expected a half-standing castle and battlements, dirty streets and beggars. Damien had hinted that Lustraya had been having its fair share in strife in the past years. If that statement were true and this was Lustraya when it was bad, then I could only imagine what it was like when things were good.

I felt a large hand make contact with my lower back, jolting me from my thoughts as I was guided to the front steps. Lining the entry way were a dozen attendants dressed in a white and icy-blue uniform. I gave a brief nod and smile to those who I made eye contact with as I passed, the castle quickly swallowing us in its embrace.

The inside matched the exterior; large glass windows adorned the uppermost portions of the tall walls. White marble flooring spanned as far as the eye could see, white rugs scattered over them. It should feel cold and empty due to the lack of color, but somehow, I felt anything but; the plush softness offering a light comfort. I clenched my jaw in irritation that I could find anything about this place remotely comfortable.

I could feel my resolve waning as I was ushered further into the castle. Introductions to the head of staff were made and pleasantries were exchanged with the King, but I paid none of it any mind. My eyes devoured everything as we navigated the hallways and moved up the stairways.

My breath left my chest when one corridor opened out onto a breezeway of marble, the bright light from the sun glinting off its smooth surface.

"Oh wow," I whispered, utterly taken aback by how beautiful the sight was. "This is . . ."

"I know," Damien said, stopping just ahead of me and turning. "It's one of the only remaining pieces from the original castle."

"Original?"

"Lustraya has had to rebuild and adapt over the decades. But this . . . this is our one piece of connection to our ancestors."

I walked to where Damien stood admiring the view. From here I could see the parts of the castle that were left in ruin, parts that were in repair, and the part that led to where we were going—into the mountain side.

"Come," Damien instructed. "There is more to see."

I nodded, letting Damien and the staff we walked with lead the way to the rounded door that led into the mountain side. Two guards clad in silver armor and blue-and-white capes opened the doors with a creak and a groan. The doors, much like everything in Lustraya, were tall and large, dwarfing everything around us.

The marble of the breezeway transferred to smooth, hard rock. The chill, dry breeze from outside replaced by damp and humid air.

"Where are we going?" I asked after a while, the silence between our group stretching on for too long.

"Your rooms. Just as you asked," Damien replied.

"In the mountain?"

"Yes."

"But there is a whole castle right behind us. Why am I being shoved into the crevices of a giant rock?"

"Because that is where your rooms are."

"Yes, but why?"

"You ask a lot of questions. Did you know that?"

"You give a lot of vague answers. Did you know that?" I threw back in a mocking tone, my eyebrow quirking up for effect.

Petulant and almost childlike; I know. But there was a whole castle—a beautiful one at that, even if parts of it were in ruin—and I get sent to the dark depths of a damn mountain? Ridiculous. Especially without a proper explanation.

Our path curved further into the mountain till it opened to a large cavern, a gentle waterfall flowing right through the middle of it. It reminded me of spring back in Imeria, just on a much, much larger scale. The collection of rock wall stretched a hundred feet into the air, a large opening at the top letting in the daylight and illuminating what I gathered was the central hub to the mountain.

The path continued to curve in a spiral around the central fall, other paths branching out from it like a main highway. Damien and his attendants veered left from the main path, taking us down an arched hallway illuminated in translucent blue-and-green light.

"What are these?" I asked, unable to hide my curiosity as I reached out a hand to touch the blue bubble attached to the top of a torch. My hand recoiled quickly as it made contact with the jelly-like substance.

"It's a bioluminescent alga we've recreated to help light the walkways and rooms of the mountain," Damien responded proudly.

"Why not just use fire?"

Damien chuckled, the sound reverberating off the rock as we took a right turn into another hallway.

"We live in compact quarters down here," he replied. "Inhaling all that smoke day in and out would begin to affect you after some time. Not to mention the soot clings to everything and makes a mess. I don't have enough people to dedicate to round the clock hallway cleanings like Imeria does."

Okay, uncalled for.

"So why build into the mountain side anyway if you don't want to maintain what you've built?"

Damien's footfalls came to a halt in front of another set of doors. He turned around to face me; his expression riddled with annoyance at my incessant questioning.

"I liked you better when you were sulking."

I kept my face composed, but anger boiled up inside me at his arrogance. I stared at him with contempt, keeping my mouth shut instead of snapping back at him like I knew he was beginning to expect from me. Good, let him know I wasn't happy about this arrangement and would never be.

The doors to our right were pulled open and Damien gestured with a large hand to the room that awaited beyond.

"Your rooms, Princess."

I scoffed at the title but nonetheless shuffled forward into the room that was to be my new place of refuge.

"Dinner is at six. I will send an attendant to help you get ready and escort you to the dining hall when the time comes."

"And until then?"

"Sleep. Bathe. Read. Whatever you wish to do, but you are not permitted to leave this room."

My nostrils flared, my eyebrows getting lost to my hair line as I spun back around to look at Damien's smug expression as the doors closed behind me. I doubled back quickly, tugging aggressively on the door handles to no avail. With a sharp click, I heard the lock latch into place, sealing me in.

"You can't just lock me in here, you bastard!" I shouted, pounding my fists against the doors viciously.

This was too far, too much. I smashed my fist against the door again, this time following it with a swift kick of my foot. I repeated the motion again. And again. And again, till the tears began to flow ceaselessly down my cheeks and a repressed sob ripped its way up my throat.

Despair and hopelessness smashed its way through me as I crumbled to the floor, my hands sliding down the wood of the door till they met the stone beneath me. I was a prisoner in my own life and as the realization sunk in, I began to cry harder and harder.

All the tears I refused to shed the moment I stepped foot into Damien's carriage unleashed themselves in a fury. I cried for my sister and for the friends I left behind. I cried for the love that slipped between my fingers. I cried for my mother, because this felt exactly as it did when I found out she was never coming back all those years ago. I cried even harder for myself, for the little girl that was still so clearly hurt and angered at the world that refused to give her a break.

I don't know how long I sat on that floor, my knees curled beneath me and my face against the cold stone, but it was long enough for my tears to run dry and my body to ache like I had been out in the forest for training drills for weeks. When I could stomach the floor no longer, I moved my body into an upright position slowly, turning to press my back against the wood and taking in my surroundings through puffy eyes.

Before me was a sprawling, crescent shaped room, the floors and walls a light grey stone littered with rugs and sheer curtains billowing against a breeze. A large four-poster wooden bed with white bedding sat off to my left; a small cobalt couch and chairs sat around a fireplace to my right.

I audibly groaned as I shifted to my knees and then my feet, my body swaying with the effort it took to right myself again. Without hesitation, I unclasped the pin holding my cloak in place and let it fall to the ground. My shoes were next to follow, the pair falling against the floor with a clatter.

Aimlessly, I wandered further into the room, losing my socks next, my fingers coming up behind me to begin unfastening the laces of my dress. Now that I was left alone and no one else was around, the stench that was me hit full force. I needed to bathe immediately before I began to wilt any of the plants that were crawling their way around the outside balcony.

The laces were undone by the time I found my bathing chamber on the backside of the crescent room. As much as I didn't want to admit it, I loved the space already. It was enormous, much like the sunken bathtub at the back of the bathing suite. The water flowed over the edge and into the void below, steam billowing off its surface still. The green-and-blue tiles reflected against the surface, sending rays of lights bouncing around.

All other thoughts emptied from my head as I let the dress slip from my body in a quiet whisper. A shiver ran down my spine as my skin was left bare to the open air. I made my way over to the pool, gingerly placing my toes against the water to test it. It was blessedly warm, and I sunk my foot down onto the first step all too eagerly.

Slowly, I eased my aching body into the pool until the water reached my neck, and eventually fully submerged, a moan escaping my lips as the warm water flowed around me. After the hell that was traveling in a cramped carriage and sleeping on frozen ground, this was paradise.

I dunked my head under the water, needing to feel the heat against every inch of my body. When I resurfaced, I paddled to the edge that ran along the balcony side.

"This is unreal," I whispered in disbelief as I looked out to the view.

The room faced the outside of a mountain; the rock wall covered in plants and pine trees as it sloped down into a valley that ran below the exterior castle. It was unlike anything I had seen before. Soon, the mountain would be fully covered in snow, and all the liveliness of this place would be gone.

A knock echoed through the chamber; no doubt it was probably the attendant Damien said he would send me. My stomach rolled at the thought of the King. At the thought that he physically *locked* me into this room, despite its interior being comfortable enough that I didn't want to leave. The knocking echoed once more before I heard the doors being swept open.

Footfalls replaced the knocking echoes as a young woman rounded the corner into my bathing chamber. She had a round face and pale skin, her hair a cascade of white and black.

"Princess," she said with a soft voice. "My name is Nic. I have been sent to be your personal attendant. Whatever you need, I am at your disposal."

"I don't need an attendant," I ground out, turning away from the ledge and to look at the girl.

"Yes, miss," she replied but remained rooted to the spot, her hands clasped in front of her.

I waited a moment, then two before asking her, "Is there something I can do for you, Nic?"

"No, miss. I am here for you."

"I just said I don't need an attendant. I am a grown woman and am perfectly capable of bathing and dressing myself."

"I understand, miss, but the King has requested I stay with you and escort you to dinner. If you'd like, I can wait in the other room."

My irritation flared as I realized that this girl, Nic, was no more than a glorified babysitter sent to check on my every move.

Of. Fucking. Course.

"Very well, then," I relented. "Can you please hand me the vials in which I can clean myself, then?"

Nic nodded once, moving over to the far side of the room where a tray of multicolored glass bottles were kept. She lifted it, bringing it to the edge of the pool where it would be within my reach.

"Thank you," I said.

"The blue is for cleansing the hair. The green for softening. The rest is for cleaning the body."

I reached for the large blue bottle, dumping an obscene amount of the potion into my palms, and began the task of scrubbing my hair clean. The moment I felt the lather on my locks, I could feel the tension begin to leave my body. To be clean was such a gift I had taken for granted over the last six days.

"*. . . rolling around in wet mud is not my ideal form of training. I do have some standards.*"

That's what Aeddan had said to me all those weeks ago, and a pang of hurt struck me as I thought of him. What I would give to just see him one more time. To tell him I was sorry and that this sacrifice was going to be worth it.

I dunked my head under the water once more, ridding myself of the potion's lather and my sad thoughts. When I resurfaced, I continued cleaning myself, taking my time with each step.

Nic watched on from the far wall the entire time. While I was used to being doted on by attendants, or being given limited privacy because of the military, Nic looked about as comfortable as someone wearing shoes two sizes too small.

"Nic," I said, moving onto the softening potion. "If you'd like, I am going to need a robe and some clothes to wear. You can pick them out for me instead of standing awkwardly against that wall."

"Right away, miss," she said, dipping her chin down before disappearing behind a set of doors along the back wall.

I smiled to myself, glad for the few more moments of privacy I was being given. I continued my time in the pool leisurely, not wanting to leave the warmth of the waters just yet. Not even when Nic reappeared from the doors with a pile of clothing and moved into the main sleeping room.

Time was catching up to me now and I knew I had to make a decision about how I wanted the rest of this day to go. So it was with reluctance that I left the bathing chamber and meandered over to where Nic left a plush robe waiting for me on a chair.

I slipped my arms into the sleeves and tied the chords around my waist tightly. Not the silk of Imeria I was used to, but I liked this one all the same. Nic stood near the balcony, waiting for me.

"I picked out two different variations of clothing for you to wear this evening. Either one would please the King and be suitable for this evening," she commented.

I looked to where she had the two outfits splayed out on the bed for me to review. One was a simple light pink, wool dress completed with white fur trim and gold embroidering. The other was a white version with grey accents instead of gold.

I recoiled away from the white, my stomach doing flips at the thought of being put into that color so soon. The pending engagement was something I did not want to recognize right now. As I stared at my options, I felt the walls around me begin to close in and I knew in that moment what I must do in order for me to breathe.

"Nic," I asked, looking from the bed to the woman who stood eerily still.

"Yes, miss," she replied.

"Is it just to be the King and I for dinner, or will there be others in attendance?"

"Just you and the King, miss."

As I suspected and hoped. The next words out of my mouth came all too happily.

"Then please inform His Majesty that while I thank him for the hospitality, I will not be joining him this evening. I will take my food in here." I watched the surprise ripple across Nic's face as she processed what I was telling her.

"Miss, I don't think His—"

"I wasn't asking, Nic. I am telling. Now if you would." I gestured to the doors that led back out to the hall. "I'm sure His Majesty is keenly waiting on your update."

I was being harsh and a bitch; I knew that. Nic was not the source of my frustration but unfortunately for her in this situation, she was representing it. As I watched her knock on the door to be let out and it quickly be closed and locked once more, I decided that if I was going to be locked in a gilded cage, I was going to do it my way. And that started today.

3

GET IN LINE

My first day as future queen to Lustraya came and went as easily as the tides changed. Nic brought my dinner to me soundlessly and I ate it all with nothing but the brushing of the curtains against the floors to keep me company. It was at that moment that I wished I had a book to occupy my thoughts. Maybe today I could convince someone to bring one to me. Or better yet, I be allowed to go get one myself. But I wasn't going to hold my breath on that one.

I was still laid up in the soft, white sheets and fur blankets of my bed when a familiar knock sounded and Nic was let in, a breakfast cart in tow.

"Good morning, Your Highness," she announced with a small curtsey. I groaned at the formality.

I sat up straight, tucking the blankets around my hips and fluffing the pillows as Nic began bustling about setting up my breakfast.

"Nic," I said as she handed me a cup with a dark brown liquid in it. "I can prepare my own food, you know."

She ignored me, instead continuing her shuffling about to make up my plate.

"Nic," I said again. "Please. I can do this."

"Yes, miss. If you insist."

When I thought I had won one battle, she laid a tray on my lap with a plate of assorted foods. I frowned as I watched her back away and come to stand at the foot of my bed.

"I have a message from His Majesty," she said. "He would like you to know that you will be accompanying him on a tour of the grounds today followed by a luncheon with his council. I have been given firm instructions to help you dress and escort you to him. You . . ." Her eyes dropped to the floor briefly before looking back to me, almost like she didn't want to say what she had to next. "You are not allowed to say no. And if you do so refuse, then the King has given the two guards outside permission to use force to see these instructions fulfilled."

I narrowed my eyes at Nic, at her message. Damien was a prick. A righteous one at that. Clearly, my refusal to have dinner with him angered him more than I expected and he was ready to take that anger out. He was a King to be obeyed by any means necessary.

"And did Damien have anything else to say?" I asked.

"No, miss. That was all."

"Right then," I said, bringing the cup in my hands to my lips and sipping its contents. The liquid was bitter and earthy, but at least it was warm. I reached for the fork on my plate, digging into the food I was given before that turned cold as well. Nic moved about the room, cleaning up the piles of clothes I had made.

"When you are finished," she said. "We will begin the process of getting you ready for the day. I will be in the other part of the room to give you some privacy." She turned without another word, disappearing around the bend of the room. I swallowed the bite that was in my mouth, knowing all too well that today was going to be a test of my patience and my sanity.

An hour later, I stood before a mirror in my dressing room as Nic finished securing the last of the small braids she had made in my hair to the crown of my head. She has me dressed in the white dress laid out for me for dinner last night. My stomach churned at the symbol it created, what today meant for everyone's future.

I was a soon-to-be bride, a prize from the King's conquest. This was also his message to me that I would obey and fall into line with his plans. And if not, he would have his way of making me.

"All finished," Nic announced as she stepped back and allowed me to look at myself in the mirror.

"Let's get this over with then," I ground out.

I stepped down from the stool I was on and followed Nic to the doors of my room. She rapt on them twice to signal the guards we were ready to leave, and a moment later, we were walking through the blue-and-green hallways of the mountain stronghold.

I counted our steps, counted the turns and the curves of where we walked till the hallway opened into the large spiraling cavern. It was quiet, for all intents and purposes. Only a few people milling about the walkways as I was guided down and around to the floor below the one where I stayed.

Nic walked behind the two guards from outside my doors, her back ramrod straight and hair a curtain of silk against her white robes. If it weren't for the two guards that had materialized behind me, I could slip them. But this was another one of Damien's messages: he has eyes everywhere and they report to him.

So, it was with great disdain that I followed them through another dark hallway that merged into another large, rounded room; the sounds of shuffling feet and the grinding of door hinges greeting us as we passed through and in the doors that awaited us.

Damien sat poised on a large throne at the back of the hall. The piece was chiseled from white marble, blue veins rippling throughout it and onto the floor below. He was relaxed, adorned in a dark brown-and-grey wool ensemble. There were two additional guards behind him, but that was it. He was in his element, a predator dominating over his prey.

If I was anyone but myself, I would cower. I would let the fear bubble to the surface and spill over. I would let the effects of hopelessness begin to take root while I rolled over and played perfect princess.

But I was me. I was Daniella Castielle—an orphan who became one of Imeria's most deadly warriors. And I would be a victim in my life no longer.

Our party came to a halt at the bottom of the dais where Damien waited. I squared my shoulders back and lifted my chin lightly as Nic cleared her throat to speak.

"Your Majesty," she spoke. "May I present her Highness, Princess Daniella."

Nic dropped her head and curtsied before stepping to the side to let Damien take me in. He grazed a finger back and forth along his lips, his eyes trailing me head to toe in a not-so-subtle inspection.

"Thank you, Nic," he said to the girl kindly. "You may go."

She left without another word, and I remained still in my quiet defiance.

"How did you sleep?" Damien asked.

"As good as any other night," I responded tersely.

Damien chuckled. "As any other night . . . like sleeping on frozen ground in a tattered cloak is any better than a warm bed and blankets?"

"At least it was my choice."

Damien's eyes narrowed, his hand dropping from his face to grab the side of his chair. He pushed off it slowly, standing and shoving his shoulders back to stand at his full height. He took the stairs down slowly. With each step, his boots echoed, the sound piercing through me each time like a nail through stone.

He stopped with only a foot of space between us, and I could feel the anger simmering off him as he stared into my eyes.

"I was hoping a real meal and comfortable accommodations would lessen the stubbornness and sass from you. But I can see it is just as alive and well today as it was on the road."

"If you think you are the only one who has had an issue with my personality, you should get in line. It will not be changing anytime soon."

He paused. "We'll see about that."

It was his tone that had my stomach plummeting into the depths of my being. He didn't raise his voice or speak in anger. No, he was much too calm for such a bold statement. Damien wasn't threatening me or scolding me—he was promising. And that promise held more weight than I cared to admit because I knew it was one he could keep.

"Before our day begins, Daniella, I wanted to remind you of a few things." He stepped back from me, starting a slow circle as I stared straight ahead. Prey and predator. "Your obvious disdain for this arrangement has been noted, but I expect your full cooperation as this new venture begins. As future Queen of Lustraya, you will be a symbol of hope to these people that the bad days are behind us.

"You will be polite. You will shake hands and smile with those you meet. You will talk about how excited you are, how fortunate it is that you could be a part of this kingdom. By default, you are now an extension of me, and my people need to be led by someone strong. I will not have you sulking and pouting about just because you couldn't get your way." He stopped in front of me again as the last of his words pierced through my ego.

"This is the only time I will ask you nicely. I am not an inherently cruel man, but I will exercise my might if I must."

I looked past him and to the throne that sat above us. It glinted in the small shafts of light that came in through the tops of the ceiling. One throne for one ruler. Damien has mentioned several times how I am the soon-to-be Queen of this kingdom. The single throne stood as a reminder that I wouldn't ever be his equal.

My eyes roved back to his, his expression patient, yet annoyed with my lack of response.

"Am I allowed to speak?" I asked as casually as possible, but the sarcasm that followed was too natural.

Damien's left hand twitched at his side, the only indication that I was now truly pissing him off. Was he really the type of man that hit a woman when he was upset? I didn't want to believe it, if only because something like that had never happened to me before, but I locked the information away anyhow.

"Yes," he spoke slowly. "You may speak."

"Then I understand."

Damien puffed out a breath and ground his teeth. With a turn of his back, he waved for the guards in the room to form position around us. For the first time in a very long time, I felt helpless.

"The repairs are coming along as best we can, Your Majesty. There were some issues with transport. A rockslide and . . ." A casual yet pointed glance to me. "Blockages. We had to alter our route, but it will only extend the completion by a day or two."

I poked at my plate, taking note of how the man next to Damien was pointedly toeing around subjects I was not allowed to hear about.

"Thank you, Callen," Damien said as he cleared the last of his lunch from his plate. "If you can get that report to my desk by morning, I can look into sending you extra hands to help."

"Thank you, Your Majesty," Callen replied with a lift of his glass.

For what it was worth, I didn't think it was Callen's fault he had to tiptoe around conversation topics. In the hour we have spent at this lunch table, I could gather that he was a calm-minded and intelligent man. If I had to guess, he was an adviser or high-ranking official in Lustraya's forces. His clothes were well-pressed and tailored in the Lustrayan icy blue. His silver hair hung long and silky like he took care to keep it so.

I wanted to ask him this, to know more about the person with whom Damien clearly trusted, but one glare from the King had me leveled to submission. Instead, I was to field the two women of our party of eight. They took an immediate interest in me and my journey here, something I was not too keen on talking about, yet alone making a pleasant tale.

"You must have been so scared," the woman to my right said.

"I know I would have been," the second echoed.

I sipped at my water glass—no wine. Another tragedy, as I fought the urge to roll my eyes at them.

"On the contrary," I said as politely as I could. "I've faced such conditions many times in my life. It was just an average day for me."

"But you were raised inside the Imerian palace, were you not? I doubt Clara Demontier would make camping a family past time," the second woman laughed.

"Actually, I—"

"Spent a lot of time tending the gardens of the palace," Damien chimed in from down the table. "Or reading. Daniella is fond of a happy story. Isn't that right, Princess?"

Damien leveled me a look that dared me to argue with him. I clenched my jaw tightly, a half-smile stretching across my mouth as I fought against the urge to correct him.

No, I actually am used to the elements because I am one of the best warriors in all of Imeria's history. I can gut a man just as swiftly as I can notch an arrow and release it. Clara doesn't like camping, no, but she allowed me the ability to choose my own path. I can't say the same for our King here.

"That is correct," I responded simply.

"How wonderful it is that you know your bride so well already, Your Majesty," the first woman crooned. "Why, if only my husband paid attention to me like that, we may have had more heirs."

The table erupted into laughter at the woman's remark. But it seemed only Damien and I understood how sad the statement she made really was, as neither of us laughed at all.

As I sipped my glass once more, I wondered how Damien did know such small details about me. Or was he just assuming correctly for the sake of building up my image to his people?

Our people, I quickly reminded myself. This was my new home, and these were to be my subjects too. No matter how much I wished I could run away from it.

With the most impeccable timing ever, a servant entered the veranda we sat in and bent down to whisper something in Damien's ear. He nodded and thanked the man flatly before he looked to Callen and the three other men that accompanied him.

"Apologies ladies, but we must be off now," he said standing.

Thank the gods. The rest of the table stood as well and just as I made to move from my spot, Damien cut the motion with a wave of his hand.

"Daniella, dear, why don't you let Mrs. Hapsborg and Mrs. Fallon accompany you on the rest of your tour? They make wonderful company."

He smiled sweetly to me; an action I know wasn't forced because of the daggers I threw at him the moment the words left his mouth. He was winning the battle of today and he knew it. Just as I'm sure he knew I would rather face the Gauntlet again than be accompanied by these simpering women for the rest of the afternoon.

"A wonderful idea, Your Majesty," I responded just as sweet.

The men left without another word; leaving me, the two women, and four guards to carry on.

By the time the sun reached the horizon, my body was aching to be off my feet. We had toured every inch of the main cavern. I smiled and carried on conversation as I was shown the different shops that lined the main pathway through the inner city. I shook hands with dozens of citizens, introduced myself and played the part of excited princess.

We walked what seemed like miles as I was shown to the inner villages and homes carved into the mountain, the hot springs where people went to bathe and wash their clothes, and the schools where there were children playing and studying.

Mrs. Fallon and Mrs. Hapsborg prattled on, their need to fill silence with mindless chatter a quiet blessing as I only had to pipe in a few words of conversation to keep them happy. They meant well, and if I were half the princess Ary was, I'm sure I would have appreciated their company more than I did. But alas, I was not my sister, no matter how many times I tried to emulate her during the tour or during conversation.

"Well," Mrs. Fallon said, stopping at the end of our pathway. "This is the end, I guess. We have shown you everything Avalla has to offer."

"Avalla?" I asked curiously.

Mrs. Hapsborg piped in, "Avalla. The Hidden City. That's what we call this place."

That's when it clicked. The castle outside, the way it was half in ruin and half inhabited. The way the architecture sprawled and connected in arches and bridges. It was intentional. For whatever reason, it was all for show and the real thing remained encased in this mountain.

I bid the two women a goodnight and followed the guards appointed to me back to my rooms. As much as I had tried memorizing paths and exits today, the city sloped and curved too much for me to fully grasp its layout. Yet. But I would get there.

When we finally made it to my doors, I felt the tiniest glimmer of relief flow through me. Finally, I could strip myself of the white clothing and relax in the bathing pool—its hot water courtesy of the natural hot springs that ran through the mountain. The doors closed behind me and just as I kicked off the first boot I noticed Nic standing in front of the balcony, still as stone.

"Shit," I exclaimed as I saw her for the first time. "Nic! Don't stand there like a statue and scare me half to death. Are you insane?"

If it was an overreaction on my part, I didn't care. I was tired of being watched every second of every day.

"My apologies, Your Highness. I did not mean to startle you."

"Don't call me that," I snapped, tossing the second boot by the first. The coolness of the floor soaked into my feet, sending a shiver up my spine.

"Yes, miss." She paused, her eyes following me as I made a break for the bathing chamber of the room. I could feel those eyes burning into my back with the might of seven fires. It was with reluctance I turned and faced her again.

"Forgive me," I said. "It has been a long day, and I am tired. Was there something you needed from me?"

For a second, I watched Nic's serene face drop, a hint of sympathy shining in her eyes before it was smoothed over again. I felt a pit form in my stomach.

"The King sends me to dress and escort you to dinner. I'm afraid we don't have enough time to bathe you fully, just enough to change your clothes and be on our way."

I mentally punched the wall with agitation at the thought of having to share another meal with that condescending, controlling man.

"And did His Majesty say who would be in attendance this evening?"

Again, though I knew they meant well, I could not stomach entertaining those women again for a whole evening. I'd rather eat rocks.

"It will be just the two of you, miss."

"Right," I said, turning my back and walking around the bend to the bath. "You can tell the King I'll take my meal in here then."

I shed my wool ensemble to the floor, the cool air blowing in tickling my bare skin as I walked over to the steps of the pool. Modesty be damned.

"Miss," Nic pleaded as she followed in my stead. "The King was not happy you snubbed him last night. I do not recommend doing it two nights in a row."

I dunked my head under the surface, feeling at peace for just a moment before my head resurfaced. Nic watched on from near the entryway, fear and concern etched across her features.

"Nic, I wasn't asking for permission. If you must give a reason to Damien, then say I wasn't feeling well or that I went to bed early. I do not care. But I will not be leaving this room, and I ask for my dinner to be brought to me. Please."

She nodded once and disappeared, leaving me in the quiet of the chamber. Peace at last.

4

ALONE

I had never been one to like the cold. Mostly because I had lived much of my life near the ocean. The salty brine and citrus of the coast was as familiar to me as my own hand. It felt a part of me, and me it. But as I stared out onto the mountain side, a thin layer of snow beginning to stick to the ground, I felt a cloak of familiarity drape itself over my shoulders.

The sight was something to behold and a thing of its own beauty. There was a stillness in the nature that made me want to slow down and just . . . exist. And as I sipped at the bitter brown liquid in my cup—coffee, Nic had told me—I felt my contempt at my prison ebb ever so slightly.

Ten days. That is how long I had been in Lustraya already and secluded in this damned room. Nic was right when she said Damien would not take kindly to me rejecting his dinner again. The morning after I was greeted to a breakfast cart and nothing else. Every meal for the last five days had been brought in by Nic, and she left without a single word.

I had no books, no music, nothing. It was just me, this open landscape, and my thoughts. At first it was nice; not having to be worried about being monitored or having to engage in pointless conversation was a breath of relief. To quell the boredom, I came up with a training routine I could implement in the morning and afternoon to keep up my strength and agility. It took up two hours of my day usually and once that was over, well, I did this—sat on the balcony and watched as the days past.

I was beginning to grow agitated. I wanted—no, needed—out of this room, but the locked doors and guards outside them told me that would not be happening. At dinner, Nic would offer to help me dress and escort me to the dining room to join Damien, and each night I refused. I knew the game he was playing. Each refusal that I gave added one more day of isolation. He wanted to break me into submission, which was something I was not going to give him the satisfaction of doing. I was isolated, sure, but I could remedy that. And it was precisely that thought that had me standing from my chair the moment I heard the door swing open and Nic entered like she did every night.

"Nic," I greeted her a bit too brightly as I walked back into the room where my bed stayed.

"Your Highness," she responded warily.

"I would like you to escort me to the dining room. I think I will take His Majesty up on his offer this evening."

Nic's shoulders slumped in relief, a small smile spreading on her lips as she responded, "Of course, miss."

She rapt twice on the door, the guards opening them and following us happily into the hallway and to the dining room. We veered right down the path that forked instead of left, something I made sure to note.

I was brimming with anticipation as we moved into another natural cavern of the mountain, this one smaller and more intimate than the others.

Damien waited for me at the head of the table made for six but set for two. A wrought iron chandelier was hung above it, the blue-and-green light source strung up in bulbs along it. The effect made me feel like I was under water.

"Look who decided to join me," Damien drawled, his lips pulling up in a smug smile, his eyes twinkling with victory.

Nic and the guards peeled away to their posts, leaving me exposed to the open room and Damien's attention.

"Under one condition," I stated as I squared my shoulders, thinking of the conditions that came to me last night. The only reason I would entertain coming to dinner this evening.

Damien leaned back in his chair, threading his fingers together and placing them on the back of his head, his smugness faltering as he took in my words.

"This should be good."

I inhaled deeply through my nose, raising my chin with courage before saying, "I want to write to my sister."

Silence. Cold and deafening silence.

"And I want to see the library," I tacked on last minute.

The smug satisfaction from earlier drained from Damien as he mulled over my demands, his jaw twitching as he clenched his teeth in hard thought.

"I shall have a writing desk sent up to your rooms in the morning. You can write to your heart's content tomorrow."

"And the library?"

"Out of the question."

"Then you eat alone," I spat and turned away from him, ready to walk out.

I made it all of two steps when two guards blocked the exit with the cross of their two spears, effectively cutting off my plan.

"You cannot keep me caged here like some common animal!" I roared as I turned back around and marched to where the King still sat at the table. Without thought, I swept my hand out and across the table, sending his dinnerware flying around the room. He was on his feet in a heartbeat; his hands balled at his sides like he was readying himself for a fight.

"I can do what I please," he growled, getting close to my face, his left hand lifting to point a finger between my eyes. "I told you I would have you behave by any means necessary. You have no one to blame for your isolation except yourself."

"I have done everything you asked," I bellowed, my hands flailing at my sides as my anger rose. "I have met your council, I have toured the city. I've met the people and shook their hands. I have played along with your bullshit story about how our arrangement came to be. All I ask is to write a letter to my sister, and I want a damned book!"

He narrowed his gaze and pulled back to analyze me, dropping his finger from my face; it flexed in irritation at his side. "I said no, Princess. And that's that."

And that's when I lost it. There was only one person who could get away with calling me that and he was beyond my reach now.

"I am not a princess! I am a fucking Captain!"

The slap that ripped its way across my cheek, reverberated throughout the cavern, enough so that even the guard's spine stiffened. I raised a hand to cup the right side of my face, a lone tear spilling out and down to the rock floor beneath me as I kept my head down.

He hit me. He . . . he hit me.

I righted myself slowly. The shock, adrenaline, and anger stanching the pain I know I would feel later. Damien's chest was rising and falling heavily, his eyes wide with shock at what he had just done.

"Daniella, I—" he stumbled out, moving to grab me, but I hurried backward on shaky steps before he could.

"Don't touch me," I whispered in shock. "Don't you ever fucking touch me again or so help me, I will kill you." The guards didn't like that statement, and neither did Damien. All of who's backs straightened as the tension in the room grew to near suffocation. "You will have your dinner," I continued. "But that is the last thing you will ever get from me."

Before he could respond, a messenger came flying up the pathway and into the cavern, a letter with a yellow seal pressed in his hands, as the doors creaked on their hinges. He and Damien exchanged quick words before the messenger was off and running again.

Damien's shoulders slumped forward, his left hand coming to rest atop the back of one of the chairs, his right sliding down his face.

"Looks like you get your wish tonight, Daniella. You can have your supper brought to you in your rooms or stay here if you'd like. The choice is yours, but there's a matter I must attend to and it's of great emergency."

He walked out, leaving me alone with Nic and my two guards. They watched me with worried expression and sympathy, none of them saying a word in case I exploded again. I straightened back up and schooled my face into as neutral an expression as I could, the pain beginning to prick the surface of my skin.

"Let's go," I demanded in a hushed tone. Nic was at my side immediately, following the guards and me back to my cell in silence. I counted each of my steps as we closed the distance, each number an effort to keep my mind occupied and me from unraveling at the seams before I had privacy.

Nic watched me from the corners of her eyes the entire walk, her concern obvious which only made the situation worse for me. I hated to be pitied. When the doors to my room were opened, I walked through and to my awaiting bed. The ties to the dress I had picked out loosened swiftly and the fabric fell to the floor. I kicked the shoes into the crevices of the room, and I climbed between the furs in nothing but my undergarments.

"Miss," Nic asked from behind me. "Would you like me to bring your dinner to you?"

"Don't bother," I mumbled. "I'm not hungry."

"As you wish, miss."

I heard the door close as I cried silently, "Dani. My name is Dani."

I was used to being battered and bruised by other humans. But when it happened, it was usually under the context of training, or me being able to defend myself. As I stared at my face in the bathing room mirror, I realized that I had never been attacked quite like I had last night.

There was a cut across my cheek bone and black-and-blue bruising sprouting underneath my eye. After Nic left last night, I allowed myself a moment for the silent tears to fall before I rolled over and fell asleep. When I woke this morning, it was to Nic shaking me awake, a breakfast tray set at the foot of my bed.

"The King would like to see you this morning before he rides out," she told me gently.

That was an hour ago; now she rakes her hands through my long brown waves, twisting and pinning them away from my face. I'm dressed in an emerald green long sleeve dress, the color an attempt to pull attention away from my face. When she offered to smear cosmetics over the area, I declined. I wanted him to see what he had done. For everyone to see it. And I wanted him to feel the shame of it.

I told myself last night that I would not get angry. Nor would I make a fuss over the situation. When his court inevitably asks what happened to me, I will turn and stare at him with trepidation and make him feel as small as he made me feel in the dining room last night.

"Okay, miss," Nic said, smoothing my hair over my shoulder. "You are ready."

I grabbed her hand, looking at her through the mirror's reflection. "Nic," I said, letting my eyes soften as she looked back at me. "Please . . . call me Dani. At least within these walls. We both know I am no actual princess. So, let's drop the formality."

"As you wish . . . Dani."

I smiled to her softly in gratitude, to which she returned. I stood from the vanity and followed Nic out of the doors and to wherever it was Damien resided in this mountain city. As we walked, my steps lightened ever so slightly. Finally, there would be at least one person who would let me be who I was. It was a small win.

Our party ventured up a steep slope of stairs, winding us into a new section of the mountain that I knew was far off the central pathways of the city. The blue-and-green lights were sparse in this area, and I found myself tripping over the hem of my dress one too many times. And if that wasn't enough, I was brought to a halt by smacking against one of the guards who had stopped ahead of me. He ran his hand on the rock above us, blue-and-green bioluminescence illuminating the doorway and its sigils ingrained in the rock. He tapped the center sigil thrice, the door jumping out from the stone so it could be moved to the side, and we could enter.

Damien sat at a plain desk littered in paper and ink. His one wall was a floor to ceiling bookshelf stuffed to the brim with old texts, some even finding home in stacks along the rung before it. He had his head bent over a long scroll, his back silhouetted against a solid wall of glass.

"Your Majesty," one of the guards spoke, bowing and stepping aside so Nic and I could be shown. "Princess Daniella and her attendant are here to see you."

"Thank you, Gunnar. You and Kristian can wait outside. You as well, Nic."

The three of them bowed once more to the King, walking back out into the dark of the corridor. I stood rooted to my spot, my hands clasped in front of me. I would not curtsey. I would not speak. I would, however, stand here in uncomfortable silence for as long as possible if it meant proving a point to Damien.

He set his paper down with a heavy sigh, rubbing his palms into his eyes before looking at me. I watched as a glimmer of emotion passed through them and disappeared just as quickly. With the amount of light that was streaming in through the window, it would be hard to miss the damage that was my face.

Damien stood carefully from his desk, his eyes never leaving mine as he rounded it and came to stand in front of me. He began to reach a hand up to inspect his work, but I took a lofty step back before he could make contact. His hand dropped back to his side.

"Daniella . . ." he began. "Last night . . . last night was inexcusable. I cannot begin to explain how incredibly and deeply sorry I am for hurting you in the way I did."

My heart began to beat rapidly in my chest as the memory resurfaced, and a wave of shame stirred in me. Tears pricked at my eyes as I fought to restrain the words and feelings I had toward him about what transpired the night before.

"I know it will never right the wrong that has been done, but I have instructed your guards to grant you leave to walk around the city. And access to the library."

"And my letter?" I asked in a shaky voice.

"A writing desk is being set up in your room at this very moment. Write as many letters as you wish."

I nodded my head in thanks but said nothing more. When Damien realized he would be getting no conversation from me, he went back to his desk and rolled up the scrolls he had been reading when we entered.

"Something has come up along our mountain borders," he said. "I will be leading a scout team out there. I should be gone for two days. Maybe three." Begrudgingly, my curiosity piqued. What happened in the mountains?

"And I take it that that is all I am allowed to know?"

He sighed heavily again. "Until you are officially Lustraya's Queen, it is all I'm allowed to offer."

"Allowed?" I asked. "You're the King. Is it not you who gets to decide what I can be told and what I cannot?"

"That is true. And I know Clara exercises that authority, but when it comes to this kingdom, I have a council. And my council . . . well, we operate differently than the others. For now, until they can be absolutely sure of your allegiance to Lustraya, they would prefer certain information remain guarded until the time is right."

"And what about you?" I asked because I couldn't contain myself. "Are you sure of my allegiance?"

He paused, weighing my words and their accusation. "No," he admitted. "But I do know one thing."

"And what is that?"

"You're loyal to a fault, and I don't know if that is a good or bad thing because does that loyalty still lie with Imeria or does it now live in our bargain?"

I stalked over to the desk, resting my hands on the edge as I leaned into the King.

"I gave you my word the night I left with you. I thought that I had proven it just the same the last two weeks," I offered as evidence that I was a woman of my words.

"Perhaps," he mused. "Or perhaps your loyalty to your sister outranks any other loyalty you have. Any soldier who is willing to step forth and aim a blade to a King's throat, proclaiming the words 'over my dead body' earns some respect in my book, but no less caution. You won't turn your back on this bargain because then that would put your sister in jeopardy, but it cannot also mean you wouldn't seek to warn those you love what you have learned here. And that is the last thing we need."

"Are you threatening me?" I asked incredulously as he said the most honest words since I had been here.

"No," he breathed. "I'm merely explaining the why."

He moved away from the desk, walking toward the door, his cape making a hissing noise against the stone floor. He stopped only once to turn over his shoulder and say to me, "I meant what I said earlier. You are free to explore in my absence and to write your letters. But should you try and take advantage of this kindness and hospitality, well . . . I would hate to become a man who took back his word once it was given."

He left without another word, the door letting in a draft as his footsteps echoed away.

Damien was a bastard alright. An insidious, fucking bastard.

5

PAINFUL REMINDERS

All I wanted to do was be angry. I wanted to plot and plan my escape from this hell, but that would only prove Damien's point further. But that anger fizzled to an ember as Nic brought me into another large cavern of the mountain fortress. This time, one that housed the library.

Stacks and stacks of bookshelves lined the rock floor, built-in's circling around the perimeter overflowing with different spines. A large chandelier hung down the middle of the room, illuminating everything in the blue-and-green light I was becoming accustomed to.

"Oh wow," I whispered in awe.

"I know, right?" Nic concurred next to me. She smiled brightly as she looked around the space, the action lighting up her features and making her look younger than I thought she was. "There's five levels to this place," she continued. "Each dedicated to an era of Lustrayan history. For those, you have to be granted access." She pointed to the top three floors. "But down here," she motioned with a hand to the ground level shelves. "Anyone can come and grab a book for learning or enjoyment."

"Anyone?"

"Anyone."

Not that Imeria didn't have her fair share of libraries, but they were either in the palace or a part of the universities. The public had to purchase their own or get special permission to borrow from the kingdom.

"So, where shall we begin?" Nic asked, turning toward me.

"You're going to stay?" I asked skeptically.

Nic looked behind us to where the guards—Gunnar and Kristian, as I've come to learn their names—stood at the entrance.

"I should not be saying this," Nic whispered as she walked us forward to the awaiting shelves. "But . . . How do I say it? The King has been under immense stress the last year. It has almost completely transformed him from his former self. He is the most gracious King Lustraya has had, and we all serve him loyally and faithfully. With that being said, last night was a shock to all of us. I have never in my years of service seen him lash out like that. It rocked us all." She glanced at me with sympathy in her eyes. "I think the King feels exceptionally terrible for what he did to you and is wanting to atone for it. And since he's gone for the next few days, I think I can get away with giving you some company. That is, if you wish that."

We stopped in front of a shelf, the books whispering for me to pick them up and look inside. I reached out a hand, letting my fingers trail along their spines in curiosity.

"I think I would like that," I responded, feeling nothing but gratitude toward the woman next to me. I may have wanted to isolate myself from Damien as much as I could, but I wasn't naive enough to know that I would be absolutely miserable here without someone to lean on.

Nic squeezed my free hand gently. "Besides," she said, moving us along again. "My brother works down here. Should anyone want to question why the future Queen's attendant is with her so frequently, I can say I am visiting him."

"You have a brother?"

"I do! He's a scholar and archivist for the kingdom, and one of my favorite people in the world."

The way she talked about her brother is how I talked about Ary, with nothing but love and admiration.

"He's lucky to have a sister like you," I complimented.

"Indeed, I am," came a joyful voice from the shadows of the shelves.

Nic pivoted quickly, turning to the aisle of where the voice came from. She chuckled under her breath while crossing her arms across her chest.

"Leave it to you to appear the second your name is mentioned," she teased as a tall, dark-skinned man stepped into view.

"Only when I'm in such fine company," he replied, showing off his white teeth behind a blinding smile. "Treysen Kemp, my lady." He reached out his hand for me, but it was quickly swiped away by his sister.

"Brother," she said tersely. "May I present to you Princess Daniella of Imeria, our King's fiancé and future Queen of Lustraya." Bile rose in my throat as Nic introduced me by my titles with formality. It took every ounce of training I had to keep my face from showing my disgust with the arrangement.

Treysen's eyes went wide, his face slackening as he realized his misstep.

"Your Highness, please forgive me. I had no idea—"

"Please," I demanded, reaching out the grasp his hand in mine. "I take no offense. The title is just as new to me as it is to you."

Treysen's shoulders relaxed as he registered the sincerity in my words. He nodded once, looking to his sister.

"A warning next time would be great, sister," he declared.

"How was I supposed to know you would be here on the day you're technically supposed to be taking a rest?"

He narrowed his eyes as Nic smiled in triumph. I laughed at their exchange, a pang of sadness cresting my heart as I thought of Ary and how their bickering once mimicked ours.

"Well, it's wonderful to meet you, Treysen," I said. "Nic here was just going to show me around the library. I've been without proper reading material for too long."

"Well, that's a tragedy if I have ever heard one. Let's remedy that, shall we?"

They set off, arguing over which department to show me first. Should we go by era in history or genre? Perhaps giving me a tour of the place first would help. Their back and forth was incessant, but in the best way. I could tell that the duo was close.

In the end, they agreed that a tour would be best first. We kept to the first two levels only, the remaining three staying off limits, even to me.

"I apologize, Your Highness," Treysen said as we concluded the tour and went about actually finding me some reading material. "Even us archivists have to have permission to enter those levels."

"And why is that?" I asked curiously. "As an archivist and scholar, shouldn't you be able to have access to as much information as possible?"

"Well, yes. We're granted access by the Grand Master if need be. But . . ."

The siblings looked at each other once and that's when it dawned on me.

"It's a Damien rule, isn't it? He's given the order that it be off limits to me. And to others."

"In all fairness, Your Highness, they are his books. They date as far back as before the creation of the first kingdoms. The fact that he even allows us to get permission to read them is a generosity not many can have."

The first kingdoms he says . . . now, that is interesting. I remember catching a short chapter in the book I borrowed from Clara about that part of history, but the details of it remained vague. And the book remained lost. If Clara hid hers, I wonder what Damien's collection had to offer.

"Well," I said. "Let's not dwell on it then. Can you show me to the history section I am allowed to be shown?"

Treysen nodded eagerly as we set off on the second floor and down the fifth row of stacked shelves. He reached for three books in particular for me: *Lustraya: A Brief History*, *The Life & Death of Lyria the Wise,* and *The Royal Families of Lustraya.*

"Best to get your feet warm. *A Brief History* will hit the high points from our inception till now. Lyria the Wise was King Edgar's most trusted adviser during the Second Wars. Her battle strategy is some of the best I've ever studied. Then, The Royal Families . . . well . . . because best know the people you're marrying into, I guess."

Nic pinched her brother's arm fiercely, glaring at him like she would throw him over the mountain top.

"Thank you," I laughed lightly, cradling the books in my arm. "I suppose you're right on the family part."

I would be throwing that book into the depths of my cell once I got back to it. While Treysen had given me an excellent selection, I preferred not to acknowledge the family I was marrying into quite yet. That reality would be for a later time.

"What else would you like to see?" Nic asked me to change the subject.

I thought about it a moment. Now that I had the freedom to mill about, what did I want to see? It felt like I had seen everything available, willingly or not. What more could I see? And then a thought occurred.

"I've seen most of what I can about this inner city," I said. "But if I could, I would really enjoy a broader tour of the castle."

Nic smiled broadly. "Of course, Your Highness. I know just the places to show you."

We met Gunnar and Kristian at the doors, but not before handing my newly acquired books off to an attendant, who would see they made it to my rooms.

Treysen and Nic filled the silence in our walk with stories of their childhood. Their mother was a maid for a wealthy noble and met Nic's father when she reached her twenty-eighth year.

"It's actually a crazy story once we talk about it," Nic prattled on. "My father was revered—supposedly—and designed things as an architect that my mother drew up for him. He just wanted her to be as happy as possible and made it his life's mission. But then the plague came."

I felt her sadness as she talked about the time when an aching sickness sucked the life from Taelle. No healer anywhere on the continent could find its origin or it's cure. It was a nasty sickness that took no mercy.

"When he passed, my mother was devastated," she continued like she had told this story too many times to feel it's weight anymore. "She met Niklaus on a sporadic trip to the many small islands of the Cashian Sea. She told me it was the love that saved her."

Nic's eyes lit up when she spoke of Niklaus, Treyson's own smile mirroring hers.

"They married within months of knowing each other," Treyson filled in. "My father knowing that there was no other woman he could possibly love in his whole lifetime."

"It's true," Nic supplied as we turned down a walkway I did not recognize. "My mother tried to warn him that she was a heartbroken widow with a child, but Niklaus said he would love us both all the same. I was only three years, but the love was felt instantly. And then they had Treyson and our family felt so complete. So right."

"She says that now," Treyson teased, to which I laughed heartily. "But there was a time when she hated me."

"Okay, hate is a strong word," Nic said, pointing a finger at him.

It reminded me of when Ary and I used to get into our petty squabbles, one of us always trying to prove the other wrong. We began ascending a small flight of stairs.

"Anyway," Treyson continued, swatting his sister's hand away. "I threw myself into studies, and Nic over here, threw herself into anything and everything she could to piss our parents off."

"Wrong!"

" . . . In order to make a name for herself. Me? I just wanted to be like our dad and be an archivist. I love knowing things, no matter how obscure."

Nic huffed out a breath, punching Treyson lightly in the shoulder.

"I wanted to open my own shop," she said in defense against her brother's accusations. "I wanted it to be a place where women from all over could share clothing and ideas and just . . . be. I have never liked the fact that this land was so separated by which kingdom they came from and how that affected their identity. Personally, we all benefit from what this land gives us, so why not share? It would have been a great place for a crossroads."

Treyson scoffed lightly, but there was an undertone of mockery to her dream from him.

"It didn't last long though," Nic said solemnly as light began to grow greater and brighter in front of us. "Pretty soon, the village we were living in was attacked and burned to the ground. My dreams of a shop burned with them. I took a position working for the King once we moved from our village to the mountain."

"We left in the night," Treyson quickly cut in. "Threw the smallest of means in bags we could carry on our backs and made haste for the mountain. It was rumored to be a safe haven, but we were taking the chances as a family to find it."

"I know what that's like," I admitted quietly. They looked to me confused so I added, "I had no family when I was left in Imeria. I was told of the family—my family now—that looked over the land but . . . some things you have to see to believe."

Nic and Treyson gave me sad but knowing smiles each as they noted what I meant.

"My sister is not blood related, but I thank the god's everyday she is mine."

"You must miss her," Nic said sympathetically.

I could only nod as the thought of Ary and I cozy in our parlor with stolen cookies played through my mind. "Only every minute of every day."

Soon, we reached the breezeway, its opulence as stunning as it was the first time I saw it. Treysen began to rattle off facts about the architecture and history of it, but it was all noise to me as I breathed in the chill and crisp air. Despite the balcony I was lucky to have outside my room, nothing compared to actually being outside those walls.

I felt the heaviness of the last week begin to melt from my shoulders with each step we took away from the stronghold. Nic looked back to me, noticed how relaxed I'd become and smiled.

"Enjoying the sun, Your Highness?" she asked me playfully.

"You have no idea," I replied.

"Well, just wait till you see what I have in store for you."

We entered the marble castle, the light and airiness of its creation a stark contrast to the dark and eerie one we had just come from. Nic took us down the main staircase, Kristian and Gunnar right on our heels. When we reached the bottom we veered to the left, taking a long hallway that stopped at two large glass doors. Nic flung them open wide, stepping aside so that I could walk through first. Any words I could have said left me as I took in the sight before me.

It was the most spectacular garden I had ever seen and not because it was perfectly manicured like the ones in Imeria. No, this one was wild and stretched all along the mountains base. Swaths of purples, yellows, and golds coated the ground as I followed the stone path further into the gardens waiting arms. When I had reached the middle, I sank to my knees, taking in its beauty.

My chest stirred tightly, and I felt the beginnings of tears well in my eyes.

"How do you like it, Your Highness?" Nic asked timidly from behind me.

I turned my head as the first tear fell silently. Nic and Treysen watched me with concern as the second tear fell.

"I think I should like to write that letter now."

6

HIGH STONE

Ary,

I'm sorry I haven't been able to write sooner. It was a long ride into Lustraya, one that left me sleeping in a ball gown and on the frozen ground. But don't worry, that was my own doing, so you shouldn't be surprised. By the time this letter reaches you, I will have been here over two weeks, and it could not be any more different from home. It's cold and everything is white. My only comforts are the library and a rare garden in the valley of the castle, though it's slowly freezing over. I'm afraid both make me miss you *more each day. I hope you're not too angry with me. I know you most likely don't approve of my choice in this matter, but I need you to understand that I did it for you and Imeria. It's not as bad as you think, and I think I could eventually like it here. I hope to hear from you soon; there is still a wedding to be planned after all.*

With love,

Dani

Nic retrieved my letter the next morning, telling me she would send the fastest rider she could to deliver my message. Her conviction raised my mood for the day, allowing me to finally start to feel at ease with my new circumstances.

I could do this. I could live this life. I didn't have to be cut off from my old life entirely. If I received a reply back, I would write to Maddox and Harrison immediately. And Aeddan . . . I wouldn't even know where to begin when it came to writing a letter to him.

You didn't think I would be worried about you leaving . . .

I guess letters were never my strong suit toward him. Then there was the challenge of putting my thoughts and feelings onto a piece of parchment for him. A simple 'I'm sorry' wasn't going to cut it.

Gods, I had made such a mess.

Luckily, I had Nic for company now. While I couldn't trust her just yet with the details of my life, it was nice to have someone to talk to. The cloud of apprehension that was Damien's presence vanished in his absence. Even Gunnar and Kristian managed to smile at me and greet me with a cheerful hello now, versus their usual stoic faces and quiet demeanors.

As we all were making our way back from one of the shops in the mountain city, a messenger in a black cloak ran up to our party, holding out a scroll to Gunnar. The guard took it hesitantly, reading it quickly and handing it off to Kristian.

"Nic," Gunnar instructed. "Go with this man. No questions. Your Highness, I apologize but we must get you back to your rooms immediately."

"Why?" I asked as Nic looked back at me stricken. "What's happened? Is the King alright?"

"The King is fine, miss. But we must carry out his orders, and right now that is to get you to your rooms."

He took point in front of me while Kristian took the rear. We moved swiftly through the caverns and pathways until I was dumped back into the place I was just starting to get used to not feeling like a cell. How quickly everything can change because of one letter.

"What did the note say?" I asked on a whim before the door was shut.

"I'm afraid I can't answer that, Your Highness. We'll send a servant later with your dinner. Should you need anything else in the meantime, just knock and we'll do our best to accommodate it."

I ground my teeth in frustration. The door closed with a click and once again, I was left all alone in a quiet room, against my will.

That was yesterday and today didn't look any brighter.

I woke this morning with a noticeable shift in the air. It was chillier than normal when my eyes cracked open, the sky outside grey and angry compared to the sunshine we had experienced since my arrival. I threw a log onto the fire first thing.

Nic didn't show up today either. In her stead, was a girl no more than her fourteenth year. She was timid and quiet, and I sent her on her way after she set up my tray. No use in making us both uncomfortable so early in the day. That wasn't the only thing I noticed that was different either. No matter how much I knocked, Kristian and Gunnar ignored me. Enough so that I had no choice but to sit down and attempt to read the books I had been lent.

The afternoon came and went and when my dinner arrived—still no Nic—my impatience grew to anger. No. It grew into rage. Violent and steaming.

How dare they. How dare they *all*. I had held up my end of this bargain, and this is how they were going to treat me? By locking me in a room with pity books and ink? I had every right to know what the hell was going on outside of these walls. It was my life they were messing with, and I refused to not have a part in its outcome. I had worked too long and too hard to forge myself into someone I was proud of; only to have her set aside to play the role of some simpering, damsel of a would-be queen.

As I stared out into the cold night, I let myself plan. Damien said he would be gone two days, maybe three. That would mean his time was up. Which also meant that, tomorrow, I would be putting his promises to the test.

"Gunnar! Kristian! Open this door right this moment!" I shouted as I pounded my fists on the doors like I did my first night here.

I paused just long enough to hear if there was a shuffling of feet, or a hand on the knob of the door. But there was nothing but that persistent silence that permeated the space since yesterday.

I had braced for this, though. My guards were loyal to their King's word, which I could respect, but right now it was a thorn in my side.

"If you do not open this door this very second, I will have no choice but to leave via the balcony, and I'm sure you don't want to have to explain that one to your chain of command."

Silence.

Fine. I prepared for this too. I moved away from the doors and to the couch where I had strung together all the dresses in my wardrobe till it created a chain long enough to reach the mountain side. I tied one end around the marble pillar of the balcony and sent the other end flying over the side. But I had no intention of actually escaping this way. This was just for show.

I grabbed a glass from the tray that was brought this morning and clutched it tightly in my fist as I walked back to the doors, pressing my back to the wall just beside them. I took a deep breath and threw the glass across the room just far enough that it shattered just before the balcony and was clearly audible.

I heard my guards stir on the opposite end, a smile creeping on my face as Kristian burst through the door and stared in horror at my fake escape. I used his moment of panic to slide through the opening he left, coming up behind Gunnar as he guarded the hall to my doors.

I hated what I had to do next, but they left me no choice.

"Gun," Kristian exclaimed. "She actually went out the balcony—"

He stopped mid-sentence as he took in the scene before him, which was me holding my knife from dinner to Gunnar's throat, his sword thrown to the ground.

"You two do remember that I am a highly trained soldier from Imeria, correct?"

Kristian took a step closer, and I dug the knife harder against Gunnar's throat, the skin growing taught under the pressure.

"I wouldn't do that, Kristian," I said, like I was scolding a young child.

He narrowed his eyes at me. "What do you want?"

"What was in the letter?"

I felt Gunnar swallow hard while Kristian blew out a frustrated breath.

"Just that something happened in the White Passage, and we needed to get you back to your rooms. You were not to leave under any means until His Majesty returned."

"And Nic?"

Kristian looked to his friend, the two of them having a silent argument. My impatience grew when the silence stretched on, and my hand began to cramp with the force I was using to keep Gunnar under my control.

"Kristian," I demanded, my grip on Gunnar tightening as my patience thinned. "Look. I really like you both, so it will cause me grief to have to spill blood in this hallway. But I will do it if you don't give me an answer, and I have to go off on my own to figure it out. And believe me, I will figure it out."

I could see the war within my guard break out as he deciphered whether he stood by his King's word or obeyed what his would-be Queen demanded of him in the name of his fellow soldier. It was a decision I was sorry to force on him.

It was Gunnar who finally succumbed to me. "She's been taken to High Stone."

"What's High Stone?"

"It's where we send recruits, where we train. Soldiers not in direct service of the King live there," Kristian said.

"Why did they take Nic?"

"We don't know," he said earnestly as he squirmed against my grip.

Fair enough. I would be pissed if I was in this situation too. I released Gunnar, shoving him gently in the direction of his friend. He gasped for breath, clutching the side of his neck to check for any blood. The two of them looked at me with trepidation as I tossed my dinner knife to their feet, letting them know I was no longer a danger to them.

"Well, then," I said, placing my hands on my hips. "Looks like I know what we're doing today, boys."

The ride to High Stone was worse than the days long trip coming into Lustraya. The cold sliced against my face like shards of glass, despite it being covered with a wool collar. Luckily, the destination wasn't far from the castle and the horses we rode were impervious to the conditions. They rode just as well as any other.

Kristian and Gunnar were on either side of me as we approached a stone structure, its exterior nearly black with age. The entrance in was barred with a metal grate; a watchman standing just outside it. The posts inhabiting the four corners of the fortress had fires lit within, showing me that there were even more guards watching the grounds than anticipated.

We slowed the horses to a trot, Kristian continuing forward and exchanging words to the guard. I watched as Kristian motioned toward me with his hand and the other man's eyes followed. He looked surprised at first, then narrowed them in suspicion.

"Are you sure you want to do this?" Gunnar asked next to me.

I looked at him, then at the red mark that was now on his neck from my earlier desperation.

"I'm sorry about that," I said to him meekly, pointing to the mark. "If there is anything you must know about me, it's that I don't like being told what I can and cannot do. If the King wants to make me his Queen so fiercely, then I will fight for the limited freedoms I am given."

Kristian waved a hand toward us, motioning for us to come forward.

"So, yes. I am sure I want to do this."

I moved my heels against the horse, the pressure spurring it forward and to the waiting gates. Gunnar trotted alongside me, his gaze weary and watchful as the residence of the Fort looked upon my entrance.

But it wasn't them I was concerned about. First, it was the smell. Like rotten food and stables that hadn't been mucked out. It was revolting and I had to forced down the bile growing in my throat. Second, it was the rows and rows of young people—men and women—that were lined up in formation in the center of the courtyard. They looked scared and cold, the youngest looking no more than their fourteenth year and the eldest at a mighty twentieth year. When my gaze finally caught onto who I was looking for, my blood ran cold. Colder, actually.

There was a man, his short, white hair whipping backward against the wind as he shouted down to a girl with white and black hair—Nic. She was on her hands and knees, her shoulders shaking as she flinched away from the man's encroaching steps. He threw a sword down at her, screaming at her to pick it up.

My heart broke as I watched her pick it up with red hands, her grip slipping on the hilt as she fought to hold the metal up. Her uniform was cut at the shoulder, a line of red visible through it. The man—I'm assuming he was the head of this place—knocked his sword against hers, effectively displacing it from her hand and skittering across the stone till it settled in front of me. He yelled at her again; new tears flowing down her cheeks and her chin quivering uncontrollably.

My temper rose as I watched with horror at the treatment she was receiving. Being a recruit was hard enough, but to be recruited against your will and in this winter hellscape? My temper changed into fury.

"Who is that man?" I bit out to Gunnar.

"Colonel Anders," he said quietly, but I knew he was just as angry as me at the display he was putting on. No one should be humiliated like this.

Time seemed to slow in the next moment as I watched Colonel Anders draw back his free hand and send it flying down across her face. Before I knew what I was doing, I was off my horse and unbuttoning my cloak; Kristian and Gunnar protesting furiously behind me as I charged to the fallen sword and to the coward standing over Nic.

My vision went red as I watched him rear back once more, and then I lost all control.

7

MORE THAN A PRINCESS

The hilt of the sword bit into my palm as I held its icy grip. It was nothing compared to the one Samir had given me, this one merely meant for training purposes, but I would be a liar if I didn't say that the frozen blood in my veins didn't begin singing the moment I held the steel.

It felt good to hold something that made me feel like me again, and as I swung out to stop Colonel Anders' sword from cutting across Nic, I felt more power than I had in weeks.

He did me the honor of looking surprised as I stepped between him and my crying friend, the clashing of our swords ringing out into the icy air as a warning.

"You will not touch her again," I growled.

Anders yanked his sword back, dropping it to his side as he looked me up and down, his stare settling on my face—my black-and-yellow eye.

"You would do well to mind your place, girl," he snarled. "Or else your eyes will become twins."

At that, I chuckled darkly.

"I'd love to see you try."

His eyebrows rose, a chain of gasps coming from behind me and from some of the guards. Kristian and Gunnar exchanged a panicked look, but I halted their approach with a small shake.

"Do you know who I am?" he exclaimed angrily.

"From what I can tell? A piss poor Colonel who's only way to control those in his command is with fear and intimidation. A coward's tactic."

Colonel Anders did not like that response.

"Raise your sword," he demanded. "You think you know so much. Prove it."

I smiled wickedly. "Gladly."

He lashed out first, catching my blade as I swung around him and away from the lined up recruits. He followed me, his breathing coming in fast spurts as he launched a volley of swings and jabs in my direction. I met him head on, parrying and slicing my own sword around with grace and ease.

Anders was a sloppy swordsman. He placed too much weight in his back foot and utilized his upper body rather than his torso to build strength and balance. He went stumbling back as I struck out against him. *Proving* that I was more than capable of taking him down.

"You think you're clever, girl?" he mocked. "A few party tricks with a sword and you think you know what it takes to be a leader? A soldier?"

I straightened up, cocking my head to the side as I thought over his words. Not for the first time in my life was someone undermining me to my face and blatantly disregarding my skills when I had bested them. It was a tale as old as time, and so I did the only thing I could in this moment. I tossed away my sword.

It clattered to the ground a couple feet from where we stood. The courtyard drew in a collective breath; Gunnar dropping a whispered "shit" from behind me. He and Kristian were there the night of the ball; they knew exactly what I was capable of. Colonel Anders followed suit, chucking his sword to the ground as well.

"You think hand-to-hand is going to be any better for you?"

"Well," I purred. "They are party tricks, after all."

It was me who went on the defensive first this time. I ran full speed, cocking back my fist like I was going to punch him, but faked and instead slid between his legs. I twisted halfway through the movement, shoving my boot into his ass and knocking him off center. He stumbled forward, sliding along the frozen stones as I rolled to my shoulders and popped up into a fighting stance. Anders spun around, charging forward as he reached for my middle. But his age showed and he was too slow to stop the gut punch I landed to his abs as I darted to the side. He grunted loudly, the breath leaving his lungs in a long whoosh. He reached up, grasping a few strands of my hair and yanking me down to the ground.

I cried out in rage at the cheap shot, sending a foot flying into his shoulder to get him to release me. His fingers loosened, allowing me to drop down and swing out my leg once more, but this time through the back of his ankles. Anders went airborne and smacked down against the stones loudly. I clambered onto him, my legs straddling his torso as I drew back my fist to land it against his face like he did Nic. But I was stopped in my tracks by a loud and booming voice echoing over the courtyard.

"Enough!"

I looked up to find Damien dismounting his horse and storming forward toward us. His anger was palpable as he pulled me up from my collar and to my feet, pushing me away from the downed man. I brushed him off, stepping away with satisfaction over the situation. When Damien had pulled the Colonel to his feet, he leveled me with a seething glare.

"Would either of you care to explain what the hell you are doing?" he asked in a calm rage.

"Apologies, Your Majesty," Anders began. "The girl just rode in here and demanded a fight."

I scoffed loudly and laughed.

"Is this true?" Damien asked me.

"He was beating her," I bit out as I pointed to Nic, who was now back in line, her face puffy and red. "Someone had to stop him."

"I was teaching, you insolent little bi—" Anders roared but was cut off by Damien grabbing him by the collar and getting in his face.

"I suggest you choose your next words carefully, Anders."

"She is just a girl."

"She is your future Queen."

The air around us shifted as everyone within earshot looked to me with renewed interest and awe. Damien released Anders roughly, rounding his attention back to me and lowering his voice as whispers began to work their way around.

"I thought I instructed your guards to keep you in your room?"

"And I thought I told you I wanted out of that gods forsaken cell," I spat back, not caring who heard me.

A muscle in Damien's jaw twitched as he ground his teeth together, his temper rising once more. His eyes darted behind me, no doubt looking for Kristian and Gunnar.

"You two," he called. "And you," he said back to me. "Follow me. Anders, get these recruits back inside before they freeze half to death. Get these horses tended to as well."

He turned with a swish of his cloak and began walking toward the heavy doors that led into the side of the Fort. I felt my cloak get draped along my shoulders again as Kristian and Gunnar came up behind me, ushering me forward.

"Now you've done it," Gunnar murmured.

"I'm sorry," I said and meant it. "I didn't mean for it to go that far. I just wanted to make sure Nic was okay."

"It's okay," Kristian said from my left. "It was nice to see Anders get his ass handed to him for once."

"Kris, don't say that out loud," Gunnar grumbled as we turned down a hall, keeping Damien in our sights but far away enough he couldn't hear us. "We'll be lucky if he doesn't punish us for not stepping in sooner and letting everyone know who she was immediately."

"You think he was watching that long?" Kristian mused, his face suddenly turning worried as he thought of the consequences Damien could dole out.

I snorted softly as I was hit with memories of Maddox and Harrison arguing in a similar way. The four of them would be fast friends; I was sure of it.

Damien stormed in through a door, leaving it ajar for us as we stepped through behind him a moment later.

"I want to speak to you two first," Damien demanded with a point at my guards.

"They have nothing to do with this," I said evenly, stepping forward in their defense. "I forced their hands. They had no choice but to follow me."

He looked to me and then the men, his eyes narrowing in on one of them.

"She held a knife to my throat," Gunnar confessed sheepishly. I heard him shift his weight from foot to foot with embarrassment at being so easily bested.

"Seems she has a penchant for that . . ." Damien replied dryly. "Fine. Wait outside."

The men complied, closing me in with Damien. Alone.

I remained rooted to the spot I was in while he skimmed over me quickly, making sure there was no extra damage done while he was away. I could sense the irritation coming from him as his forehead creased and his mouth smashed into a hardened line.

"Why have you not put a healing salve on your eye?" he asked in a gentle tone.

"I—I—" I stammered because I hadn't expected him to sound so regretful and not angry. "I wanted you to be able to come home and see your handiwork. Consider it a welcome home present."

Damien's face slackened, his shoulders rounding forward as he pinched the bridge of his nose. "I told you I was sorry for that."

"And I told you," I said, trying to match his tone, "that I didn't want to be held up in that room anymore!"

"It was for your protection!"

"I can protect myself!"

The calmness that started the conversation had now turned to shouting. Kristian and Gunnar surely were able to hear us, a realization we both had as we stood staring at one another, our breaths coming in short burst as we tried to calm back down.

"I will not keep having this argument with you," Damien said tensely, placing a hand on his hip and rubbing the other down his face as he walked away from me. "I know you think me insensitive to your current position here, but you have to trust me that I know what I'm doing and that I know what's best."

"Trust you . . ." I said incredulously. "Trust you? You wouldn't know the definition of the word! How am I supposed to trust a man that goes back on his word when it's convenient to him?"

"I have done no such thing."

"Really," I said, tossing my hands in the air in frustration. "So then why was I relocked in that room just recently? What happened in the mountains?"

His eyes narrowed as he understood the point I was trying to make.

"I understand that it was Arabella who you were seeking," I pleaded. "But you have me. I am a warrior, a soldier. I have sworn oaths and kept secrets for my kingdom. I have been entrusted with the lives of men and women in a unit. You're either delusional or an outright idiot for thinking I would come here and play the role of a docile princess, which by the way, I have been trying to do. But I will not allow you to sequester me into a hole in the mountain when clearly there is a way for me to help."

Damien crossed his arms over his chest and began pacing the room, letting the idea of me doing something outside the mountain ruminate.

"You think," he started, "that just because you were something in Imeria, it means you can be something here?" The words were like a punch to the heart. "Daniella, this is Lustraya, not Imeria. Here, our terrain remains in an everlasting winter. It is unforgiving and harsh, not to mention the enemy we battle closes in more every day. I cannot risk your safety nor that of my people to fulfill your ego boost."

"I do not have an ego . . ."

Damien cocked his head to the side and chuckled lightly under his breath.

I couldn't help but wonder if he was right, though. Was this a way for me to feel useful to the people or a way to make sure they all knew exactly who I was? And what did that even matter?

I huffed out a breath as I slouched into one of the chairs by the fire. Damien took note of the frustration, our earlier argument dissipating as we both collected ourselves together for the better.

"Look, Daniella," he said, coming to sit in the chair opposite me. "I will not pretend to know what you struggle with while being here. I know this was not the life you envisioned for yourself. But I can't have you out in the mountains with no training and no knowledge. It's too dangerous."

I went to open my mouth with a retort, but he cut me off with a raise of his hand.

"How about instead, I let you stay here and teach this new batch of recruits?" I sat up straighter, the hope in me blooming for the first time since I had been here. Damien continued, "You could teach them your fighting techniques, and then you can learn from the rest here what it means to be a Lustrayan. Something you probably wouldn't be able to do in the mountain."

"Yes. Yes, that would be amaz—"

Once again, he stopped me in my tracks, but I hid the annoyance because the chance at having this small freedom was too good for me not to take a chance on.

"There will be stipulations to this, of course," he said, his voice turning serious and king-like as he laid out his rules for me. "For starters, you will have a weekly check in with me. I want a full report on the recruit's progress, good or bad. Second, they will need to accept you. This will only work if they see you as a leader. It will also be a test for you too, Daniella."

I nodded my head as he spoke each condition. Leading? I could do that easily. Getting these people to like me . . . well, that could be a challenge, but I would try my hardest to win them over.

"And lastly, you will come back to the mountain once a week for dinner with me."

I felt a groan threaten to release from my chest, but I held it back. How was dinner with this man really going to be the deal breaker for me?

"If I agree to all this," I finally spoke. "Will that mean I am trustworthy to you? To your council?"

The need for information was great, I realized, the longer I lived here. Never had I felt so blindfolded to the events happening around me that I no longer felt I was a part in something. I was purely existing and that wasn't okay with me.

Damien nodded his head thoughtfully in confirmation as his hands clasped together on his stomach.

"It will be a step in the right direction," he concluded. "I will not get your hopes up about anything further."

"I accept your terms, then," I said, reaching my hand across the space between us for him to shake. He clasped it back with a firm grip, our hands rising once before settling and ending the agreement.

Damien rose from his chair with an exhausted grunt and I followed his lead, knowing that this was his way of excusing me from these chambers. I walked straight for the door before he could change his mind, but just as I was about to grab the door handle, Damien called my name.

"Yes?"

"Don't forget," he warned. "You are still a princess, and when duty calls, you will answer it without a fuss."

"Of course."

"It's settled, then. Now if you'll excuse me, I have other matters I must see to," he said gruffly. "I'll have Gunnar and Kristian show you to where you'll be staying and I'll let you be the one to tell them that they will be relocated back here."

Damien smiled ruefully as he settled in behind the desk, my eyes rolling in annoyance that I had to tell my guards that they would no longer be enjoying the comforts of the mountain, but instead this cold and unfriendly Fort.

The two men turned around with expectant looks, and I squared my shoulders as we walked away from Damien and into our next chapter together. Today, my new mission began.

The pair took the news of their reassignment surprisingly well, offering to help me move any of my preferred belongings from the mountain and to the Fort the next day.

"That shouldn't be necessary, but thank you," I told them as they concluded the mini tour of our new home.

The Fort was large, but its makeup was rather simple. A mess hall, strategy room, and barracks flanked the eastern side, while the training facilities were north. The south had a few extra rooms for indoor lessons, but according to Kristian, that happened very rarely.

"So, what now?" Gunnar asked as we found ourselves in the courtyard once more.

"What do you mean?" I countered.

The two guards looked at one another and back to me.

"Well . . . you kind of saved us earlier with the King. It's only right that we help you in any way that we can," Gunnar explained.

"Besides," Kristian piped in. "We hated seeing you locked in that room just as much as you. We've never seen him so protective before."

Their words comforted me in a way I didn't realize I needed. Having Gunnar and Kristian at my side was a breath of relief, almost like I had Mads and Harrison with me once again.

"That would be appreciated," I said to them with a warm smile. "We can start in one of those extra rooms you were talking about—"

"Gunnar."

I was abruptly cut off by a woman storming her way toward us. She was striking and bold, with half of her head shaved short and the other side cropped to her chin and wore the Lustrayan grey-and-black wool-lined leathers like everyone else.

"Poppi," Gunnar croaked, like he was surprised to see the woman now standing with us. "What are you doing here?"

"I could ask you the same," she said pointedly, turning to me. "I take it you're Princess Daniella?"

"I am."

"The King sent me for you. Follow me."

Maybe it was her tone, or the way she commanded herself with confidence, or maybe it was the fact that I didn't like being told what to do and wanted to tell her that, but I followed her all the same. Gunnar and Kristian stayed on my heels as she took us away from the courtyard and toward the barracks sector of the Fort.

"Poppi," Gunnar said, annoyed. "We've already shown her the room she's going to be occupying."

The woman—Poppi—turned around abruptly, glancing between the two men behind me.

"I know you two have been with her since the Imeria mission, but the King has ordered she stay in my room." She looked directly to me now. "Don't worry, Your Highness. I'm not keen on sharing a space either."

Truthfully, I didn't care whether or not I shared a room with the woman. What I cared about was that I knew Damien had something to do with this woman being placed here specifically and I didn't like being monitored.

"Sharing a room doesn't bother me," I replied, trying to keep the conversation moving forward.

"Excellent. We'll be on our way to the female wing, then. Boys, you can go . . . do whatever it is you do."

They grumbled, readying to continue the argument.

"It's okay," I assured them. "We'll meet back on the eastern side of the courtyard in an hour. Sound good?"

They nodded in agreement and departed, heading straight toward the mess hall. Poppi motioned me forward silently, taking me down a narrow hallway and up a short flight of stairs that led to my new residence.

The room was bigger than I was expecting; a fireplace bisecting the two beds that were pushed against either side of the walls, a small dresser accompanying each of them.

"The right side is yours," Poppi said. "The King is already sending your things over."

Of course he was. Gods forbid I be able to do anything on my own.

"Thank you," I said with feigned politeness as I stepped further into the room to examine it. Poppi closed the door behind us with a thud.

"Look," she said, rounding on me. "Now that we are alone, I want to get something straight. I know who you are—who you really are. I admire what you did for your kingdom, but it's not going to win you any favors here. Lustrayan's have been through hell and the last thing we need is an egotistical Imerian coming in and telling us what we're doing isn't good enough."

My eyebrows rose at her boldness, but it made me like her slightly.

"Anything else?" I goaded.

"Yeah," she said, crossing her arms. "Your little display earlier? That's not going to win you any favors either. Colonel Anders is a prideful man, and most of our soldiers look up to him like a savior. What you did, embarrassing him like that, just made them all less likely to follow your lead."

"So, what you're saying," I replied, sitting down on my bed, "is that everyone is most likely going to hate me and want to see me gone before the week is up?"

"That's correct."

"Well, then. If you know me so well, Poppi, then you'll know that this is not territory I'm unaccustomed to. The people want to hate me, fine. Let them. But it won't be for my lack of trying or for lack of preparation. I know this kingdom is fighting something and I'll be damned if any more innocent lives are lost because they can't handle it."

Poppi leveled me with a look that was equal parts skeptical and impressed.

"You sound like you've already got a plan."

"Lesson one, Poppi; I always have a plan.

8

NEVER BACK DOWN

The plan was falling apart.

Over two hours we had been sequestered in this cold and damp room, with half-rotted desks and chairs. We had several different pieces of parchment splayed out on the one desk that was in decent condition, the efforts of our time written hastily among them.

My initial plan was to have the recruits stay together and utilize these extra rooms to teach them all the basics first. They needed to know theory, weaponry, and above all—history. And that's where the arguments began.

"What the hell does history have to do with taking these people and making them soldiers?" Poppi asked, annoyed.

"Everything," I said. "They have to know that when times were hard before, this kingdom lived on. That they lived on. We need to give them something to hold onto. We need to give them hope, and we do that by showing them what worked and what didn't, so that when the day comes and they're in battle, they'll remember."

"They can learn that while they're holding a sword," Poppi snapped. "The quicker we get them used to holding steel, the better. They can learn this . . . theory or whatever it is you do in Imeria, later. This is not the time."

I narrowed my eyes at her.

"Why are you pushing so hard against this, Poppi? Is it because you know something about what happened in the White Passage?"

She snapped her jaw shut just like I knew she would. One of these days, I would know the depth of the shadow that haunts these people.

"I'm not saying it's not important," she admitted. "I'm just saying that it shouldn't be the priority."

"As much as I hate agreeing with her," Gunnar spoke up from his spot next to Poppi. He held a sheet of paper that had names and ages of everyone recruited to the Fort on them; his boyish face marred in worry lines. "I have to take her side on this one, Your Highness. Time is of the essence, and the King expects to see heavy progress."

"You leave the King to me," I said with a huff of breath, rubbing my temples. As I thought over their requests, I also remembered my conversation with Damien, and what it was going to take to win everyone here over.

It was begrudgingly when I said, "Fine. We'll do it your way. We'll separate them into four groups, each of us heading up one. We should implement strength training and agility exercises first, and I want to start them off with staffs or wooden swords till their confidence is better. We all saw how much Nic—an adult—struggled to hold hers up."

The room remained silent as the memory sat in the stillness. Even on my worst days in Imeria, I was never treated like that from a person in command. Maybe in the sparing ring, but that was after we had been given proper hand-to-hand instruction.

"We should consider keeping the women and the men separate as well," Kristian added to break the tension. "Perhaps we should consider leaving the women out entirely and let them focus on the theory you were talking about."

To this suggestion, Poppi and I's back's went rigid, my head snapping to the side to look at the man brashly.

"Excuse me?" Poppi asked like she couldn't believe what she was hearing. "You want to try those words again?"

"I–I just meant—" he stumbled out, suddenly realizing how ignorant those words sounded.

"One day you'll learn how to shut up, man," Gunnar scolded him, shaking his head as he dropped the paper down.

"Women are just as capable at fighting like the men are," I stated plainly. As if Poppi and I weren't proof of that statement.

"Of course they are," Kristian replied, trying to back track his words. "I only meant—"

"He's trying to say that up until ten years ago, women were kept from the fighting," Gunnar supplied, saving his friend, and aiming the explanation mostly to me so I would understand. "They mostly stayed back at the camps or here, away from the danger."

Poppi let out a sound of disgust, rolling her eyes at the absurdity of the old law.

"So, what changed?" I asked.

"The attacks got worse. We needed people to protect the villages left, and that meant bringing them in. The law was never intended to be malicious; it was made to keep families safe. Keep children from becoming orphans." The last words clanged through me, drawing up a feeling I knew well.

"Well," I said, trying to move the conversation along. "That was then, and this is now. The women learn how to fight alongside the men. End of discussion."

Poppi's shoulders released their tension, the woman herself walking back to the desk from where she had paced over to the lone window in the room.

The rest of the afternoon was spent drawing up a curriculum and milestones we all could agree were necessary. With all our combined years of experience and skill, the new plan should be attainable, and within a few months if the gods allowed it.

By nightfall, Poppi and I had returned to our shared room, my meager belongings scattered throughout and ready to be placed in their new home. As I stuffed a pair of wool pajamas into a drawer, I suddenly longed for one of my silk sleep sets. Or maybe I longed for something that made me feel like myself in a place that threatened to take away who I was piece by piece.

That night I dreamed of my mother, of her ability to move us town to town without a second thought. We never had more than a few belongings. Making attachments to things was not conducive to my mother's plans, and for the first time in my life, I hated her for it.

***

I awoke the next morning to Poppi already gone. Her bed was tightly made, her things tidy and neat as if she was never here. It allowed me the peace of getting ready alone and to prepare for what the day was going to bring me.

We had decided last night that it was best to present a unified front for the new soldiers. They needed to see that I was going to be a capable leader and had support from other Lustrayans. But as Poppi pointed out yesterday, I gave myself no favors when it went to garnering respect from those higher in the chain of command. I had disrespected one of their leaders in front of them and that was not going to go without its repercussions. Not to mention, if people didn't know already, I was a princess from another kingdom—an outsider come to challenge who they were. Yet again.

I looked at the sword and sheath Kristian dug up for me yesterday. It was old, the hilt almost smooth from the number of hands that had passed over it. I did my best to polish and sharpen it so it would be an effective weapon, but there were no guarantees when it came to this kingdom. I buckled the sheath and sword around my hips, savoring the weight of it like a long-lost friend. I had been given a set of grey leathers that hugged me almost too closely, but they would have to do for now too. I would add the lack of supplies to the list of things I needed from Damien next time I saw him. And that time would be here soon enough.

I left the room with one last glance in the mirror and a prayer to whatever god would listen to it. As I navigated my way around the Fort, I was hit with the familiar feeling from when my journey in Imeria began. Although this was a battle I had fought before—and I could do it again —I hated that I had to keep proving myself to people who would rather see me fail.

"You ready for today?" Gunnar asked me as he exited the men's barracks and joined me in my walk.

"As ready as I'll ever be," I said nonchalantly.

"That's the spirit."

I laughed at his attempt to brighten my mood, something Maddox would have done for me. I had to remind myself that this challenge was what I asked for and that I was more than capable of doing it. It was that little dose of confidence that kept my shoulders back and my chin lifted as we found our way to the meeting room from last night.

Kristian was already there when Gunnar and I arrived. His head was bent over our notes, a piece of bread clutched in his hand as he chewed.

"Good morning," I announced. "You ready for today?"

"Absolutely," he said cheerfully. "It's time this place got shaken up. In a good way, that is."

Gunnar shook his head while I chuckled lightly at his enthusiasm.

"I take it Poppi is gathering everyone like she said she would?" Gunnar asked, going to stand by Kristian.

"I hope so."

Though I had known her all of twenty-four hours, I knew that Poppi had a commanding presence here, and if Damien trusted her then the rest of the Fort would too. I didn't know how I felt about her personally yet, but I wasn't exactly in a place to be picky about what allies I was given.

"How are you feeling, Your Highness?" Kristian asked me, he and Gunnar each looking at me with mixed emotions.

"Dani," I told them. "Here and to you two, I'm Dani. And I'm fine. This isn't the first time I've had to stand in front of people and remind them that I belong somewhere, that I am on their side; I doubt it will be the last."

They nodded appreciatively as the door to the room swung open and closed. Poppi pulled the hood from her wool jacket down, cursing the gods and the winter they were bringing as she did.

"Well, good morning to you too," Gunnar teased her.

She shot him daggers before leveling her gaze to me.

"You sure about this? It's not too late to go back to the mountain and spend your days in luxury."

"Is that what you'd like me to do, Poppi?" I scoffed, crossing my arms over my chest. "Walk away from something just because it seems hard? Well, here's lesson two." I walked over to her leisurely, letting the tension build between us, wanting her to know I was not scared of her nor would I ever be. "I never back down from a challenge."

I shoved passed her, purposely hitting her shoulder with force as I moved toward the door and forced it open against a blast of icy wind.

"Let's go," I commanded from the three people that had been entrusted to help me on my new mission.

I heard the scraping of a chair followed by footsteps rushing to catch up to me. Gunner and Kristian flanked me on the right and left side, Poppi right behind them. With each step I took closer to the courtyard, the more my resolve grew.

I can do this. I am Imeria's Gauntlet champion, team lead of the Serpentine Guard.

Or so I was. As we rounded the corner and the lines of recruits came into my view, I felt the energy around me shift. It hit me that once I stepped up to the platform and gave my speech, I would no longer be Captain Daniella Castille of Imeria. No. Instead, by accepting this new path and giving myself in servitude to these people, I would officially become Princess Daniella Castille of Lustraya.

My heart leaped in my chest as my boot made contact with the first step and began to beat rapidly as I ascended the remainder of them. My breaths were like clouds in front of me, and I urged myself to steady my breathing, so as to not show my sudden nervousness to the soldiers I was now in charge of.

There were more of them than I remembered from yesterday. Easily two hundred to two hundred and fifty pairs of eyes found their focus to me. Gunnar, Kristian, and Poppi formed a line behind me, signaling their allegiance and full attention.

I swallowed the last of my hesitation and took a step forward. It was now or never.

"Thank you all for gathering here this morning. I know it's not the warm, sunny day we all wished it was," my voice rang out confidently. "Many of you were there to witness my actions yesterday. It is regrettable that that is the first impression you have of me. For those of you who are wondering just who I am, my name is Daniella Castille . . ." I had to swallow my distaste for the next words. "And I am your new Princess."

Sharp intakes of breath and gasps of disbelief chorused through the courtyard. I heard a snicker or two from some of the guards on the wind, but I continued on.

"My story is not so different from your own. I fought against great odds to get to where I am today. In Imeria, I was a captain." A damn good one. "But I started off just like you—a recruit. I know the fear and uncertainty you all might feel. Some of you have never held a sword or thrown a fist. But I can help you fix that." My voice grew stronger with each word I spoke.

"Lustraya may be new to me, but the challenges we will face together are not. I am not the type of person that likes to sit idly by while the people and places I love suffer. If you will allow it, I'd like to help in the best way I can, which is teaching you how to fight. How to survive. So that when it is time, you can go home, and your families are safe. It may take time, but I'm asking that you allow me the honor of earning your trust with this. Will you accept my offer?"

The courtyard was silent aside from a small cough that sounded from the back. Neither the recruits nor the guards made a move. Even the three people behind me made no noise as we all waited on bated breath for a response.

Just when I was beginning to lose hope, a woman bravely stepped forward from her lineup. Her white-and-black hair was braided back tightly, revealing the large cut across her face. Nic.

"I accept your offer," she said loudly, her answer carrying on the icy wind.

A young boy stepped up next to her, proclaiming the same sentiment. Then another boy followed, and another, and another; till the courtyard was filled with choruses of acceptance.

I looked to the watch towers where dozens of guards had gathered to hear me out. I looked each of them in the eye, roving my gaze high and low. Some nodded their acceptance, others remained stone faced and skeptic. But my heart seized beating when my eyes met Damien's.

He looked down at me from the top of the crosswalk between towers, a black fur cape pulled around him and a silver circlet on his brow. I puffed my chest up slightly as I looked at him, waiting for him to make some kind of gesture that would let me know our deal was sealed. Something akin to pride ghosted his features as the last of the acceptances rang through the air and he gave me a dip of his chin in approval.

I looked back to those who stood in the cold, waiting for me to say something more. A quick glance behind me revealed Gunnar grinning wildly, Kristian and Poppi remaining impassive and most likely impatient for the task before us to start.

I turned my head back around, a smile gracing my own face at last. I raised my hands out to the side; a gesture I had seen Clara do so many times when addressing a crowd. If only she could see me now . . .

"Then let the work begin!"

85

9

ACHES AND PAINS

The grunts and groans of untrained recruits filled the entirety of the courtyard. We had split everyone into four groups: Gunnar, Kristian, Poppi and I each taking control over one. Much to Kristian's disapproval, we kept everyone blended. The women trained alongside the men, the young with the old. Should there ever come a day when they had to be sent out into whatever was going on in the mountains, they had to be able to adapt. And throwing as much diversity at them now was the best solution.

My unit of trainees took over the center of the courtyard—Poppi's idea.

"They need to see you be in control and sure of yourself," she told me last night. "They'll never want to follow you if you shelter yourself in the corner. You need to make a show of it. Show them that you are capable of leading not only these new faces, but an entire kingdom."

When she put it like that, I felt acid rile in my belly. I wasn't ready to lead an entire kingdom, I don't think I ever would be. But I could do this, and for now, that's all I was focused on.

"When throwing a punch, it is important to center yourself, really harness the power from your abdominal muscles to punch straight and fast," I instructed as I walked up and down the rows of trainees.

They had been at it for almost an hour now. Their hands red from the cold and breaths coming in heavy as I instructed them through the basic moves of hand-to-hand combat.

"Give me a two-three combination, five times," I shouted for everyone to hear.

They did as told, some better than others, but that was to be expected. I glanced around as I walked through the lines, getting glimpses of the progress of the other groups.

Kristian was personally instructing one of the youngest recruits, the kid looking as lost and confused as the day he was born. Gunnar on the other hand seemed well-off. His group had begun their introduction to staff work, progressing them a bit too soon in my opinion. When I looked to where Poppi was, I couldn't help the frustrated sigh and spike in temper that accompanied it.

Her group of trainees were gathered in a circle, two of the trainees in the middle locked in a scuffle. I ground my teeth as I watched one of the opponents swing out sloppily and connect with the shoulder of the other. The man that was hit fell and fell hard. His uniform hung loosely on his shoulders, a sign that he wasn't the most bulky or muscular member of Poppi's group. He let out a wail, holding onto his shoulder and sliding back from his encroaching aggressor.

I looked to Poppi, hoping she would call the match, but all she did was stand on the edge with her arms crossed, a look of satisfaction in her eyes. It was enough to have me moving from my group and over to hers. This wasn't how we built morale or soldiers. This also wasn't part of the plan we came up with to help these recruit's progress.

The closer I neared, the angrier I grew. I pushed through the bodies of the circle, my presence there allowing me to move swiftly to the center of the chaos.

"Finish it," I heard Poppi instruct and the man standing did as told. He straddled the downed man, sitting on him to prevent any more movement as he cocked his fist back.

"Yield!" I shouted, grabbing onto the raised fist.

The man whirled to face me, his eyes growing wide as he realized who had stopped him. He relaxed his arm, standing up and moving away from the man who laid crying in the snow.

"Are you okay?" I asked quietly to him as he attempted to sit up and stand back on his feet.

"I–I think so," he whimpered, still holding his shoulder.

"Go get that looked at. You're done for the day," I told him as Poppi chimed in with her protest.

"Like hell—"

"*You*," I called, turning and meeting Poppi head on. "This was not what was agreed upon."

"We agreed to hand-to-hand basics today," she ground out, stepping even closer to me till we were only inches apart. "I am teaching them that. You are out of line to step in during my instruction."

"You call that instruction?" I asked tersely. "He was injured. On the ground. The fight was over."

"The fight is never over."

I drew in a sharp breath, my hands balling into fists at my side.

"You're dismissed," I shouted, never taking my eyes off Poppi's. "Get yourselves cleaned up. Your assignments are pinned in the mess hall."

"How dare you . . ." Poppi growled. "How dare you undermine me in front of them."

"No. How dare *you*. We are building soldiers, not bloodthirsty barbarians."

"They need to learn how to finish their fights and not pull their punches. The enemy will be worse. They need to be prepared."

"Not on day one, they don't!"

Our argument had garnered attention, those that remained in the courtyard looking to us with confusion and piqued interest. What would Ary do in this situation? What would Samir? It was with great discipline that I took a step back from Poppi and drew in a deep breath, channeling the patience both of them would exercise in this moment. This was not the time, nor the place to be having this argument.

"I will talk to you later about this," I said before storming off and excusing the rest of the courtyard from training.

Gunnar caught up to me first, while Kristian went to Poppi.

"What was that about?" he asked me as I shoved open a door to the corridor of the Fort.

"Has she always been like that?" I asked, unable to contain my attitude.

"Been like what?" he asked, working to keep pace with my stride.

"Difficult! She doesn't listen. We had a plan. Hand-to-hand basics for the first few days before we let them start sparing. That man . . . he had nothing to him. He is skinner than a courtier trying to seduce a man into marriage and what does she do . . . she was going to allow him to be beaten till he surely passed out!" Gunnar remained quiet as I thought and spoke.

"Not to mention I know she detests my presence here. Well, I have news for her. This wasn't my first option either! I am trying to make the best of this whole situation, and she is making it ungodly hard. What is her deal? Gunnar?"

"Hmh?"

"You're quiet. Why?"

We rounded a corner, the hallway opening to a foyer with four different staircases. We took the one to the left, heading toward the barracks side of the Fort.

"I don't think it's my place to talk about why Poppi is the way she is," he confessed. "I think this is something you two need to figure out yourselves."

"I would if she spoke more than two words to me outside of our meetings," I grumbled.

"Just try. Think, if it was you, what would your friends back in Imeria do? Your sister?"

A burst of laughter escaped as I thought of the scenario.

"My friends . . . well, they'd suggest a good bottle of wine and a duel. My sister would bring me a tea tray piled high with pastries and then she'd offer to take me shopping."

"Shopping?"

"I love a good trinket, Gunnar."

"I see . . ." he mused. "On second thought, don't do any of that for Poppi. Accept maybe the wine. But she prefers akava more, so I guess either will work."

Akava, the clear drink of choice in Lustraya was worse than the Rilunaean firewater. It was odorless and almost tasteless until you felt its afterburn down to your belly. At least firewater had a sweet and smokey flavor. Akava sent you to your dreams sooner rather than later.

"No promises there."

"Well, if you two don't do something about your rift, we're going to lose the small amount of support we just got."

Ary,

I hope by the time you receive this letter, you would have gotten my first. Things are looking up around here. Finally. ~~Damien has let me~~ *Damien and I have come to an arrangement. I'm finally getting to do what I do best, but it's not without its work. Some days are easier than others, but I miss you more as they pass. How do you do it? The whole princess thing? It's exhausting. Frankly, I've never felt so tired in all my life, and I am only a few weeks into it. I wish there was more I could tell you. Maybe one day I can. I hope to hear from you.*

All my love,
Dani

I let the ink set in the parchment before folding it up, sealing it with navy blue wax. The week was finally over, but I still had my dinner with Damien tonight, one of the conditions I had to accept in order to gain my small sliver of freedom. A dress was delivered earlier while we worked with the recruits in the courtyard, the shimmering silver fabric trimmed with matching fur. Arabella would have loved it.

I took the letter from the desk and shoved it into the hidden pocket of the garment I was expected to wear. I tossed a black cloak around my shoulders to complete the look and took off to where Kristian and Gunnar would be waiting for me at the front gates.

The walk there was humbling; the eyes of guards and trainees all looking at me like I had morphed into a completely different human being as I passed. Aside from my fighting with Poppi, the people here were beginning to see me for more than the shiny new object the King brought home. I was solidifying myself as a leader, as someone who had a lot of knowledge to share and was capable of teaching it.

The leathers I wore daily here helped everyone know that I could be just like them; that I, too, was a warrior. The dress served as a reminder that I was in fact royalty now, and I would always stand apart from them, no matter what.

I passed through the last door that would lead to the gate, winter in full force as I was met with the frigid outside. Gunnar and Kristian stood right where they said they were going to be, their faces passive in the torch light as I approached. I grabbed my horse's reins from Gunnar, thanking him as we all swung up onto the saddles.

"Let's get this over with," I said to no one particular as I fussed with the hem of the gown.

Once more, I was grateful that the road back to the stronghold was a short one, my lungs screaming in protest with each breath I filled them with as we rode. It was a silent trip, though what else could I expect. At least the view was stunning as the sun set behind the mountain tops and gave way to the purples and blues of twilight.

"This way, Your Highness," Kristian instructed from my right. "We'll take the back way in."

I followed him and Gunnar through a crowd of pine trees and down a narrow road. It snaked its way up the side of a small peak, opening up to a cave that had three guards at its entrance.

"State your business," one of the guards demanded.

"Lieutenants Halle and Greyborne escorting her Highness Princess Daniella at the behest of the King," Gunnar supplied for the man.

Without another word, we were ushered through, our horses clopping the only sound to accompany us as we moved farther down the cave. When we reached another fork, Gunnar and Kristian dismounted their horses, the latter coming to my side and offering his hand.

"I can do it," I said as I ignored his hand and swung my leg over the saddle and hoisted myself down. I felt instant regret as the dress caught under my slipper and sent me falling back, but not before I felt a pair of strong hands reach out and catch me.

"Want to try that again?" Kristian asked sarcastically.

"Stupid dress," I muttered as I stood up straight again. "I can't wait till this is over."

Kristian ushered me forward, Gunnar leading the way as I was taken up hidden stairwells and down narrow passageways that eventually brought us into a larger cavern I recognized. If we went right, it would lead to my rooms, and the warm and glorious bath water within. But instead, we headed left down the corridor that would take us into the King's sector of the mountain and our shared dining space.

Each step felt like a note in a death march, the door leading into the dining room its crescendo. I felt nervous walking in as Kristian and Gunnar halted their advances at the door, but that was quickly wiped away as I saw Poppi sitting at the table with the King.

What the hell . . .

"Ah, Daniella," Damien announced. "How good, you're here. Send for the food please," he instructed a servant behind him as Poppi stood, bowed, and walked out the doors behind me. All without a single word.

"Please, sit," he said, gesturing with a hand to my waiting chair across from him.

"Why was Poppi here?" I asked, still standing. I was trying very hard to keep the irritation from my voice, my hands clasping in front of me in an attempt to keep them from making fists.

"Sit down, Daniella."

With an eye roll, I did what he asked in the hopes that he would answer my question. But the servant had come back in the room, and had three more in tow, all carrying platters with them. They made quick work of serving us, Damien tucking into his portion with a mumbled thank you.

It was the most awkward dinner I had ever sat through, and that was saying something after all I endured in Imeria from people like Lord Andrews. The room was quiet, save for the clattering of our utensils and chewing. There was no attempt to answer my earlier question nor any attempt to make conversation whatsoever. It set my teeth on edge. What was he hiding?

"Damien," I finally said to break the silence. "About Poppi—"

"It's not important, Daniella," he sighed, drinking from his goblet. "Don't ruin the evening."

"What evening?" I bit back. "It's been nauseatingly silent this whole time."

"A rare gift for me these days."

The words felt like another slap to the face. I had obliged him with his weekly dinners for almost three weeks now. His words were probably not meant to hurt me directly, but the least he could do was find his manners.

"Damien, I am trying. You could at least do the same."

"Fine," he said, pushing his plate away and folding his hands on his lap. "What would you like to talk about?"

"Well," I said, straightening my shoulders. "I have a report on the new trainees if you'd like to hear it. Or maybe after supper is cleared, we can discuss their progress somewhere else."

"That won't be necessary," he said plainly. "I have all the information I need."

"How? We haven't even talked . . ." Oh.

It clicked then and there. The rug slipped out from under me as I put together the reason why Poppi was here when I entered.

"Is that why she gets back to the Fort late? Keeping tabs on me and my recruits?"

"I would hardly say they're yours . . ." Damien chuckled lightly.

Red sparked along the corners of my vision.

"You said that I would be in charge of the trainees and getting them up to speed. That you wanted a weekly report from *me*. This makes it feel like you're undermining me, Damien. Was it all a lie?"

"You're not being undermined," he said, standing and throwing down his napkin. "This isn't a conversation to have here."

"Fine. Then where would you like to have it then?" I barked, following in his stead.

He left through the door the servants came in, the hall winding left until we came to a staircase. Upward we went, silent as the grave, until we stopped at his study door. He threw it open, and I threw it closed, my anger becoming harder to maintain.

"Damien," I pressed. "You really need to start telling me what is going on."

Despite my frustrations and anger toward him, I had to admit that it was valiant on his effort that he didn't lose control on me again. That was something I was not eager to repeat.

"Daniella," he began, leaning against one of the large windows. "There are things happening in this kingdom that are of no concern for you. I brought you here because Lustraya needs a Queen; that Queen, truthfully, was supposed to be Arabella. Me and my court planned for Arabella. But we have you. And that is something we didn't plan for." He leveled me a tired, yet empathetic look.

"Change doesn't happen in Lustraya quickly. You should be grateful that the new recruits have taken to your expertise in the first place. As for Poppi, I owe you no explanation. You two are more than welcome to sort out whatever." He gestures with a wave. "It is you two have going on between yourselves."

"You have her doing what's supposed to be my job, Damien," I retorted. "It's going to confuse the recruits if you tell them to report to me, but Poppi is the one that's in your ear."

"They know who to look to."

"Not if Poppi is going against the set plan and defies me at every turn in front of them. There is no order. There is no communication. There most certainly is no respect from her, either. I'm beginning to wonder if you even respect me."

His eyes narrowed. "I respect you."

"Do you? Because from where I'm standing, it looks like you want me to fail and come crawling back on hands and knees for your forgiveness, just so I can be shoved back in that room until it's time for me to come out when it's necessary for you."

He remained quiet, a solemn affirmation that I was at least right on that account.

"Are you going to say anything?" I asked, exasperated.

"I have nothing left to say," he responded. "I've told you everything. I have given you your opportunity. Now it's time you do something with it instead of complaining how unfair everything is to you."

"My whole life was ripped away from me and *that's* what you choose to say?" And because my temper was high and I had no ability to hold my tongue, I added for affect, "I should've cut your throat in that hall. Your blood should have spilled that night. Let all of Lustraya know what a coward you truly are."

His nostrils flared and he was moving away from the wall of windows before the last words fell from my lips. I caught the balling of his fist out of the corner of my eye and felt my body twitch ever so slightly to the right. The memory of the last time he made the same gesture in a similar setting flashing through my mind.

Damien's footsteps halted as we locked eyes from across the room. His face slackened in recognition, his hands going limp at his sides. I waited for him to say something of authority, to dismiss my feelings about this.

"I will talk to Poppi," he said in a low timbre. "Just . . ."

He couldn't finish his sentence and honestly, I didn't want him to. I could feel the remorse radiating off him as our imaginary weapons fell. With the fight in me gone, I turned my back and made my way out of the study. Kristian and Gunnar were just outside the door waiting for me, the expressions on their faces telling me that they heard every word between me and Damien.

I waited till we were further down the hall before asking, "Where is she?"

"She left for the Fort already," Kristian confessed.

The thudding of our boots was the only sound for a while; until I couldn't take it anymore and I had to ask them.

"Am I wrong?"

Silence. Uncomfortable, mind-numbing silence ensued as we rounded one last bend that would lead us to where our horses were being kept.

"Listen, Dani," Gunnar started in a low voice. "We like you. We do, and we respect what you are to this kingdom. But there are some things you are just going to have to figure out for yourself. The King is right. If you are having trouble with Poppi, or anyone else for the matter, you have to take it up with them. This isn't Imeria. We don't dance around the problem; we meet it head on. You need to meet Poppi head on with this. Or else it could get ugly. Really quick."

10

REDO

Ary,

The days grow colder up here. Nothing like what we ever experienced in Imeria. I find that almost every item of clothing I now own has some sort of fur lining or trimming to it. Where does it all come from? This is a question a future Queen should know but alas, I know nothing. You of all people should understand how badly that gets under my skin, frozen as it is. Oh, how I miss you and our garden, and the tea cakes we used to have as kids. Lustraya has its charm but the food . . . well, that's something that can't be helped, from what I'm told. I hope to hear from *you soon. Maybe the weather is what is delaying your letters to me. Stay strong, sister.*

With love,
Dani

Poppi avoided me like a sickness. She was never in our room anymore and only communicated with me when we were also in Gunnar and Kristian's company. The whole thing set my teeth on edge. Luckily, training with the recruits faced no more obstacles, and within the week, we could start blending our groups together to make one unit.

Members of Damien's court would come around every now and then to see the progress being made or not made by some of their standards. It reminded me of the nobles in Imeria, and how they used the Gauntlet as their own sort of entertainment. I guess this is what my life would look like as a Queen.

Not for the first time I considered what Kristian and Gunnar told me about how to cope with Poppi, but she didn't strike me as the type to have a conversation and let the situation ebb away. She was like me in that regard, I guess. Stubborn and with something to prove.

The idea struck me then.

My first time ever speaking to Poppi, I knew her—I *liked* her, even—but I knew her because something deep down recognized that we were not so different from one another.

She was where I stood my first year with the Imerian military and wanted to desperately prove that I deserved to be there. And each year, I proved it time and time again, until I did become what I had set out to do. Poppi had her own story too. And that's what I needed to get out of her—her why.

But I just needed to figure out how.

The sun was less than an hour from rising, at which time our unit would gather and begin their training for the day. Poppi was already up and gone, and if my revelation about her proved any sort of correct, she would be somewhere on her own. Somewhere where she felt safe and could release her frustrations.

I stood from the desk and folded my letter to Ary, sealing it with wax and tucking it into the pocket of my jacket to drop off later. It haunted me that I hadn't heard from her yet. I would have thought she'd gotten one of my letters by now or written one herself. But the weather had been taking a turn for the worst lately, so that had to be why there was a delay.

The Fort was extra frosty these days, but graciously I could maneuver around without Kristian or Gunnar at my heels. It seems that everyone had finally come to the realization that I could take care of myself and didn't need to be lorded over like some precious jewel.

There were three places in this Fort I knew Poppi wasn't: our shared room, the mess hall, the abandoned rooms, and the courtyard. Correction: make that four places I knew she wasn't. Which meant that she had to be in the north sector, where only the highest-ranking soldiers were. And where I was entitled to be.

I moved down a foreign corridor, an icy blast of air greeting me as I shoved through the door leading into the secluded courtyard, if one could call it that. It was a small area open to the air, the door to the dorms off to the right, a watch tower to the left. The morning was still young; most would be asleep still, but I heard the low murmur of voices coming from the tower and turned my direction toward it.

My steps echoed off the stones as I wound my way up the tower. Through small cuts in the stone, I could see the mountains encasing us in. The longer I stayed here, the more I appreciated them. In their own way, they were a thing of beauty, much like the waters of Sapphire Isle.

During my second year—post winter river fiasco—part of our training was to go aboard one of the naval vessels. Our goal was to become accustomed enough that should we ever be involved in a war, we could do the bare minimum of navigation. Let's just say it's a good thing I belonged on land.

I reached the top of the stairs, the landing opening to a circular space and there, in front of a window opening, stood Poppi with Gunnar right next to her. They halted their conversation at the sound of my approaching steps and turned toward where I stood on the landing.

Gunnar couldn't hide the shock that showed in his eyes any more than Poppi could stop the magnificent eye roll upon seeing me.

"Gunnar," I asked nicely. "Can you give me and Poppi a moment?"

"Is that a good idea?" he questioned.

"No," Poppi replied flatly.

"I just want to have a quick word with you, Poppi," I stated and then added, "Please," for extra affect.

Poppi slumped forward on the ledge, knowing I wasn't going to let this conversation go until it was had. Gunnar patted her shoulder before he made his leave from the tower.

"I'm going to go get Kristian," he said, turning back before descending the steps. "We'll see you two in a bit."

He left on quick feet, and I waited till I no longer heard the echo of his steps before approaching Poppi where she still leaned on the ledge. We stayed there for a moment, the both of us looking out into the grey, frosty morning.

Did she think of the morning as a precious gift like I did? Or did she see it as another day coming to pass and get over with?

"Whatever you have to say, just spit it out already," she said sassily.

I gathered up my courage and set my pride to the side, making sure I approached this conversation with the delicate hand needed. But that was easier said than done because I knew Poppi just wanted me to leave her the hell alone.

"I don't want to fight," I said with a tinge of defeat already in my voice.

"Could have fooled me," she replied sarcastically, turning her gaze to me as she leaned on the stone.

"Look," I said, leveling with her. "I know you don't like me, and I know we haven't gotten off on the best start, but I hope you will just listen to what I have to say, so we can put whatever this is behind us."

"Fine," she conceded. "I'll listen, but don't expect me to feel any different about you in the end."

I drew in a deep breath, looking her in her brown eyes, so she knew that I wasn't scared of her or this conversation.

"I know what my life in Imeria looks like from the outside," I started. "I grew up in a palace with a family who loved me like one of their own. I received an education most wouldn't dare to hope for, and I made a name for myself by choosing my own path. I should be the happiest and luckiest person in the world."

Poppi scoffed, her eyebrows raising and lowering as she crossed her arms, turning to stand and look me straight on now. By her reaction, I knew I hit her judgment of me dead on.

"The truth few people know here is that my mother—my actual mother—abandoned me when I was a kid. I don't know why. No one ever told me. But it's left me with this hollow feeling inside, something that to this day I can't shake.

My mother was my everything. She was wild and free and smart and everything I wanted to grow up to be. It pains me that I'll never know what happened to her."

"I'm struggling to see what this has to do with me. Or with Lustraya . . ."

"The point I'm trying to make is that I understand the pain of losing something you hold dear, like everyone in Lustraya right now is facing."

She dropped her head and kicked a pebble away from her boot. When she looked up again, her hardened expression had softened.

"I took my sister's place at that ball because I didn't want one more thing to be taken from me. Or to have another family ruined. I chose to come here because it was the only way I saw to protect my family. And now that I'm here, I want to protect this place too."

"I really don't care—"

"I know you don't," I interjected, my temper slipping slightly at the last word. Poppi raised her eyebrow, turning away from me in dismissal. "But I want you to give me a chance, Poppi. A real chance. If not for me, then for everyone we have to lead out in that courtyard. We cannot go on being divided any longer. It's time for us to figure out how to be a team."

She shook her head, her half-bob tickling her chin as she rejected me for the umpteenth time.

I knew there was nothing more to say than what I already had. So, I turned from the ledge, giving her a curt nod before I left her in the tower.

"One day, I hope you will tell me your story, Poppi. And when you do, I'll be ready to fight for you all the same."

I took the stairs back down and out till I was walking the halls of the Fort, the weight easing from my shoulders the closer I neared the courtyard. The recruits should be waiting in their lines when I got there, ready for morning inspection.

Today was the day we began the next phase of their training. Kristian and Gunnar were heading this one up; giving the recruits a dose of what Lustrayan soldiers would be required to endure in this terrain. I would be learning alongside them today, my status report for Damien pending on the desk in my room already.

Poppi would be assisting them in the rearranging of groups, helping to start sorting the strong and the weak from one another to create frontliners and second units while I watched on. These were direct orders from the King himself; therefore, I would obey with no fit.

So, as I entered the courtyard of the Fort, I stuffed down my pride and watched the morning walk-throughs and discussions from the back. Today I would be putting myself in the shoes of these recruits and letting the boys shed their knowledge of this land on me.

Poppi joined us all soon enough, her demeanor calm and transfixed as she waited at the front for Gunnar and Kristian to meet her. Our eyes locked for a moment and instead of being met with her usual annoyance and disdain, there was a glimpse of understanding. Like a white flag being flown on a ship, and I felt a glimmer of hope begin to break through.

Gunnar finished his last circle of the recruits before nodding to Poppi, who stepped forward with a piece of parchment she had tucked in her back pocket. She began barking out names and ordering them into new lines. This would become their new unit, should they make it through the end of this exercise.

When the reordering and restructure was complete, Poppi looked to me still hanging in the back of the crowd.

"We begin the next phase of your training," she said steadily, her voice like a strong wind against a sail. "As we leave these gates, you will be handed a pack. In it will be all the things you need to make camp in the mountains. We move as a unit, and we move quietly. If you fall behind, you will be left behind. The mountains are as beautiful as they are deadly." She moved her gaze to my right, looking at Nic, who was first in her new group. "First group. Move out."

They wordlessly began to file out of the courtyard and through the west gate, a whistle of winter air following them like a quiet guide.

Gunnar and Poppi took the front lead, their horses kicking up snow as they made their way away from the Fort. Kristian came to find me in the back, two packs in each of his hands.

"Dani," he said, reaching one out to me. "For you. Horses should be ready to go."

I took the pack wordlessly and slung it onto my back, the strap crossing along my chest.

"Everything okay?" he asked as we moved through the gate and to the waiting steeds.

"As good as it's going to get, I suppose," I replied blandly.

I could tell Kristian wanted to push further but he let the topic go, for which I was thankful. My guess is that he knew exactly what was weighing on my mind and didn't want to exacerbate the circumstances further. If I were to guess, Gunnar filled him in on me going to the tower this morning.

I swung myself up onto my horse in one swift move, settling against the saddle for what was sure to be a long and very cold journey.

The boys had shown me a map of the mountain range and the trails we would be passing through. They looked steep and treacherous, and I prayed to whatever old god was listening that I was wrong for once. This was one of those moments that I would choose the boats of Imeria over an unknown terrain like this.

We steered the horses into a trot just as the wind and snow began to pick up. It was merciless. I tried to shrug further into my fur coat but not even that could keep the chill from seeping into my bones.

I envied the way Kristian managed to take the chill on the chin. The cheery tune he whistled carried in the air, a few of the recruits in front of us chirping in when they found the extra energy.

I couldn't think of a time when I was in my first few years of training with Imeria that anyone would be allowed to do something like that. Our protocols were strict and rigid. There was no room for games, no room for merriment. It probably explained why when we got a chance, we all acted like fools.

But it was in those moments that I became friends with Mads and Harrison. How I was able to bond with my unit like I did. It was the silly moments that brought us all together, not the ones where we were being relentlessly yelled at or told to keep fighting when even raising a sword took all of our energy.

I understood why Kristian was doing what he was doing.

This trip and this weather were terrible, but it could be tolerable by making a small moment feel not so bad. I wonder if that's how Poppi and Gunnar felt or if we would be the lone wolves in the cause.

Either way, anything that took my mind away would be acceptable. We still had nearly another hour of travel before we reached camp point one and my mind began to wander into the sadder topics of my life.

My new life in Lustraya I could begin to accept, but it never came without the pang of nostalgia for my previous one.

I missed my sister every day. It hurt that she had yet to write back to any of my letters—and I wrote her weekly at this point. Not hearing anything from Maddox or Harrison crushed me more.

What had become of them and the Serpentine Guard since I left? How would they be handling the situation of the border and Lustraya's clear breach of them? No way Clara let anyone in command get away with that one. They had gotten too close to Ary and that was Clara's biggest fear after losing her husband.

What could I do in my position now to assure our neighbor that something like that would never happen again?

My mind circled through the possibilities and the changes I could summon. Damien had to let me have a say in that one day. Which brought my thoughts around to my—gag—wedding. A shiver that had nothing to do with the cold slithered down my spine. Marriage. A concept and life path I had never wanted waited on my horizon.

Queen Daniella Castille of Lustraya.

Double gag. I couldn't be a Queen. I wouldn't even know where to begin when it came to fulfilling that duty. Astride this horse, I knew who I was and what I could accomplish. It unsettled me deeply to know how much of myself I would be losing to give my new kingdom the Queen they were promised. The one they deserved.

I looked over to Kristian as we climbed higher into the mountain pass and wondered what he actually thought of all this? What did he see me as? Afterall, he and Gunnar were there the night of the ball. Gunnar was the one who scooped me up from the frozen ground and into the King's tent. They saw everything.

He caught me staring and shot me over a small, comforting smile; as if he could see the storm spiraling in my mind. A storm that mirrored the one coming in from the west.

"Is that something to worry about?" I shouted, pointing a finger at the large clouds gathering over one of the peaks.

"No," Kristian shot back. "Looks like standard cloud cover."

It, in fact, was not just standard cloud cover.

Fifteen minutes later, Gunnar and his horse were running at us, panic stretching along his features as his eyes darted to us and to the sky.

"We need to circle up and get these recruits together. There's a storm coming in fast and it's a big one."

"What about the horses?" Kristian called.

"Get them into the trees," Gunnar replied, pointing to a barely visible hole through the snow in the line of trees to our left. "The deeper the better, but we better hope the storm passes quick or we're going to have to let them go."

He spun away, kicking up mud and snow as he traveled back to the front. Kristian and I worked quick against the rapidly increasing wind, nudging the horses into the tree cover and securing their reigns to a low-lying branch. I took the extra minute to throw a blanket around my mare in an attempt to keep her warm.

By the time we had them secured in place, the rest of the recruits had made it to the front of the group; all of whom were huddled together against the rock face of the mountain, their shirts pulled up to cover their mouths and fur caps dropped down as low as they could go. Body heat would be their greatest ally.

The beginnings of the storm were upon us now, which left Kristian and I in a precarious position with two options. One: we could run like hell through the foot of snow and join the others as our best chance of not dying of cold. But they were easily sixty yards away. Two: we could run like hell to the very small rock opening we passed and pray that it led to some sort of cover where we could ride out the storm.

I tapped Kristian's shoulder, getting him to look to where I wanted us to go.

"What are you pointing at?" he tried to ask over the howling of the wind.

"I think I saw a break in the rocks back there," I shouted. "There might be a cave or something we can hide in."

"That's too risky. We need to get to the others and shelter there; it's the safest option."

"But that way is faster!" I pleaded, hoping he sensed the urgency in my tone.

"Of all times to argue, you're really picking now?"

I glared defiantly in response, hoping he would see things my way. When he growled and reached for my elbow, I knew I had won. We took off at as much of a sprint as we could toward the rock, the snow slowing us down considerably as the storm began to bear down on us.

The wind gusted stronger as we ran against it, pushing us to the side as our feet lost their traction just before we reached the opening. I was knocked into Kristian, a strained grunt chorusing from his lips as my elbow met his ribs.

"Sorry!"

The opening was small—maybe too small—I realized as my fingers reached for the crack that turned out to be the edge of a rock wedged in front of another. I pulled with everything I had, and it budged very little. I pulled again and it moved only a millimeter more.

Kristian wrapped his hands around mine and tugged with me, the rock finally moving enough for me to check what was behind it.

The hole was no cave, but it was large enough for Kristian and me to settle in against if we sat on top of each other.

"I still say we should've gone back with the others," he scowled as he made room for me to crawl in first.

The smell was awful. Like rotting leaves and whatever animal had died in here. It was also so cramped I had to tuck my knees into my chest tightly as Kristian squeezed in behind me. The wind howled fiercely again outside as the storm increased in strength.

"Is this normal?" I asked, my teeth chattering loudly.

"Not in the least bit," Kristian stated, his eyes darting around the small space as if there was any way for something else to get in or out. It raised the hairs on the back of my neck in worry.

The longer I lived in this new kingdom, the more I realized how many secrets haunted its land. How the air here seemed to be coated in mystery and sadness. It was not the sparkling mountain kingdom I had been taught about, but I supposed that's what Damien wanted. It wasn't a good look to your enemies if they knew how bad you were falling apart.

I attempted to stretch my legs out from my chest just as another bought of wind blasted against the stone, the sound of an animal growling accompanying it. These were not the rough waters of the Cashian Sea anymore. This was the cry of a kingdom in pain.

"We can't sit like this forever," I said into the void, my breath coming out in puffs.

Kristian looked at me in agreement, his jaw working to keep his teeth from chattering against the frigid cold. We were curled on opposite sides of the cave—if we could even call it that—our knees tucked tightly under our chins, muscle cramps forming as the storm raged on.

"Okay, fuck it," I said, uncurling myself and moving toward him. "Open your legs."

His eyes went wide in shock, and he shook his head fiercely.

"Not like that," I scoffed. "Just do it."

He begrudgingly complied, untucking his knees and extending them forward and out as he maneuvered to the side to accommodate the space. When he had found a comfortable angle, I wiggled to the free spot in between his legs, settling my back against his chest.

"Warmth," I stated. "We'll need it to get through the worst of this, so our limbs don't cease to exist."

"This is weird. No girl has ever—"

"Please don't finish that sentence. This is for survival."

"This could get my head cut off, *Your Highness*."

Shit. He was right. This crossed a line of propriety that I never thought of. But then again, we were alone, and it was doubtful anyone would brave the force of the winds to come and get us. For the moment, we were okay. And if he kept his mouth shut, Kristian could keep his head.

"Just . . . keep quiet and get through this storm. N-no one will come to look for us in this, and we can meet up with the rest of the group once this b-blows over. No one has to know."

He remained quiet but I took that as a mutual understanding between us. We huddle down for warmth and then when the worst was over, we make our way back to the others. Simple. Easy. Effective.

Locked in with this knowledge, I let myself relax against Kristian, snuggling as close as our layers of clothing would allow us. The storm outside raged on and soon I found my eyes getting heavy, my body weak.

The trek and weeks in the Fort had been more draining than I realized and now that I had a moment to relax . . . it was nice. Too nice. Kristian's heart was a steady beat, like a lullaby, and eventually when my eyes closed, they stayed closed.

How long we were in that cave, I don't know, but the grogginess I felt when blinding white light entered the small space was immediate.

I groaned and Kristian tensed up.

"Princess!" someone yelled. "Princess, are you in here?"

The person was panicked and out of breath. Like they had been on the search for me for a while. It wasn't until the rock covering the opening was fully removed and Gunnar's silhouette revealed that the panic made sense. So did his look of distress as he beheld the way I was cradled against Kristian's chest; he, too, having dozed off with his arms around my shoulders.

He reacted quicker than I had the capacity to, pushing me away from him and to the opening where Gunnar was waiting to pull me out. The motion was quick and my feet drug under me as I tried to right myself and adjust to the light of day. I heard rather than saw Kristian scuttle out from our hiding spot, the two men exchanging strangled whispers.

"What the hell were you two—"

"It was cold and cramped. We had no choice."

"If Poppi gets wind . . ."

"And how would she know?"

"How would who know?"

Like a spell being cast, Poppi found herself outside the circle of our huddled bodies.

"Nothing," both men said, the lie written on their faces.

"Uh-huh . . ." Poppi mused, unconvinced. She leveled her eyes on mine, taking in my appearance: rumpled clothes, wild hair, ice-bitten skin. Kristian's was no less intense, and I could see her putting the pieces together in her mind. As unfortunate as it was, we did have a similar way of working out scenarios.

"We need to get back on the move," she stated plainly. "There's a pass between those two ridges ahead. Should take us half the day to get to, but once we do, we'll be blocked from most of the wind elements and can make camp. The work can begin afterward."

She spoke decidedly and surely, like she was the top commanding officer under Damien. Maybe that was what Poppi wanted, just like I had once wanted. Perhaps something I still wanted. It was another thing we could add to our similarities.

I squared my shoulders back giving the men a nod with my chin to follow Poppi's snowy steps back to the rest of the unit. I watched the curious eyes of the young recruit's rove over our appearances, taking in our strained silence and lack of congeniality. If this was Imeria, Armas and Samir would lose their heads to see such lack of discipline in their leadership.

"Everyone grab your rucksack," Poppi ordered, swinging up onto her horse. "We've got our work cut out for ourselves."

The bite in her words was not missed as she turned her horse away from us and sailed to the front of the line.

"Kristian, why don't you meet up with her. I'll hang back with the Princess," Gunnar suggested.

Kristian nodded his agreement, resting his hand gently on my shoulder for a brief moment and then he, too, was off.

I turned to Gunnar. "Why do I get the feeling I'm being put into some kind of time out?"

He shrugged his shoulders and walked off to fetch the horses that had not run away during the storm. I follow after, because what choice did I have?

I swung myself up on my horse the moment she was in front of me, lingering stares from the recruits never leaving.

"Well, you heard the woman. Move," I barked.

11

STRONGER TOGETHER

The canyon pass was a blessed reprieve from the torment of the winds and looming storms. Before the snow had fallen, this place would be riddled with wildflowers and tall grasses lining the long river that wound its way through. Seeing the frozen water now though only made the tattoo on my hip pulsate with longing.

I thought of Rivers and Tanner. Were they okay? Had they been removed from guard duty at the city and placed somewhere else?

They should've been here with me. They all should. I should be making this grand adventure with those that I trusted the most. The ones I had gone through the worst with. As much as I was grateful that

I had this new role to fill and minds to teach, it couldn't and wouldn't ever be the same as those I had made so many memories with.

I stole a quick glance over to Gunnar, who was watching me with a sad curiosity. It wasn't written plainly on his face but in his eyes. I held them as I let my shoulders sag and my own sadness cloud over my features. Vulnerability has never been my strong suit, but in this moment, I felt I could truly trust Gunnar. The realization that I had no one to lean on anymore seeped through my aching chest.

But just as quickly as I let the sadness show, I closed it back up. Yes, I wanted someone to know and see my pain, but I couldn't let it consume me. Not now. No matter how wide the hole was being ripped open.

I kicked my horse, jolting her back into motion. The recruits had already begun the process of fanning out and making camp the best they could in the conditions. I could hear Gunnar following right behind as we rode in search for Poppi and Kristian.

We needed to talk strategy and planning for what was to come over the next week or weeks, seeing as the snow could become detrimental. Poppi was in the middle of instructing Nic and another recruit about which stretch of woods would be the best to find dry wood for a fire when we found them.

"Remember," Poppi said to Nic. "Large logs and heavier pieces of wood to sustain the fire, but we need the kindling most. Find the dryest grass possible and small twigs. We have no shot of sustaining warmth without a proper starter." She placed a large leather satchel into Nic's arms and sent the two on their way.

"Come to grace me with another one of your stories? What, did you go camping once as a child and have better instruction on how to get a fire going?" she called to me, hands going to her hips.

Was she really trying to pick a fight here and now?

I shuffled through the snow, coming to stand in front of her, aghast. I raised my arms out to the side and let them drop back down heavily.

"Anything else you want to say to me?" I asked her.

Her nostrils flared and pupils dilated as I saw her reel in her anger, and work to not make a scene right here and now.

"You are such an arrogant asshole, you know that?" she ground out. "You think telling me one story about your oh-so-tragic childhood is going to me make me like you? Think again."

"Yeah?"

"Yeah!"

She paused, the restraint she usually kept slipping as she let all her pent-up words toward me fumble out.

"And another thing," she said, stepping closer to me so no one else could hear. "I don't care what anyone tells me about you; you will *never* be my princess. You will always be a spoiled brat in my eyes with no *right* to lead these people, and tell them how they should feel and live their lives!"

"Is that it?" I said, matching her slick tone, egging her on so we could let out all our animosity.

"No! Actually . . ." She stepped closer, pointing her finger right between my eyes. "I don't like your attitude toward the King, either. You have no idea what he has done for us as a kingdom. The sacrifices he has made and is willing to make. You should be lucky he accepted you and has brought you into the fold as he has, you ungrateful bitch."

Normally, I would have hit her by now for getting so close in front of my face, but I was willing to overlook it for the sake of this moment.

"What else?"

Maybe it was the steady calm in which I delivered the line, or the way I refused to back down to her intimidation, but her spine straightened and her hand dropped. Honestly, it was a line Arabella would have been very proud of. Calm, fierce, slightly egging on the situation. Picture perfect princess.

"We have to make camp and get these recruits set up for the next leg in their training. Pitch your tent and then we begin."

Poppi said everything with a finality to it, stomping away like someone who was used to calling all the shots and not having to back down to anyone. What a sight it would be to see her go up against that heinous Colonel with an attitude like hers. Now, that would make me Poppi's number one fan.

Gunnar and Kristian busied themselves by tending to the horses and removing the packs from their backs, like they weren't just watching us with concern seconds ago. And there I was, left looking around aimlessly for something to busy myself with like the others. How embarrassing.

People will never see you the way you want them to, Daniella. All you can do is lead with your best foot forward, and chin up, and hope that they see you for who you are . . .

That's what Clara told me after she had found out I ran away and Sam found me. That moment was my turning point in this life, and it seems to me that there is still a lesson I have yet to learn from it.

I took another look around the snowy area—at all the troops scattering about, doing what they can to make the cold tolerable—and then an idea occurred to me.

It would have to wait till sundown, of course. When Poppi's temper had fizzled, and everyone was more at peace with being locked in between a mountain pass that was equal parts terrifying and beautiful. But it would help boost the morale of everyone. Or so I was hoping.

I would need Nic's help too. As much as I had gotten my crew of recruits to trust me, I know not everyone was in the same mindset. I found her by a stack of wood, doling out the kindling and dry branches like they were precious gemstones—which I guess was true, considering the harsh climate we were about to have to survive.

"Nic!" I said happily, approaching the group as pleasantly as I could.

"Yes, Your Highness," she replied with a small bow of the hips.

"I need your help with something."

Nic listened intently as I explained my plan to her, a small and hopeful smile cracking along her features as she began to plan out how she would achieve my request.

It took no matter of time before the sun descended over the peaks and the fires illuminated the dark, the perfect setting to my plan. Gunnar sat to my right, Kristian to my left, and Poppi was across from us, slouched over her knees, cradling a bowl of stew—if we could even call it that. Conversations were whispered amongst the flames; the tones hushed, concerned, and dotted with the occasional chatter.

I felt their nerves, the panic that would be taking root in their stomachs as their realities came to fruition. Whether they were carpenters, blacksmiths, seamstresses, or castle workers; all these people had new identities. And if anyone knew what it felt like to start over, it was me.

After the final bowls from dinner had been collected, Nic arrived into our circle at precisely the right moment, a few of her newly formed friends trailing behind her. She caught a stray look from Poppi, and quizzical ones from the gentlemen seated on either side of me. Why would this young recruit dare enter the campfire of her superiors so boldly?

"Your Highness," she asked timidly as she settled on a log adjacent to mine. "I was wondering if you had any advice to offer . . . perhaps from your early days of being a soldier? I-I . . ." Nic let her words trail off but anyone around could sense where her thoughts were taking her. Fear. Anxiety. Concern. Anger. Every emotion could blend into one and create its own inner chaos.

"It wasn't without its own difficulty," I admitted. "Even I have to admit it was all harder than I thought, and I had had some training prior to making the decision to join Imeria's ranks."

Nic locked eyes with me, hers encouraging me to keep going.

"The truth is, I have never been exceptionally good at anything in my life," I continued, cradling a mug of tea in my hands. "I just got really good at trying. Clara—Her Majesty the Queen—often referred to me as her stubborn child unable to quit once I started something. I wanted to be the best, always. Perfect, even. Before I never really knew the job I was signing up for, I thought to myself 'head down, eyes forward. And if that doesn't work, then run them over.'"

A few stifled laughs worked their way around the small circle. I noticed three new recruits standing behind Nic, their ears trained on the conversation.

"That philosophy only got me so far though, because after two weeks in, my ass had so many bruises from being shoved to the ground, I could no longer sit, no matter how hard I tried."

More laughter, more people gathering around. Exactly as I wanted it. Kristian and Gunnar seemed to release the tension in their shoulders the more I continued to talk, and the more people came around to listen.

This wasn't my Imerian unit and the river— *that* I would never be doing again—but I realized the same process could be applied here.

Gain their respect. Well, diving headfirst into snow and a cold river was not an option now. But story telling . . . that was a tale as old as time itself. Everyone loved a good story, and boy, did I have a lot of them to share. That's what everyone here needed, I realized. They needed to be seen, to be heard. To be reaffirmed that their experience is not uniquely their own. That their leadership also bared scars and embarrassment from their early days, and at the end of it all, we were all human.

And then there was Poppi.

"What about you, Poppi?" I asked, extending whatever fragile peace we had even further into her hands. "What was it like when you joined Lustrayan forces?"

She gave me a deadpanned look, let her eyes rove around those that had gathered, and crossed her arms. Silence. As was her favorite form of punishment toward anything I tried to do.

"I'll go," Gunnar said, raising his hand softly. We all looked to him with anticipation. "My brother . . . he was my hero. Undoubtedly the greatest man I've ever known. He was kind and sincere, a hardass; but gentle all the same. He loved Lustraya with everything he knew. When we were boys, he would talk about the battle strategies he would use in the event someone would ever try to overtake us.

"Then the First Raids happened, and he got his opportunity. He was one of the first people to step forward and commit himself to the kingdom and keeping it safe. The rest of our village followed suit because that is who he was. Fierce, steadfast. A true leader who knew what he wanted to do with his life."

Gunnar sniffled ever so quietly, something that caught me off guard and sent a shiver down my spine. One that told me this story didn't have a happy ending, and he was doing his hardest to keep it together.

"When the First Raids were over, my brother changed. He was hardened and more reserved. He carried his pain on his shoulder, the loss of all his men heavy on his heart. Then the Second Raid came . . ."

Many of the people that had gathered were now poised on the edge of their seats or toes, the only sound to be heard was the cackling of the fires around us.

"He held the battle front to the very end. Never faltering, never giving into the exhaustion that plagued him. Because of his sacrifice, seven villages were able to heed the warning calls and get to safety in the mountain. My own village included. While I may have kept my own life . . . I lost my brother, my best friend."

He let a few tears fall down his cheeks in memory for his brother. But when he spoke again, his voice was steady as a drum. "It's for him that I fight. For him that I walk down the road I never wished to. But I couldn't let my brother's memory, his accomplishments, be of waste. I promised him that night I would carry on his legacy. I keep that promise to this day."

"Your brother was Igo. The White Blade," came a voice from three rows back. A collective intake of breath chorused its way around as the history of Gunnar's words took root in some people's minds.

"I was eleven when I lost him," Gunnar continued. "But his loss feels just like yesterday." He then looked to me, his eyes glassy and face set in stone resolve. "It is why I admire our new princess so much."

Gunnar turned his head from me and made eye contact with all those that stood around us.

"You all weren't there the night she gave her life for her sister's. You did not see how she cut through men to defend her family. Or how she held a blade to our King's neck fearlessly, knowing that it could cost her her life. In the end though, she chose to take her sister's place. A life for a life, without the bloodshed. It was the honorable thing and an act born of love. Love for one's family and for one's country.

"Now I don't know about you, but I think everyone has at least that much in common. Lustraya has seen better days, and Dani may not be the princess that was promised but she is the one we deserve. And I will gladly follow her into battle."

Tears welled in my eyes as Gunnar took my hand and squeezed. I folded my other over his, embracing him in the best way I could. My heart broke for the loss that haunted Gunnar, a loss that I could understand. For the first time ever, I finally met someone who could meet me eye-to-eye on the pain and duty that weighed on my shoulders.

Silence coaxed everyone into somber thought. The embers of the fire crackling against the quite night.

"The kingdom roared . . . And in the light, it burned. Her kingdom come," Poppi cooed in a low timbre.

"The retreat she mourned.

Two thousand men, in a grave with snow.

To the wintery night, she raised her sword.

For her people, she'd defend the way.

A sworn oath, she released a cry.

She held the line through the screams of *night.*

The ground turned red, the debt finally repaid."

When the last verse finished, I felt my bones vibrate with the love and hate of a thousand ancestors. Of those that came before and sacrificed everything they had for what they loved. The tune chilled me to the bone yet somehow erupted a fire so deep within me that I couldn't make sense of the sudden pull to this land, to these people.

A lone tear slid down my cheek, and then another. I looked to Nic, and then to those around her, and then finally to Poppi who—for the first time—seemed to get me.

"What was that?" I asked through a hushed breath.

""The song of Lost Souls." Of Alita the Brave," she explained. "Said to be born of the light between sun and shadow, she was Lustraya's first protector. Legend says she held the line between Fae and witch. Light and Dark. She was the protector of all man and womankind, the first of her name. The stories also say the gods of old blessed her with wonderful capabilities to end the strife that has always riddled this continent, but in the end . . . the hatred of one group spoiled it for all.

"Alita was everything good and pure the gods had to offer, and everything dark and enticing the world had to offer. She now lives on in the stars, her blood given to the ground in which she sacrificed herself for the protection of others. Lustraya's first Queen."

Mist clouded Poppi's eyes, as did it everyone else's. I still clutched Gunnar's hand in my own, the touch offering a comfort I didn't know I needed. When I looked over to Kristian, he had his hands clasped in his lap, wringing his hands in an effort to self-soothe.

I reached over my free hand, offering it to him in solidarity. He looked at it for a heartbeat before gingerly accepting it and lacing his fingers through mine. As another tear streaked down my face, I steeled my spine, wanting all the words I spoke next to be heard loud and clear.

"I may not be the princess you all desired and hoped for. I may be a foreigner, and ill-educated on your customs, and perhaps a bit ill-tempered, but I swear to you this from this night forward: I will fight for you. For all of you. For your mothers and fathers, brothers." A look to Gunnar then Nic. "And sisters. I won't rest until this kingdom has been restored to what it once was. What it always should have been." I looked to Poppi as I said the last of the promise I would make to all that were here.

"Until my dying day and final breath, I shall call Lustraya my home."

Poppi raised the chipped mug into her hand high above her head, others around following suit. Some even crossing their fists over their hearts.

"The Princess Daniella," she boomed. "Long may she reign."

12

LEGEND HAS IT

Dani, get up, we've got to go!"

Never had I ever been shaken awake with such urgency, such panic. Immediately I went into fight mode, reaching across my tent to latch onto the hilt of my sword and remove it from its sheath.

"What it is it?" I screeched as I was yanked out of the tent and toward waiting horses.

"I don't know," Gunnar roared. "It's not an ambush but—"

A blood bath.

Red coated the white down of the snow, the crimson mingling with the grey and white to create a landscape of absolute horror.

A scream caught in my throat as I took in the scattered bodies, the eyes of my recruits lifeless and vacant. Gunnar tugged at my hand with all his might, jerking me to his side as an arrow came whizzing past my ear; a thunderous roar echoing against the clashing of steel and screams.

"I don't understand . . ." I mumbled as a scuttle of movement in the tree line caught my attention.

I watched in disbelief as three large grey-and-white spotted beasts prowled out from the tree line, their maws bared with red coating their teeth. It was something out of a nightmare, something that not even my fears in trial three could have replicated.

They pulled back on their haunches and launched themselves at the scattering recruits, some managing to escape and others becoming not so lucky. Some bravely wielded their blades against the monsters, their warrior instincts kicking in as they fought to defend the camp.

"Dani, move! Now!" Gunnar screamed again, this time my feet stumbling under me as I was pulled to where the horses stood waiting for us. But still, I couldn't move my eyes from the carnage.

Had I not just promised to defend these people till my dying breath last night? It would seem that that oath was being put to the test and what was I doing? Standing here frozen and not fighting. The one thing I was good at.

The realization snapped me back to reality and I yanked my arm from Gunnar, spinning on him as I shouted, "We have to help them!"

I entered the fray manically, swinging my sword at the beast who charged for my people. With each stroke of my blade, I drew blood, the whimpering and retreat of the animals a song of victory as I worked closer to where the real damage lie.

But just as I thought the retreat was almost done, the unexpected happened and I felt my heart bottom out. There, in the middle of the snow, stood Nic, her sword raised and her face defiant as she looked at one of the beasts with no fear. I would be proud of her determination if I wasn't so terrified. Nic, the young girl who never wanted this life, whose brother was a scholar, continued the fight with all her might.

The beast swiped at her but missed as she ducked right and rolled. But the snow slowed her momentum, and as she stood back up to face it, the monster slashed out its claws, lines of red spurting from her chest as it made contact with her.

"Nic!"

My vision went red, redder than it ever did in the Gauntlet, redder than I thought I could see. Fury whirled its way through me, and I gripped the hilt of my sword so hard I thought I would bend the steel.

"You stay away from her!"

My battle cry rang out clear enough that the beast turned, his icy-blue eyes locking with my own. I didn't think; I just acted on pure instinct, running full speed to where it stood, and swinging my blade around to cut the creature's flank.

It dodged the full might of my blow, but not before the tip of my sword was able to catch the barest of flesh and leave a trail of . . . purple?

Its blood was purple? How had I missed that?

The moment of being stunned was enough for the animal to leap at me, baring those long teeth once more.

"Bring it on, fur ball!" I taunted.

It lashed out again with its claw, the nails almost as long and sharp as the finest dagger. But I anticipated it would do this, and side stepped to my left, swinging the blade around to connect with the other side of the creature's flank.

"Is that the best you got?"

Where this well of confidence came from, I do not know, for I felt more fear than anything else in this moment of time. But from my side vision, I could see Nic being dragged to safety and most of the camp running into the safety of the rocks of the passage, and that seemed to give me the ego boost I needed.

"C'mon, I expected better," I cooed, lashing out once more.

The creature evaded, coming close to swiping me along my shoulder with its claws.

"Is that the best you can do?"

That was where my ego and confidence died. In the shadow of the tree line emerged two more of the large beasts, their maws foaming and tongues licking their teeth like they were ready for dinner. And gods knew they were about to have the best meals of their lives.

"Well, come on then," I roared, flipping the hilt of my sword. "Do your worst."

They lunged with a vengeance, and I slashed out, darting and ducking their advancements. Steel met claw in a resounding clash, the creatures growling their displeasure for every blow I dodged of theirs. Swiftly, I was pushed to the small river's edge, the ice licking at my boots. I was already unsteady in the snow but this? How the hell could I run away on ice?

In the distance I heard Poppi roaring orders and Kristian and Gunnar doing their best to get to me. But who were they against three fearsome beasts; the likes of which I had never seen or heard of. Never in a history book, never a passed down legend.

The leader—I assumed, anyway, due to its immense size—was taking slow and calculated steps toward me, each one accompanied by deep, guttural growls. It stopped its slow advancement when my boot hit the ice, the slickness of it sending me off my balance for a mere second.

The creature smiled—*smiled*—tilting its head up to the sky to roar its accomplishment to its comrades.

I felt something in me stir just then, something deep within me, past the pit that usually sat hollow in my gut. No, I felt this feeling in my bones. Felt it vibrate and shake me in a way that felt like my blood was humming.

The creature snapped its jaws at me again, licking its foul lips as it took another step closer.

The adrenaline that pulsed through my veins was no match for the feeling that surged in me now. I felt my vision go spotty, the corners of my eyes sparking, as I felt myself lose control to the feeling.

My pulse thudded in my ears as I reached my hands down to the snow, feeling for the ground that was frozen beneath it. The monster snapped at me again but this time I let a new instinct take hold, and soon I felt the burning vibration of my bones roar back at the beast as a scream ripped its way up my throat and at the monsters looming.

It was a roar so loud that it shook the snow from the trees and made the ground tremble. My hands dug further into the mud as my scream intensified, the monster's ears flattening in surprise as I roared back.

The creature reared back to its friends, their steps stumbling backward from me until they turned all together and bolted for the tree line; tails low, and purple blood leaving a trail.

When I felt the threat fade, I released my scream, my throat going raw and my head spinning in exertion. As my head fell forward, I heard the rushed screams of Kristian and Gunnar come toward me.

"Are you okay?" they called as they raced toward my precarious position to the ice. I tried to speak but my voice wouldn't allow it. I managed to mumble an incoherent "I'm fine" before a rush of lightheadedness. I began to fall to the ice as Kristian swept me into his arms seconds before impact, my body going limp with exhaustion.

"Get her on the horse and let's *move*," Poppi shouted from atop her own before flying to the front of the remaining units.

"Wait," I coughed. "The bodies . . ."

"There's nothing we can do, Princess. We must go."

Princess. A word I once loathed. But when said in a tender and loving way, I had come to see it as a privilege. Particularly when it was said by one person.

"Aeddan . . ."

And then the world went to black.

". . . did you see?"

"Of course I saw. Everyone around her saw."

"What do you think it means?"

"It means we need to get her back into the mountain."

"Do you think . . ."

"She can't know or else she would have been hunted."

The words were barely whispers of breath and my head barely comprehended what was being said. She? Hunted? Who were they talking about and what did they see?

I tried to open my eyes, but the effort was too much, my head too heavy. I tried to move my hand to get their attention, but it was being held down by an invisible weight. I would have tried words, but instead a low grunting noise slithered out of my throat.

"Get the sleeping tonic, she's awake again," someone nearby barked. The voice was feminine, but deep. Commanding. Poppi? No, it couldn't be. She went back to the front to get the recruits out of the pass, right?

I tried to refuse the tonic as it was put to my lips, but someone grabbed my jaw and ripped it open. The sickly-sweet fluid dripped down my throat and into my gut, my breathing growing heavier by the second.

"That's enough. Get her back on that horse and don't stop till you've reached the gates." That same commanding voice—Poppi, I was certain—ordered. "And take this. In case any more surprises occur. And give this to His Majesty and His Majesty alone."

Feet shuffling and the whistle of swords being returned to their sheaths were the only sounds occupying wherever we were. A pair of strong hands slipped under my shoulders and knees, cradling me to their chest and eventually heaved onto the steed.

Before the tonic took me once more, I heard the voice of the person who cradled me against their chest whisper in my ear, "Hang on a little while more, Dani. We have you."

I felt the softness of the furs first, followed by the sweet chilly breeze caressing my face. I was relaxed and comfortable, something that was not familiar for my body as of late. But it was none of those things that had my eyes peeling themselves open to the twilight of my mountain room; it was the pang coming from my stomach.

Hunger. I was really, *really* hungry.

I tried to sit up, and the motion caused my head to go into the spins, for which I readily put my head back to the pillows. I groaned. Gods, I felt so weak, so feeble.

The doors to the room burst open and Damien swept in in a flurry, Poppi right behind him. The ladder joined Kristian as the door closed, the duo taking up rigid stances in front of it as if those monsters lurked near.

Damien's breathing was heavy as he checked over me for any signs of harm. I could tell by the way his brows creased together, and his hands shook, that he was worried. Panicked even.

I tried to reach out and touch his hand for comfort, but I felt too weak to accomplish that. Once Damien had finished his inspection of my well-being, he sat at the edge of the foot of my bed, patting my foot for reassurance.

"So," he drawled. "I heard you had an eventful few days."

It had to be his attempt at a joke, but it was delivered with none of the comedy it needed to elicit a laugh. Instead, his words hung heavy as the events came back to me.

"H–how . . ." I tried to say but couldn't through the burn in my throat. I coughed dryly, my chest convulsing as I tried to stanch the pain that landed there.

Damien was back on his feet in seconds, his arm snaking around my shoulders and propping me up so I could better breathe.

"Fetch her some water," he instructed to Kristian or Poppi.

Kristian obeyed without hesitation; his steps fast and sure as he crossed the room to the tray and pitcher that was settled near my couch.

Damien watched over me closely as I righted myself, the deep sleep from the tonic ebbing away and leaving behind a pounding headache. It remained quiet in the room for a while, the only sound coming from the running water of the soaking tub in the bathing room and the slow sips I took from my cup.

Oh, how those warm waters called my name.

Damien caught my gaze lingering on the corner where the pool lay just beyond.

"Would you like to bathe, Daniella?"

I nodded my head gingerly, taking Damien's outstretched hand to steady myself as I stood up. My head spun for only a moment and as soon as I felt right, he helped me shuffle to the entrance.

Everything was just as I had left it, including the tray of bottles on the edge of the pool I used to pamper myself.

"Do you need help," he asked. "Or should I go ahead and give you some privacy?"

I pointed to the edge of the water, my throat still not able to form tangible words. Luckily, he understood and escorted me to the ledge, disappearing once I set my feet in the water and butt on the step.

I peeled off my clothes slowly and surely, days of sweat and grime still caked on my skin. And that smell . . . vile.

I pushed out further into the water, letting the heat wrap me in an embrace and sooth the aches and pains. It felt like magic. The longer I stayed in the water, the more I lathered myself in the vanilla jasmine soap, the more alive I felt. The more human I became.

I had no idea the amount of time that passed, but when I finally padded my way back into the main room, swaddled in a robe, I felt like a new person.

"Is that for me?" I croaked, pointing to the bronze two-tiered tray that was next to Damien.

"Yes," he said, standing up and helping me back into bed. "What can I bring you?"

Everything.

My stomach roared loudly, a small smile pulling at the corners of Damien's mouth as my body replied for me. Without another thought

Damien placed a bread roll, broth and pudding on a plate for me, carrying it over and setting it on my lap.

"Eat," he said. "When you're ready, I would like to hear your story on the events that happened on the road."

I nodded my head, taking my first bite of warm food in days. It was divine. A gift. Something I ended up scarfing down in a manner that would make both Sam and Clara stick their noses up with distaste for my lack of manners.

He waited till my first plate was cleared. And then my second. When I felt satisfied, I looked to Damien, his expression amused and waiting.

"Are you ready?" he asked with a gentle tone.

"What do you want to know?" I replied hoarsely, sipping at some water.

"Take me to the snowstorm," he said. "Anything you may have noticed that was different. No detail is too small."

"The storm," I said. "Came on very suddenly. We shouldn't have hit bad weather like that for a few more days, according to Poppi's calculations. I've never been caught by anything like that in my life, but I guess one could compare it to catching choppy waves right before a hurricane.

"Kristian and I got separated from everyone else and had to hide in a small cave to ride out the worst of it. Poppi found us and we quickly altered course for the passage. I was told it would be the safest place because the rock faces would block out most of the wind and snow that would be trailing after the storm."

"And that's it?" he asked, clasping his hands in his lap, his head cocking slightly to the side as he listened.

"To the first question, yes. What else is there you want to know?"

Poppi and the King exchanged a glance.

"What?" I asked.

"Tell me about the ambush." Damien stated.

"Your Majesty, she—" Poppi started to say but was cut off with Damien's raised hand.

"Dani. Please. If you would."

Something felt off in the room. I couldn't place a finger to it, but Damien's kindness and patience in this moment led me to believe something more had transpired at the camp, and I wasn't aware of it.

"I was woken up to it," I said, sitting up further in bed. "The screaming of the recruits . . . we ran out as fast as we could. There was so much blood in the snow, it was . . . I have never seen anything like it. Gunnar and Kristian wanted to get me on a horse and out of the way, but I didn't. I hurled myself into battle, so please don't punish them."

"Why wouldn't you go?"

"Because I made a promise," I said tersely. "I promised them that I would fight for them—with them. I would be a coward if I turned my back on them right after promising to defend them the night before."

"But you've hardly been here a few months. Why make such a promise?"

"Because I am their princess and future Queen as everyone likes to constantly remind me." I rolled my neck, the joints cracking with tension. "I did what I thought was necessary to save lives and to distract the enemy. I will not apologize for that."

"You put yourself in danger. Put the crown in danger. If you die, Dani, there is no one to replace me. Do you understand how dangerous that could be for Lustraya?"

I would have thought by now Damien would be yelling at me, but he surprised me again by keeping his voice smooth and gentle. And when I saw the slight sheen coat his eyes, it hit me that he was genuinely worried. That he truly cared.

"I'm sorry," I said sheepishly. "You're right, I didn't think. I just acted. But Damien . . . nothing could have been as dangerous as those monsters were. I mean," I took a sip of water to help the dryness taking root in my throat again. "I have never read about or seen those animals in my life, ever. It was the thing of nightmares."

"And yet, you. . . " A quick glance to Poppi again. "Yelled at one?"

I had forgotten about that. My cheeks reddened in embarrassment, as that moment came back to me.

"I was looking death in the face. I did what my instincts were telling me to," I admitted as I played with the fur trim of my blanket.

"So instead of running . . ."

"I was pushed up against the ice. Even if I decided to run, I wasn't making it far."

There was something I was missing in this moment, something I was too tired to try and figure out. But Damien caught my quizzical looks, a large breath leaving his chest as he settled an internal debate. He looked over to Kristian and Poppi once more, a silent conversation passing between them before he turned back to me.

"Come," he said gently. "There is something I want to show you."

13

ROYAL TALES

I threw on one of the dresses from the wardrobe, the ensemble tailored to fit me instead of billowing out like I hated. I smiled to myself as I took note of the small change.

I hastily followed Damien and Poppi through the cave corridors to the library. Though the top part of the dress was tailored, the skirt remained long, and I tripped often over the dark blue wool as we traveled up a ramp to the doors that led us to our destination.

"Everything okay back there?" Damien asked, his voice echoing on the rock.

"Oh, just perfect," I growled back. "Nothing some hemming couldn't fix."

"But I had them retailored for you?"

"Seems to me that the seamstress forgot I am not the height of a man, then."

He chuckled and I resisted the urge to smack him playfully in the back of the head.

The library doors came before us and opened on a phantom wind, the musty smell of old books wafting out to greet us. We stepped into the hollowed cave, the blue-and-green lights winking as we passed the first rows of shelves, quickly veering left and into awaiting darkness. I hurried my steps forward, saddling up next to Poppi and grabbing her hand.

"I hate the dark," I confessed with a murmur.

She answered with a small pat to my hand as we followed Damien up a secluded and dangerous set of stairs. They wound down and around, only one sparse blue light illuminated our feet enough to see the step in front of us. When we finally reached the bottom, we had to jolt to a halt in order to keep from smacking into Damien's back.

"Poppi," the King said.

"On it," she replied expectantly.

She dropped my hand back to my side and drew her sword, turning her back to us and taking up a strong, rigid stance before us. A protector in action.

The clanging of keys and the turning of a lock brought me back to the task at hand. Damien shoved open the door, the hinges squeaking with disuse.

"Follow me," Damien instructed as he disappeared into the dark.

Well, shit.

It was with blind faith that I followed Damien into the damp space, the door closing behind me. Aside from a small trickle of water from somewhere, the room was absolutely silent. The room itself was also cold, something I wouldn't have thought possible considering there was no access to the outside from here.

A scuffle and groan from Damien echoed along the rocks as the blue-and-green lights that accommodated the rest of the top side of the mountain fortress glowed to life.

"This is my personal library," Damien commented, walking from around a back row of bookshelves. "My family's library. Only those of royal blood are allowed in this room."

To say the books on these shelves were old would be an understatement. I ran my finger gingerly over the leather spine of the one closest to me and I could practically hear it purr with need to be opened.

"What do they contain?" I asked in wonder, walking further into the shelves.

"History, mythology, genealogy, random journals of my ancestors. Anything that they thought important enough to pass on is down here. It's my greatest treasure."

"I didn't take you as one for appreciating books."

"Books are our only portal to the past. For without them, we cannot learn, and learning is something I think stops at no age. Especially now, there is much the past can teach us."

"Is that why you brought me down here? To teach me?"

"I wanted to show you."

Damien stepped around the last bookshelf, carrying a small leather journal and a larger book beneath it.

"These have been in my family since the first Kings and Queens ruled. They are very fragile, but I think you could benefit from their contents."

"Or you could just tell me what they say . . ."

"I could. But if I told you, you wouldn't believe me. And I need you to believe from the firsthand accounts of the tale."

"Tale? As in a story? Myth?"

"Who said stories don't hold truth within them, Daniella? What I am offering you is a look into a window of who you could be. You must already know that what you saw in the mountain pass was nothing short of abnormal.

"Poppi already told me she shared with the camp the tale of the Alita the Brave, our first Queen. I think you will find this journal most instructive if you were so moved by her story to give your life for recruits you hardly know."

I looked from the books in my hand to Damien. His face was calm and steady, no hint of ire or annoyance. Just pure devotion. For the first time I felt I could relate to the man before me.

He wanted to protect the people he loved and would stop at nothing to accomplish it; something I related to. In a way, he reminded me of Clara. In a different time maybe, they would have been friends.

"I will read them and report back to you," I said, clutching the leather to my chest and looking the King squarely in the face.

"I know you will."

Dear Ary,

Why haven't you answered me? I know I've sent more than enough letters to get one reply from you. So much is changing, and I need to tell my sister. Mostly I need your advice, which is so rare for us.

There was this mountain pass, and as much as I wish I can tell you about the details over paper, I cannot. But what I can say is that for the first time, I finally understand why you complained so heavily about becoming a Queen. It's terrifying.

I was faced with the harrowing truth a few days ago and all I want is to ask you how you handle it. Won't you please answer?

Damien has become more pleasant since I've been here. He has been more amiable and a good conversationalist. We talk about books and history, about duty and military strategy. We never speak of the wedding, which I am grateful for because every time I think of that, my heart breaks.

I won't ask you for an update on Aeddan because knowing is almost as painful as not knowing. But if this is the letter you decide to answer, perhaps you can tell me how Harrison and Maddox are?

It's torture not being around you all, but don't fret. I've managed to make two friends. Maybe three. Poppi is growing on me like a wart. I fear we become more similar every day and it irritates me because I want to hate her. After all, she has been nothing short of unwelcoming since I got here. But I understand her; at least I think I do. Only time will tell, I guess.

Please give Clara my love. You two mean everything to me.

Your sister,

Dani

I had a new routine these past weeks. I rose every morning in my mountain room; I had breakfast with Damien and then made my way over to the Fort where I worked with my team and the recruits.

The Colonel and I still didn't see eye-to-eye on things, but even he couldn't deny the valiance and bravery our new unit showed in the mountain pass. The experience changed something in them all. Made them more hungry, more willing to be molded into soldiers that could win a war.

At lunch, we would all eat as one in the mess hall before leaving for classroom instruction. Battle strategy, geographic understanding, and lessons in history were alternated on a day-by-day basis. Kristian thrived in this environment. He was most enthusiastic putting together lessons and then taking them to the courtyard for practice. The beast attack changed something in him too.

At night, I would ride back to the castle and dine with the King once more where we would talk about the new unit's progress and anything else. It still startles me that he is actually a good man. Sure, he slapped me so hard I was left with a bruise, but I know now if he ever did it again, I would beat him into a pulp without anyone stopping me. He would have earned it. Like he has now earned my friendship.

"How are you finding Queen Alita's journal these days?" he asked me from my right.

"Sad," I stated plainly. "She really seemed to carry the burden of everything and everyone on her shoulders. And to be a widow too? No wonder the woman sacrificed herself—she was miserable."

"Miserable, maybe. But she saved countless lives, don't you think?"

"Well, yes of course. But there had to have been another way, right? Or have all the kingdoms silently hated each other since the beginning?"

"You tell me. Does a wedding between Imeria and Segall sound like a contract of hate?"

"More like a contract of convenience. Much like ours, I suppose."

Damien remained quiet as I let the last words out, his head solemnly dropping as he placed his silverware down.

"That's not to say Theo and Ary don't love each other," I blurted. "They're . . . madly in love. But the circumstances in which they came to marriage were not born of it. I'm glad my sister has found what her heart has always desired."

"And you," Damien cut in. "Have you found what you desired?"

It was my turn to slowly drop my silverware to the sides of my plate. I folded my hands in my lap as I turned to look Damien squarely in the face.

"All I have ever desired was a family. To have parents to care for me. Maybe even a sibling." The wound in my heart thudded. "Clara did the best she could and I got Ary. It was never the happy ending I pictured but it's enough. They are my family, as I guess now you are."

A small smile cracked on Damien's face.

"We're family?"

"You're not as bad as you once were. And I'm stuck here for the rest of my life anyway. Might as well learn to tolerate your presence, right?"

"Tolerate," he chuckled. "So, there was never any other suitors? No one that ever caught your attention?"

I drew in a breath. I had not told anyone here about Aeddan. I wanted his identity and life protected at all costs. Not to mention the disaster that was the ball, and if anyone had seen us at any point in the evening, Aeddan's life would be placed in jeopardy.

"No," I said finally. "No one."

"So," he pressed, a twinkle of knowing in his eyes. "Aeddan is?"

My eyebrows shot to my hairline. "How do you . . ."

"You mumbled his name right before Gunnar scooped you off the ice in the mountain pass. I've been curious if you'd ever bring him up, but you haven't."

"It's not relevant. He's not relevant," I said defensively and suddenly scared of what might happen if anyone here knew that their Princess and future Queen had feelings for another. Would it be something as dramatic as a hanging or something just like pure hate? The hate I think I could live with. Consider it an old friend of mine.

"Alright then," he conceded. "I was just curious. You don't talk much about the people you left in Imeria, so I figured he was important to you somehow."

"We just competed in the Gauntlet together," I managed. "But that's it. What is it we have to do tomorrow again?"

"The advisers are back," he replied, letting me change the conversation. "We need to rethink strategy and numbers. We're losing this fight."

"And the fight is against . . ."

"Have you finished your reading?"

"No."

"So, then you have been chosen to be kept in the dark."

I rolled my eyes. "You've given me a journal of a sad queen and a book of old stories and mythology. One which died centuries ago and the other nothing short of a bedtime story for kids."

"You mean to tell me you're too grown for stories?"

"I'm too grown to believe in the unbelievable. These are ghost stories, Damien, not fact."

I could see the disappointment brush his features, but it evaporated quickly.

"Finish your reading, Dani."

That was the last thing he said to me as we finished our dinner, and I excused myself for the evening.

A guard that wasn't Gunnar nor Kristian escorted me back to my room. This was around the time I would settle into bed and read more of Alita's journal. Though her thoughts were sad, I appreciated them. The young Queen had a hard life.

A widow by thirty, a martyr by thirty-six. She did everything she could for her people all while mourning the man she had loved, had hoped to have children with. It was sick fascination that had me combing through the pages every evening.

But tonight—tonight, I would open the larger book of children's tales. If I was being honest, I hadn't even touched it. Not one page.

I didn't need stories, I needed facts. I needed truth. If I was going to help Damien lead these people, then I needed to know exactly what we were up against.

So, it was begrudgingly that I grabbed the book off the table by the fireplace and swept it into my hands. The spine cracked as I opened it for the first time in who knew how long and flipped to the first page.

A small piece of parchment fell out, landing in my lap. It was wrinkled and brown stained with age. Resting the book in my lap, I took the folded paper in my hands and began to unravel it.

In a thin scrawl, it read:

To my dearest daughter: One day you will discover your destiny, and I hope that when that day comes, you will not be afraid. You have always been who you are meant to be.

There was no name to address the mother nor the daughter, but Damien did say that these books had been in his family for centuries, so I could only assume that this was from a previous Queen to her daughter. Something I knew Damien had neither of.

The pages were old and yellow, their edges crinkling in and making it hard for them to turn. The blue ink adorning the picture of a girl in a white gown was chipping and fading.

I turned to the first chapter, flakes of gold crusting onto my fingertips as my hand found the edges and turned.

The book was spared no expense when being made; nothing short of fit for royalty. The girl who owned this was loved by her parents.

The first story was a tale of a princess who was loved by a knight, a knight that was cursed on a black sun and the spell could only be broken by the one who accepted him for who he was. It was a sweet and heartwarming tale, and I could see why it would be passed down to a daughter.

The story after that told of a prince on a quest to save his people, and along the way made friends with a god, who granted him exceptional powers to conquer his foes. The prince would later go onto become a King and set up a beautiful shrine for the god that helped him achieve his future.

As the night wanned on, my eyes grew increasingly heavy. I read through tales of witches and warlocks, beasts and maidens, greed and good. Each story an impactful lesson on the whims of humanity.

As my eyes closed for the final time, I drifted into a deep sleep consumed with the dreams of a hazel-eyed prince on a battlefield, swinging his sword to save me from peril. He sent me a lopsided smile, one that stopped my breath, and then it was over.

148

14

THE COUNCIL

This morning was bright and crisp, a stark contrast from the grey and cold of the previous days. After being here for so long, my body has adjusted to the cooler temperatures; as I found myself pulling a sage green dress out of my wardrobe, sans the fur trim.

It skimmed over my skin like a soft breeze; the long sleeves opened at the elbow freely flowing around the lower half of my arm. A silver braided belt cinched in my waist and the deep plunge of the neckline met it.

My new handmaid Elle helped tame my loose natural curls, so they lay smooth as she braided the top section around the small silver crown across my brow.

I wanted to look regal, ethereal. Today was a day of importance. One Damien and I had been slowly and steadily building up to. We agreed that today I needed to look every part of a soon-to-be queen. The way I walked, talked and dressed today would be on display for multiple members of Damien's council as well as other leaders of Lustraya's military.

I no longer felt afraid or upset with my circumstances. I realized—much like Alita—that my circumstances were above my control and that to make it here, I would have to become the new version of me. I would have to finally accept that yes, I am a princess by title now, and yes, that meant I had to play the game of court.

Don't get me wrong—the thought of sitting and conversing with people who looked down their noses to me still didn't sit right with me. But I would do what I must. For the people of Lustraya, for my new unit of troops; I would do this for them.

With one more final pin, Elle examined her work in the mirror, smiling thoughtfully.

"Is there anything else I can help you with, Your Highness?" she asked.

"I think this is as good as it's going to get," I said, standing from the chair and smoothing the fabric of my dress. "You did a wonderful job. Thank you."

Her cheeks turned a blush pink at the compliment. She was young, maybe not yet seventeen years. I did not know what her story was, if she had any family or what brought her into this new position, but I could tell she was a genteel person. The type that harbored no ill will toward anyone and seemed genuinely happy with her life.

"Shall we be on our way then?" I stated, moving from the dressing room and into the main section of my suite.

Elle just curtsied and stood to the side as I opened the door to my room. No longer did they get locked but guarded they still were. I expected to see Gunnar or Kristian waiting for me but was pleasantly surprised to see it was Poppi instead.

The right side of her head was freshly shaved down, the other half expertly cropped to her chin. Her leathers were fresh with polish and her sword glinting from the sheath of her back. She was ready for a different kind of fight.

"Are you ready, Your Highness?"

I gave a small squeeze to her hand, flashing her a timid smile.

"Let's get this over with."

She laughed lightly with me as we began winding our way through the mountain corridors. The air around the mountain had changed substantially, especially between me and Poppi. The threads of hope that her and I could move forward strengthened.

The attack in the mountain pass spurred something within those closest to the destruction. Towns had begun to be evacuated and relocated to just north of the Imerian border. Trade routes had been closed and changed. Even the citizens that resided within the safety of the mountain changed their tune.

I was still kept in the dark about a lot of things since then, but with my relationship with Poppi finally mending and trust growing, Damien had loosened the reins on me and allowed me into the political hellscape that was this kingdom.

Today was the day that signified my acceptance into the circle of trust. Months I had been here now; time and time again I had proved my loyalty to my new people. It was time that I step into my role without abandon. Not that I expected a warm welcome or anything, but something was better than nothing.

Poppi pushed open the large set of doors and allowed me to step through first. The room was expansive; large floor to ceiling cutouts onto a balcony jolting my eyes wide as I beheld a frozen waterfall behind it. A large circular table adorned the center of the room, over a dozen chairs placed neatly around it.

"Her Highness, Daniella Castille," Poppi announced for me, coming to stand at my right hand side.

Damien was sitting at the tallest chair, his crown glinting in the firelight that sat at the opposite wall. It roared with life, keeping everyone and everything in the room from freezing to death. He met my gaze with a small smile and nod of the chin, a chair next to him open and waiting for me.

As Poppi and I moved into the room, the rest of the council that had been gathered stared in our direction.

Callen sat closest to Damien, his long silver hair again pressed so straight it looked ethereal. I gave him as warm a smile as I could, doing my best to imitate Ary if she were here.

Colonel Anders sat a few chairs down from Callen. His disdain was written plain as day on his face; our squabble in the courtyard not yet forgotten.

I sat down in the silver chair waiting for me, Poppi taking the one on my left. Damien looked on at me with approval, a glint of pride in his eyes.

I told him at dinner last night that I was going to give this day everything I had. That I would show these people I could be the Queen they needed. Maybe even deserved. We just had to take it one day at a time.

A small cough across the room broke the tension as a wrinkled and hunched old man lurched into his handkerchief.

"Lord Thribil, are you alright?" Damien asked the old man.

"Quite," the Lord replied, though the pain of his fit was evident. "Nothing that I can't handle."

Damien nodded in a way that told us all that he accepted the man's words but did not believe them.

"Then we will begin," Damien said simply. "First, seeing as it is her first time in a council meeting, I would like to formally introduce Princess Daniella to you all. Daniella, these are the Lords and esteemed military leaders of my council.

"We have Lord Thribil, Lord Ronark, Colonel Anders, Lord Callen Hornborn, and of course, you know Poppi."

"It's very nice to meet you all," I said in as lovely a tone as I could muster. "I look forward to getting to know you all." I chanced a look at Anders. "Or reacquainted."

Poppi covered her mouth to hide the snort that wanted to come out. Damien cleared his throat, unamused at my subtle jab to the Colonel.

"We will start with you, Callen," Damien directed to the Lord. "What news do you bring from the west?"

Callen Hornborn sat forward in his chair, lacing his fingers together on the table.

"The villages have been raided thoroughly. Only embers remain of some of them. We've been able to relocate the women and children to the southern borders, but they are weak. And they are scared."

"And the men?" Damien asked, running a finger over his top lip.

"The fathers are already within the ranks or dead. The boys that remain are just that; boys. Some don't even have hair on their balls yet." A brief look in my direction. "Apologies, Your Highness for the crudeness; it's just the simple fact of the matter."

I waved a hand. "Don't let my presence stop you. I can assure you I've heard worse."

Damien grunted and Colonel Anders scoffed.

"What a lady you must have been in Imeria," Anders goaded, then added, "Your *Highness*."

"Watch yourself, Colonel Anders," Damien warned, his tone protective and powerful.

I narrowed my eyes at the bitter coward of a Colonel. In his position, Samir would never talk to someone with so much irreverence, not even someone he hated. Anders was a different breed of difficult.

"Please continue, Lord Hornborn," I said sweetly, putting Anders' words out of my head.

"Rations have begun to get low," Callen continued. "Routes into the towns have been blocked; the ground moving and changing every day. We cannot get anything new to the people."

"What do you mean by the ground changing?" I asked.

"Our enemy likes to dig long and deep trenches through the roads. Block them with boulders that would take the might of twenty men to move."

"If it takes twenty men to move, then how do they get there?"

"That is the part we can't figure out, Your Highness."

Poppi was tense next to me, as was Damien—the latter rapping his knuckles lightly against the armrest of his chair.

"Anders," Damien snapped. "Grab the map."

Anders stood without question or word walking over a cabinet near the fireplace and procuring the map the King had requested.

The parchment was ripped along the edges. Anders walked back to the edge of the table and began to unroll the large scroll. It whispered across the surface, the smell of fresh ink on parchment carrying through the space and reminding me of the comfort of a good book.

The map itself was a highly detailed landscape of Lustraya. Every creek, town, rock, and garden was accounted for. The images were painted in fine blues, greens, and greys. Occasionally there was a red or black slash through the towns, an indicator I was unfamiliar with, but no less incredible. The attention paid to create this rivaled any map of the continent of Taelle I had ever seen. I was mesmerized.

"And the map pieces?" Damien asked, just as Anders placed a slender box next to his hand.

Damien rose from his chair, circling the table with strong scrutiny.

"Callen," he ordered. "Show me the roadblocks."

Callen did as he was instructed, placing several small pieces on the roads that were now closed around his land.

"Lord Thribil," Damien ordered next. And then Ronark and Anders; each of the Lords planting multiple silver pieces around the map. It was absurd how many roads had been blocked off.

"How did this happen?" I asked, standing up, unable to hide my curiosity.

The room turned toward me; Poppi heaving a sigh because she knew who I was and knew this would be the first question of many.

"We've been at war for years, girl," Ronark said, interjecting his voice into the conversation for the first time. "It has not been easy, especially when our neighbors have declined our pleas for help."

The last sentence was personal and as I looked at the section of the map that he claimed his casualties were at, it was the closest to Imeria.

Visions of mutilated bodies strung up and dotted along the border flashed in my mind's eye. The memory had me drawing my shoulders back, my spine going tight.

Ronark realized his misstep and attempted to replace his comment.

"Your Highness, I—"

I held up a hand to stop him. "You speak to me of aid when you strung up helpless people to be eaten alive by the crows? Carved and mutilated their bodies like it was some sick game?"

The room went silent as Ronark glanced between the rest of the council, all of them sharing the same confused look.

"Dani," Poppi asked for them all. "What are you talking about?"

"He knows. He knows what he did," I accused but suddenly I was unsure. Based off the response of the room, I knew they had no idea what I was talking about, which meant they couldn't have been behind the village attacks in Imeria.

"The bodies," I explained instead, walking over to Ronark where his part of the map met Imeria. "Seven of them," I pointed to the locations. "Each carved with a letter in their abdomen and strung up for the Imerian patrol to find."

"And when did this happen?" Damien asked, his face grave as he took in the new information.

"During the Gauntlet," I supplied for everyone.

"Mhmm. I see . . ." Damien mused. "And these letters—did they spell something out?"

I nodded gravely, the memory turning my stomach sour.

"It's Time."

The table broke out in a series of whispered curses and heavy exhales. Lord Callen stood and began pacing. Ronark turned to mumble something to Anders and the King.

Poppi remained in quiet thought as did Thribil, but to the former, I pleaded with my eyes to fill me in on the information I was missing. She shrugged her shoulders and shook her head, pointing a light finger to Damien as if to say, 'Ask him.'

"Forgive me," I said tentatively, catching Damien's gaze as I did. "But is there something else you're not telling me?"

"Don't tell her yet, Your Majesty," I heard Ronark warn in a low whisper.

I kept my gaze trained to my King though, hoping that this would be the day he trusted me with one-hundred percent certainty, and I was brought into the fold at last.

Damien looked at each of his advisers; his shoulders stiff and mouth clenched as he fought to make a decision. Finally, when he turned back to me, his resolve broke and I knew I would learn this piece of the puzzle.

"It sounds like it's the work of the Fae," he said at last.

It wasn't a dramatic unfolding of information, more like a state of fact. My first instinct was to laugh, to tell Damien to tell me the real truth. But as I glanced around the room, waiting to see if anyone would join me in my disbelief, I realized they were all deadly serious.

"The Fae?" I questioned.

Damien nodded.

"I'm sorry," I said with a disbelieving laugh. "You mean to tell me, that the people behind the attacks in Lustraya—and potentially the ones that happened to Imeria—are due to a group of mythological beings that haven't been around since the beginning of our continent?"

"We actually don't know that specifically," Lord Thribil said in a willowy voice. "There is still so much we don't know about what lies beyond this land; only that the Fae hunt us for their own sport and Lustraya has taken the brunt of their attacks for a very, very long time."

I stepped away from the table, pacing about the stone floor as I let this new information settle in.

How could this be? If the Fae were real, then that left the door open for all mythological creatures to exist, and what a harrowing thought that was. The existence of Fae went against everything I was ever taught. Never once in my education did I have one tutor that alluded to the possibility.

I turned around, wrapping my hands around my middle as I looked to Damien once more.

"How can you be certain of this?" I asked, still reeling.

Damien responded with, "I'm just sure" as Callen responded with, "We have witnesses."

The King looked at his Lord with displeasure, the Lord looking at his King confidently, and with no remorse for the outburst.

"Witnesses?" I repeated.

The table of men all looked to Poppi, who had remained quiet during this whole exchange. She tilted her head back against her chair, closing her eyes as she mumbled something to herself. When she opened them again, she righted herself to look at me.

She looked sad and tired, like she had told this story before and would rather not repeat it. That was when the pieces of Poppi's puzzle clicked together. This was her story. This was her version of being left behind by her mother and suddenly I understood fully who Poppi was.

"The Fae killed my parents," she stated matter-of-factly, like she had done this a hundred times. It seems I was the only one to catch the twinge of guilt on the underside of her words.

"I'm so sorry," I told her, feeling her pain through my own hurt.

"It is what it is," she said but I knew that wasn't true. She leaned forward, hands clasped onto the table and continued. "They came in the night. It was without warning; our watch guards never seeing the intruders as they splintered our gates to shreds. They burned everything that night. Homes, shops, barns . . . you name it. Burned it to ash."

I saw the picture she created, felt the carnage and fear those poor people must have felt.

"They took prisoners too. Mostly men, an occasional boy if they could find them." She leveled me with the most pained expression, and I dreaded her next words. "They took my brother."

There it was; the dagger to my heart. My stomach rolled at the thought of how she must have felt that night.

"How old were you?" I finally asked when I knew emotion wouldn't cloud my voice.

"Eleven."

An awful age to lose your family.

"He was my twin," she continued. "We've been separated over a decade, and to this day, I do not know if he is dead or alive. But one thing I do know is that the monsters that used to haunt my dreams had long pointed ears, impossible speed, and were taller than any human I knew. I've been fighting ever since."

"Is this why you came for Arabella?" I asked Damien.

He nodded in return before explaining further. "The amendment in part of the Accords Lustraya holds with Imeria was a caveat neither me nor Raddison ever thought would be necessary. We were friendly at the time and two Kings who never wanted to take a bride, so we thought nothing of having a marriage pact tacked into the document for protection of a later time. But all that changed when Raddison met Clara, and they later had their daughter.

"He became closed off to me after she was born. Started trading with us less; damn near closing our border all together. His fear over losing his daughter began to invade every aspect of his life. I never had any intention of ever calling in that pact, but the last few years have drained us. And Imeria has sources we desperately need."

"I'm sorry—"

Damien held up a hand. "You were not the daughter that was promised, but you may have been a better blessing from the gods than we thought."

Anders scoffed from down the table, rolling his eyes at the King's words.

"Did Clara know about this? Or King Ambrose? Hell, does Rilunae have anything hidden in those Accords?"

"We alerted the Queen of the South years ago, but she's been reluctant to believe us, and has since carried on her husband's fears," Lord Thribil said.

"We've been able to hold the Fae at bay for the last seven years, but they know our defenses are weakening. They get bolder by the day," Callen chided in.

"But why," I asked, still confused. "What is their reason? They've let the whole continent believe they were myth for centuries now. Why attack? Why make their presence known now?"

"We believe they're after something," Lord Ronark spoke. He had his hands clasped behind his back and was now pacing the side of the table. "Perhaps an artifact, a book, a relic. We don't know. But they have only attacked Lustraya, so we must have it. We just don't know what."

My head was spinning with all the new knowledge. Usually, I would take all this information in skeptically, but something in the way they all spoke on the matter had me believing them with little questions asked.

"So, Clara knew?" I asked incredulously.

"It's probably why she brought back the Gauntlet," Damien replied. "If what you say about the bodies is true, it would have been her first clue. She would have been scared for you and Arabella's lives. For what it means for Imeria. She never told anyone about it?"

"Not that I know of," I said with my heart threatening to beat out of my chest. "If anyone knew, it would have been General Armas. But Clara wouldn't divulge any plans like that to just anyone."

"Not even King Ambrose?" Callen asked.

I shook my head. "If what we're speculating is true, then Clara is living in fear. And if I know her any bit as much as I think I do, she wouldn't want information like that to get out. Our Lords and Ladies would revolt. Run."

"Cowards," Anders scoffed. "Your Lords run, while ours stay and fight!" He slammed a fist to the table, rattling the figures nearest him. "Our Lords have died on the battlefield. Side by side with their subjects; all while you wore your fancy dresses and attended your fancy parties." Spit flew from his mouth as he spat the last words.

"I'm growing tired of your insolence, Baylon. You will do best to watch your tone when speaking to your future Queen." Damien seethed next to me.

I looked to the man at the opposite end of the table from me. His face was red with rage; his fist still curled on the table.

"I will not pretend to know the horrors you have faced," I started, keeping my voice smooth so as to not add to the Colonel's growing agitation. "You may brand me in any way you see fit, Colonel, but you do not get to tell me that I don't know what it is like to lose a family or to have everything I had ever known ripped from me and be forced to start over. I came here to save my sister, and now I will stay to save these people. Whether you like it or not."

"Your Majesty," Ronark interjected. "Come here if you would."

Damien did as the Lord asked, swishing his long red fur behind him and standing at the man's side.

"Are you seeing what I'm seeing?" Ronark asked the King, changing the subject back to why we were all here. The Lord pointed to a section on the map void of figurines and said, "Just there. Beyond those old roads . . . there's nothing."

I made haste to the King's other side to see what they saw. It took me a moment of analyzing from this new perspective before I understood.

"Imeria . . ." I breathed.

Ronark nodded again. "There's only two more roads left open before the Fae have us completely boxed in." The Lord placed two figurines down. "If they succeed with blocking them, we will have no routes left out of the kingdom. And if I were a betting man, the Fae will start to push inland, possibly here to this mountain. If they succeed, we're trapped."

Trapped. The word vibrated in the air like the threat it was.

"Say this theory is correct," Damien said tiredly. "What do you suggest we do?"

"Well, thanks to her Highness' help, this new unit of troops is capable enough to be sent over to keep the roads open," Ronark mused. "If they can keep those roads from closing, then we have a shot of moving the rest of the refugees from these villages." He pointed to the villages in the northeast section of the map. "Into the mountain or even near the Fort."

"There's no room in the Fort, and the village next to it is abysmal at best," Callen countered.

"Then what would you have them do?" Poppi piped in for the first time since sharing her story. "If the Fae are closing in, then they will have scouts out watching our every move. They will attack and take whatever is left. We need to get as many people here as possible;

secure the gates, secure the mountain. From here at least we have control; we have numbers."

"We'll be a bunch of sitting ducks," Anders added. "It'll be suicide. The Fae could wipe away this entire kingdom if we're all scrounged together like that."

"Ronark," the King asked. "Do you have any men left to spare that can go to the Imerian border and scout what's there?"

"Unfortunately, not sire," the Lord replied sadly.

"Lord Thribil?"

"All are already patrolling the western end, Your Majesty."

Damien's shoulder slumped as an idea rose in my head. A desperate and selfish plan.

"I'll go," I said, too readily. "I mean . . . if there are no troops to be spared, I'll go. I know the border like the back of my hand. I can be swift and thorough, and back before you know it."

Damien eyed me skeptically, the idea enticing but risky since I would be close to Imeria. Close to home.

"Poppi," Damien ordered, the woman becoming more alert as the King's tone demanded. "You'll go with Dani."

Poppi's mouth dropped. "But sir—"

"I wasn't asking. I was telling."

"But the new unit . . ."

"Will be ran by Halle and Greybourne until you two return. I trust you can keep the Princess safe, or do I need to find more soldiers to accompany you?"

Poppi looked at me, displeased. "It shouldn't be an issue, Your Majesty."

"Excellent. Can you leave by dawn, or do you need more time to prepare?" he asked both of us.

"We'll be ready," I said swiftly before Poppi could shoot me down.

Damien nodded his confirmation, and my heart soared in my chest. This was it. The closest to Imeria I had been in months. Closer to my sister, my friends, my home . . . Aeddan.

Damien lowered his head down to my ear, and under his breath whispered, "Don't make me regret this or by the old gods, you will never leave this mountain ever again."

I didn't bother to relish him with a sassy quip. It didn't matter to me. All that mattered was that I would be free.

15

ASHES TO ASHES

Speed. Wind. Freedom.

Everything I had been craving but had been denied. Poppi rode strongly next to me; her expression as withered as the day we left the mountain keep.

We had made progress in our friendship before leaving, but as of late she was back to her usual gloomy self. Always muttering under her breath or giving me the cold shoulder. I couldn't care less.

We were finally nearing the Imerian border, something I had only dreamed of seeing again, and I would not let Poppi ruin that moment for me. Gone was the cold and snow of the mountain, and in its place were rolling hills, dotted with patches of green and brown.

At night, the stars glistened above us, quietly guiding the way home. On our second night, I tried to point out a few of the constellations to Poppi; to which she turned over and pretended I didn't exist.

Fine.

She could have her bad attitude. Mine remained unchanged. I felt lighter and happier than I had in months.

Yes, Lustraya was growing on me. Yes, I have accepted my role as being the princess of a kingdom I was not born into. And yes, maybe I was creating a life there that fulfilled what my life in Imeria had begun. All of it, though, couldn't compare to the rush of adrenaline coursing through my veins as the sun rose above the horizon and we were now less than a day's ride away from our first stop on this trip.

The steed under me grunted as we pushed against the rising wind, its grunts coming in bursts as the creature filled its lungs.

"That's a good girl. Do you feel it too? We're almost home," I cooed to the horse. She tossed her mane in delight, eliciting a laugh from me. A laugh that turned into a long cry of pure, unadulterated joy. Poppi was taking no part of it.

"Shut up, you idiot," she hollered over the wind. "You're going to give our position away."

"Oh, Poppi, lighten up," I squealed. Yes, I squealed. "Take it in! The air, the sun, the *warmth*!"

I thought I would never feel that again. Even with the fires that were kept awake constantly in the mountain, the savage bite of cold never truly left me. Until now.

The thick fur coat I had worn leaving the gates of the Silver Castle was now tucked safely into the pack on my horse's back. For the first time in a while, I wore nothing but a loose tunic rolled to my elbow and pants tucked into boots.

"Isn't this the most amazing thing ever?"

My excitement could not be contained.

Home, home, home . . . my blood chanted.

In an instant, Poppi turned her horse to the right, cutting me off and forcing us off our course and to a halt.

"This might be your ideal day, Your *Highness*," she hissed. "But it is not mine." She narrowed her eyes further. "There could be Fae in these woods right now, listening to your shouting. You're giving away any ounce of surprise we may have on them. Shut the hell up and take this seriously."

"I understand," I replied. "And I am taking this seriously, but Poppi . . . it's *warm*. That's something to rejoice about, is it not?"

She smiled softly against her will. "Yeah. I'll admit. It's warm."

The angst dissipated after that, the camaraderie we had achieved before we left the castle snapping back into place. The closer we drew to the first road we were instructed to scout out, the heavier the importance of this mission became. I threw a leash on my excitement, pulling it inward, so I could focus on what lied ahead.

My head went on a swivel the moment we neared the edge of the forest that sat between the two kingdoms. Poppi was right; there could be Fae in these trees watching us. Though something told me intrinsically that that wasn't all we should be worried about.

Call it a gut feeling.

The horses grazed in the brush behind us while we undid one of the packs carrying our supply of food. While I set about making us something to eat with the rabbit we caught earlier, Poppi opened the map of this section of the land.

"Alright," she said. "If we head southeast through those trees, we should be able to find a spot to keep watch over the road. At the first sign of anything too suspicious, we go. Agreed?"

"Whatever you say."

Poppi squinted her eyes at me; knowing well and true that if I suspected anything out of place, I would be doing anything *but* leaving the premises.

"Dani, I'm serious," she double downed. "The first sign of any danger, we have to get you out of here. We don't have to go back to the castle, but we can at least make it to the second location. I can't risk anything happening to the Princess."

"Damien doesn't have to know if anything goes awry if you don't tell him," I reminded her. "He knows who I am. If it's information we need, it's information we will get."

"I will not lie to my King."

"Not even for your Queen?"

"Soon-to-be Queen," Poppi corrected. "And no. I won't."

"What did he do to earn such loyalty from you?" I asked, biting into my piece of rabbit. Chewy.

Poppi tossed a stick onto the fire. "After my brother was taken, my father went off to find him, leaving me and my mother behind. We went two years without hearing a word from him until one day, the King rode into our new village. He strode right up to me and my mother and asked if we were the family of Emil Provost . . ." she trailed off, tossing her rabbit carcass to the grass as she fumbled to get through the explanation.

"Poppi, forget I asked," I said, reaching out to place a hand to her arm in comfort.

"I'm fine," she said, wiping her eye and continuing. "The King told us my father was killed in a raid, and my brother was still yet to be found. My mother died of a broken heart soon after, and I guess the King took pity on me. So, instead of shipping me off to another village, he let me come live with him in the mountain when it was in its early stages of formation."

"Sounds like what Clara did for me," I muttered.

Poppi nodded. "I was able to heal, to learn, and to grow because of his generosity. If it wasn't for him, I have no idea where I would be—most likely dead. I owe him my life and giving him loyalty is the least I could do. That, and protecting the future Queen, of course."

Her gaze lingered on my left hand where a new ring had taken up residence on my middle finger. A gift, Damien had told me just before we left.

"It's a family heirloom. Passed down between the women of my family for centuries. It represents strength and bravery of those that came before you."

I looked down at the aquamarine gem inlaid in a silver band. It was simple yet elegant and glinted against the sunlight. A symbol of my newfound royalty.

"We can't afford to find a new Queen. Begrudgingly, one with your skill set. So please, when I say it's time to go . . . we leave." She meant the words playfully, but I knew she was dead serious underneath it all.

Very rarely did Poppi ask me kindly to do something for her. Even more rare, was I willing to comply. For the good of the kingdom and for the good of Poppi's sanity, I nodded my head in agreement, effectively ending the conversation.

The rest of the afternoon passed us by uneventfully. We fed the horses the remnants of our lunch before hoisting ourselves back into the saddles. From there, it was about another hour ride to the lookout point Poppi wanted.

It was here that another familiar feeling began to take root: boredom.

I forgot how much I loathed this part of a scouting mission. The uneventfulness, the quiet, the urge to do something—anything—and yet not being able to; because what if something happens the moment you move? This was torture.

So, I did what anyone else in my position would do: I trained. I flicked the dagger from my hand, releasing it so it whirled through the air before slamming home in the bark of the tree five yards away.

I released another right behind it, then a third. The grouping close together and high enough that if the tree was a person, well . . . they'd be dead.

"Can you please stop it?" Poppi called down from her perch in the tree above me.

"I'm bored," I said nonchalantly. "And when I get bored, I need to move. Need to do something."

"Well, don't."

I walked the five yards to my target tree, rolling my eyes along the way at Poppi's ability to remain calm and still all these hours.

"We've been here for hours, Poppi, and no sign of any Fae. We should go ahead and make note of it in our report and begin moving to the next road."

"No," she said with finality. "We need to see what happens come night fall. These trees are easy to keep hidden in and based off past patterns; the Fae like to move in the night. I want to see if that is still holding true. If not, we leave by daybreak."

But the night came and went with not so much as a hoot from an owl, and soon the sun was back over the horizon. We rode to our next location in that same silence, only stopping to water and feed the horses, and ourselves.

I knew Poppi wanted to scour every bit of land we touched to report back to Damien, but her wanting was costing us precious time. We had to make way to our second location sooner rather than later.

"What is that you're writing?" Poppi asked, leaning over my shoulder.

"Patrol points in Imeria," I replied. "They could be changed by now, but before I left, they were adding more units to this border. I wanted to see how close they were to these roads. Maybe there is a reason the Fae are waiting to attack them last."

The thought interrupted my sleep last night and hasn't left me since. The lingering explanation of why the Fae left those bodies for us to find was a nuisance to my mind.

"But why would they want to leave an open road to a neighbor?" Poppi questioned. "They have only been attacking Lustraya for years. Why now would they choose to go after Imeria after all these years?"

"I don't know . . . that's what I'm trying to figure out."

"Right. Well, while you figure that out, I'm going to close my eyes before taking the night shift. Wake me if anything interesting happens."

I grunted my agreement to her, but nothing interesting happened all day. Our report back to the council would be nothing short of lack luster and a waste of resources. Well, maybe not a full waste. At least we know that the roads sit unoccupied. A blessing for now. With any luck, the last road tomorrow remains unopened, and we can begin the trek back to the castle sooner rather than later.

By nightfall, Poppi had taken up her watch in the tree, and I laid with my back up against its trunk with my sword placed over my lap like I had done the last few nights. As I gazed into the sky, I felt the familiar pull to look for a certain star.

It lay just passed the North Star; a mere freckle to the other larger ones next to it, but I knew it well. My mother—my real one—once called it "Gods Key" because even if you knew it existed, you'd never be able to find it without someone telling you exactly where it was. It was on no map and only talked about in books; like it was a fable. Funny how those all seem to be coming to fruition these days.

My mother told me that if you asked the star for something, it would give it to you. But you had to be careful how you asked or else you may get your wish in a manner that you did not ask for.

"Please don't let all this be for nothing," I whispered. "Please show us the path. Lustraya is dying. Please help me save her."

I was stark tired; the last of my words no more than a mumble on my lips. As my eyes dropped closed, I could have sworn I saw the star wink, but that would be impossible. Stars didn't do that.

My eyes snapped open at the touch of Poppi's hand on my shoulder, shaking me awake.

"Get up," she ordered in a hushed tone. "Something's happened."

I was alert within seconds, springing to my feet, ready to take action at a moment's notice. Poppi handed me my sword as we moved through the underbrush to the edge of the trees that opened to the clearing ahead of us.

We saw the smoke blooming up over the trees ahead and knew it could only mean one thing. Fae.

I looked to Poppi; her own panic-stricken face mirroring mine as we moved on swift feet back to the horses.

"What are we going to do?" I asked, letting her take the lead.

"I don't know."

Harrowing words from a woman who always seemed to know what to do. I untied my horse from the browning tree, and with one leap, was on its back. Poppi did the same, nudging her heels into the animal's flank, her sword at her side.

We rode straight to the danger, my heart racing as fast as the hooves below me. The closer we neared, the stronger the smell of ash became. I could feel my lungs being assaulted by it, and by the time we came upon the carnage that was once a camp, my lungs were coughing their pleas.

It was awful.

The smell of ash clung to the stench of death, the earth scorched everywhere. It was destruction like I had never known; a grey fog slowly cloaking its way around the encampment.

"Poppi?" I asked in a low voice.

"Stay close, Princess," she instructed in a no-nonsense tone. "They could still be here."

She let her steed take the lead, its pace slow and steady as we passed down the central trail of the camp. I nudged my horse to follow, my heart catching in my throat at the sight of burned corpses and tents with burn holes billowing in the small wind.

The deeper we went, the more destruction we saw. The camp itself was large, spanning as wide as I could see. My stomach churned uncomfortably, the meager food I had had today wanting to come back up.

Poppi's back stayed rigid, her right hand gripping the hilt of her sword like a death promise as her head stayed on a swivel.

This wasn't right. This level of destruction was downright cruel and unnecessary. What had these people ever done to the Fae?

Poppi pulled up abruptly, her horse letting out a unhappy whinny, its hooves stamping the ground.

"What is it?" I asked hesitantly.

Poppi remained quiet but turned her head around to meet me with a sympathetic gaze. I furrowed my brows in confusion, trying to sense what she was telling me.

"Poppi . . ."

"Princess, we should go."

I pulled at my horse's reins, moving so I was next to her and could see what she saw.

"Dani, I'm serious. You don't want to see this—"

A horrified gasp left my mouth as the flag of Imeria was left piercing the ground; the only thing left unscathed in the carnage. It's sea serpent emblem the only light in this dark.

"I don't understand," I gasped in horror, turning to Poppi just as an arrow whirled past my right ear.

I turned to look behind me, monitoring the ash for any signs of movement and came up with nothing. Poppi was off her horse; her own bow and arrow notched as she circled to guard my front.

"Princess, you need to leave. Now."

"I'm not going anywhere without you."

I leaped from my horse, pulling the sword from my back as I came up next to her. She glared at me but held firm in her fighting stance. A small nod of her chin told me she wasn't going to argue this decision.

We remained there, poised for a fight. A minute passed. Then another. By the time I was ready to tell Poppi this was our opportunity to flee, the sound of distant hooves beating into the ground stopped me.

"What happens now?" I asked, my hand clamming up as I held my sword.

"They'll attack us high and quick and try to leave us with no way to move. We have to go low; play our difference in heights to our advantage. If we can cut their feet out from under them, then we stand a chance."

I nodded as the hooves came closer.

"Dani," Poppi said forcefully. "The second you can get out of here, you do. Don't wait for me. Get to safety. Lord Thribil's estate is not too far from this place. You get there as quick as you can."

"What about you?"

Poppi looked at me with a cocky grin painted on her features.

"I'll be right behind you. But not before I have some fun of my own."

I felt the warrior in me crawl to the surface; felt the confidence and years of training straighten my spine and cloak me like a second skin.

If Poppi and the rest of Lustraya could stand against this enemy for as long as they have, then I could too. And I would.

I planted my feet firmer into the ground, watching the horizon for the approach of riding horses. Standing by this flag, we were an obvious target; but the enemy lost their advantage for surprise, and for that I couldn't be more grateful.

The ash and soot clouded around in a fog, my eyes straining against the grey to find their approaching silhouettes. Poppi pivoted around next to me, her body waiting for the moment she could release her first arrow.

I hated that I could hear our enemy but not see them. It sent a cold fear slithering down my spine. The horses behind us stomped their hooves once again, their displeasure with staying in place rattling through the decimated grounds.

"Well, they certainly know where we are now," I huffed out.

"And we them."

I turned my eyes to where Poppi had hers trained to the right. There, surging at us fiercely, was the darker grey silhouette of two Fae riders. It was seeing this for the first time that I had an epiphany: I was at war. Officially, and truly, in it.

The ball was my initiation, but for the first time in my life, I was about to go up against the true enemy of us all. And that was . . . humbling. This wasn't a field exercise, or the Gauntlet, or a sparring match in the Ring. This was my life, and so many others were at risk now. If Poppi and I didn't succeed in ending the two approaching riders, what would that mean for Lustraya?

Damien said it once already—if I die, there is no one else in line to assume the throne. Lustraya will be plunged into even more chaos than it can hold. The kingdom could, and probably would, crumble.

"Remember what I said, Dani," Poppi repeated as the silhouettes grew closer. "The second things get too dicey; you have to promise me that you'll run."

She chanced a glance over to me, her eyes determined and panicked at the same time. Her duty and honor to protect me, and all that implies, was a direct mirror to the situation I found myself in not too long ago with Ary and Clara. My respect for Poppi surged.

"I promise."

We waited with anxious heartbeats as the riders were nearly to us, their shapes growing taller and more muscular by the second. To think, Poppi had been dealing with this size of Fae since she was a child. I hated that too.

I flipped my sword in my hand once more and ripped the dagger from its holster on my other hip. The Fae flew through the fog; their black cloaks billowing behind them, their horses' panting forming small clouds in front of them.

"Steady . . ." Poppi hummed. "Steady . . ."

I could hear the strain of keeping the bow steady drip from her words; my own body tense and tired as my muscles strained in anticipation.

"One," I counted down. "Two . . . three!"

Poppi launched her arrow at the first rider, his body just barely pivoting on its saddle to avoid being impaled. She had another arrow notched before the first had disappeared into the ashen air. She let the second sing free in one more heartbeat. This one grazed the shoulder of the second rider, his roar of pain filling the air.

"Nice one," I praised.

"Let's hope third times the charm," she replied coyly.

The third arrow went flying, except this time, there was one problem—only the second rider was charging at us; his sword out and ready to strike.

I placed my back up against Poppi, my eyes roving through the fog to find the first rider. They were smart to use the fog around us to hide them, but it was not advantageous for us. The rider could be closing in on us from any angle now, which sent my stomach plummeting.

Poppi let loose another arrow, but I couldn't see if it hit its mark or not because out of the corner of my eye, I saw the ash and fog created puffs and swirls that shouldn't be there.

I pivoted my stance ever so slightly to meet the disturbance head on, and just as I did, rider number one came charging through, their blade held high.

I took off away from Poppi, bringing my sword up with me to stop the rider's advancement. They struck out first, their blade going straight for my chest. I brought the steel of my sword and dagger together as I caught the length of my attacker's blade and stepped around them.

He was fast and powerful, that much I expected, but as I parried away from a second jab aimed at my shoulder, I couldn't help but feel . . . underwhelmed.

I expected more from the mighty creatures of myth Poppi and the council warned me about. They were supposed to be stronger and faster than any man, but as I swiped my blade at the rider, nicking their wrist, I believed that sentiment less. We twirled around in a battle dance; the ash shadowing the face of the Fae, preventing me from looking the enemy in the eye as I fought for my life and Poppi's.

The latter screamed out, a loud thud following in its wake. Something was going wrong, and I chanced a look back to see what it was.

Poppi's rider was advancing on her quickly; his moves coming fast and short as he sought to wear her out, keeping her on the defensive. The side of Poppi's head that remain cut short clung to her face in exertion. The Fae male was unrelenting, his long copper hair blazing around them like flames.

"Poppi!" I screamed, taking a step forward to rush to her aid. But I was forced back by my rider, who was grabbing at my hair and yanking.

I let out a wail of pain, his grip only tightening further.

"Who are you?" my assailant yelled, his voice tired and angry.

"Fuck you!" I shouted back as I pawed at his hand still firmly in my hair.

I felt the man still and his grip loosen just a fraction; it was all I needed. I sent an elbow flying back into his ribs and my dagger into his opposite thigh.

He cursed mightily and released me, but not before I caught the eyes of Poppi's rider.

My stomach dropped, my heart stopping in tandem. I knew those eyes. Light green, unbearably goofy, and compassionate. I should have known when I saw the copper hair that it was my best friend, but the battle lust had shielded me.

"Maddox?" I asked tentatively, breathlessly.

I watched his chest heave up and down, saw the recognition finally hit him. His sword clattered to the ground as Poppi stood with her sword raised, waiting for an answer.

"Dani," he replied. Not quite a statement, not quite a question.

I turned and dropped to a knee next to my assailant. He was gripping his leg in agony, trying to stanch the blood pouring from his wound.

"Harrison?" I gasped, taking his face into my hands and looking at him fully. How could I not tell that these were my best friends? How had I not been able to sense it?

I dropped my weapons, reaching for the hem of my shirt and tearing it till I had enough fabric to wrap around Harrison's wound.

He looked at me in disbelief as I tightened the dressing, only wincing when I tied the final knot.

"I–I don't understand . . . How—" he stammered, reaching a hand to touch my shoulder. "How are you here?"

"The better question is: why are you here?"

I turned and found Poppi and Maddox behind me; the fight finally ending.

"I think we should be the ones asking that," Poppi spoke in an accusatory tone. "You're the ones who are within Lustrayan territory."

Neither of the men answered because Poppi was right. Why were they in Lustraya and specifically, why were they at this burned down camp?

The questions lingered between the four of us as Harrison gathered his strength to stand. He wobbled and almost fell as he shifted his weight, but not before Mads and I could catch him.

"Easy buddy," Mads said in brotherly affection.

"We need to get out of here," I said gruffly as I held Harrison's torso up and Maddox shifted his arm under his shoulders for better support. "Somewhere safe and where we can talk."

"They could still be here," Poppi agreed.

"You know who did this?" Harrison grunted.

"Didn't you say there was an estate around here?" I asked to Poppi.

I could see the aggravation cross over Poppi's face as she growled lowly and took off to find our horses; it was her way of agreeing to my idea but not being happy about it. Maddox and Harrison still posed a threat, and she would not take that lightly.

"She seems like a good time," Maddox joked.

"She grows on you," I said lightly, shooting my friend a small smile.

"Like a bad fungus probably," Harrison chimed in through a grunt of pain.

"Come on," I said, stepping toward Poppi, who had scrounged up the horses. "We have much to discuss."

16

NEW FRIENDS

The ride to Lord Thribil's estate was tedious, but by mid-morning the next day, we had arrived.

The expectation I had for the Lord's estate versus what we rode up to were two entirely different things—though I should have kept my expectations low. I'd always considered my manor of smaller proportions compared to the others in Imeria but compared to Lord Thribil's, it was the pinnacle of excellence.

War had taken its toll on the Lord's grounds. Weeds rose high, thorny vines and dead flowers littering the walkway to the wrought iron gates that protected it.

An eerie and quiet breeze floated past us as we stopped in front of the gates. I looked to Poppi.

"Any idea how we get in?"

As the words left my mouth, a guard appeared in front of us, his silver armor dull and scratched.

"Name?"

"Princess Daniella Castille and Lieutenant Poppi Provost. We come in need of aid and with . . . friends."

The guard looked skeptically past Poppi and toward Maddox and Harrison; both of whom were haggard and coated in a thin film of ash. Harrison's wound was looking more grotesque by the moment.

The guard laid his gaze on me once before signaling to someone to raise the gates. They creaked and groaned as metal-on-metal moved over one another, our horses not taking the sound lightly.

I patted the neck of mine before coaxing it through. We stopped just in front of the doors, and I slid myself from the saddle with ease; turning my attention to Harrison, who looked paler by the minute.

Maddox was at his side before me and with both of our help, we managed to get our friend down and standing upright. Barely.

"Poppi?" I asked.

"Already on it."

She was bounding up the three stairs that led to the front doors of the estate and opening them as we slowly and surely led Harrison up and through.

The estate was dark and quiet, the hardwood floors creaking as we stepped in. If the outside seemed cluttered and messy, then the interior was its near compliment. I took notice of no attendants or servants milling about cleaning or fixing. There was no butler to greet us or anyone for that matter. It was like a dark light had been cast over the place.

"Lord Thribil just arrived back," the guard from outside stated from behind. I hadn't heard him follow us. "He is in the grand room just ahead. You may meet him there."

The guard pointed forward and to the left of where we stood in the entryway. Poppi gave the man our thanks and took the lead, while Maddox and I shouldered the brunt of Harrison's weight as we walked behind.

By the time we made it to the grand room, I had hairs clinging to the side of my face, my skin coated in a thin sheen of sweat. Harrison had gotten a lot heavier since I left Imeria.

The Lord sat in a large oaken chair in the center of the room; the old man ripping off the armor from his shoulder and tossing it to the side of the room, his shin guards and shoes following suit.

He seemed agitated, the wrinkles in his forehead deep and jaw tense with frustration as he yelled for someone to bring him something to drink.

"My Lord," Poppi said, dipping her head in respect. "I hope this isn't a bad time."

"Of course, it's a bad time," he grunted. "It's always a bad time these days."

He looked to Poppi and finally realized the company that stood in front of him. His eyes went wide as they found me, his gaze darting between the two men at my side and back to Poppi. Though her back was to me, I knew her well enough to know that she was giving one of her silent looks to Thribil that said, 'this isn't what I wanted either'.

"Your Highness," he finally said, standing. "Forgive me. I did not see you at first. Please come rest."

"It is okay, my Lord," I said, my words coming out strained as Harrison leaned heavier on me. "I apologize if we are intruding but my friend here needs a healer, and we were hoping there was someone here that could help."

"Of course," he said without hesitation. He snapped his fingers and two guards appeared from the shadows behind Maddox and me. "I will have him escorted to the healer's quarters right away."

"I will go with him," Poppi spoke up, surprising us all.

"Very well."

Time sped and slowed in one confusing motion as Harrison was taken from me—my back sighing in relief—and ushered through a pair of side doors; Poppi right behind them.

The Lord and I looked to one another in awkward silence for a moment while I fumbled for something to say.

"Thank you for the generosity," I said quickly. "We won't be in your hair long."

"Nonsense," he said with a swipe of his hand through the air as he walked barefoot over to Mads and me. "I will have the cooks prepare something for us and have rooms made up."

His eyes did a pass over me, stopping at my cheek and pausing.

"You have a cut there, Your Highness," he said with a point. "You may want to get that looked at."

"I'll be fine," I replied simply. "No need to waste resources on such a small thing."

"Indeed," he mused, his eyes turning to Maddox now.

They stared intently at one another, each man sizing the other up as the opponents they were. Lord Thribil may be over a hundred years, but he held himself high like Maddox did. The two finally broke eye contact, though the suspicion remained.

"Come along," he said. "I'll show you to those rooms."

We were ushered from the grand room and taken down a damp corridor; a lone torch the only light guiding us out and up a narrow staircase. The structure was built of stone and stood firm in its place, but the walls and floor remained bare; the cold holding stagnant in the air.

We came onto the second floor landing; Lord Thribil stopping at the first two doors on the left. He hung the torch in a holder between them; the light flickering gently.

"These rooms should have everything you need," he said, pushing open the first door. Maddox and I popped our heads to the side to take in the room's contents. "They're much smaller than I'm sure you are used to. But there is a bed with blankets, a wash tub, and a fireplace to stave off the chill. Though, you will have to start a fire yourself."

"Where is everyone?" Maddox asked as he righted himself, his brow creased in worried curiosity.

"I sent many away," Thribil confessed. "I keep only the necessary personnel and do most of the other things myself."

Maddox took in the old man once again. This time, I could see his perception of the Lord changing.

"Where did they go?"

Lord Thribil sighed heavily. "To safety, I hope, but there is no telling. I've done the best I could to protect these people. I've given away most of my family's belongings to the people in town to help keep them on their feet. But war has been going on too long and I doubt there is anyone there to use it now."

I looked at the empty walls again. Had a tapestry been used as a blanket to warm a child? A painting used as fire kindling to keep warm? A chill ran down my spine.

"Thank you, my Lord," I spoke gently. "We appreciate your help."

He gave me a soft smile and left us there at the doorway.

I looked to Maddox, a somber weight resting heavy between us. We had known our fair share of pain and heartache, but this was more severe than even I could have imagined.

"C'mon," I said quietly. "Let's get cleaned up and get to Harrison."

Mads nodded, disappeared into his room, and me into mine.

Getting a fire started in here was no different from when I was living in the barracks in Imeria. Nor was the familiar routine of boiling the buckets of cold water left out or scrubbing myself as best I could in the small washtub provided in the corner.

It was tedious and the water ran cold too quick, which made me miss the ever-warm flow of water in my mountain room, but nonetheless I was grateful to be clean. I redressed quickly in the extra clothes Poppi teased me for bringing. Who was the one laughing now?

Maddox was waiting out in the hallway when I opened my door; his copper hair pulled back in a knot, two braids framing his face, and in fresh clothing as well.

"Do me a favor, and never ever get rid of your hair," I stated.

He looked at me confused before saying, "Okay?"

"It's the easiest way I can ever spot you. And I don't want to have to guess if it's you or the enemy I'm fighting ever again."

Realization clicked in place and his features softened as he pulled me into a hug, kissing the top of my head like he liked to do.

"Never again," he promised.

And with that, we left back the way we came and circled to the room we met Lord Thribil in when we arrived. The haunting quiet followed us through the side door Harrison and Poppi had disappeared behind; another damp and eerie hallway meeting us.

We heard the shouting and grunted groans of our friends before we saw them; a loud crashing noise greeting us as we pushed through the only cracked door in the hallway.

"Just take the damn tonic!" I heard Poppi shout.

"I'm not drinking a gods damned thing until you tell me what's in that!" Harrison demanded with equal fervor.

"You're being a big baby," Poppi chided. "This will make the healing process go by a lot quicker, and then we can all be on our way."

"How do I know it's not poison?"

They spared back and forth; Maddox and I standing in the doorway watching with all the curiosity and humor in the world. It was comical the way their hands were waving above their heads and the veins bulging in their necks. I had to place a hand over my mouth to stifle the laughter that wanted to leave me; Maddox biting his lip to contain his.

We let them argue a minute more before Maddox stepped inside, his hands raising to pause the fight.

"Okay, you two. That's enough," he chuckled. "What's the problem?"

"This *baby*," Poppi spat with a huff of breath. "Won't drink the healing potion we created because he thinks were going to poison him. Which is *stupid!*"

"Harrison, man, just drink it so we can get you out of here," Maddox encouraged, going to stand next to Harrison who was still on the healer's table.

Harrison leveled him with a seething look before replying flatly, "You know how I feel about getting fed unknown potions these days."

Of course. I had almost forgotten. The third trial when we all were forced into the fear dreams, Harrison was affected deeply. Come to think of it, I don't think I had ever seen him drink anything he didn't pour himself after that. No more taverns after that, either.

I walked over to where Poppi stood on the opposite end of the room; a broken vial dripping on the wall behind her, the glass scattered on the floor. My guard and friend was irritated and flustered as I laughed lightly while holding out my hand for the vial clutched in hers.

"You Imerians . . ." she ground out and I laughed harder. Poppi placed the tonic in my hand with a slap, and I turned to Harrison.

"Open up," I demanded lightly.

Harrison narrowed his eyes at me, Maddox shaking his head in disbelief.

"Now Harrison," I said, a bit sterner. "We don't have time to waste."

There was a pause before he reluctantly held out his hand for the vial. I placed it in his palm and watched as he tipped back the purple liquid. We all waited a few heartbeats, letting the potion settle into his system. When he remained in his upright seated position, Poppi crossed her arms and released a sarcastic, "See!"

Harrison rolled his eyes as he swung his legs off the table and stood gingerly to his feet, testing the weight against the injury.

"It's good," he said, taking a small step forward. "I can walk."

"And the pain?" Poppi asked, looking at him with narrowed eyes.

"I can handle pain."

"Men," she huffed.

"Well, now that we have all this taken care of," Mads said, clapping his hands together. "Let's go eat."

Everyone's stomachs rumbled in agreement; our hollow footsteps echoing out of the room as we left the healer's quarters and walked to find the dining hall.

No servant came to find us, so we had to rely on the smell of food wafting through the house, and eventually we found where we were supposed to go; Lord Thribil already waiting at the table.

The Lord stood as we walked in, his hand ushering me to take the seat at the head of the table. It was weird. Damien usually sat there, or Clara, but as the highest-ranking person in the room, it was technically mine. I sat as though the title didn't bother me, but I don't think it ever would not.

Plates were set in front of us; root vegetables and an unidentifiable meat steaming in a brown sauce.

Poppi, Thribil and I grabbed our forks without hesitation, but Harrison and Maddox eyed the food with suspicion. I watched them poke at the meat questionably as I put the first bite into my mouth.

It was tough and gamey, very bland but food was food during these times, and for that I would be grateful.

They lifted their gazes and watched as the rest of us dug into our portions, their hesitancy waning and crude acceptance taking forth. It was this or nothing. They choked down their portions, never complaining, though their faces said otherwise.

It was a quiet meal and when the plates were scraped clean, they were taken away. No dessert or after meal drink was brought to us. Lord Thribil sighed.

"I'm afraid this is about all I can offer you all," he said. I had never seen a man more defeated. I reached my hand out and gripped his where it still sat on the table. He looked at me with a mist in his eyes.

"You have provided more for us than we would have had on the road. Thank you."

Thribil nodded once in thanks; an awkward silence settling over the table. It was Poppi who finally broke it, proclaiming to the men seated in front of her, "I hope you both understand now why Lustraya acts and moves the way it does."

When they looked at her with a heavy pause, she continued.

"No one is bold enough to acknowledge the heaviness in this room, but I will. There are many things we need to discuss with you both. Like why Imeria was camped in our territory, or how and why it was attacked. But if I was a betting woman, I bet it would be to get to her." Poppi pointed a finger to me, and I saw my friends look at me with guilt.

"We cannot—" Maddox began but Harrison stopped him with a look.

"I think this is safe company," Harrison stated. "And as *your* superior . . ."

"Not this bullshit again," Maddox said, rolling his eyes.

". . . I'm inclined to share a bit of information." Harrison finished with a satisfied look on his face.

"Superior?" I asked, raising a brow.

"With Helvig attached to the Queen's hip, someone had to step up and replace him."

He gave me a knowing look, a piece of information only I would know was valuable. My heart clanked in my chest at hearing his name. Though I tried to hide and not acknowledge the longing in my heart, I missed Aeddan more every day.

"I see," I replied simply, trying to show no interest in knowing this.

"Your Highness," Thribil murmured to me. "Are you sure we can trust these people with the information we know?"

His look was pointed, and Poppi's expression mirrored his; the two sharing the same concern. I took a moment to really reflect on the decision, thinking not only of myself but also of Damien and what he would want. He would be irritated, defensive, and protective. But after careful consideration, I think even he would conclude that we needed to trust someone in Imeria with the knowledge we kept hidden.

"I think it's time we try to make a friend, not another enemy."

17

EXPLANATIONS

S o where shall we start?" Maddox asked with piqued curiosity. "Why were you in Lustraya?" Poppi asked again, lacing her fingers together on the table and leaning forward. The lack of information was grating on her nerves, and it showed in the way she clipped her words.

"We were sent to bulk up protection on the border," Harrison supplied. "Since your King decided to make a surprise appearance at the Queen's ball, she's been . . . on edge."

"Welcome to the team," Thribil laughed lightly.

"You were in these lands, Harrison," I chimed in. "You know good and well where Imeria ends and Lustraya starts. Unless you have a better reason than Clara being on edge, there was no way you didn't know *exactly* where you decided to place camp."

"Fine," he conceded. "We knew. But the reasoning is still the same. We needed to protect that border better, and if we just so happened to stumble upon you or anyone who knew where you were—well, opportunity is opportunity."

"So, you were going to come kidnap her?" Poppi said in disgust.

"More like rescue," Maddox offered with a coy smile.

It warmed my aching heart to know my friends were still trying to get to me. And as I was about to tell them so, another thought occurred to me that altered that feeling entirely.

"I wrote to you though," I said suddenly, the words spilling from my mouth as I became confused. "Why would you feel the need to rescue me when I told you I was okay and adapting?"

Now it was their turn to look confused.

"What letters?" Mads asked.

"What letters . . ." I whispered in disbelief. "What letters?"

My voice rose in octave as I sat up straighter.

"Fuck," Poppi said, leaning to the side of her chair and pinching the bridge of her nose.

I whipped my head over to her, eager to know what the hell that was supposed to mean and why the hell she looked so guilty.

"Poppi," I prodded. "What do you mean by that?"

Poppi released her nose and looked to Lord Thribil, who looked almost as guilty as her. Almost. We sat waiting for their response, a quiet conversation passing between the two true born Lustrayans.

"The King thought it best if we . . . postponed sending your letters," Lord Thribil said carefully. "In the event that you were writing them in code and giving away information that would be too dangerous once it got in the wrong hands."

Hurt, anger, and shock rocked through me as I looked to Poppi, the one person who I gave those letters to in the hopes that my family would know I was okay.

"Please tell me you didn't?" I asked, my voice wobbly as the tears stung my eyes. "Please tell me you didn't do that."

"I had my orders," Poppi said in that brisk tone of a soldier. "And I wouldn't defy my King in the name of sparing your feelings. I'm sorry, Dani, but it was before we could trust you wouldn't turn on us."

"And after?"

Heavy and dreadful silence hung in the air between us. Maddox and Harrison eyed the Lord and my guard with vengeance in their eyes. I thought of how hurt I had been that Arabella wasn't answering my letters. All the while, she had never gotten them and probably thought I discarded her after the events of the ball.

"How could you?" Maddox said through tight teeth. "To be so cruel as to not let her send one damned letter."

"It was for our kingdom's own good."

"I could give a damn about that," he retorted, slamming a hand to the table. "You could've read it and resealed it before sending it out."

Harrison rested a calming hand to Maddox's other arm, a signal for him to simmer his anger. This wasn't the time, nor the place for this conversation.

"I'm sorry," she finally said, her eyes finding each of ours with sincerity.

I swallowed down the lump that had formed in my throat, the sting of unshed tears the only lingering feeling of betrayal I felt.

"What's done is done," I managed to get out. "Let's just focus on what's important, and that's finding out why you were attacked."

Harrison nodded in agreement and Maddox grunted. Lord Thribil looked tired and Poppi, like a child, just scowled. How were we the people spearheading this mission?

"They came at us at dawn," Harrison said, getting us back on track. "They were unusually fast and the cover of darkness cloaked them, so we never saw their faces." Thribil rubbed his upper lip; Poppi nodding along like she was there with them. "They started with the fire, burning everything they could touch. I counted six, maybe seven of them on horseback. It was so much damage from so little men."

"And did they take anything?" Poppi asked cautiously, but I knew what she meant. Not just anything . . . more like anyone.

"No," Maddox said.

"And that's the confusing part to us," Harrison pressed on. "They just burned everything to ash. We got as many people out as we could, but we lost at least a dozen men and women to the fires."

"All of which I presume are back across the border where they belong?" Thribil added pointedly.

"Yes," Maddox said flatly.

"Do you know who did this?" Harrison asked, looking to me.

I swallowed again, knowing exactly who did the damage but something in my gut twisted, preventing me from telling them. I looked to Poppi and Lord Thribil, who already had their eyes locked on me.

This was it; now was the time to let the truth out. And for once, I understood where Damien stood when deciding whether to trust me with this information. Mads and Harrison were my best friends, but their oath was to Clara—to Imeria. How could I know if they would stay true to our friendship? To honor the pact that was etched in our skin forever.

"Lord Thribil?" I asked tentatively. If the Lord's age or his calmness at the council meeting was any indication, then I know he would know what Damien would want in this moment. He thought for a moment before nodding his approval solemnly.

"What I am about to tell you has to stay in these walls," I started, breathing in deep and releasing the rising tension in my shoulders. Maddox and Harrison looked at me nervously but remained calm— their silent answer to my one condition. "You're going to think me insane, and that we are lying, but I promise you with everything that I am that it is the truth."

I paused and collected myself, rallying all the courage in my body before I spoke the deadly words out loud, "You were attacked by the Fae."

Maddox's eyebrows rose to his hairline, and Harrison remained frozen, his expression unwavering as they took in the information.

"I know it sounds crazy, but I've researched it. Seen the destruction with my own eyes. Hell, Poppi has *lived it.*"

Their gazes turned toward the woman with the half-shaved head, their eyes calculating, and yet they didn't laugh or scoff in our faces once. They believed us.

"How is it possible?" Harrison finally asked.

"I–I'm not sure. I've been—"

"Her Highness is being kept in the dark for her protection," Lord Thribil said, saving me from admitting the embarrassing truth of not knowing. "As per your question, the answer is simple. They have always been here. Since the first Kings and Queens. They never left but instead bided their time and struck us when we were most vulnerable. Now here we sit; a decade later and no closer to ending this war than we were at the beginning of it."

"And you," Mads asked, looking to the old man. "You have fought them?"

"I may be getting up there in my years, but a blade is as a part of me as my hand. I've been fighting for this mighty kingdom since the day I could walk, and it is the battlefield in which I will die."

Respect lit the features of my friends and burst through my chest. Lord Thribil's words were enough for any soldier to rally onto.

"So where do we go from here then?" Poppi asked the group. "Now that you know the truth, you must finally see why we had to do what we had to the night of the ball. We need help. And your people will be reporting back to your Queen what they saw by now, no?"

"It is true we sent word," Harrison confessed. "But the detail about the Fae will remain absent from any of that correspondence."

"And it must." Lord Thribil's tone turned deadly serious. "No one can know about this. There is a reason King Damien has danced around mentioning them by name for so long. They thrive on the fear and chaos. It's what they want, how they conquer our towns so quickly. You must not speak on any of it."

My friends turned toward me, Maddox giving me an incredulous sideways glance before saying, "Dani. You know we can't do that."

"It's not forever, Mads," I protested. "But Lord Thribil is right. Can you imagine what the people of Imeria would say if they heard such a thing? What they would do?"

They took a moment to picture the outcome; both of them coming to the same conclusion.

"So, what do you recommend we do?" Harrison asked. His new role in the Serpentine Guard has matured him a way I never would have expected. He was calm and methodical, calculating and planning. It made me proud.

"You keep this information to yourself," I instructed them, then turned to Poppi and Thribil. "And we send word to Damien about everything that has happened since we left."

"And then what?" Poppi asked.

"We go to Imeria."

18

DETOUR

Damien,

Enclosed with this letter, you will find an updated map of the southern border as well as Poppi and I's reports on enemy activity. We did run into an Imerian camp that has been decimated because of them. I hope you will forgive me and find it in your heart to trust me when you read these next words, but I want to remind you that Poppi is with me and we're okay.

We're going to Sapphire Isle. We need more information about why those three roads specifically have been left unscathed and if I can convince the Queen to join our cause. I will send message when I know *something more than what I am giving you now. My heart is with Lustraya. I have to do this.*

-Daniella

I sent that letter out three days ago and I felt as sick now as I did when I sent it. Damien should be receiving it any day now and when he did . . . I could feel his wrath already. Poppi agreed on our next steps forward, but I could tell she was far from trusting Mads and Harrison.

At this very moment, we were cresting the last hill needed to see the palace overlooking the Cashian Sea. Sapphire City, the jewel of Imeria. With a swift gallop, we reached the top of the hill and my heart burst in my chest. There she was—the palace. My home.

In the dimming light of late afternoon, the palace sparkled like I remembered it.

Home, home, home . . .

Maddox and Harrison had sent word to Clara to let her know I was coming. I prayed that she would welcome me with open arms once more as Poppi and I began the final leg of our journey.

I tried and failed several times to think of what I would say to Clara when I saw her. 'Hey, how are you?' didn't seem to cut it. I struggled most with what I would say to Arabella. Gods, she would be furious about the letters.

The closer we came to the palace's doors, the bigger the pit in my stomach seemed to grow. Why was I so nervous?

Time seemed to fly by yet come to a screeching halt as we covered the rest of the distance and rounded the bend to stop in front of the steps of the palace. The memory of when my mother and I first arrived here surfaced, and for a moment, I felt like that scared little girl again.

Poppi waited next to me, her mouth tightening with concern as she watched me delay getting off my horse.

"We don't have to do this," she said in a low voice. "We can turn around right now and go back. Just say the word."

"No," I whispered. "I can do this."

I said the words more for myself than for Poppi. With a deep breath, I swung my leg off the horse and to the ground. The dry dirt crunched beneath my boots as I walked up to the guard that had come down to greet us.

"Princess Daniella Castille of Lustraya," I announced. "I'm here to see Her Majesty Queen Clara."

Recognition sparked in the young man's eyes as he took in my appearance and my name.

"Princess Daniella . . ." he said with wonder. "Of course, right this way."

"One thing," I spoke, stopping the guard mid-step. "Would you have someone show my companion to the stables? Our horses need tending."

"Of course."

"Absolutely not."

I looked over my shoulder to see Poppi glaring at me; her favorite thing to do these days. "I'm going wherever you go," she demanded.

"Not this time," I said calmly. "You are going to take our horses to the stables, and I will see Clara alone. There is no danger here, Poppi. I'll meet up with you when I'm done."

I turned on my heel without another word, marched up the steps, and through the doors of the palace.

It was just as I remembered it. Plush carpets, purple drapes, so many flowers . . .

"Your Highness," said an old willowy voice, one I knew all too well.

"Kalter," I beamed as the old butler met me in the entrance. "It's been a long time."

"Indeed, it has," he said sweetly. "I am here to escort you to see Her Majesty."

"Thank you, but you don't have to escort me. Just tell me where she is and I can find my way."

"I'm sorry, Princess, but its standard practice with all foreign visitors . . ."

Right. They knew me, watched me as I grew. But I was another kingdom's princess now, I couldn't be left unattended to waltz around the palace. Especially at a time like this.

"Of course, Kalter. You're right. Take me to my mother, please."

The old butler smiled warmly and led me through the halls of my childhood. A wave of nostalgia passed through me as memories of me and Ary flooded my mind. Memories of running and hiding, shouting, crying. Memories that I could only hope to one day replicate inside my mountain home of Lustraya.

When we turned the corner of the corridor that led to Clara's study, Kalter stopped his steps. The butler looked torn, like he was deciding between what was right and what was wrong.

"Kalter, what is it?"

He took a moment before answering, "Her Majesty would want me to tell you to wait for her in her study, as per the usual protocol. But," he paused his sentenced and leaned in. "If you just happened to find out that Her Majesty was in her War Room instead . . . well, I guess there is nothing I can do about overheard gossip, now is there?"

The old man winked at me before walking away, leaving me alone in the corridor.

The War Room. Of course. That's where she would be.

I waited till the butler had disappeared around the corner before turning and walking back the few paces from which I'd come. I stopped in front of the wood door that led into the War Room, taking in a few steadying breaths as I decided what I wanted to do.

Knocking seemed odd and storming in seemed brash, but alas they were my only options.

"C'mon, Dani," I chanted quietly to myself. "Just open the door. She's not going to get mad because it's you. You have to do this."

I let the words settle and before I could overthink the situation more, I pushed the door open and took as confident a foot forward as I could.

The door flew open easier than I anticipated and startled the room with a loud bang against the wall.

I stood there as half a dozen pair of eyes all turned toward me, some recognizing me instantly and others squinting against the light pouring in behind me.

With all the confidence I could muster, I continued into the room with my head held high and shoulders back, the warrior in me falling to the shadows while the princess made her debut.

I watched as Clara's eyes widened in surprise, her hand that was raised with a piece of parchment going limp at her side. My heart burst wide open at seeing her lovely face healthy and just as I last remembered it.

"Daniella," she gasped.

The table of advisers broke out in whispered mumblings as the shock of my presence passed around. But only one of them stood out from the rest as he was the only one to leave the table.

Aeddan pushed his seat away swiftly and stood to his feet. He had a bewildered expression on his face as he walked toward me. My heart leaped to my throat as I watched him, hundreds of unspoken words flying to the tip of my tongue as he stopped a few feet in front of me.

I wanted nothing more than to reach out and touch him, to feel his skin and know he was alive. I wanted even more for his strong arms to pull me into his chest and never let me go again. He looked like he wanted to do the same, and time stood still as we stood there taking one another in.

Aeddan had cropped his hair short since I had been away, his shoulder length curls exchanged for a short cut and stubble coating his jaw. He looked larger too, like he had put on even more muscle since I had been away. He was the portrait of a soldier. My soldier.

"Dani . . ." he whispered softly, his voice breaking on the last vowel.

"I'm back," I tried to say nonchalantly but even I couldn't avoid the emotion that threatened to consume me.

"How?"

"Daniella," Clara called loudly.

I turned my gaze away from Aeddan and remembered that he and I were not alone in this moment. It seemed that this wasn't the first time Clara had called my name since I had been standing there.

I moved away from Aeddan without a second thought, needing to put space between he and I before I could forget the reason why I was here. I stopped at the opposite head of the table as Clara, laying my hands against the mahogany to steady myself.

"Ladies, gentlemen," I greeted the table, nodding to the people sitting there as I did so. And then to Clara, "Hello, Mother."

"How are you here?" she asked, her eyes still wide and voice filled with disbelief.

"It's a long story," I replied genuinely. "One I would love to tell you, but perhaps without an audience."

Grumbles chorused around the table as Clara's advisers rejected the idea. I kept my gaze trained to hers as I felt Aeddan's eyes boring into my back. He still hadn't moved from the front of the room, like a petrified statue.

Clara listened to their objections thoughtfully and I took note of the way she carried herself with them. It was just like Clara to make everyone at that table feel seen and heard, for her to make sure that they knew their thoughts mattered to her. It reminded me of the Queen I hoped to be one day.

Eventually she held up her hand to silence their pleas and turned her attention to me once more.

"Whatever you have to say to me, Daniella, you can say in front of this council."

My gut twisted. I looked to see if I recognized any of the faces in the room, but I saw none. There was no General Armas and no Samir. Hell, I would have even settled on Admiral Luscette being my good omen but even she wasn't present.

I don't know what it was, but I knew I had to trust my instinct and keep the information I came with to myself and Clara. I shook my head.

"I'm sorry, Clara," I stated calmly. "But my request isn't negotiable. I understand if you all need some time to discuss the matter, but I plead for you not to take too long."

"Pray what could be so urgent, girl?" A rotund, short man with greying hair asked from the left of Clara.

I flicked my gaze quickly to his and back to Clara.

"It's a matter of life and death."

I willed Clara to understand the meaning in my words. After all, had Damien not tried to send her correspondence in asking for aid the last few years? Surely, she was intelligent enough to read between the lines.

"I see . . ." she mused, her head tilting ever so slightly to the side, her dark curls spilling over her shoulders. The way her lips tightened and how she shuffled the pages in front of her around let me know that she knew what I was referencing. I felt a wave of relief wash over me.

After one agonizing minute of waiting for her response, she finally said to me, "Then we shall continue this conversation privately—"

"Great! I—"

"—tomorrow," she finished, effectively shutting down my next words. "For now, let's see to it that you get some rest, hm? I'm sure your journey was long and tiresome."

"Yes," I tried again, stumbling over my words. "But Clara, please—"

"Your room is just how you left it."

Those words stopped me dead in my tracks, as did the warm smile Clara gave me after. My room. With its soft sheets and silk sleep sets . . .

I nodded in agreeance, knowing I was not going to win this argument. So, I did the only thing I could, and I began backing out of the room and past Aeddan. I didn't even bother trying to look at him as I walked out the door. We had already drawn too much attention, and the last thing I needed on my conscience was if I was jeopardizing his well-being again.

19

DENIAL

Waking up felt like a fever dream.

The smell of jasmine wafted in the air as a small fire crackled in the far reaches of my room. I was snug in one of my old silk sleep gowns; deep within the confines of my blankets. I didn't want to wake up. But I had too. Mostly because there was a relentless banging coming from my bedroom door.

I groaned as I was forced out of bed before I was ready, throwing on my old cobalt robe as I shuffled to the door. I opened it only to find a fully dressed Poppi, irritation already emanating from her.

"Oh, good," she crooned sarcastically. "You're awake."

She pushed passed me and into my room, the thud of her boots stifled by the carpets.

"I see why you put up such a fuss being in Lustraya," she said in amusement. "If I had come from a life like this, I think I'd be a brat about a lot of things too."

"Is this why you came to wake me up? To tell me that I'm a brat?"

"No," she said simply, hands on her hips. "But it doesn't hurt to remind you every once in a while."

I sighed and ran a hand down my face. "Now you choose to have a sense of humor. What is it you need again?"

"We need to go over what you're going to tell the Queen today."

I should have known. I got the sense from Damien and the rest of the council that the information regarding the Fae was to be kept within the walls of that chamber. And seeing as I was only just recently allowed within those walls, Poppi would want to make sure I kept that information where it belonged.

"Can I at least change before we have this meeting?"

"No."

She unbuckled the sword at her hip and placed herself on the couch in front of the fire. "Why does every room have one of these going? It's so hot outside."

"Imeria doesn't have the winter like Lustraya does," I replied, going to sit next to her. "This is cold for the majority of people here and Clara likes to keep her guests comfortable."

"Huh. Well, we're about to make the Queen very uncomfortable."

"Poppi—"

"Shut it. I know you want to tell her everything and confide in her, but you can't. You have to think of what the King would want you to do since you're acting as his liaison here."

I groaned as I sat next to her on the couch, a small headache already forming in the front of my head.

"Before we left, His Majesty and I had a conversation about what needed to happen should the plan deviate and we come here."

My hand dropped from where it was rubbing my temple, my eyes opening in suspicion.

"C'mon," Poppi teased. "You really thought we didn't know you'd try everything in your might to make it as close to Imeria as possible? Come now, we're smarter than that."

I threw a pillow at Poppi, which she evaded with a laugh.

"Anyway," she continued. "His Majesty impressed upon me that should we get an audience with Queen Clara, we needed to ask her not only to send soldiers, but to send ships. Our intel suggests that her admiral here was once a, uh, pirate?"

"Privateer," I corrected.

"Regardless," she said with a hand wave. "The King fears that if the Fae know we have joined forces, they'll attack us with all their might. The goal is to have Imeria's ships closest to Lustraya's northern border to ward off an attack from the sea and use what soldiers we have left to hold off the last three roads from closing. A privateering Admiral would know how an enemy like that would move."

"If she even agrees to help," I sighed. "If she's been aware of the Fae existence this whole time, she may just let Lustraya keep fighting the battle to spare her people. Her pride. It's worked for Imeria this long."

"That's what I'm afraid of."

As was I. Without the aid of Imeria, Lustraya would only be able to hold off more advances for a few more months, another year if they were lucky. Our supplies were dwindling; the winter icing over every lake and crop as we spoke.

Even if we did somehow win against the Fae, Lustraya would be rebuilding for decades to come.

"And what are you going to be doing while I talk to Clara?"

"In a perfect world, I'm in that room with you. But I know my limitations, so I will be just outside the door should you need me. The Queen can't deny me my duty of protecting my Princess; even if she is hardheaded and stubborn and can take care of herself."

I snickered at her jab. "Poppi. I think that's the nicest thing you have ever said to me."

"Don't count on me doing it often." She gave me a soft smile before patting my knee and standing. "Well, get dressed. You have more than one battle to win today."

# # #

Having on one of my old dresses felt so right and yet so wrong. I lingered in front of the mirror longer than I should have, questioning whether I needed to change. But if I was being honest with myself, I was stalling for time.

Nerves had invaded my system, the weight of the conversation I needed to have with Clara pressing down on me. I rehearsed a dozen times in my head what I wanted to say to her and how I wanted to say it. The longer I looked in the mirror though, the more I realized I couldn't do it as my old self.

After Poppi had dropped the horses off at the stables yesterday, my meager belongings were brought back to this room. I searched in my pack for the spare set of clothing I had packed in case we found ourselves on the road longer than necessary.

I donned the pair of black pants and white tunic, lacing up an icy-blue and-silver threaded vest over it. The boots came next and then my aquamarine ring.

For such a small thing, it carried immense power over me. It reminded me of my oath and my duty to my new people; a reminder I needed today. But that wasn't the only reminder I needed.

I dove my hand back into my pack and pulled out the thin silver circlet Damien had given me and placed it along my brow. It sparkled against my dark hair, lit up my blue eyes, and as I smoothed my hair down one last time, I repeated the words that would get me through the day.

"I am Princess Daniella of Lustraya, and I have come to ask for aid to my people."

I knew my mission, and I could no longer delay the inevitable.

The walk to the War Room with Poppi was a silent one, each of us anxious for our own reasons.

"If anything goes wrong in there, come and get me."

"Nothing is going to go wrong."

Poppi scoffed at my optimism.

"You have to trust me on this," I tried again, to which she answered with a long sideways glance. I shouldn't have expected anything else.

We came to a halt at the door, both of us staring at it as if it would open itself and spare us the choice of staying or leaving. Why was this so hard?

"Wait here," I instructed. And for reassurance, "I will yell if I need you."

I rapped my knuckles three times against the door before stepping into the room for the third time in my life. The large table that stretched down the middle of the room no longer shocked me. What did, however, was the amount of people gathered around it. I shoved the feeling of surprise down as I approached the end, my eyes wandering to find Clara's.

"What's all this?" I asked her tentatively.

Stationed around her were General Armas, Admiral Luscette, and Aeddan, all of whom were looking at me expectantly; their faces neutral as I came to stand at the open end of the table. I avoided the pair of hazel eyes that I knew were waiting on me, instead giving a brief nod to the others at the table.

"Daniella, darling," she said sweetly. "You're early."

I swallowed. "I walk fast."

Clara was polite enough to laugh quietly at my joke, but not everyone shared the same sentiment.

"Clara, forgive me, but I thought that I would be getting a private audience with you?"

"I received some news this morning. News that I'm sure has to do with your arrival here. You're familiar with everyone at this table. I'm sure you and your companion can find it within yourselves to trust us."

"Of course, I trust you, but Clara, it's—"

"Spit it out, girl," Luscette chided.

Oh. No. Not today.

"Girl I may be, but princess I am. And you will address me as such," I snapped backed. Eyes widened in surprise at my change in tone. I turned back to Clara. "I think you understand what kind of information I have come to talk about and unless everyone at this table is . . . up to date, I really think this conversation needs to happen between us." I inclined my head slightly, hoping she would understand the hint at my tone.

"Indeed, I do understand," she finally said. "But it's time that we open that conversation up to a few more ears." She gestured with her arms out to the leadership that stood around the table.

"Fine," I said, folding my hands together in front of me. "Then one more person needs to join us." I turned toward the door and yelled, "Poppi!"

The door to the War Room was open a half-second later, Poppi already drawing her sword from her hip and scanning the room for danger.

"What's going on?" she asked as she marched forward, eyes trained on me and then moving to the ones at the opposite end of the table. "Is everything alright?"

She let her sword fall back in her sheath as she came up next to me.

"Everything is fine," I said in a hushed tone, so no one else could hear us. "Clara wants to loop the General, the Admiral, and this Captain in on our . . . plight."

"No," she responded instantly. "The King said talk to Clara and no one else."

"Poppi, we need aid. We can't get it if we don't start working together."

She looked from me, to the Imerians at the end of the table, and back. "And what makes you think we can trust them?"

"We trusted Maddox and Harrison. We have no other choice here, either."

I watched as she rolled her eyes half-heartedly, knowing that I was right, and we were going to have to break that news to Damien at some point. I loathed the tongue lashing I was sure to get from him.

"Everything alright down there?" Armas called.

"Peachy," Poppi called back and then said to me, "You sure about this? King Damien won't be pleased."

"You let me deal with him."

I sidestepped her and walked around the table so that I was now standing on the other side of the Admiral. They looked to me with waiting stares, but I remained quiet. Where did I even begin with this?

"We once thought the bodies found during the Gauntlet were a string of attacks by pirates or someone else close to those borders," I found myself saying. "What if I told you, it was neither and that we now shared a common enemy?"

"Then I would say you're a liar," Armas stated but followed up his harsh comment with, "But then I would ask you who is behind it."

I looked to Clara and then to Poppi, both women nodding lightly at me to continue forth with our admission.

"The Fae."

Silence fell. I half-expected them to break out in a round of laughter, but to my surprise, no one moved or so much as batted an eye to my announcement. Poppi looked to me just as shocked.

"You all believe me?" I asked doubtfully.

"There have been tales of sightings on the seas for decades now, but no one has been able to prove it. Ghost stories are what the crews will tell you to keep the fear at bay," Luscette offered; like this was an everyday occurrence for her.

"Well, they're real," Poppi commented. "And they're every bit as horrible as you might think."

"And you?" I asked General Armas. "You don't seem surprised by any of this."

He sighed, rubbing a finger against the top of his mouth. "I've been at this job longer than you've been alive, Princess. Nothing surprises me anymore."

Poppi and I looked to Clara, now hoping she would fill in any of the gaps for her advisers. I watched as her shoulders rose and fell heavily, a sign that she had accepted the truth now that it was out in the open.

"I had hoped when Damien first warned me of their presence in his kingdom that it was a scare tactic to get Imeria involved with his plans of expansion," she stated. "I can see now that that assumption was wrong."

"Assumption?" Poppi scoffed. "You think the number of times we wrote to you for your assistance was all a game?"

"I've known Damien a long time," Clara stated. "Everything he says is either a truth that has been twisted into a lie, or another scheme of his to reclaim what he calls 'stolen land'. I put nothing past him, especially an opportunity to place my people in jeopardy to further his own agenda."

"Well, now you know," I said, trying to keep the peace. "So, will you help us?"

A pause passed. Then a minute. Then two. The silence stretched on for so long it was becoming unbearable; the Imerian leaders exchanging silent conversation with one another. But then Clara exchanged a look with Armas and turned toward me with sympathy in her eyes.

"I'm sorry, Daniella," she finally broke. "But we can't. The loss of Imerian life would be too great."

No.

Poppi scoffed a laugh. "Of course. Even when asked by your own daughter, you would rather leave an entire kingdom to slaughter."

Clara's nostrils flared softly, the only sign that her temper was rising and she was doing everything in her power to keep her composure. She rose slowly and steadily from her chair so she could look down on us all as she said her next words.

"I have no doubt that Damien thought to manipulate me by sending you back here to ask me yourself, but I will not waver in this. If Imeria enters the conflict now, it would mean more of a loss of life to us than Lustraya. You all have held on this long already; you can make it that much more."

I felt like I had been slapped in the face again at the callous tone in Clara's voice. How could she do this?

"Damien never sent me," I said starkly. "I came here on my own will and against his. Poppi and I were on a scouting mission when we found your camp at your northern border. You may not want to be involved Clara, but you already are." Clara turned as if to walk away from the conversation, which only spurred me into action more.

"They have murdered entire villages. Burned them to the ground. Women, children . . . babies. They take the men, and their families never see them again. How can you turn your back on them?"

She halted and turned back to me, her eyes conveying sympathy but I could tell by her posture; there was no swaying her.

"One day when you are Queen, Daniella, you will understand."

"If you do not help Lustraya now, there will be no kingdom left for me to rule!"

My breathing was shaky, my grip on my emotions loosening by the second. How could she deny us?

"Please," I begged.

Armas and Lucette turned to look at Clara, hearing the helplessness that seeped from my words, but still, she did not move.

"You have my answer."

It was all I could do to not fall to my knees in that moment. To not scream and yell for her to send aid to us. All those people . . . I failed them yet again. Some kind of princess I was.

"Come," Poppi said firmly to me. "Let us not burden the Queen any longer. She must have dinner party invites to fuss over."

She gripped the top of my arm, gently turning me to the door. I followed her guidance without an argument. But just as we were about to exit, Clara called to us.

"There is a storm on its way that will impede your traveling. You are more than welcome to stay a few extra nights until it passes."

Poppi and I said nothing back as we exited the War Room and into the corridor. I turned to look at her, her expression mirroring my own of contempt and heartbreak.

"What do we do now?" Poppi asked.

"We convince her," I declared. "One way or another, we are getting that aid."

20

CONFESSIONS

The palace felt empty—hollow, even—as I roamed around the familiar hallways. Out of habit, I found myself taking a servant's stairway down into the kitchens, in the hopes that maybe Micah was still cooking. And maybe he had a pastry waiting for me. Just in case.

But it was late, and it was entirely possible that he had cleared out for the night, and I would have to fend for myself in the storage rooms for something to ease the ache in my chest.

As my boots cleared the landing, I was delighted to see a dim light shining through the bottom of the door that led into the kitchens.

Micah was here after all. May it be the one singular blessing of this entire trip.

I gripped the handle of the door and pulled. Warm air smelling of fresh baked bread greeted me, and I smiled.

"Oh, Micah," I called into the room. "I hope you don't mind but I came down for a visit. Oh."

I stopped short as I realized it wasn't Micah who was kneading his frustrations out in the dough, but Aeddan.

He pinned me to my spot with the eyes that haunted my dreams.

"I'm sorry. I thought Micah was here. I can go."

"No, wait," he said, releasing the dough. "Stay."

My heart thundered in my chest. This was a bad idea. A terrible one. I should really leave, but something kept me rooted to the spot. Kept me from walking away from him again.

"Okay," I whispered.

The setting was all too familiar. Not even a year ago, we stood in his parent's bakery, kneading dough and stuffing pastries. That day was seared into my head, and by the way that Aeddan was looking at me walking toward him, he was remembering it too.

"You look . . . healthy," he finally said.

I sniffed a laugh. "Yeah, I'm doing okay."

"Just okay?" Concern laced his words as his eyebrows creased together. Perhaps I should have chosen a better word to describe the convoluted mess I had been thrust into.

"Maybe that wasn't the correct word, but yeah, I'm okay. I mean . . . my people are dying while I get to sleep in silk pajamas, so I guess I could be way worse."

"Your people?"

This was it. The ugly and horrible reality we had to face. "Yes, Aeddan. My people."

He ground his teeth together as he balled his fist against the wood top. It broke my heart to see him like this and to know that it was all my doing.

"Aeddan . . . I . . ." But what could I say that would change any of this? "I'm sorry that it all ended like this. Believe me, I never *ever* wanted to hurt you. I just wanted to protect my sister."

"I know," he ground out. "It's just . . . I've tried everything to get you back for the last eight months and then you just show up like no time has passed, proclaiming to be the princess of a kingdom we have a strained relationship with. I just . . . he kidnapped you and you don't seem to care."

"Of course I care," I said, stepping forward and closing the gap between us. I cupped his face in my hands like he had done to me and brought his downtrodden face before mine.

"I have thought of you every day since I left," I confessed into the quiet of the kitchen. "In another life, Aeddan, it's you and me and the house on a hilltop."

"I tried to give that to you, Dani. You wouldn't let me," he whispered, nuzzling his cheek against my hand.

"Because that is not what fate has in store for us. We were never going to be able to be together, no matter if I left Imeria or not."

A sad, but honest truth.

"Do you love him?" he asked tenderly.

I blinked twice in astonishment of the question. I knew who he meant, but how could I tell Aeddan that Damien and I were . . . complicated at best. That, yes, I had love for the King, but it was born from respect and honor for doing what was best for Lustraya, not of romance.

"Don't ask questions you don't want answers to."

That was also the wrong thing to say. Aeddan's nostrils flared in frustration. As he removed my hands from his face, I felt them trail up and down my arms till they held my hands. Aeddan's hand rubbed against the silver band on my finger, and I felt him go still. Shit.

"What's this?"

"It's . . . it's not what you think. It's just—"

"An engagement ring? You're really going through with it then?"

"It's not an engagement ring, it's a gift. A very old one," I tried to explain.

His eyes softened, his jaw tightening as he held back words.

"Just say what you want, Aeddan," I urged. "There's no need to hold back from me now."

He stepped away from me, walking back to where I had found him when I walked in. The ball of dough was in his hands without a moment of hesitation, and he began kneading his fury into it. I didn't know what to do or what to say, so I just stood there helplessly watching him. The hope in me was holding on by meager threads.

"Months," he finally broke. "Months I have been organizing and pleading with the Queen and Armas for ways to get you back . . ." He smashed a fist into the dough. "Do you know what it is like? To watch someone that you care about be taken away in front of your eyes. To have the mental torture of wondering what they were doing to you. It's been agony, Dani. Pure agony."

Guilt, sadness, and longing etched his features, his lower lip trembling. The need to go to him and comfort him were all too much for me to handle. He slammed a hand against the table.

"Damn it, Daniella, I went after you!" he roared.

I wrapped my hands around my stomach, begging my body to keep in the tears that were forming in my eyes, and the sob I knew that wanted to follow.

"You did?" I whispered.

He nodded, his head hanging from his shoulders as he gripped the edge of the table. "After we got the chaos of the party settled, I ran to the stables; Harrison and Maddox yelling at me as I did. We were ready to go that night had Connors not intervened and reminded us of the oath we just took." He lifted his head. "But I didn't listen."

I drew in a gasp as the first tear fell. "What?"

"I went after you anyway," he admitted, looking me square in the eyes. "It took some time, but I made it over the Lustrayan border. I was on my way to finding your tracks when I was caught and brought back before the Queen. She had me put in irons and placed in the dungeon. Damn near executed me for treason."

No . . . No. Clara wouldn't do that.

"Well, clearly she didn't, so what happened?"

"Samir stepped in. I don't know exactly what he said to her on my behalf but next thing I knew, I was out of irons and being escorted to the barracks."

Of course, Sam would do something like that. He always saw more than the others did. The thought of him stepping in to save Aeddan for me—because what other reason could there be for him to risk his entire career—moved me more than any words could ever do.

"So, he saved you?"

"Yeah," he breathed. "He did. He saved me and I got promoted. Whether it was from pity or spite, I don't know. But the Queen keeps me under her watchful eye now in case I misstep. My only regret is that I couldn't save you. And look where we are now."

Once again, we found ourselves at the same crossroad, having the same conversation. It would always be the same conversation with us. Always a push-pull.

"I'm really sorry," I said in all sincerity, wiping my nose. "You know I never wanted any of this to happen like it has."

"Then what did you want?"

Him. I wanted him. I wanted to be a part of the Serpentine Guard and to protect my sister. I wanted to live out my days fighting to protect the people I loved. I wanted . . . it didn't matter what I wanted now. It would never be mine.

"I wanted to protect my sister," I replied through the lump in my throat. "And I don't even know if I've been able to do that." I wiped the tears that had fallen from my cheeks. "I have failed so miserably, Aeddan. In so many things."

He moved from the table, walking a few steps back to me before I stopped him with a hand to his chest, keeping him arm's distance away.

"I may have failed you, and I may have failed my sister in some capacity. But I won't fail the people of Lustraya. Aeddan, if you could only see what they have been through. We need Imeria's help. Damien might be too proud to keep asking, but I'm not. Help me convince Clara to send aid. Please."

The last word shook as I asked him for what might be the final time, because the way he was looking at me was like he didn't know who I was anymore. Like I was a total stranger, and he couldn't stand who I was becoming.

The familiar feeling of my heart breaking followed as he shook his head and left the kitchen all together.

21

QUEEN TO QUEEN

My garden remained unchanged except for the fact that most of the flowers were no longer blooming, and the ground was starting to look more brown than green.

As far as I could remember, I had always sought out this garden for comfort. Even when things were wrong, this place always allowed me to think. But right now, I felt hollow. Empty. I had no sense of direction and for the first time in a long time, I felt entirely helpless.

Damien was going to be furious with me when Poppi and I returned to Lustraya. I could already hear the click of the door to the mountain room shutting closed. I could feel the little progress I had made slip away with each passing day.

After my kitchen escape last night, I met Poppi in her room. I told her that we needed to stay one week and after that we could leave, and I would not argue. Aeddan may have stormed away from me last night, but I had to believe that he would do what he could in persuading Clara. The man I knew wouldn't let innocents go unprotected. I had to believe in that.

If only Samir could see me now. What would he think? Would he still think me a headstrong girl capable of changing her destiny or would he think I was a simpering girl who had become a disappointment?

It was all becoming so much.

The sound of crunching grass jolted me from my thoughts, and I whipped my head around to find Poppi coming from the side gate.

"Good morning," I said, a little disappointed that it wasn't Arabella walking through the grass. Where was she?

"Morning," she replied, coming to sit down next to me on my blanket. "How long have you been out here?"

"Too long . . ."

We lapsed into one of our moments of comfortable silence, something I had come to appreciate from Poppi. She may have been one of the worst people when I first met her, but I was glad to have her here with me. As fond as I was of Kristian and Gunnar, they would not be able to understand me the way Poppi did.

"So," she said, breaking the silence. "Is this like . . . your place or something?"

"Something like that," I supplied. I was going to leave the conversation at that, but I felt the need to add, "When my mother left me here, I tried running away. And when that didn't work, I learned how to fight." I sighed. "But then I was always fighting and Samir used to find me in abandoned hallways stabbing a made-up opponent. He was the one who told me to find the balance." I spread my arms wide, indicating what I meant.

"He seems like a wise man."

"He is."

"Was he the one that was in the council room the other day?"

"No, that's General Armas. He's . . . not a man of many words. But he fought in the Great War and has seen horrors I don't even want to imagine. When he took over after the last general passed, he made sure that we went into everything with eyes wide open. Our training here could only be described as relentless."

"So, where is Samir then?"

I looked to her. "I wish I knew."

So much was changing in my life. Nothing felt consistent anymore and as I sat in the garden with Poppi, I wished for just one thing to remain in my life unchanged.

"So, Samir . . . what is he to you then? You speak of him with such . . . admiration. Respect."

"He was like a father to me," I admitted, picking at the petals on a rose. "He was the one who found me the times I ran away, the one who first started training me and encouraged me to forge my own path when everyone thought I should keep my mouth shut and get married. My life here would have been so much different."

"I'm glad you had him," she said definitively, reaching a hand through the space between us. I grabbed it, meeting her squeeze with one of my own. "You know, when we first got here, I was so mad at you for deviating from the plan. I still am, truthfully. But you seem more relaxed here than you have been in Lustraya and . . . I don't know. It's nice to see. This version of you is what Lustraya needs."

Her words struck me hard. She was right. Since stepping foot in Lustraya I have made my distaste for my situation well-known, despite trying everything I could to win over the people. But maybe they could sense my unhappiness from beneath the surface and that's why things were still so hard for me.

"I sent another letter to Damien as well," she continued. "He would want an update on what's happening here. I just hope he can get them in time."

"I will get us that aid, Poppi," I promised. "I won't let one more innocent die at the hands of the Fae."

She smiled solemnly. "I know."

# # #

The parlor Arabella and I so loved and adored was bleak and cold when I visited it. The furniture remained uncovered, but a thin layer of dust had begun to coat the surfaces that were left exposed. It seemed no one had been here in a long time. Even Arabella's room seemed to be untouched, which led me to the question: where was my sister?

The more I walked around the palace, the more it was evident she was not here and hadn't been for a while. Something about that didn't sit right with me.

She should be here.

The annoying pit in my stomach that opened during the Gauntlet opened its maw once more. I was missing something important. There was no sign of Samir nor Ary. Was coincidence or fear getting the best of me?

Experience taught me there was no such thing as coincidence, and that there was a reason for everything.

Out of habit, I looked to our bookshelf where a title less leatherbound text should be placed, but its hiding spot had been secured by another. What I would give to know where that book went, and most importantly, *who* took it.

"Princess Daniella," Kalter asked from the doorway, making me jump in my skin.

"Kalter," I breathed. "You startled me. What can I help you with?"

"Her Majesty would like to see you in her private green room for tea. I am here to escort you."

Always with the escorts.

"Of course," I complied. "Let's not keep her waiting then."

Though I didn't like being summoned like a common mutt, I would admit that the private time with Clara was something I needed. Perhaps she would tell me what was going on without three others watching her.

The unease that hit me in the parlor only continued to grow the closer we came to Clara's location. Something in me just felt *wrong*.

"Here we are," Kalter announced as he opened one of the glass paned doors. "She is in the back right corner, closest to the lilacs."

Of course she was. I smiled and thanked the butler before walking into the green room that seemed to be halted in spring. The smell was amazing the further I walked through. Roses, gardenias, peonies, carnations; all bloomed around me like there wasn't a winter raging outside.

"Clara," I called into the room. "Where are you?"

"Over here, dear!"

Her voice rang out clear as a bell, and I looped through one more gathering of trees before finding her sitting at an ornate table; papers and tea spread before her.

"Come, Daniella. Sit," she instructed. She waved a hand to the open chair facing the window overlooking the cliffs of Sapphire Isle. "How did you sleep?"

Better than I had in weeks. Months, maybe. But that yawning pit kept me from saying that, so instead I told her, "Well, thank you. It's a bit odd being back here. I'm almost not used to it."

"Huh," she snorted. "Damien finally found it in him to have proper accommodations in that castle of his. It was always so cold."

"You've been?" I asked her, surprised. As long as I had been in Clara's care, never once did she leave Imeria for any reason. Which now that I thought of it, was suspicious in and of itself.

"Once," she admitted. "A very long time ago. I had never been so cold in my life."

I smiled, thinking of the feet of snow that was surely covering the mountains near the Silver Castle. "It grows on you eventually," I said fondly.

"Grows," Clara laughed. "Oh yes, it gets everywhere. The only place on this continent where it snows more than it does bloom. That's why I love where we are, Daniella. We live in a near constant spring; this cold only persisting a few months a year. It's paradise."

"Paradise . . ." I echoed hollowly before taking a sip of the tea in front of me. It was lavender and chamomile.

It felt wrong to be surrounded by all the luxury and comfort that Imeria had to offer while my people sat in snow and haphazardly built cottages. No town in Lustraya would dare expand more than that, for fear of being taken once more. The tea turned sour in my mouth.

"Why that face, dear?"

I swallowed loudly as I composed myself, getting a handle on the rising tide of my frustrations. "You talk about the comforts of home so easily and the blights of others just as candidly." I looked her deep into her grey eyes. "The snow is cold; yes. But it's also beautiful. In the mornings, you should see the way the light dances off it like a sea of diamonds begging to be scooped up and tossed at someone's face.

That same snow also freezes our ground, making it hard for us to harvest. It cuts off our roads, so it is hard for families to travel. You live in a paradise, but my people are living in hell. More now than ever."

The last words came out accusatory by accident but there was truth in it.

"Daniella . . ." Clara sighed, setting down her tea. "There is so much you don't know."

To that, I rolled my eyes. My, oh my, how I was tired of people telling me what I didn't know and then withholding that same information.

"Are you going to enlighten me or just keep chastising me like I'm a little kid again?"

Clara's eyebrows raised at my tone. "You will always be my little girl," she said sweetly. "But you're right. You are no child; that much is certain." She paused, looking out the window to the cliffs and the fast-growing storm clouds headed our way.

"I am proud of you, Daniella. For everything you have overcome and for how you have handled yourself. Queen to future Queen; Lustraya is lucky to have you, even if it means Imeria won't. But dear, you can't be naive."

Naive? What the hell?

"I don't mean to insult you, but merely to caution you," she said when she saw my change in demeanor. "Damien is not who he seems. He is calculating and precise, and has a knack for getting to know people just so he can exploit them for both good and bad. Don't let him do the same to you. It's bad enough he sent you here—"

"I sent myself."

"Did you?"

I opened my mouth to reply but the words wouldn't come. What did she mean, 'Did you?'

"Think about it, Daniella. What happened the day you decided you were going to cross into Imeria? What happened before that, even?"

The council meeting. The meeting where I was finally trusted to hear the secrets and information that had been withheld. Damien knew that was important to me; knew that I wanted to help in the best way I could. Is that why he finally relented?

I thought about it harder, stirring in another lump of sugar to my tea. The conversation had been about Fae blockades and their constant interference with the villages to the south. Was it pure coincidence that the day I was allowed into the circle was the day that we discovered there were only three roads left untouched? Three roads that just so happen to be close to the Imerian border?

Damien would anticipate my want to go inspect the scenes for myself. He would know that I yearned for my old home or any reason to be close to my sister again. Had he manipulated me like Clara said? Or was it just coincidence?

The pit opened further.

"Damien has a way of making you think you've come up with a plan all on your own, while in actuality, it was him pulling the strings the whole time," she said, laying a hand gently to my arm.

"He wouldn't . . ." I said sordidly, not looking up from my cup.

"He would," she said the words with a surety and ferocity I hardly ever heard. They were sharp and biting, an unyielding truth. "I do not doubt the plights of the Lustrayan people. My heart does sympathize with you. But you have not known Damien as long as I have. You have not heard the way he strategizes even if he doesn't realize he's doing it."

She turned her gaze to the papers scattered on the table. Her left hand glided gently over them in a way a mother would caress the top of a baby's head.

"These are correspondence letters between him and Raddison. I should have known then what he was capable of, but I chose instead to believe he was a good man."

She lifted one of the letters up and gave it to me. I recognized Damien's writing immediately, the scrawl unique and blocky.

For weeks we have searched, and I am pleased to tell you, friend, that we have found it at last. The woman is insane at best, but her knowledge is immeasurable. She smiles at me like I am her sun and moon. I almost feel guilty allowing her to feel such a way when I know I could never return it. In the end, I do it all for my kingdom.

"He speaks as if he is a selfless ruler, one who only wants what is best for his people, but he's actually selfish and ruthless."

"What is he talking about?" I asked, waving the letter between us. "What is this 'it' he is talking about?"

"I wish I knew," Clara sighed. "It was all he and Raddison ever spoke about and in vague terms. I tried to ask one time, but Raddison said it was too dangerous to speak of. He and Damien were so tight-lipped, I just stopped asking."

"And this woman? Who was she?"

"Some lover Damien took for one summer. No one ever saw her; no one ever knew her name. He would always go to her and come back a few days later. Then one day he just . . . stopped. We all wondered what happened, but he never said."

"So, he had a secret affair with a woman decades ago?" I quipped. "I hardly think that means he is a manipulative person, Clara. Look," I said as I ran a hand through my hair. "I know what it looks like on the outside, but I have been living with him for months now and though he would probably rather I not say anything, I know he's scared.

"And me? I'm scared too. I've seen the destruction. I've seen what lurks in the mountains and in the trees. You paint this place as a paradise because it is so easy for you to go beyond its walls and feel safe, but we do not have that luxury. Whatever your past with him, I am asking—no, *begging*—you to please reconsider."

"If the destruction is as awful as you paint, then you leave no hope for me in keeping my own people safe, Daniella. You once defended these walls. Tell me, would you readily send your unit, your legions into a war with no face? One that is shrouded in mystery and myth?"

No. I wouldn't. When I was told the truth, I even laughed in its face. Clara must've known what I was thinking because she smiled sadly at me.

"It is no easy thing being a ruler. It doesn't make it any easier when your heart is so big and you care so much, too. But you'll figure it out, I know you will."

Tears of frustration welled in my eyes. "Is that what you would tell Arabella?"

It was the first time I had mentioned her name since being back. Just like something did not feel right about the 'coincidences' happening, Arabella being missing from the palace was equally worrying.

"Arabella has her own things to worry about right now."

"Like what?"

Clara did not like my sharp tone and pressed her lips into a thin line. She loved me like a daughter, but Arabella was her true flesh and blood. There is nothing that she would not do to protect Ary, and I could see that protective instinct flaring to life in her eyes.

"After Damien's little outburst at the ball, I made sure she was sent somewhere that was safe."

I waited for her to elaborate, but I was met with a wall of silence instead. I should have known she would be vague on the details.

"Is that why Samir is gone, too?"

The thought occurred to me quickly, but it made sense all the same. Ary was gone and so was Samir. If Aeddan's timeline of events was correct, this would have happened around the time he tried to leave and rescue me.

If Ary was away, she would need someone that had skill and experience at keeping another away from harm and trouble. Samir was the perfect candidate. And with him gone and the Serpentine Guard newly reformed, it would also make sense for Clara to put Aeddan in charge in his stead.

He was intelligent, skilled, and easily watchable from that spot.

"I appreciate your concern for the well-being of my family and the people who protect me, but you're asking questions you shouldn't be, Daniella. First lesson of being a Queen: tread carefully. Court is as much a battlefield as the mud and muck of a real one. One wrong question, one wrong step and you will be at war with any ally. That is something I would tell Arabella."

It was clear that I was going to be leaving this tea with more questions than answers and it made my skin crawl.

"Well," I finally said, clearing my throat. "Thank you for explaining things to me. It has been an . . . enlightening afternoon."

"Don't be like that, Daniella," Clara scolded. "This wasn't meant to demean or demoralize you. I just want you to know exactly who you're aligning your life with. It's better to go into these things with eyes wide open than with half-truths."

"Speaking from experience," I accused as I stood from my chair.

"Yes."

We held one another's gaze; sympathy, understanding, and a strong sense of duty passing through us. Queen to Princess. Woman to woman. I bowed my head and moved from the table, the conversation exhausting me. But before I could leave, I looked at Clara one more time.

"Just tell me one thing," I asked. Clara met my gaze. "Is she okay? Is she happy?"

"There are wedding bells still in her future, Daniella."

22

ROUND TWO

Training was always my center. The physical exertion would calm me down and allow me to think and to plan.

Finding my way to the Ring was second nature, my legs carrying me through the halls and down the stairs as I got lost in my thoughts. By the time I felt the outside air kiss my cheeks, I'd almost forgotten how I had even gotten here.

Twilight was on the horizon; the cold greys, purples, and blues peeking through the clouds that had begun to gather since we arrived. Torches were already lit around the Ring which meant that I wasn't alone.

Aeddan was in the middle, sword in hand, slicing and stabbing his way through his own invisible enemy.

I became enamored as I watched him from the top of the stairs. He was lethal and steady, swift and sure as he worked through the movements. In all the years I had trained next to him, I had never stopped to watch him and now that I did, I never wanted to stop.

He was a force to be reckoned with and as he stripped off his sweaty shirt, I was ready to be the cause of that force.

I snapped myself out of the trance and moved to meet him in the center of the Ring, grabbing a nearby sword from the weapons area on my way. My footsteps were muffled as I moved, his backed turned away from me and none the wiser.

"Care for a partner?"

He spun around quickly; his hands balled in his shirt as he wiped the sweat from his brow. Had I seen Aeddan shirtless before, yes. But the effect was different now that we had crossed over the forbidden line we had once drew.

I ached to reach out and touch his skin, to feel his warmth under my palm. I ached for a lot of other things too, but I suppressed that urge as fast as it made itself known.

"What are you doing here?" he asked, half-annoyed.

"I needed to clear my head," I said honestly. "There's too much rattling around up there and the best way for me to clear the fog is to train. But you know that."

His eyes danced over my face as he remembered the last time he dropped in on one of my training sessions in the abandoned room.

"I do."

The air between us became charged as we stared at one another, neither one of us daring to move just yet. I replayed his words from the kitchen over in my head, my heart seizing as I remembered how much pain I had caused him.

"So, what do you say?" I offered, clearing my throat. "Want to be my target practice?"

A smile tugged at the corner of his mouth, and I knew my teasing had won him over.

He grabbed his sword and motioned with his head for me to follow him forward. The muscles in his back rippled as we walk to the other end of the sparring field. Yes, he had indeed bulked up since I had left.

He turned swiftly, mischief glinting in those hazel eyes as he readied his sword.

"Time to see if you've still got it," he said, before coming at me quick with a left jab.

I brushed it off with my borrowed sword, feigning right and stepping away from him, a smile ghosting my face at his challenge.

"Try to keep up, Helvig."

And then we were off like no time had passed at all; our bodies falling in sync as we moved around each other, the familiarity releasing all the pent-up stress of the last months. But as the relief came, so did the pain. The words we had left unsaid the other night spurred to the surface and released themselves through the clashing of steal. No longer was this a friendly round of sword practice, but instead an unleashing of locked away emotions.

As I brought the steel behind my shoulder to block a pass from Aeddan, I felt the vibrations of the hit travel through my hands and arms. My muscles quaked under his strength.

The pace intensified, my breathing becoming more labored as I had to work harder to avoid his advancement. He lashed out more; his moves becoming more frenzied and angry. Aeddan was losing himself to whatever he battled inside and as I twirled away from yet another blow, I saw the hurt behind the mask he kept up.

I could see the night I left with Damien playing over in his head. I could feel the betrayal that he battled with day after day. I could taste the words he wanted to scream at me on my own tongue.

In the next moment, I knew what I had to do. For him and for me. Aeddan regripped his hilt and swung for my neck, but instead of backing away and preparing to counterattack, I stepped into him. He bent his elbow last minute, the blade stopping at my throat between us, his breathing rapid and crazed.

I held firm, feeling the cold metal pressing against my skin as I looked into his eyes in surrender, my sword dangling at my side.

I watched the battle haze clear from his eyes as they blinked rapidly. I reached my free hand up to touch his cheek, my thumb stroking the smooth skin there in reassurance.

"It's okay," I murmured. "It's okay."

He swallowed hard, his hand shaking as he clutched the sword for dear life.

"Why?" he asked. It pained me to hear the slight crack in the word. He was keeping it together but only barely.

"You know why."

He pushed away from me and tossed the blade to the ground. I dropped my own with him; our conversation picking up right where it ended.

He turned his back again, his hands running through his short hair and tugging it roughly as he walked away from me. My heart cracked as I scrambled for something to say to him. But what more could I say to him? How many more times could we have the same fight?

His shoulders slumped forward, and I did the only thing I could think of. I walked to him and wrapped my arms around his middle, my forehead pressing into his back.

We stayed there, our heartbeats finding the same rhythm, our pain mingling, until that too was in sync.

He turned around to face me, my grip loosening and finding home on his hips, the anguish written on his face for anyone to see.

"I am so mad at you," he whispered, his bottom lip quivering ever so slightly as he pushed a strand of hair behind my ear.

"I know," I breathed. "I know."

"And you come back," he reached down and grabbed my hand. "Wearing his ring and acting like none of it meant anything to you."

My hands slid up his chest, capturing his face between them as I said, "You know that's not true."

I felt the warmth of a tear hit the tops of my fingers and I brushed it away. I couldn't bear to see him cry.

"Why couldn't it have been enough?"

I pushed the lump forming in my throat down, forcing myself to keep my composure. There were so many things I wanted to say to him, so many declarations I wanted to confess that it was scrambling my sense of thought.

"Of course it would've been enough," I said, gripping him tighter. "It always would have been enough. *You* would have been enough. But that was never going to happen, Aeddan, no matter how much we want it."

"I know you love Arabella, but even she would want you to live your life the way you wanted."

"And I am."

He didn't like that answer. Aeddan removed my hands from him not so gently, backing away from me again, his jaw clenching in frustration.

"Look, Aeddan," I said, lifting and lowering my arms in exasperation. "What's done is done. I don't regret what I did, and truth is, I would do it again. My duty has always been to Ary and Clara, and I will protect them, no matter what."

"You could have done that here. With me!"

"No, I couldn't," I yelled. "I never would have been able to focus on them because I would be too busy focusing on you!" Titus had given his life for Phaedra. Turns out I would give mine for not only my sister, but also Aeddan. That thought chilled me to the bone as I pictured Ary with an arrow through her chest, while I protected Aeddan with my body instead.

"I told you I would give it all up," he roared back. "I would walk away from all this, the consequences be damned, and wait for you. There was always another choice, and you have always been too scared to take it!"

"You're the one who is scared, Aeddan. Not me. You!"

"Bullshit!"

"No," I stamped out, trying to reign in my temper. "It's not. You're letting feelings cloud your judgment and you're just upset that I am not. You're scared of losing something that wasn't there to lose. But guess what? I have already lost everything once. And now twice. So, I have no problem rebuilding because I no longer fear it."

I walked to him; his hands balled at his sides to keep from shaking and took them.

"I want nothing more than to be at your side, every minute of every day. I want to be able to wake up every morning, and have your eyes be the first thing I see. At some point, Aeddan, you will have to reconcile that I can and do want to be with you, but my duty will always come above it. It is who I am, and I will not change."

I placed a kiss to his knuckles, feeling him tense as our skin met and prayed that one day he could forgive me. Or at least understand why I had to keep my feelings for him at bay.

The Fae closed in every day, their threat an ever-looming storm over my head and time not on our side.

"Dani—"

"Thank you," I interrupted him. "For coming after me the night of the ball. I don't know if I ever said that. No one has shown me that much devotion in a long time."

He looked at me tenderly, his face softening and hands unclenching to hold mine.

"I can't keep losing you," he broke. "And I don't want to be angry at you, but you make it so hard not to. Every time I think I might get my way, you ruin that hope."

My heart caved in on itself, his last words throwing guilt into the firestorm of emotions that were already cascading within me.

"I think it's time I retire for the night," I said quietly as I dropped his hands. He remained rooted to his spot, the fight leaving his body. I reached up on tiptoes to plant a small kiss to his cheek in goodbye before taking off for the stairs back into the palace.

As I walked back to my room, I felt nothing but hollowness. It was an inescapable feeling; one I wouldn't surrender to but one I was learning to walk hand in hand with. All my life I just wanted to be wanted; wanted to belong to something. To someone. And here I finally was, with just that at my fingertips, walking away because this world was becoming bigger than me.

Duty, honor, loyalty.

All of which bound me to Lustraya and to being their princess. As I shut my door to my room, I felt the Dani that used to walk these halls—desperate for love and hope—evaporate into the shadows.

23

IDLE SCHEMING

The next morning, I did what any sullen princess would do, and I woke my favorite guard up for more target practice. By guard, I mean Poppi, and by favorite, I mean the only person who was around that could challenge me.

Clara had placed her in the rooms next to mine—not the usual practice for Clara, since I was still in the family wing—so when the sun began to crest the horizon, I was the one banging on the door to wake Poppi this time.

She was irritated with me at first, but when I told her I had something fun in mind for the morning, she was out of bed and dressed within seconds.

Watching as she took in the Ring for the first time made me feel like a giddy kid.

"I get why you are the way you are . . ." she breathed in amazement as we walked down the steps and to the edge of the weapon's keep. "This is massive."

"Mhm," I agreed. "And it's ours for the morning."

She looked at me quizzically, her brow quirking up.

"I may or may not have called in a favor to get the Imerian training moved. They should be hitting their first mile soon."

"How many miles are they running?"

"Five."

Poppi burst out laughing, clapping a hand on my shoulder as she tipped her head to the morning sun.

"You're evil," she chuckled, walking to inspect all the Ring had to offer.

We spent a while chatting and figuring out what we wanted to do. Afterall, we had the morning to ourselves and no one to bother us. The possibilities were limitless. But eventually, we decided it would be best to train like we were going head-to-head with a Fae warrior, the incident at the Imerian camp just a teaser of what could be.

In no time at all, Poppi and I had shed our vests and were now wearing just a thin tunic tucked into our pants, boots laced up tightly. The morning sun was rising higher, the sweat running freely down our backs as we sparred.

Poppi wanted to start with swordsmanship, but after my night with Aeddan, my palms were aching and shoulders too sore to hold up a sword right now. So, we decided hand-to-hand was the way to go.

"That's all you got?" Poppi taunted as I swung for her again, my punch missing her and my foot stumbling forward. Gods, I was tired.

"Fuck off," I spat, catching her wrist and spinning till I had it pinned behind her. "What do you have to say now?"

She leaned back into me, using her weight and momentum to throw me over her shoulder, her body rolling over mine as I held her still. I was now pinned under her and to the ground.

"What was that you were saying?" she said in a mocking tone. I could hear the smile on her face as she taunted me, the breathing leaving my lungs with a woosh.

I let go of her wrist and shoved her off my chest, both of us rolling up and into a crouched fighting stance.

"Yield?" I asked.

"Never," she grinned wickedly.

We launched at each other again, fists flying and feet dancing as we ducked and jabbed our way through the morning. When she had me in a headlock, I tapped her arm, letting her know I was done.

My body felt like jelly, my lungs wheezing and burning as I struggled to keep them filled.

"The Fae won't be as nice as I'm being," she said as she handed me one of the canteens we brought. "You'll have to rethink the way you approach hand-to-hand, should it happen. Remember, you have to use their height against them, and keep low, keep their footing unbalanced. It's the only way you'll get the upper hand until back-up comes."

"How do you know all this?" I asked, leaning against the stone wall, my hands reaching up and lacing behind my head.

"King Damien taught me," she said simply. I looked at her expectantly, knowing there was an explanation about that around the corner.

Poppi sighed, laying her canteen on the top of the wall.

"You're going to make me tell you this story too?"

"Yup!"

"Fine," she said, rolling her eyes. "Then I'll try and make it short and sweet. The night the Fae came to my village, they not only took my brother, but killed my mother."

I jolted up straight because I had not expected her to say that.

"Oh, shi— Poppi, I'm so sorry."

She brushed off my apology. "Don't worry about it, it was a long time ago. Anyway, my father tried to run after them—the Fae, I mean—and left me all alone. Damien found me the next morning hiding under the remains of my father's old workshop. He was a jewelry maker, if you can believe that."

Truthfully, I couldn't.

"He brought me back to the mountain keep, back when it was still forming into what it is now and taught me everything I know. I was like you in that regard. Always asking questions."

She said the last part with loving sarcasm, and I punched her lightly on the shoulder as she laughed with me.

I knew Poppi and I were more similar than we were different, which was a reason we probably fought so much in the beginning. I hated that the thing that was bonding us was the loss of family. Why couldn't it be over anything else?

A twig snapped in the trees, setting Poppi and I both on edge and into fight mode. There was supposed to be no one here but us. A twig snapped again and this time Poppi grabbed her sword and reached out an arm in front of me, ever the present guard.

The rustling continued until we saw two people come from behind the trees, their hands raised in front of them.

"Easy," Harrison said. "It's just us."

Poppi and I relaxed, letting out breaths we didn't know we were holding.

"You guys damn near gave me a heart attack," I scolded as they hopped over the stone wall and into the Ring with us.

"Our apologies," Maddox said. "We heard the fighting and came to check it out. We didn't realize it was the two of you beating the lights out of each other."

I took in Poppi and I's appearance. Wrinkled shirts, frizzy hair, dirt smears on our cheeks and hands.

"We weren't beating the lights out of each other," I said defensively.

"We were training," Poppi said at the same time.

"Who the hell beats up their crowned princess?" Maddox asked, crossing his arms over his chest.

"Someone who isn't afraid that their princess will get mad because she is covered in mud," Poppi sheathed her sword. "Besides, she needs the practice."

Without thinking, I let my left hand loose, slapping her in the chest lightly.

"I'm not the one who needed practice," I joked back. "You could barely keep your feet under you that whole time."

"Lies."

"Great," Harrison groaned. "There's two of them."

In unison, we level Harrison with a glare, one that reads 'don't mess with me' and 'please never compare me to her again.'

Maddox chuckled under his breath. "Never thought I'd see the day . . ." he mused.

"Anyway," I said, changing the subject. "Why are you guys out here? Are you just getting back from somewhere?"

The men exchanged a quick glance before Maddox responded. "Can I tell you where it's a bit warmer and I can have some wine?"

Poppi cocked an eyebrow. "Since when was it cold?"

At that, I laughed. She had a point, though. After being in the Lustrayan cold, the Imerian one was child's play. In fact, I think Poppi and I both were still sweating. Harrison clapped Mads on the shoulder and led the way out of the Ring. He halted abruptly once we were back in the palace, his head darting right and left, trying to figure out which way he wanted to go.

"Uh, Dani . . ."

"We can go to Ary and I's parlor, or my rooms," I suggested.

The Serpentine Tower would be out of the question for us to visit now, despite the fact that I lived there myself not too long ago. I was a foreigner in my own home.

I showed them the way, passing a few guards stationed at entry points, but they didn't say anything or try to stop us. Probably because they recognized Mads and Harrison and thought they were escorting us.

Soon, the gilded door handle was in my palm, and I was pushing the doors open for us. The smell of books and dust welcomed us into its fold.

Maddox closed the door quietly behind us. He and Harrison removed their swords from their hips, settling onto the couches. I moved to the fireplace, setting about making a small fire in the hearth that would satisfy my two friends. In the meantime, Poppi perused the perimeter of the room, stopping every once in a while to read a book spine or admire a piece of artwork.

"Dani," Maddox said from the couch. "How about that wine?"

"Fourth bookcase, lower cabinet behind the old flowerpots," I instructed.

Back when Ary and I were barely in our teen years, we used to sneak a bottle or two from Clara's stores and keep them here for when we wanted to have a real fun night. I'm sure looking back now Clara knew, but in the moment, we felt so clever.

I heard Maddox dig through the cabinet, his copper head disappearing before reemerging with a bottle that looked like it had been sitting in there for years.

"Think this will be okay?" he asked, coming to place the thing in front of me. "It's got a solid layer of dust on it."

"The last time I saw this label was when I was in my eighteenth year. I'd say that it is good and aged by now."

"Excellent," Mads beamed and went to work getting the cork out with a knife.

"You're really about to have wine for breakfast?" Poppi asked as she found a spot in a chair across the couch from where Harrison laid with his legs stretched out.

"Of course," he said smugly. "And because Dani girl over here loved to be a little troublemaker back in the day, I know this is a good one."

"I was not a troublemaker," I said in my defense.

"Whatever you say, Your *Highness*," he teased. I grabbed a pillow from the chair I was about to sit in and lobbed it at his face.

"You try being pawned off into marriage and see where it leaves your sanity!"

We all laughed as the pillow connected with its target, Maddox revealing a grumpy pout as it fell to his lap.

"So," I said, pivoting the conversation. "Care to tell me what you two were doing spying on us?"

"You said some interesting things that caught our attention," Maddox said carefully. "We wanted to see if you further elaborated. What we didn't expect was to hear . . . that."

"We're sorry for your loss," Harrison interjected with the most sincerity. "I can't imagine losing my family in that way."

Poppi nodded her thanks before replying. "My family was just one of many decimated by the Fae. Our only hope is that your Queen finally sees the light and sends us the aid we've been desperate for. Otherwise, there's going to be many more orphans in this world."

I knew Mads and Harrison wanted to say something in defense of their Queen, but they held it in. If not for my benefit, then for Poppi's. Arguing was not going to solve anything.

"So, what do you suggest we do?" Harrison spoke. His cool calculation evened out the sadness, then dissipating it all together. Battle strategy; our one common thread.

"As of now," Poppi chimed in. "We do our best to keep those last three roads between our kingdoms open."

Harrison and Mads nodded in agreement.

"We noticed that on the maps, too," Mads said, taking a swig from the bottle. "It's why Clara had us out there in the first place."

"Maddox . . ." Harrison chastised like he was the father of a child that couldn't keep quiet.

"Harrison, I think we're past the point of secret keeping," Mads countered. Poppi and I exchanged a quick look in agreement with the sentiment. "Besides, if the Fae are coming, then we need to be ready sooner rather than later."

"That's what we've been trying to tell you . . ." Poppi muttered.

I shot her a side-eye before turning to Harrison to say, "We have no more men at our disposal and they're catching onto it. The southern border is our weakest point, but we can't do anything unless you can help us convince Clara of the severity of it."

"You're her daughter," Maddox countered. "Shouldn't your word be enough?"

"It should, yes," I confessed. "But it's not enough—"

"She wants physical proof," Harrison interrupted, already knowing where the rest of my sentence was going. I nodded in agreement again.

"What, like their head on a spike?" Poppi asked. We all know she meant it sarcastically but unfortunately, that was correct. And unless we wanted an attack sooner rather than later, we were at a dead end.

"So, this is it then . . ." Poppi sighed, leaning her elbows onto her knees and looking us each in the eye. "This is how hope dies? With idle scheming and a massacre."

She stared into the fire, her eyes glazing over slightly as she lost her train of thought to its beauty. I reached out a hand to Mads, taking the wine from him and tipping a large mouthful down into my stomach. Oh, how I missed it.

Poppi moved to her feet quietly, grabbing her sword from the table she had laid it on without a single word.

"Where are you going?" I called after her.

She stopped when her hand was on the handle to the parlor door and turned her head only enough that we could hear her say, "To get our proof."

That afternoon we were greeted by one of the largest storms ever to hit Imeria. Wind and rain thundered against the windows, whipping plants around and threatening to uproot trees.

Palace tenants swarmed about, trying to save anything from the outside they could or else face an airborne attack from them. It was absolute madness.

"Your Highness," one attendant called to me as I tried to enter the hallway from my room. "Get back into your room and wait for a guard to retrieve you. They will take you into one of the bunkers for safety."

"No, I can help," I argued as a strong wind blasted against the glass window next to me, causing it to splinter.

"Please!" the man tried again; but one more gust, and the glass was shattering and raining over us and into the hallway.

"Ahh!" we screamed, my body covering theirs as we fell into the rug. I felt the glass cut through the sleeves of my shirt and tear into my pants, sharp pricks of pain greeting me as I rolled.

"We can't wait! We have to go now!" I hollered over the roaring wind.

I stood up as quickly as I could, snatching the attendant by his collar and pushing him through the hallway and to safety.

"Poppi!" I called as we ran. "Poppi, where are you?"

The fact that she was not in the hallway with me twisted my gut. Something was wrong and if I found safety without her by my side, Damien would never forgive me. I wouldn't forgive me. And Gunnar and Kristian . . . what would they think?

I threw open her bedroom doors; another burst of cold, rainy wind surging through the broken balcony doors. I scoped out the room from the doorway, hoping to see her come out from her hiding spot, but when I didn't, I began to move. The balcony doors swished in the wind, a sign that they had been opened. When I made it to them and out onto the marble balcony, I gasped in horror. There was Poppi, slumped over, eyes glazed white and skin turning paler than snow.

"Poppi," I screeched as I knelt next to her frozen form. "Poppi, please wake up! Wake up, we have to move!" I shook her shoulders to no avail, my heart catching in my throat at the thought she might be dead.

In my bought of strangled screaming, I never heard the footsteps come in from behind me, nor did I hear the quiet swear, or the grunt of frustration. All I could remember was the feel of a cloth against my mouth as an arm pulled me against a chest and my final cry for Poppi was still ringing out.

24

AWAKENING

My head throbbed painfully as I slowly woke to the smell of a sickly-sweet perfume in the air. It was oddly familiar and sent my body tensing for a fight. I let out a groan as a full body ache tore through me.

"Sit still," someone told me. "You're going to make it worse if you move too quickly."

"What did you do to me?" I groaned again.

"I just put you into a deep sleep," the person said again. I tried to open my eyes, but they felt like they had been sewn shut. Panic swept through me, and I tried to move once more, a shooting pain coursing up my arm in response.

"Would you stop moving?"

They sounded irritated now and I could hear the shuffle of boots moving closer until I felt their presence by me. I felt a hand scoop under my jaw and force my mouth open. I thrashed against it, hoping for dear life that this wouldn't be my ending.

I felt a cool liquid slither down my throat. I coughed and hacked, trying to prevent it from going down but only managed to make myself choke. I tried to spit it back out but then my mouth was being slammed shut and I had no choice but to swallow it.

"Relax!"

I used the little energy that returned to me to bite the palm of the hand keeping my mouth shut. They snatched it away and I drew in a shaky gasp of air.

"Ow! Calm the fuck down, Dani. I'm helping you."

As my senses slowly regained, something in the back of my mind tickled in recognition. I knew that voice. It was raspy and willowy, but it held a tone of authority now. Their name was on the tip of my tongue as I forced myself to calm down enough to crack open my eyes.

A man loomed over me, their face blurry and split in two. I blinked once. Then twice. The image of them coming in to focus with each passing heartbeat.

Long black hair, pale skin, a jaw cut so sharply he didn't need a sword, lanky limbs that packed a powerful hit . . .

Viper.

"What the hell is going on?" I asked, my voice groggy and raspy from the tonics.

I made to sit up but felt the motion restricted. I looked down to my arms, to my wrist and was horror-struck that they were bound and tied to the table. Cold panic swept through me as I looked down to my ankles next and saw them bound too.

I thrashed against the restraints, trying to loosen them but to no avail. He tied the knots well and there was no budging them. Only a knife would set me free from the ropes.

Viper stepped forward hesitantly. "The ties are just a precaution. I've seen what you look like when you come out of an induced sleep. I didn't want to be tossed on my ass. They're more for me than they are for you."

I would laugh if I wasn't so angry.

"Viper," I said as evenly as I could. "Undo these restraints right now."

He removed a knife from his pocket and twirled it between his fingers as he assessed me. In the meantime, I laid as still as possible, not jerking on the restraints or spewing obscenities at him to show him that I was no danger to him or myself.

I heard the sawing of the rope before I felt the relief on my ankles, then my wrists.

I raised myself up slowly and tossed the remaining rope to the ground, my hand going to my head as it spun.

"Ugh," I grumbled, rubbing at my wrists, the skin tender under my touch. I swung my legs over the edge, letting them dangle as my head settled itself from the spins.

"Where are we?" I asked. "Where's Poppi?"

The image of her frozen body flashed in my mind's eye and I shuddered. Viper pointed to a small bed in the corner where my companion laid. Her skin was no longer white and frozen, but pink and warm.

I exhaled a sigh of relief.

"Thank you for saving her," I said as I placed my hands on either side of my legs, letting the table be a stabilization point for me.

"You're welcome," he replied, letting me take a few moments to collect myself.

When I was sure I wouldn't vomit, I asked him again, "Where are we?"

"In my . . . workshop? I guess that's what we can call it."

I looked around the space, not recognizing any of it. The stone down here was browned, a slight musk hanging in the air. Against the walls were long worktables piled high with herbs and vials; some of them steaming, some stoppered and ready for use. Bookshelves stuffed to the brim were behind me, crates stacked in front of it. The whole room was a cluttered mess.

"Are we still in Imeria?' I asked, confused, trying to gain a sense of my surroundings.

"We are," he assured. "Just in a hidden level of the palace. This used to be an old archivist room. I took it over once I was assigned here, needing a private place where no one would know what I was up to."

The old archives I had heard about in rumors growing up . . . but why he would need the privacy as a soldier was something else entirely.

"Assigned here?"

"The three of us," he motioned between his body that was leaning on the desk in front of me, Poppi's sleeping form, and mine still perched on the edge of the worktable, "Share more than just the inner knowledge of the Fae. We all serve Damien—someone I affectionately call The Frost King."

I couldn't stop the gasp that left my mouth, or the shockwave that sent me teetering back on the table. Viper reached out to steady me, his hand grasping my forearm gently.

"How?" I asked in wonder. "How do you know of the Fae?" And then accusatorily, "Why are you in Imeria?"

Viper competed next to me in the Gauntlet, won with me and the others. He was a traitor, a snake. Maybe that's why he went by that name.

"I will tell you what you want to know," he said, Poppi stirring at our commotion in the corner. She grunted something in her sleep, something I couldn't make out from this distance. "But I doubt you'll believe me when I tell you."

"Try me," I responded, crossing my arms over my chest as he released me.

"Fine," he said, matching my tone. "My real name is Baltasar, and I am an Oracle over two hundred and twenty years old. I am here because our world is in danger, and only you can help me stop it."

He was right. I didn't believe him. I stared at him dumbfounded.

"I'm sorry. Try that again?"

"Daniella," he urged. "I know it sounds improbable—"

"Extremely."

"—but what I speak is the truth. I sought out King Damien the moment I knew the Fae had decided to come out of hiding twenty years ago. He didn't believe me then either, but together, we have been able to hold off their advancement to the rest of the continent for the last decade."

"So, what's changed?"

Poppi coughed in the corner, her eyes fluttering as a sign she was waking up.

"The magic that has remained locked away is finally returning. It's waking up as its old foe threatens to tear apart the land once again."

"Magic?"

He nodded gravely. Poppi coughed again, this time enough that she gasped and jolted awake, her arms flying out and legs thrashing against the blanket. Viper—Baltasar—moved to her side, snatching up a cup from the small side table as he did.

"It's okay, it's okay," he cooed to her, placing the cup gently in her hands. "You're okay. You're in my workspace; the storm is gone. Daniella is safe. Just breathe."

He spoke his assurances like he knew they would be answers to questions she had yet to ask. All the while, Poppi worked to steady her breathing while taking small sips from the cup.

I, on the other hand, sat still trying to digest the wild explanation he had given me. Magic? In Taelle? It would seem crazy, if only I didn't believe him. After coming face-to-face with the mountain beasts and seeing the destruction from the Fae, I was more inclined than ever to accept this as truth.

When Poppi had calmed herself, she looked over to me, her face relaxing as she saw that I was unharmed.

"Thank the gods," she said, closing her eyes to the sky and reopening them to look at Viper. "What did I miss?"

"Nothing much," he said, standing and shuffling back to his worktable. "I've only just told Daniella here that I am an Oracle, magic lives in these lands once again, and she will be a cornerstone in us defeating the Fae, once and for all."

"Oh, just the easy stuff," she said mockingly. Viper chuckled.

"You know about this too?" I asked Poppi, not letting the hurt hide from my voice.

She nodded, tucking her half-bob behind her ear.

"It's just one of the many secrets I've had to hide for the well-being of Lustraya," she said. Then added, "And for me."

"Yourself?"

"Poppi is what we affectionately call a practitioner," Viper interrupted. "She is a conduit for the magic to flow through and use at its behest."

"So . . ." I mused, looking between them. "Like a witch? Like the kinds they tell us about to scare us as kids?"

"The one and the same," she confirmed, pulling one of the blankets around her shoulders.

I hopped down from the table, no longer able to sit still. I began pacing in front of them as I let this new information settle. The hurt of information being withheld from me again was nothing compared to the bewilderment I was feeling. I ran a hand through my hair and looked to Viper.

"So, what happened this afternoon with Poppi and the storm . . ."

"I used the atmosphere's magic to speed it up, intensify it so that Clara would heed our pleas. Give her proof," Poppi explained. It clicked then just what she meant when she left the parlor that morning. This is what she thought would change Clara's mind.

"Yes, and you almost killed yourself in the process," Viper scolded. "I taught you better than that."

Poppi made an obscene gesture at the man before going quiet again.

"Always genteel," Viper muttered. "Magic always comes with a price, Daniella, and it does what it wants. You've already experienced those side effects yourself."

I dropped my hand from my hair. "I have?" I asked breathless.

"I was not there to witness it myself, but according to the reports I received you caused quite the stir in the mountain pass."

I looked to Poppi, hoping she could fill in the gaps for me. I probably looked crazed to her right now.

"Do you remember when we got attacked by those beasts? How when you reached the ice, you reached down to the ground and roared back?" she asked.

"Vaguely . . ."

"When you touched the ground, you opened yourself up to the magic that laid deep within it. Whether you knew it or not, you were drawing up its power and using it to defend us all. It was stronger than anything I have been able to do before today, stronger than even that. And I've been training awhile."

"So, everything that is happening right now . . ." I asked the both of them, desperately trying to connect the dots. "The Fae, the magic . . . it's all because of me?"

Viper nodded and said, "I have been at this a very long time. As an Oracle, I am attuned to have the gift of reading prophecy, predicting events, and even hearing that of which cannot be heard. There have been whisperings in the Unknown of a practitioner that will come and restore the magic and beauty back to this land. They say she will be able to harness all the elements and to rid the world of evil. Daniella, I believe that person is you."

"Okay, now you're finally starting to sound insane," I hedged. "Viper, I am one person. I cannot do what you're saying. I-it's . . ."

My last words came out in stammered remarks because the thought of being anything but Daniella of Imeria now sickened me. I should have ran away with Aeddan while I had the chance.

"It's a lot to take in now," Viper assured, his hands reaching out to hold my shoulders. "But now that you know, we can get to work. Poppi and I will be with you the whole time. You won't be alone."

"Viper . . ."

"That's enough for today. I promise to answer the rest of your questions, but only after you have rested."

I nodded because there were no other words I could use. My body felt tired, my head numb. Viper was right. I needed a nap.

262

25

TRANSCEND

I insisted Poppi stay with me that night so I could monitor her. What I didn't say is that I feared for what would happen if I let her out of my sight. Before we left the archive room, I manage to weasel out a few more pieces of information from the duo.

"So, how does it work?" I asked them.

"Magic is always a give and take. It requires a balance. That can look like many things, but at its basic form, it is the circle of life and death," Poppi explained.

"So, what you did today, conjuring the storm . . ."

"To conjure that storm, she tethered herself to another source of power," Viper explained. "And depleted the resources she was allowed in that same time. Put it this way, Poppi does not hold a well deep enough to hold that amount of magic. She could have been killed."

"You said magic is like a living being, right? So, it just picks a favorite practitioner to give all its power to and moves on?"

"For the most part," Viper confirmed. "It was gone for so long that there is not enough documentation for us to confirm or deny suspicions. That is why I have taken the liberty to do it myself while I have the life span to do it."

I shot Viper a confused and curious enough look that he laughed.

"My age is new to me too, Daniella. While I may be an Oracle, I don't have all the answers, particularly when I am going to die. I only have the answers that I figure out myself. The moment I had my first premonition, I began documenting my journey. I cannot tell you how many courts I have served in my time since. Imeria and Lustraya are just new homes in passing."

They tried further to explain what they knew to me, but I was at my capacity for bullshit for the evening. I had survived a chaotic magical storm, been told that I was slated to be a powerful witch—*practitioner*—and that the entirety of the continent rested on if I could get my shit together or not. It wasn't exactly a peaceful mealtime conversation.

So, here I sat in front of my fireplace with Poppi's head in my lap as she slept peacefully and deeply, while I laid awake with even more questions. In the morning, I was writing Damien about this, and I didn't care how long the damn thing took to get to him. He would face my wrath one way or another.

The only thing that worried me most is how I was supposed to keep all this from my friends now. Maddox, Ary, and Harrison deserved to know the truth. Afterall, they were the ones to see me for me and love me because of it.

And Aeddan . . .

The soft voice in my head never let me be when it came to him. Even if I did tell Aeddan all I learned, would he believe me? No. No, I don't think he would.

I thought back to my conversation with Clara and what she said about Damien being a manipulator of people. Did he know who and what I was when he saw me, or was it Viper who led him here?

I longed for the life I used to live. It was simple yet predictable. Wake up, change and head out for training, then breakfast. After that, it was guard duty or route running through the city. Dinner would follow and then you go to sleep. Whatever happened in the meantime was your own business.

But now? Being told that the fate of the continent rested on my shoulders as well as the well-being of a kingdom? It was more than I ever bargained for. The Fae were one thing to deal with, but to add an entire mythology of nonsense on top of it was a hard tonic to swallow.

The fire crackled before me, its energy stoking me into a calm trance. The flames danced and danced, the flames growing brighter and louder until suddenly . . .

Was that . . . Damien? The vision before me was no longer a hearth in Imeria, but a marble stone in a too small study.

Damien smacked a hand against the desk, spit flying from his mouth as he yelled at someone. No, not someone. Gunnar. He was yelling at Gunnar.

" . . . they have to be ready. We cannot face another attack like we did in the mountains. It's bad enough I have to deal with the shit in Imeria and then you bring me this half-assed excuse of the newest troops being scared to fight now? What the fuck is this, Hale?"

"Hey!" I screamed from my spot on the couch. "Leave him alone!"

Damien's head snapped to the left, his eyes searching till they found mine, and then his eyes widened, his jaw slackening. "How are you . . ."

"You have no business talking to him like that. We have enough to worry about without you demoralizing the only people we have left willing to fight!"

The words came from me fluidly and without hesitation, almost like it was a dream. That was the only thing that made sense all day. This was a dream. And this wasn't the real Damien; this was a man locked in my mind.

And if this was a dream then I could unleash my fury and pent-up words upon him because it wasn't real. Right?

"If there is anyone to be mad at, it's *you!* You, who has manipulated and deceived your way into war. It's you who has failed to secure our borders, and you who we have to blame for the lack of preparation. How could you keep such a secret from the continent? How could you not call for aid sooner? Was it pride? Was it ego? You owe an explanation not only to me but to all Lustraya!"

In this dream, Damien was dumbfounded and Gunnar stunned. Neither of them moved from their spots nor offered a counter argument.

"I'm taking your silence as acceptance," I spat. "Now get your asses in gear and get a unit down to the southern border. Something is going to happen and when it does, Imeria and Lustraya will need to work together to fix it. Make it happen and fast."

The vision ended with a shudder through my body, like I was being pulled back through a rip current. My lungs gasped for air as I reared back on the couch, my hand dropping from Poppi's hair and beginning to pat my own.

The room remained unchanged, the fire crackling in its hearth. When I looked down to see if Poppi still snoozed peacefully, I was met with her brown eyes watching me in wonder and amazement.

"What—what just happened?" I stuttered.

"You transcended," she said, a smile tugging at the corner of her lips.

"I . . . huh?"

"Transcended," she repeated once more, this time sitting up so we were level. "It's a form of communication we can do. Fireplaces are the best because they harness a lot of energy. It's usually a harder skill to attempt as a practitioner but you just did it without any practice. You're stronger than we thought."

"It was a dream," I explained. "I saw Damien and Gunnar, saw his study. How can I do that if I never left the couch?"

"Magic does what it wants, and right now I think your magic is itching to figure out what it can do."

"I—I . . ."

"Don't worry," she said, reaching for my hand. "I'll be here every step of the way. No matter what. It's you and me, okay?"

I nodded because words were lost to me as my heart continued to race in my chest and fear crept in. We remained on the couch for the rest of the night. Blankets and pillows found themselves being piled high as we relaxed further into the night. By the time our eyes closed, my will to understand what was happening evaporated. I just hoped the gods would let me sleep peacefully.

A thunderous banging rang through the room, jolting Poppi and I awake, pillows flying high in the air as we raised up from the cushions.

"Dani!" Maddox called from the other end. "Dani, are you in here?"

I slammed my head back down, my fingers rubbing at my temples.

"Do you have to be so loud?" I groaned.

They shoved their way into the room, their heads on a swivel as they checked to see if anyone else was here with me.

"Dani, where the hell did you go yesterday? We've been looking everywhere for you," Harrison cut in. "You can't just disappear like that. You're not a soldier here anymore. Tensions are too high between Clara and Damien for us to lose his princess."

I had thought of that at some point last night, but by then it had been too late. I sat up straight, pushing myself up against the pillows to look at them more evenly.

"I'm really sorry," I said. "We were just so tired, and we crashed in the first non-destroyed room we could find." A partial truth, but they couldn't be told the full scope of it yet.

They eyed me skeptically but dropped the subject. Maddox turned to look at Poppi.

"Where were you yesterday?" he asked, his tone laced with accusation.

"I got stuck under some furniture in my room that knocked me unconscious," she lied smoothly. "I only managed to gain consciousness a few hours later and by that point Dani had already found me, and the storm was over."

My friends watched her closely and I knew from their posture and the quirk of Harrison's eye that they didn't believe her. If I recalled correctly, one of them went to her room yesterday to try and find her and said they couldn't.

Which, now that I thought of it, they should have been able to if they had made it to the balcony. Or maybe they didn't see Poppi because she didn't want to be seen. Another mystery solved because of magic?

My head began to spin.

"Dani, are you okay?" Harrison asked, his voice laced with concern. "You look really pale."

"She's fine," Poppi said reassuringly. "She just needs to rest, is all."

"I am fine," I said on everyone's behalf. "You guys don't have to worry. We're safe. Tell Clara I am sorry for running out and disappearing, I didn't mean to scare her."

Harrison puffed out a grunt, casting a quick glance in Mads' direction.

"Thank you. Now, is there anything we can do to help with the clean up? How did the city fare?"

They stood straighter, eyes taking on their skeptical glisten once more. "It's fine. It's like the storm didn't even touch it." Mads offered, his tone flippant and accusatory in the same breath.

"How is that possible?" Poppi asked, reciprocating his tone. She was good at feigning innocence; I'll give her that.

"We don't know. We're sending out scouts to see if they see anything out of the ordinary." Harrison answered, taking the role as the serious one in their duo.

"Can we come?"

"No," Mads and Harrison said in unison. Maddox crossed his arms over his chest and continued, "You're to stay here where we all can keep an eye on you."

I threw my hands up. "Oh, so we're prisoners now?"

"No," Harrison interjected. "Like we said earlier, you're another kingdom's princess now. There are rules we have to follow and one of them is keeping you safe and away from danger. We may be friends,

Dani, but Clara and Damien are not. She won't allow you to go anywhere at this point without a heap of guards following."

I had to admit; he had a point, and when I looked at Poppi across the couch, she tossed me a look that said she agreed with them too. I pinched the bridge of my nose.

"Okay, fine. I'll stay put."

They relaxed finally, the tension in their shoulders slumping away. "Good," Mads replied as Harrison said, "We'll have a guard stationed outside for you both, should you need anything."

"Who is it?"

"Viper," Harrison answered matter-of-factly.

That sneaky, cunning, manipulative man. I should have known he would volunteer for the job. I could see from the corner of my eye Poppi trying to hide a smile by the ticking in her jaw. She must be thinking the same thing.

"I take it you are both going out on this scouting mission then?" I asked, refocusing my gaze on my male friends.

They led with silence, and I took that as a 'yes'. Of course, they wouldn't be allowed to tell me forthright; that would be a breach of trust within their ranks. The fact that they had been so forth coming with what they have told us already is a gift of its own.

"Well," I said, breaking the quiet. "Thank you for coming to find us. Wherever your day takes you, please be careful."

Before they walked out, each of them gave me a hug, placing a small kiss to my head as they did. My best friends. My brothers. My heart clenched as I watched them go and when the door closed behind them, I turned to Poppi.

"They're going to hate me when they find out what I am."

"Why would you think that?"

"I'm not sure," I confessed. "But I get the feeling that I'm not really going to get a choice in the matter anymore."

"Your magic will only manifest as strong as your belief in it is. The stronger the belief, the stronger the connection. You have the potential to be one of the greatest practitioners in the history of this continent. Perhaps greater than Alita herself."

The last part had my ears perking up with curiosity. "Alita?"

Poppi smiled smugly, knowing she had me with that small bit of information.

"She was a strong practitioner too," she stated, grabbing a pillow and hugging it across her belly. "One of the strongest we have record of. It is why she was able to rule as long as she did and alone. Her greatest strength was fire magic. In her presence, it danced and sang like a moth to the flame.

"In those days, Lustraya was not the frigid place you have come to know now. Cold it was, but it was alive. The fire magic Alita wielded burned through the worst of the temperatures, her flame cast in most of the hearths in the city that was around the Silver Castle."

"What do you mean by 'her flame'?"

"I mean, her magic was so strong she could cast it out, and as long as she was alive and in good health, it would continue to burn."

"Wouldn't that deplete her well though? I thought you and Viper said there were limits."

I was leaning forward now, my hands turning to fists to tuck under my chin as I listened intently while she filled in the gaps in Alita's story.

"And there are," Poppi continued. "But that is how deep her well went and she was known for constantly training the magic too. Some journals said she could become the flame itself."

I thought back to the story Poppi sung by the fire that night in the mountain pass. How it told the gory details of a Queen's death and the love she had for her people.

"So, Alita . . . burst into flame to save the village? She let it consume her to the point of no return?"

"Magic requires a balance, remember? To save that many lives, the magic demanded payment of equal magnitude. Alita was that equal. Her might and powers were the sacrifice to keep the balance."

"And what happens when the balance is off?" I asked, standing to my feet. "What if someone overextends or uses too much without giving something in return? What then?" I began a slow pace as Poppi answered my slew of questions.

"Magic gives, and magic takes all the same. Do you remember the stories of the first creation of the kingdoms?"

"Vaguely," I admitted. Most of those lessons were for Arabella, given that she was the heir and I wasn't.

"Before the first Kings and Queens, we were a united land. There were no kingdoms and there were no monarchs. We were run by elected leaders of all factions of life. Witches, Fae, humans . . . everyone got a say in how the continent operated."

I had to resist the urge to roll my eyes, turning and pacing the opposite direction. "So, what happened?"

"They upset the balance. One group got greedier than the others and I bet you can guess which one that was."

"The Fae."

"Exactly. And they didn't just want more power, they wanted more land, more control over the waters. They wanted total domination. And they started this process long before anyone ever realized. Slowly and subtly, they began terrorizing witch and human villages, burning and taking what they believed was theirs.

"When the leaders of the witch and human factions realized what was happening, it was too late. They did the only thing they could, and they fought back using magic and human ingenuity. In the end, they sank the capitol and the witches drained all their magic in order to extinguish the Fae from Taelle."

"By extinguish, you don't mean . . ."

"I do. And they knew what they were doing, which is why the magic ripped itself from them and nearly disappeared from Taelle altogether."

"So, why reemerge now? If the magic laid dormant for so long, what caused it to suddenly come back?"

"That's the thing Viper and I have been trying to figure out," she confessed, fixing her hair behind her ear. "We don't know the exact cause, just that everything shifted dramatically when you joined the Gauntlet. All documentation of any of this has been picked from stories and cross-referenced from written accounts, which are extremely hard to come by. We can only theorize so much."

"Poppi, I can't be a part of this. There have to be other ways to handle a situation like this. If Imeria won't give us help, then we go to Rilunae. They're our mountain neighbor. Surely they've had to deal with the Fae at some point."

"The King has tried. He reached out to their leader several times with no answer. They have buried their heads quite literally into the sand. No one has heard from them in years."

I dropped my head into my hands. This was a disaster. Just when I thought I was forming a grip on my life, bam! Something weird and unexpected comes rushing in, changing everything I knew.

At that moment, there was another knock on the door, this one lighter and more precise. A second later, he pushed the door open and slithered in.

"Well, you two look well rested," he commented.

"No thanks to you."

He raised an eyebrow. "Glad to see you're in good spirits, Your Highness. Do tell me; are you always this cranky and I've just never noticed?"

"You try having your life completely upended—again—only to be told you're part of an old group of people called practitioners, and tell me if you'd wake up on the right side of the pillow?"

"Yes."

I threw my hands into the air. The way Poppi and him were treating this whole thing like it was no big deal was starting to really irritate me.

I walked over to the back window and flung it open, the morning air rushing in and filling my senses with its calming scent. I rested there while Poppi and Viper chatted quietly behind me. It was hard to hear exactly what they were saying but for the most part, I gathered that they were wanting to write to Damien about the advancement here.

". . . well, she wanted evidence, Viper . . ."

"But the cost was almost too great. He won't be happy about this."

"He's never happy when it comes to us touching magic," Poppi countered, the rustling of blankets falling to the ground following her sarcasm.

"No, he's not, but that's not why I came here." He held up a folded piece of parchment, the seal on it recognizable as one from Lustraya. "I received correspondence this morning. It seems you two may want to tell me about something that happened last night."

I groaned while Poppi grinned.

"She transcended," Poppi said excitedly. "You should have seen it. She did it so effortlessly."

"Transcending is dangerous," Viper chastised her. "You should have stopped her when you saw what was happening. What the hell were you thinking?"

"I was thinking that we finally have what we need to reestablish the balance. I wanted to see just how far she was going to go. I wouldn't have let anything happen to her."

The scathing look on Viper's face told another story.

"You should know better than to test magic like that. You know what happened the last time we pushed a novice too far."

My stomach sank at his tone. "Wh-what happened?"

They looked at me, Viper running a hand down his face in frustration. "She bled out from her eyes, ears, and nose. The magic consumed her, and she couldn't make it back to the natural realm."

Lesson one of magic: never take what you cannot give back. Noted.

"So, the attack in the mountain pass. When I . . . screamed. Why didn't that happen to me?"

Viper waved me over to the couch where he took a seat, Poppi standing right next to him. I walked over cautiously, my mind going on alert for what would be perhaps another improbable explanation in this never ending charade.

"Magic can be spurred in many different ways," Viper explained. "Either by emotion, physical ailment, and for some, they are born knowing that they possess it. In your case, I believe it was brought on by all three.

"The first being your fear and desire to save the new recruits in the pass. That feeling was then amplified by the physical exertion and injuries you took as well. Your scream was born out of pure instinct. Somewhere, deep down, you called on the magic for help, and it came. Do you remember what you were thinking in that moment?"

I took a deep breath and closed my eyes, letting my thoughts drift back to that day. "I remember seeing Nic getting clawed by the beast and the panic that surged through me at seeing her hurt. I remember thinking of Alita and what she would do in this moment, and that was to hold the beasts at bay. I wanted to be brave like Alita, to become a distraction so the others could get away."

"That was noble of you," Viper reassured.

"It was incredibly stupid," Poppi said at the same time and then followed up with, "Damien nearly threw me in the pits for that one."

Viper ignored Poppi's comments and pressed on with his questions. "And what happened when you got to the end of the ice?"

"I . . . I . . . don't know. I remember looking the beast in the eyes. They were cold and malicious, and triumphant. The thing released a howl, and I just thought, well, two of us can do that and if I'm going to die, I would rather do it in defiance than in subjugation. So, I screamed back."

"And what happened after?"

"The ground shook and I just felt this . . . this *thing* boil up in me."

"She had sparks coming off her," Poppi murmured. "Blue and orange just radiating off her shoulders. And her eyes, Viper, they were glowing like the lights in the mountain keep."

"Did you know that, Dani? Did you know you were emanating sparks?"

I opened my eyes. "No," I said simply. "But I remember putting my hands to the ground and feeling it hum under my hands. It felt like the right thing to do."

"So, you unknowingly tried to tap into the source?"

I shrugged my shoulders because I didn't know what that meant or why I was doing it. "I guess . . ."

"Oh, to be so powerful and willfully ignorant at the same time," Viper sighed.

No one knew what to say, so we sat there awkwardly, until Poppi looked down at the paper Viper held and asked, "What's that?"

"What I also came here for," he said. "Damien sent a new report. He's sending two legions of soldiers south."

My heartbeat sped as Poppi and I locked eyes.

"I assume this has to deal with your trance too?" he surmised. I nodded my head once.

I could see it in my head strategically. We would have bodies at the border but none near enough the cliffs to cover the Fae coming in from the sea and overtaking the docks and the harbor. We would be cut off from not only the ability to flee, but to also get any resources through. Not to mention that if the palace fell, everything else around it would.

But the walls of Sapphire Isle hadn't been breached in centuries and even then, the palace stood strong as an impenetrable fortress. They could do it again.

"So what," I mused. "We seek an audience with Clara. Tell her that—surprise—we have connections to magic, and the Fae are on their way here; let's get ready for war! She would laugh us out with escorts. I may be her daughter, but even Clara has her limits. She sent Ary away for this exact reason."

Viper paused. "Is that what she told you?"

I stared back confused, Poppi also waiting on bated breath for an explanation. "Is that not what happened?"

Viper stood up, tossing the letter from Damien onto the couch. Poppi scooped it up instantly to read the full report, her eyes moving over the paper swiftly.

"Arabella didn't get sent away by Clara; she sent herself away. Her and the rest of the Segallian court left shortly after your departure. Your mother and sister haven't spoken in months."

I reared back. Clara and Ary weren't speaking to one another? That was one of the most unrealistic things I had heard in the last few weeks, and that was saying something considering we are about to go to war with creatures of myth.

"But why would she do that?" I asked to no one, mostly myself. "Arabella, she would never put Clara through something like that."

"I think you underestimate her, Princess. Your sister exhibits more cunning than what anyone here is willing to give her credit for."

"And Samir?"

"Volunteered to go to keep her safe. He would send a report back every week or so but even those stopped coming. We have no contact with her or the royals."

Warning bells tolled in my head. All this was completely out of place for Arabella, and I struggled to believe she would abandon her mother and kingdom to run off somewhere to hide.

"If you want to know more, I suggest you ask that friend of yours, Helvig," Viper quipped, tossing me a knowing smile. His use of Aeddan's last name told me that he knew about us but wasn't about to out me to Poppi.

"How do you manage to know all this? Oracle or not, you seem to know something about everything."

"These palace walls hold many secrets. If you listen close enough, they will tell you anything you want to know."

26

A BREAK

The damage around the palace was, well, out of this world. Trees had been uprooted and fountains turned over. Glass was sprinkled everywhere, random scraps of fabric hanging from windows and shrubs. Palace attendants buzzed around the grounds, cleaning up the mess. If Poppi wanted to make a point, she achieved her goal. The palace was a mess, and its people scared.

I didn't know where I was walking to, all I knew is that I needed out and away. I needed to think, to breathe, and to process. Doing it here was not going to help and that is how I found myself in the stables, saddling up my mare, and flying down the drive and to the city.

If anyone saw me, they didn't say anything. My absence from the palace would eventually be noticed and by the time that happened, I would be out of their reach.

The thought of watching Poppi and Maddox fighting over who lost me first sent a wave of laughter and satisfaction over me. Imagining Maddox's red face arguing with Poppi's as she pointed a finger up at him was the prettiest picture I could imagine. I should have someone commission it when all this was over.

The ride to the city wall went by too fast and soon I saw the gates come into view. The guards outside it had doubled in number since the last time I had visited. I veered my horse left, going off the usual road, and heading for the back entrance Ary and I used. If any of the guards recognized me, then this trip away would end before it could even begin.

I slowed my horse to a trot as we arrived at the patch of apple trees. I chose the one with the most shade coverage and abundance of apples for prime snacking while I was gone. I swung my legs down, landing on the ground with a soft thud.

"Alright," I said to the animal. "You be good for me and stay here, okay? I'll be back shortly." I planted a kiss to its neck, making sure that he was tied securely before heading for the city wall. I crept along the tree line, keeping to the shadows until I could find the right moment to sneak through the guard change.

I waited for a while, enough that I grew bored and restless, and decided that if I got caught coming in this way, I could fight if I needed. I scaled the tree closest to the stone, testing its highest branch for security before crawling out onto it and jumping to the top of the wall.

My balance wavered for a moment, but I caught myself before I completely toppled over the edge. I checked once more to see if any guards were coming and to my surprise, I saw not one body. How odd.

But that was not my problem any longer. I took the window of time to scale down the wall as swift as I could and disappear into the crowds.

It was amazing that everyone here was carrying on like there wasn't a giant storm that destroyed the palace yesterday. It was business as usual here and there was only one business that I wanted to visit.

Two hours later, I was slamming a mug down on the bar top and waving the barmaid over for another ale. I felt lighter, my body more relaxed than it had been in months. Was getting drunk my best plan? No. But it was a lot more fun than ruminating the possible end of human existence due to *magic*.

Misty walked over, a sly smile on her face.

"Another one already?" she asked.

"Oh yeah," I said coyly. "And keep them coming."

She laughed and walked away to procure me a new drink and when she returned, she leveled me with a serious and concerned look.

"Dani, dear," she said, lowering her voice so no one else would be able to hear. "What's going on, sweetie? Why are you here?"

It was a loaded question for many reasons. First, I was supposed to be in Lustraya. By now the news of the Queen's ward's departure would have made it through the kingdom, so there should be no reason for me to be sitting here. Second, why was I at her inn getting drunk at her bar?

Well, how did I politely tell her that my whole life has been a lie? That I was actually a witch with deep magical powers I didn't know how to use yet, and that the fate of this kingdom and the one north of it depended on me mastering them or else we would be overrun by Fae and cease to exist?

"Just needed a drink," I said simply, taking a long pull from the new mug. Misty eyed me skeptically.

"You're a shit liar, Dani," she stated before walking away to tend to a group of men getting rowdy at the other end of the bar.

That's what I loved about Misty; she was blunt and honest and not afraid of me nor Ary because of our titles. She treated us just like any other patron.

I spent my time at the bar watching the people of town come and go, listening to their conversations of everyday life, and wondering if I had never been left in Clara's care, would I be one of them?

Would I have become a flower shop owner? Maybe an academic? No. No, I couldn't sit still long enough. I would need to be out in the open air. Perhaps then a merchant, that way I could travel and see what all Taelle had to offer. I'd have the ultimate freedom. Yeah, I liked the sound of that.

"Another one?" Misty asked thirty minutes later, leaning against the bar top.

"Oh yeah," I slurred lightly. "Keep them coming."

She obliged my request, sliding a bowl of stew and warm bread next to the mug when she returned.

"Wait, I didn't ask for this."

"No," she said smartly. "But you need it. You're looking a bit too skinny over there for my tastes."

I smiled warmly at her. "I'm not skinny."

She chuckled. "Yes. You are."

Misty turned to walk down the bar again and tend to her guests, but the ale was flowing through me, and I stopped her in her tracks before she could make a single step.

"Hey, Misty." She turned back to me. "Can I ask you something?"

"Always, dear." She threw her towel over her shoulder and leaned forward, giving me her full and undivided attention.

"Did you always want to be an inn owner? Or did you have another dream?"

She laughed to herself, her eyes glazing over with memory. "That wasn't what I was expecting to hear, but yeah, I always knew I wanted to have my own inn. My parents used to run one in Segall, and they loved it, and I wanted to be just like them. So, when I moved here at a ripe twenty years, I set about building this place. It took some time, but we got there."

"Do you believe in fate?"

Misty watched my face closely and I saw her eyes turn soft. She reached out a hand, taking mine in between her own.

"I believe that we make our own destinies and even if we get waylaid in the process, there is always an opportunity to choose the path that best fits you." She paused a moment and then added, "Whatever it is you're questioning, Dani girl, just know you are on your best path. And it may be hard right now, and you may be angry, but everything will work out. Have faith in yourself and trust that you can and will make the best decision; come what may."

"But what if I mess everything up?"

"Then you learn, and you grow. And continue forward." She placed a kiss to my knuckles and walked away, leaving me to my thoughts and dinner.

I stayed long enough at The Mist to watch the sun go below the horizon and the dock drunkards come in for their late night debauchery.

They were loud, obnoxious, heavily intoxicated, and having the time of their lives. I watched in fascination from my corner of the bar, completely enamored by their lack of decorum. Tankards of ale were brought out as the small bar area filled to capacity, the room growing louder by the minute.

Men of all backgrounds gambled away their earnings for the day, their poison of choice for the night being dice. How very trivial a concept; yet it brought out anger and frustration like no other. I had no choice but to laugh to myself as I watched.

When I felt my stomach shift and my head begin to ache, I knew it was time to head back to the palace. There was no telling the amount of trouble I was going to be in for abandoning the palace with no notice of where I was going. Poppi would be livid.

As I waited for Misty to bring me my final tab, a sharp wailing from the corner had my head spinning to the side. In the far corner of the room stood a woman with two ale mugs in her hands and five men.

One of them stood behind her, his hand cupped around her mouth and the other one crossed over her chest. Three of his friends watched and laughed as the other roved his greasy paws over her, the woman straining against them to get away to no avail; his friends cheering him on.

I checked around to see if anyone had also heard her scream and was already on their feet to help, but the room was too busy and too loud for anyone of sound mind to be aware.

The man's advances continued until he was dangerously close to exposing her to the whole room. That was all it took for me to slide the dagger out from my hip and throw it in their direction, the blade slicing the man's ear to plant itself into the wood behind him.

His advances stopped and the woman's eyes widened further in fear. I watched as his hands dropped from her body and his head snapped around, looking for the culprit. His friends followed suit, loosening his grip on the poor woman just enough for her to wrangle herself free and run as far as she could from them.

I was off my bar seat the moment the dagger landed, my steps coming surer and more steady than I would have thought.

"Who did that?" the grease trap of a man called.

"I did," I said, right before I sent my fist flying into his ugly face. There was a satisfying crunch under my knuckles just as blood came spurting out of his nose. I didn't give him a chance to yell for help as I sent a spinning throat punch in his direction; his fat body toppling to the ground seconds later. I shot my knee up as he fell, catching him one last time in the face and knocking him unconscious.

I turned to the man that held the woman's mouth shut. "Your turn."

The man scowled as I launched an attack on him, his friends jumping out of the way as I sent a punch to his gut and groin, turning to rip the dagger from the wall and then slicing it through his cheek. A long line of red ran down his face as his friends began to join in on the fray.

The room around us halted briefly and then spurred into action, fist and egos flying as people turned on each other for no other reason but a chance to join in the chaos. I kept my sights clear as I took down each of the men, one by one, making sure that their injuries would be visible and severe.

If I truly had it my way, I would cut their throats right here, but I didn't want Misty to have to clean up so much blood. As I turned to the last man, the doors to the inn burst open, the night watch pouring in to control the fighting.

I was shoved to the side and jostled around as people made their breaks for the back door. I would have joined them had a golden-brown head shorn short not entered the room. Time seemed to slow as his eyes found mine like it was the most natural thing in the world.

"Shit," I breathed out as Aeddan clenched his jaw and stomped over to me.

He was mad, no—not just mad—furious. He reached me in four quick strides, his hand grabbing my arm, pulling me from the inn and back out into the street.

I thrashed against him, none too happy with being manhandled. A few patrons from the bar room shouted their praise as I was forced out into the night; a few of them shouting because they hadn't noticed that the fighting had ceased already.

"Let me go!" I ordered as the inn door slammed behind us. Aeddan obliged my request, but threw my arm out of his grip angrily, sending me stumbling a few steps forward. I looked at him in disbelief as I grabbed the spot where his hand was and rubbed against it.

"Well, ow! What the hell is your problem?" I spat.

He glared at me in bewilderment, his right hand coming to his hip while the left ran down his face.

"Are you . . . are you being serious right now?" he asked.

"Well, I didn't ask to be polite."

Once again, he stomped forward, except this time his hand reached out to grab my jaw and force my eyes to look into his. Oh, how I could get lost in those eyes.

"You're drunk," he stated, his grip not faltering.

"No, I'm not," I responded as defiantly as I could.

"Then why are you slurring?"

Well. He got me there. As I stared at him, his face did blur in and out of focus, only further proving his point, but he didn't need to know that. He released my jaw, a tingling sensation rushing back to it as I rubbed it.

Aeddan paced back and forth to me, each time opening his mouth to yell at me and then thinking better of it. I was too tired and too annoyed to give him the satisfaction of feeling guilty or sorry, so I waited for him to calm down instead.

He halted his pace finally, coming back to stand just inches from me.

"Why are you here, Dani?"

There were so many excuses I could give, so many scenarios I could concoct to avoid the embarrassment of the moment, but I couldn't lie to him.

"I just needed a break," I admitted sheepishly as I crossed my arms and looked down at my feet. "I needed to breathe, to think without someone telling me everything I should and shouldn't be doing."

His face softened and that concerned, loving look returned to his eyes. He wrapped his hands around me, pulling me into his chest and placing a kiss to the top of my head as I breathed in the scent of him.

If I was being honest with myself, I could have stayed in that moment forever, just listening to his heartbeat and basking in his hold. It was cruel that this couldn't be us.

"Why the inn? Why get in the middle of a fight?"

I lifted my head, the searing memory of what those men were doing reigniting my anger. "They were touching one of Misty's bar maids. They were going to—they deserve to die," I said plainly.

"Who?"

"The men I left unconscious on the floor."

"I'll see that they are brought to the dungeons immediately."

Short. Sweet. To the point. No questions, no doubts, just pure trust. My heart ached in my chest at the loyalty he paid me, my body wishing and begging that I could have him in my life for good and not just in this moment.

"Poppi is beside herself," he said with a small chuckle. "I think you're going to get an earful when we get back." I groaned loudly, bumping my head against his chest in a smooth rhythm.

"How did you even find me?" I asked when I was done being dramatic.

He ran a thumb over my cheek, stroking the skin there lightly. "I didn't. I was on my way to the bakery when I heard the commotion coming from the inn. I just knew it was you."

Something about that felt so intimate and it made me feel nauseous. Wait, no. That was the ale fighting back against me.

"Oh, I think I'm going to be sick."

He laughed at me again. "Alright, Princess, let's get you back."

He reached his arm under my legs and scooped me up, cradling my body against him as he walked over to his horse.

"Wait," I argued. "Wait, my horse . . ."

"I'll have one of the guards grab him and bring him back to the stables."

"Okay," I conceded as he placed me back upright and held me as I struggled onto the back of his horse.

I wobbled like a toddler until I felt his arm wrap around my waist and brace me against his chest. I had a vague memory of this happening once before in a wagon under the stars, surrounded by the strongest warriors in Imeria.

I settled back into him, letting my hand wrap around his and hold fast, the silver and gold rings adorning my left-hand glinting in the moonlight; a symbol of the lines of the life I straddled.

He kissed the top of my head as he jolted the horse forward and down the cobblestone road back to the palace. Tonight was the first night in many that I had felt a glimmer of security.

Though the thought of being a practitioner was daunting, without realizing it I had accepted this new fate of mine. As is, I had already achieved what I set out to do initially—even if it was a short-lived victory, it was mine. And now there was something different in store for me.

If I looked at the reality from a different lens, this new probability was absolutely amazing. And to be chosen as a vessel for such power? I would have a lot to learn, but I had never backed down from a challenge before, so why would I back down now?

I wouldn't. Couldn't.

A simple and easy decision, yet one that was laced with firm determination to set the balance right.

"You've gone quiet," Aeddan observed. "What's going on in that head of yours?"

"Too much," I half-slurred, half-whispered. "Too much . . ."

His arm tightened against me in comfort. "You needn't always try and face things on your own, Princess."

When he said that word, my heart sang in sweet nothings; reveling in the way it felt like a caress on my skin each and every time.

"This one is a battle I have to fight on my own," I responded without any context. Just like I wasn't ready to believe in magic, he wouldn't either. Maybe Clara, but anyone around her would be skeptical and think us mad.

Aeddan veered the horse to the right, keeping us out of view from the palace and taking us closer to the cliffs. I let the cool breeze wash over me, the ale working its way out of my head and giving way to vision that wasn't so foggy.

"Aeddan, the palace is that way," I commented with a point.

"I know, Princess," he said sweetly. "But if I take you up the main road then Poppi is going to be waiting there for you, and I don't think this is the state you want her to find you in."

Damn it. He was right.

I could hear the scolding she would give me already. Would Viper give me one too? What was he up to in the Guard these days? Why had I never asked? I should not have drank that last ale.

Aeddan pulled the horse to a stop just at the edge of the palace's east garden where we would be more hidden. It also happened to be the garden where he kissed me for the first time.

He dismounted silently, his departure from behind leaving me feeling empty and cold as he escorted the horse to a tree and away from potential prying eyes.

"Okay, you," he said, walking back to the saddle and lifting his arms to me. "Come here."

My first instinct was to argue, but the gentle nature of the moment had me succumbing to his ask and placing my hands against his shoulders, letting him lift me down. He caught me tightly against his chest, laughing as I fumbled to find steady footing.

"I may be a princess now, but I certainly lack the grace of one," I teased against my own struggle.

"That's okay," he said, keeping one arm around me while the other came up to tuck a stray hair from my braid behind my ear. "You make up for it by being one hell of a champion."

I smiled warmly at him, letting his praise shower over me.

"I missed you."

And I had. As I looked at him now, under the moon with no watchful eyes, I shocked myself by how true my words were. I missed his touch, his smile, his smell. I missed the way he teased me and pushed me even when I didn't want to be. I missed him arguing with me.

"I missed you, too."

And without hesitation, he leaned down to plant a soft kiss to my lips. It was sweet and delicate, one that made me want to sink further into his embrace and forget the world and everything that went on within it.

I kissed him back, deepening the kiss a little further. He met me eagerly, his hands moving to wrap around me fully and pulling me close. My own hands found purchase on his shoulders as my body begged to be closer to his.

Home.

Home wasn't a place. Home was Aeddan. And as he kissed me so thoroughly and completely under the night sky, I felt every wall I had dissolve into ashes. How could something so right, so beautiful, be so forbidden?

"Wait . . ." I breathed, pulling away. "Wait, Aeddan. I can't . . ."

I saw the truth reflected in his eyes; saw the way he equally knew that this was a dangerous path to walk. A path that we couldn't walk.

"I know . . ." he said, placing his forehead to mine. "But I had to. I'm a selfish bastard when it comes to you, Dani. I missed you too much to not let you know."

A single tear fell from my eye, and he quickly swept it away with his thumb.

"Don't cry, Princess. I can't bear to see you sad."

"Why did it have to be like this?" I whispered. "Why are the gods so cruel?"

I know what he wanted to say. It was written on his face as plain as I saw it in my head. He offered us a way out once. Said he would leave everything he had worked for here just to maybe have the chance to be with me. To wait for me.

But that night was long gone. And I no longer belonged to this kingdom—or belonged to Aeddan.

I rubbed my hands on his chest, wanting so desperately to touch the skin that was there, to feel him on me. To feel him over me.

"I feel like I have made a mess of things and I don't know what to do," I confessed.

"We'll figure this out, Dani. We can be together—"

"I'm not talking just about us, Aeddan," I said, my voice quivering with effort to keep it steady. My gods, why did I drink so much ale tonight? "I'm talking about everything. I have just made such a mess, and I no longer know what to do. I have no direction. No purpose. Some days I think I should've just done what Clara wanted; married for title and gone about my life."

"Don't say that," Aeddan said, firmly grabbing my face in his hands and turning my gaze back to his. "Don't you ever say that, Daniella. You're the most capable person I know. The most stubborn too, but also the most intelligent and determined. Whatever it is you think you can't face right now, I know you can because you are you. And that is a beautiful thing. You're right where you're meant to be."

I reached up and kissed him again, unable to stop myself.

"In another life . . ." I whispered on his lips. "Would you like to sit with me?"

He looked at me, puzzled.

"Come sit with me, Aeddan." I pushed away from him and undid the cloak around my shoulders, laying it on the ground and following it.

I tapped the spot next to me, silently telling him to sit down. He chuckled under his breath, taking up the spot next to me, and wrapping an arm around my hip, pulling me close.

"I like you like this," he said, leaning his cheek against my head.

"Drunk?" I laughed.

"Soft."

I turned my head to look at him again. He ran his thumb over my cheek again. "I like it when you're soft like this. Because you only ever do it for me."

"You're the only one who's ever made me feel safe," I replied without thinking. My eyes went wide in terror when I realized what I had said, panic setting in at being so vulnerable.

"That . . . I didn't mean to say that."

He kissed my forehead and didn't press further, the quiet acceptance something I was grateful for as we sat there looking at the stars. Time passed gracefully and warmly, our arms wrapping around each other and holding tight; our hearts beating in tune.

If the Fae came now and destroyed everything in sight, I decided I would die a happy woman knowing that it was in the arms of this man.

I knew when I woke up, my life and duties would resume, and I would have to force this moment from my memory. For now, though, I was going to enjoy every last drop of peace I was being gifted.

27

ELEMENTAL

The scent of flowers tickled my nose as the wind stroked me awake with its early morning perfume. I nestled my nose further into my pillow, wishing and wanting a few more hours of sleep before I had to face the day.

But it wasn't a pillow, and I wasn't in my room. I was still outside on my cloak, and my pillow was Aeddan's chest.

His arms were still wrapped around me tightly, his breathing deep and relaxed. The most relaxed as I had ever seen him.

I moved one of my hands out from under me and pushed a loose hair from his forehead. He was beautiful. Probably one of the most beautiful men I had ever met from the inside out. He deserved someone that could love him and give him a big, happy life.

I tilted my head up just enough to lay a gentle kiss to the tip of his nose, taking one more moment to enjoy laying there in his arms, and appreciating the few hours I was able to sneak with him. I would cherish them forever.

When I could delay no longer, I quietly and slowly released his arms from me, and crawled away and onto my feet. He stirred slightly but slept soundly; exactly what I wanted.

I looked to the sea and the layer of fog that covered the water and beach below. The first light blue and yellow began to peak through the cloud cover on the horizon. My favorite time of day.

I closed my eyes and breathed in deeply and released it, thanking whatever god I needed for last night. When my eyes opened again, I steeled myself for the day ahead.

I would have to forget this night and shove these renewed feelings down deep in order to become the battle-ready princess that my kingdom deserved and needed. I had one night of selfishness, and it would have to last me the rest of my life; to know that moments like that were real and worth fighting for. I looked at Aeddan's sleeping form one last time, knowing this is all I could do before disappearing from our hiding spot and back into the palace where my real life awaited.

Poppi was waiting in my new room when I got back. She looked every bit as furious as Aeddan had said she would be.

"Where the *hell* have you been?" she screamed. "I have searched everywhere for you! Do you know the lengths I have been going through to try and find out where you have been?"

I dropped my head guiltily, looking at the mud and muck caking my boots.

"I'm sorry," I said finally, lifting my head once more. "I really am, Poppi. I just . . . I needed to get out of here for a while."

Her mouth dropped open, her face bewildered as she looked at me, scanning my face for a better excuse.

"Oh, who *cares*, Daniella! You have responsibility. You have a duty. We are at *war,* and you think you can just run away from that? You don't think the rest of us would like a break too? Get over yourself!"

She was right. I needed to do better, to be better for everyone involved. Though it seems it was never meant to, the direction in which this war would turn rested solely on if I could step up and do what needed to be done.

I had had my time with Aeddan, said my goodbyes to him this morning. I looked down to the two rings on my hand—one mirroring my past, the other my future—and I felt a calm settle over me. One of determination and acceptance for who I knew I needed to become.

"You have every right to be disappointed in me, Poppi." I walked over to her, grabbing her hands in mine and squeezing them tightly. "But I promise from this day forth—everything changes, okay? I'm ready to be who you need me to be."

She blinked. "Are you talking about the magic?"

I nodded.

"Truly? You're ready to begin training it?"

"I am."

"Then we must get to Viper immediately."

She wasted no time releasing one of my hands and yanking the other as she tore out of my room and to the hidden archives of the palace. Her pace and grip were intense, my feet barely keeping under me as she sprinted down the narrow staircase and into the dimly lit passage to Viper's workshop.

Poppi burst through the door, catching Viper off guard, his eyeglasses halfway down his nose and his face shoved in a book.

"Glad to see you're in one piece after all," he said nonchalantly.

"Tell him what you told me," Poppi demanded as she shoved me through the threshold and slammed the door behind us.

Viper closed his book with a snap and removed the glasses from his nose, his arms crossing expectantly as he leaned against his desk. I took a deep, steadying breath.

"I'm ready for you to teach me about magic."

His eyes quivered ever so slightly, the only way I would know Viper showed shock or surprise on his otherwise cool and collected face.

"You're sure?"

"Yes." I was tired of having to double down on that statement.

Viper cast his eyes over to Poppi and the two of them shared a silent conversation before Viper discarded what he was doing. He clasped his hands together; his shoulders taught with renewed purpose.

"Then let your training begin."

I sat and watched as he and Poppi scurried around the room, setting about lighting candles and placing herbs in bowls. They talked to one another in hushed tones, quietly arguing about what was necessary and if they could somehow speed up the process. I believed in the magic simmering in my veins, but what process were they talking about?

What had I agreed to get myself into?

Viper placed the last bowl onto the table and turned to face me with a grim expression.

"Are you sure you're ready for this?" he asked. "Because the magic will know if you're lying. There can and will be consequences if you try and take advantage of it."

"I'm ready," I said confidently as I stood on my feet.

"Good. Then come here."

I walked over to him, swallowing the nerves that were boiling in my stomach as I did. Viper stepped to the side, so I was standing in the middle of his workstation now; Poppi in the corner, becoming a silent observer.

There were four bowls in front of me. One with water, one with flowers and herbs, another with a piece of coal and ember, and another one with a pebble in it. Behind them was a lit candle, the warm lighting casting shadows against the back wall.

Viper moved behind me, placing his hands on my shoulders.

"Close your eyes," he instructed. I did so against my instinct. "Take a deep breath." I did that, too. On my exhale, Viper moved me to the left, right in front of the water bowl if I had to guess. "Now, place out your hand."

I swallowed but did what I was told again. "Now what?" I asked hesitantly.

"Now," he continued. "I want you to visualize the water. What it feels like, tastes like. Is it moving or stagnant? Salty or fresh?"

The first thing that came to mind was the crashing sea of trial one. The rain, the waves, the salt in my eyes and the burn of my lungs. Despite living in a fisherman-led kingdom, I didn't take to the water well. Never have. I respected it, sure, but I knew to keep my caution and wits about me when I was near it.

"That's enough," Viper whispered. "You can drop your hand now."

I did so, cracking open my eyes in the process. The water from the bowl had splashed around, a small puddle forming under it. I chanced a glance back to Viper, but his expression remained neutral.

"Again, with the next bowl," he said.

I stepped over to the bowl of soil and repeated the process of closing my eyes and placing out my hand. Viper remained quiet behind me as I did, thoughts of my garden swimming around me. I could feel the softness of the petals in my hands, the sweet scent of them on an early morning, the way their roots ran deep into the ground. Stronger than what their faces allowed.

I felt my fingertips tingle and my belly tighten. My thoughts furthered on until I felt something touch my fingertips. I opened my eyes and gasped. There, in the bowl just under my hand, was a flower in perfect bloom. Impossible.

"Excellent," Viper said ecstatically. "Try the next one."

The bowl with the ember. Fire. I knew what I had to do. I envisioned what a fire would look and smell like, how beautiful it could be; but then my thoughts turned sour, and suddenly I was thinking about Lustraya. I could see the burning villages as if I had been there myself for their destruction. Could hear the echoes and screams of the families slaughtered. I could feel the sweltering heat as if I was there, holding the line of safety.

My breathing had turned quick, and my eyes flew open in panic to make the memories stop. When I did, the flame on the candle burned high and unruly. The ember in my bowl had been used up and all that was left was a chard circle in the middle.

I removed my hand from it, rubbing the center of my palm as if I had been burned. The memory . . . it had all felt so real. I looked to Viper, and he nodded his chin down once in encouragement for me to keep going.

The pebble.

I didn't know what to think of this one. We had water, earth, and fire. I could only assume this bowl was for the element of air. But what did a pebble have to do with air? I held my hand out and closed my eyes, tried to envision what it would be like to move air. Could one move air? I waited to feel the tingle on my fingers again but felt nothing.

I didn't know how long I stood there, but after what felt like five minutes, I opened my eyes to see if I had moved the pebble by any means. Nothing.

Viper was scribbling something down as I stood there confused.

"Is that all?" I finally asked.

Poppi remained quiet in the corner as Viper finished whatever it was he was working through. His glasses were perched on the end of his nose once more, and he swiped them off and tossed them to the table with his notebook.

"For now," he said simply. I waited for further explanation or instruction but was met with only more silence.

"So, are you going to explain to me what all this is then? What my training is going to be like?"

"This was a test," he replied, sweeping his hand in front of the table. "When magic begins to form in a Practitioner, it usually manifests in one of the four elements. You have an aptitude for three of them which is rare and what we need. Earth and fire seem to be where your power mostly lies. Water seems tricky and well, air . . . that one is not for you. But nonetheless, you've already shown great potential."

"Great!" I said, clapping my hands together. "Now what?"

"We do nothing."

". . . We do . . .nothing?" I repeated.

"Nothing," he confirmed.

That seemed counterintuitive, and I looked to Poppi once more for her to step in and say something, but she didn't.

"I don't understand," I finally said, a bit of the anger and confusion rising in me seeping into my voice. "I thought that was the point of this. To begin to learn how to use my connection to my magic and build it up?"

"And we will. Just not at this moment. Right now, we need to write to Damien about your advancement and the rising threat looming over both Lustraya and Imeria. We cannot spread ourselves short, and as far as the Queen is concerned, I am still part of her Serpentine Guard. I do not possess the proper time to teach you. I can give you small exercises and reading material in the meantime, but not much more than that."

"So, this was all just a waste of time then?" I practically shouted. Now I was angry, truly and rightfully angry. All this time they just spent convincing me of my potential magic connection, preventing me from persuading Clara to give us aid. It was a waste of time.

"Unbelievable," I scoffed, making my way to the door.

"Where are you going?" Poppi shouted as I stepped back out into the hallway. "Daniella, get back here!"

I took off at a sprint, and I heard Poppi's footsteps pick up soon after. I had to decide on which direction I was going to go, what I wanted to do. No—*needed* to do—and I was struck with the idea the moment I flew out the side door and into the palace proper.

I ran toward the Ring, my focus razor sharp as I ducked around corners, trying to shake off Poppi. She was gaining on me fast and I heard her curse my name as I descended the stairs to the outside and launched around the corner that would take me toward the cliffs.

Muscle memory kicked in and my body screamed in delight as I moved closer to the stone wall and eventually through it. My lungs ached and my hair slowly slipped from its braid as I pushed myself further to the woods and to my old running trail. I didn't even stop to see if Poppi was still following me because I didn't care.

Time ceased, the birds sang, and I felt free.

I pounded against the ground further into the tree's embrace and when I felt myself want to go right, I turned left off the path and toward a deeper part of the wood. One that remained loosely explored because of the thick canopy cover. Poppi wouldn't be able to find me here.

I almost felt guilty running away from her again, but what choice did I have? If they weren't going to train me, then I would figure it out myself. Just like I usually did.

I ran until my legs were numb and head cleared.

I could smell the sea water coming from below the cliff's edge, hear the crash of the waves against the rocks. I could feel the gentle, cool breeze skimming past me.

I felt that tingle again. This time not in my hands, but in my belly. I knew what it was now that I had gone through Viper's test. I knew that it was an indication that my magic was stirring. But how did I touch it? Could I touch it? What did it all mean?

"Okay, Dani," I muttered to myself. "Time to get it together. Focus. Breathe. You can do this."

I had been faced with obstacles my whole life. What was a little dose of magic to add to the insanity of it all?

For Viper's tests, he had me close my eyes and hold out my hand, therefore I needed to focus on something. I was more apt with fire and earth, he said. Fire, if not controlled, would burn this whole wood down and I didn't want that damage on my conscious. So, I chose to focus on earth.

"Alright, Dani, here we go."

I held out a hand, closed my eyes, and thought of that tingly feeling. I felt a small tug rise from the core of my being, felt it slither up my chest and down my arm. I thought of flowers and a garden, of a warm sunny day when it was best to grow things.

I felt the tingle leave my hand.

When I opened my eyes, I was met with a blank canvas of trees. Nothing had changed; nothing had grown. I frowned.

"Try again," I encouraged myself. "Think about what you did last time to make the flower grow."

Again, the tingling feeling returned, but something was different about it and I couldn't place it. It was more difficult to control it this time. I thought of a simple red rose, thought of its roots firmly in the ground, and of its big round petals.

Once again, I was met with nothing.

Frustration flared in me, and I scowled down at my hands. "Seriously! We're really going to do this."

I closed my eyes again, opening my palms to the ground and focusing hard on the magical pull. The tingle felt sluggish this time, almost like it was resisting me. I yanked and pulled on the invisible tether, pleading with it to come forth.

It did, but it slipped from my grasp even quicker.

I tried again. And again. And again. Until I was dripping with sweat, and the birds had retreated from the tree canopy, and it was nothing but me and the rushing of the sea nearby.

An hour had gone by, and still I had yet to make a flower bloom again. Why was it so difficult now? Why would the magic not listen?

I told myself to try one more time. One more time to throw all my might into calling up the magic and letting a single flower bloom before me.

I closed my eyes, envisioning the garden. I held onto the picture as I called up the magic; the tingle coming through forcefully and . . . and . . . was that anger I felt?

Without knowing what I had done, I felt that tingle evolve into a full-on lightning strike to my body. My arms went wide, my knees collapsing below me and hitting the ground hard. A scream escaped my lips and echoed through the hollow as I felt like my insides were being eviscerated.

I was in agony.

My throat was being screamed raw, the magic crashing through me and around me without restriction. I knew then and there that I had done something wrong, and the magic was mad. But I didn't know how to make it stop, didn't know how to make it come back in on itself.

The trees began to sway, lower vegetation getting caught on the brisk winds as they circled around.

Stop, stop, stop. I pleaded to the tether but there was no stopping it now.

The magic would pull me apart, make me cease to exist. If I let go of it completely, I would fall and fall, and no one would know what had come of me. I was naive to do this alone. Too arrogant to think I could control something like this.

I felt the trickle of water on my face; felt it slide down to my arms and soak the ground in which I kneeled. The rain advanced harder until suddenly I couldn't breathe.

I felt my body waver, my limbs growing limp as I collapsed to the side. My head hit the ground with a squelching thud, my arms splayed out to the sides uselessly. Deep in the depths of my head, I could hear the shouting of my name. The echoing continued and I couldn't stop myself from wondering if someone was calling on me from beyond the veil. Was it my mother? Had she truly been dead all these years?

Something warm stirred in me, starting in my chest and spreading to my neck and shoulders, then my hips and legs. My fingers and toes were the last to feel the warmth and then I was burning. I felt as if I was standing in the middle of an oven, my bones and muscles quaking with heat exhaustion. I tried to scream again but it got muffled out by something around my face.

I thrashed in defiance, desperately needing air in my lungs and for the fire to be put out. It was one of the worst times of my life, and then it was done.

I could breathe: the fire had stopped, the lightning was gone, and I was left on the ground in exhaustion. I had to be beyond the veil now. There was no other explanation.

"Dani," came the soft voice again. "Dani, wake up. Wake up. Damn it. Wake up!"

Something tapped against my cheek. No, not a tap. That was a slap. And another one. And I felt the sting on my cheek. I tried to crack my eyes open; tried to tell the person I was aware. On the third slap, my body jolted awake and upright, my lungs taking in a deep and sharp breath.

It was Poppi.

She had found me and my hollow. Her eyes were sunken in, face ashen, and her hands covered in . . . was that blood? It coated her shirt and hands; seeped into the knees of her pants.

I followed the trail till I noticed it flowed directly under my hand. Directly under me.

I let out a small yelp and scurried away from the blood as quickly as I could until my back hit something hard and squishy. I turned my head over my shoulder and began to hyperventilate in horror. There, just a few inches from where my head had been, lay a dead stag. Its eyes were black and cold, his abdomen sliced open from neck to center.

"Poppi, wh–what . . ."

"Magic demands a balance."

I looked back to her, the copper tang of blood filling my nose as I realized that I was covered in it. Not just plastering my shirt to my back, but all over my hands and chest. The water I thought I felt on my face, I had no doubt was blood now.

My stomach churned, my head spun.

"Poppi . . ." I pleaded through my growing fear. "What . . . why?"

I heard her shuffle closer to me, felt her hands grab the sides of my face to bring my eyes to hers.

"Magic is not something you can forcibly mold. You have to work with it. Control only what it gives you. If you take too much, you must pay the price for it or risk your own death." She paused and looked around at the hollow, her eyes growing sad and tender. "Come on. Let's get you back and get you cleaned up."

I had only enough energy to shakily nod my head as she reached for my hands and gingerly pulled me to my feet. It was going to be a long trek back. We were nearly two and a half miles away, not a horse in sight to help us.

"I just wanted to grow some roses . . ."

"I know," Poppi said sweetly. "I know."

And as we began the tedious walk back, roots began to bloom under the soil of the stag, the ground claiming its prize and producing the most gorgeous and vivacious blood-red roses.

# # #

It was late afternoon when we finally arrived back at the palace and to my absolute horror, Maddox and Aeddan were outside in the

Ring training when Poppi and I came through the stone wall, blood soaked and exhausted.

The men turned their attention to us as we passed through the entrance of the wall, their faces slack with panic.

"Dani!" Aeddan called and sprang into a run, Maddox hot on his heels.

"What the hell happened?" Maddox asked. "Were you attacked?" He looked to the tree line from whence we came, his body tightening for a fight.

"Everything is fine. Just a training exercise gone wrong," Poppi replied for us. It wasn't an outward lie; it wasn't the whole truth either.

"Is that all blood?" Maddox asked her, his voice seeping with distrust.

The silence that followed was loud and tense. Aeddan reached out and grabbed my wrist. "We need to get her inside before anyone else sees them like this. We can ask questions later. And there will be questions." He aimed the last bit at Poppi.

The men escorted us back to our rooms, careful to use the servant's entrances and exits to not bump into anyone.

When I was situated behind closed doors, I turned to look at myself in the mirror. My eyes were the first change I noticed. They were blue, but not just any blue. They were . . . how did Poppi describe it? Glowing? Like the walls of the mountain keep. My hair seemed shinier too. I traced a hand down my curls, down my face and neck, and down my stomach. I ripped off the blood-soaked fabric and tossed them into the fire that roared on the other side of the wall.

On the outside I was beautiful and pristine, but on the inside, I felt used and burned; a feeling I knew I wasn't making up because when I finally was able to dip my toe into my bath water, it sizzled. And then it kept sizzling the further I sunk my body into it. Steam rolled off the top of the water as I settled in up to my neck.

I could stay here for hours, and the water would not turn cold. I washed slowly and tiredly, my body fighting against every small movement I made in jest. I had pushed too far. Tested a magic I knew nothing about and I almost killed myself for it.

Damien was going to be angry when he found out about all of this. I wouldn't be surprised if he came back to Imeria and plucked me from this palace once more. The sad part is, I think I would let him.

What good have I done here anyway? We were no closer to gaining aid against the Fae than we were before Poppi and I arrived. I knew about magic now, sure, but if I couldn't figure out a way to work with it and quick, I would be useless in this war.

It had all become a mess. I thought about writing to Damien myself as I rinsed my hair for a second time. Maybe if he heard from me, he would know that I was trying my best and not finding a way out. That I was doing everything in my power—literally—to help Lustraya as best I could.

Poppi had done the most to help by summoning her storm as a beacon for the Fae. They would be here any day now. Was that fair to Imeria or was it a blatant point to be made? They wanted proof; they were getting it.

I stood from the tub, the water brown and red tinged. If only magic could snap me clean, I would feel immeasurably better. It was with great effort that I dressed for the day once more. As I secured the last knot on my pants, I heard the swish of paper on floor and turned to the door.

There by the threshold laid an envelope with an Imerian seal on it. I walked over, snatching it up and unfolding its contents as quickly as my fingers would.

We need to talk. Meet in our garden. Come alone.

Aeddan. I huffed out a breath, the memories of last night breaking through my fatigue. Oh, Dani, you stupid girl. You've done it now.

28

PROGRESS

I expected to find Aeddan waiting for me under the tree where we kissed for the first time; the one we slept next to each other under last night. But instead, he was waiting for me near the hedges, behind a bush of pansies, Maddox and Harrison flanking him on either side.

My stomach dropped and I paused halfway up the path, half-tempted to turn my back and run in the opposite direction.

"Don't you dare," Maddox called. "Get over here, Dani." A nudge from Harrison. "Please."

I swallowed my pride and closed the distance to my friends. The pit that had taken up residence in my stomach opened once more, the beast within it roaring with rage. I shoved against it, telling myself that I had known these men all my life and I had nothing to fear from them. Except disappointing them, that is.

"Dani," Harrison said gently. "It's okay."

It's like he could hear my thoughts.

"I guess I owe you all an explanation," I sighed when I reached them.

"Yes, you do," Maddox spoke for them all.

I swallowed again. "Where would you like me to start?"

"Why are you here?" Harrison asked.

"You guys know that. I'm here for Clara's aid."

They made sounds of outrage and frustration; Maddox's hands flying up and Harrison lowering his gaze to the ground. But Aeddan, he knew better than to make me feel small. He kept his composure.

"Aid on your faceless war?" Maddox spat. "No, wait. I'm sorry. The war with the *Fae*?"

His tone and behavior set my teeth on edge. Had my absence wounded him more than I anticipated? He had never talked to me in such harsh ways. "Dani, we want the truth. We are owed the truth after everything we all have been through together."

"I know," I breathed. "I know. I was told what you guys did for me the first week I was gone. What lengths you tried to use to come get me." I placed a hand to my heart. "It means so much to me that you all would do that, and I am forever sorry everything has happened the way it has."

"So, what are you hiding?" Maddox pressed. Aeddan shook his head back and forth ever so slightly. Deep in my bones, I knew I could trust Mads and Harrison with the truth. I wasn't worried if they would tell anyone. I was worried what they would do once they found out.

"If I tell you," I said anxiously. "You wouldn't even believe me."

"Try us," Maddox challenged.

"If I tell you what I know, you have to swear to me now, swear on our blood oath that you will not tell a soul until the time is right."

"I swear it," Mads and Harrison said at the same moment. I looked at Aeddan, at the stern look across his face. His forehead was scrunched in thought, and finally he relented.

"I made no blood oath, but I would follow you anywhere, Princess. You have my word."

At the use of my nickname, Mads and Harrison exchanged a sideways glance.

"We have been raised on a lie," I said softly. "Our world . . . it is not as it seems. And it has finally come to catch up with us. A debt needs to be paid, and if we do not help one another, we will all die."

A pause, then Harrison asked, "What debt?"

"The world works in balances, and the scale has been tipped to one side too long." I took a pause, looked each of them in the eye and revealed the truth that weighed down my heart. "Magic has returned to Taelle."

It wasn't the answer they were expecting as evident by the confused looks on their faces.

Aeddan remained expressionless as Maddox and Harrison did what I initially did: laugh. I understood their reluctance to believe. It was absurd. There had been little proof of its existence outside of stories and fables fed to us as children. But when they noticed Aeddan nor I were smirking or laughing, they sobered quickly.

"You're being serious?" Harrison clarified.

"Yes."

"That's outrageous"

"I know."

The three of them exchanged more silent conversation. But I understood what they were asking one another. Could I be believed? How could this be possible? Both great questions. So, I answered them before they could ask.

"I will admit there is very little that I know. Damien has kept me in the dark on a lot of things, and rightfully so. A secret of this magnitude isn't something you just share with a person from a foreign kingdom. Trust and time——two things no one has——cannot simply be bought off whimsy."

"So, then how did you find out?" Harrison asked, rubbing his hand against his chin.

"Because there was an attack." I paused, my gaze drifting to Aeddan's. "I was almost killed. As were dozens of my unit. We were out training and there were these beasts . . . I have never seen anything like it before. And when I was about to be eaten alive, I stopped it."

"You stopped it?" Maddox asked.

"How?" came Harrison.

"The event spurred Damien into action," I continued. "Made him realize that he could no longer hide what was out there from me. Once we realized the Fae were slowly sealing us within our borders, Poppi and I came down to check out the last three free roads. The ones between our kingdoms."

"That explains why we saw you in the woods then," Harrison mused. I nodded in agreement.

"Coming here was my idea, not Damien's. He's too proud to ask for more help but I'm not. I know how this all sounds, what it all must look like to you. But I need you to understand that what I am saying is true and if Imeria does not start giving aid to Lustraya, the world as we know it will burn."

They took in every drop of information I gave them. Each man concocting his own theory, their minds going straight to battle strategy.

"How did you stop them?" Aeddan asked me tensely. I could see the pain laced behind his eyes, the edge in his tone. If the roles were switched, I would be thinking of every which way I could to slaughter the thing that dare hurt the man in front of me.

I knew the thing they wanted most right now was for me to give them proof, and I wanted to give it to them so badly, but I was scared now. After what happened this morning . . . if the magic didn't kill me, Poppi would; if she wasn't already tearing through the palace right now to drag me back to Lustraya.

They continued to watch me as I wrestled with myself and in the end, I felt myself reach for that internal tether once more.

"Please . . ." I whispered to it, as I closed my eyes and held out my hand.

I felt it stir, felt it snap its jaws at me as I touched it. But instead of grabbing onto it, I envisioned my hand caressing it, coaxing it into working for me. I felt the familiar tingle of magic shoot through my core and to my fingertips; the feeling faint and fuzzy, but there.

I had my hand poised over a dead pansy. I didn't know what the magic wanted to do with it, but I let it flow freely from me without restraint.

When I heard the gasps of my friends, I opened my eyes. Not only had the pansy come back to life, but the whole bush sprung into full bloom. I smiled softly, thanking the magic within for not killing me and giving me this last gift before tucking it safely back within me.

"Magic," I finally said, relieved that they were looking at me with belief now.

"And who else knows about . . . this?" Maddox asked, running his hands through his long copper hair.

"About me," I clarified. "Just Damien and Poppi. Like I said, most of this is a secret kept with Lustraya. Those that have been witness are either murdered or taken as hostages to the Fae. Theres been only so much we could do to protect them."

I saw the weight I had been carrying the last few days—the last few weeks—settle on their shoulders now.

"We need Imeria. And I need you all to help me convince Clara to provide it."

"You know," came the scratchy call of a pissed-off Poppi. "I'm going to start sleeping in your room and chaining you to my side."

I let out a low groan.

"I'm guessing by this secret little meeting of yours, you've told them?"

When her question was met with a resounding silence, she grimaced. "Of course you did. Is this a game to you? Do you think just because you think you know these people they won't go run to their Queen and out us? We could be killed before we reach the border, Dani!"

"Watch how you talk to her," Maddox growled.

Aeddan nodded his head slowly, menacingly, in agreement. I knew the words Poppi threw toward me angered him, because they angered me too.

Just being back here made me more attuned with him. More attuned with the world around me.

"So, what now?" Poppi asked. "Where do we go from here?"

It was the question on everyone's mind, but the answer eluded us all.

"What was with all the blood this morning?" Aeddan finally asked.

I looked to Poppi, wanting her to explain this because I knew my knowledge was limited and if I spoke wrong, it would set everyone in this garden off.

"Dani decided she knew best and tested her magic's boundaries this morning. What you must understand about magic," she supplied, eyeing down every man there. "Is that there is a give and take. A balance that must be maintained. When Dani wielded her magic this morning, untrained and untapped, she upset the balance. She took too much without giving anything back. Luckily," she side-eyed me quickly. "I found her just in time. The blood was from a stag. A sacrifice to even the balance of give and take. No one said magic would be pretty."

I hung my ahead, ashamed of my lack of control but only for a moment. I wouldn't let my insecurity show in front of these men, in front of the people who had seen me at my worst and best. There was nothing to be ashamed of when it came to them. They would have my back no matter what; that I knew.

"Are you okay?" Mads asked in the brotherly tone I was used to.

"I'm okay," I confirmed. "It's what Poppi said. I'm new to this and pushed too far, too soon. There's so much I don't know, but I'm working on that. You all know me better than anyone else. I will stop at nothing to protect our kingdoms. I just really need you to fight by my side when it matters."

"We're with you," Maddox stated.

"Through the worst and the best," Harrison added.

Aeddan and I exchange a heated stare. I thought about how much the last day had changed for us. He would be angry with me for leaving him right here this morning, and now he's finding out a truth I had been keeping.

There was never going to be a solid foundation of trust between us. Never going to be a perfect time. I knew that with everything in me, but I could still see him fighting.

"I will talk to Clara. Try to make her and the General see reason," he offered. "We have units at the border and soldiers to spare. Let me see what I can do."

"About time you stepped up," Poppi countered. She looked to me now. "We have to go. There's been an update."

I knew immediately what she meant. Before we turned and left, I looked to the men in front of me. "Thank you. For always believing in me and walking by my side."

Poppi tugged on my arm, pulling me away from them and back toward the palace without a second glance.

"That was reckless and damn near treasonous, Dani. What the hell were you thinking?"

"I was thinking that my friends know me and deserved an explanation as to why I was smothered in animal blood this morning. I can't lie to them, Poppi, they would see right through me and when it comes down to it, we need them."

"You should have ran it by me or—"

"And what would it matter? You say I am your princess but sit here and scold me without second thought. You would never do the same to Damien or any other royal. What? Do you think you can do this job better?"

And then it hit me. Suddenly, brashly.

"Oh, my gods . . . you do."

Poppi kept her mouth shut as we walked closer to the servant's staircase that would descend into the lower depths of the palace. How had I never seen it before? Poppi worshipped Damien and was a trusted confidant in all this chaos. Was Poppi the princess Damien wished for? Did they have an arrangement before he thought to act on the Accords?

"Poppi," I demanded, pulling her to a stop. "What did Damien promise you?"

"You're making up things, Dani. Damien never—"

"Oh, look," came a clear and commanding voice from in front of us. Clara. "Just the two people I was looking for. Come, meet me and the others. I have received word that would be of interest to both of you."

Great. As if this day couldn't get any better.

We followed Clara and her two guards back to the War Room: the tension between Poppi and I thicker than the blood-soaked ground under the stag.

General Armas and Admiral Luscette were already there when we arrived, followed by a few of Clara's top advisers. Whatever news had come for the council, it was important. Perhaps important enough to spur Clara into action.

Clara took her spot at the head of the table, those around her standing on her entrance and sitting back down only once she had done so. Poppi and I remained at the other end of the table, our separation from the rest not going unnoticed.

"What is this all about, Your Majesty?" I asked, no longer able to contain the burning curiosity or tension growing in the room.

"We have received word from King Damien," she said bluntly. "He's rode south to his borders and found a number of my soldiers there." Poppi and I looked to each other, neither of us surprised by the news that the camp we found was not moved. "Dead."

Now that was a surprise.

"The Fae?"

Armas sighed heavily, looking over to Clara, the two of them sharing a strained look with each other.

"They left little evidence," Armas started. "But with you being here, it's a reasonable suspicion to have."

"So, where does that leave us? Have you tracked their movements?" Poppi asked out of turn.

"It's as you said once before," Luscette interjected. "They left a trail of carnage but no trace of themselves. Like thieves in the night."

"So, does this mean you're finally ready to fight with us?" I asked Clara in dead seriousness.

"It means we are open to terms. But there are no guarantees. We will have to wait until Damien gets here," she said matter-of-factly, like she had already been in communication with him and was just now cueing us into the plan.

"And in the meantime?"

"We would like you to do what you do best," Armas said smartly. "Share your wisdom with the Serpentine Guard. Train with them again. Give them the best advantage if this thing escalates further."

I looked to Poppi, her jaw clenched tight, but her eyes as determined as I'm sure mine were.

"We can meet with them," I said for the both of us. "Poppi can take the lead as she has dealt with the Fae firsthand. But we will need your cooperation when it comes to strategizing where to place soldiers—"

"We will wait for Damien on that account," Armas interrupted.

"And how long till that happens?" I asked icily as I was cut off.

"Three days according to his last message," Clara confirmed.

"And how far out are the Fae?" Poppi pushed.

"About a week. If they come from the north border, it could be sooner."

Great. Just what we needed. If Damien was delayed even half a day, the Fae could strike, and we would have nothing because Clara and Armas were strong-arming me out of the planning. Why, I wish I knew. They should know better than anyone that I was capable of concocting a battle strategy.

Was this another one of those royal protocols that I was susceptible to now? No princess can make a decision for her kingdom without express permission from her King? It could mean the difference in life versus death.

"Is there anything else you would like to share?" I asked with annoyance.

"That is all," Clara said. "Best get to meeting with the Guard, Daniella. The sooner, the better."

"And telling them about this. You're all okay with it?" Poppi asked quickly.

"They can be trusted. But see to it that this happens covertly. I don't need panic to rise amongst everyone else. They will know in due time."

This was it then. The final board being placed on the ship that would take us into war.

"We'll see to it," I said confidently.

Poppi nodded in agreement as I turned from the table, and she followed at my right. Only when we were safely in the hallway again, the door firmly closed, did we look at one another in agreement.

"They're withholding from us, aren't they?" Poppi asked.

"Most definitely," I confirmed. "But there is nothing we can do about it now. We have to find Viper."

We wasted no time finding the stairwell and descending into the lower parts of the palace. When we arrived, there was no Viper in sight, just his vials and plants; one of the bowls emanating a purplish smoke.

I took the chance to wander around the room, poking around and seeing things for myself without Viper's piercing gaze on me.

He had stacks on stacks of notebooks, random papers scattered along the desk next to an ink well half-empty, and an empty teacup accompanying it. I picked up one of the papers, squinting my eyes to help interpret the writing.

Phenathyl: purple in nature, sweet. Inhalation may cause sleepiness, muscle relaxation, slurred speech, violent dreams. Good for keeping people subdued. Can this be weaponized?

"He really does plan, doesn't he?" I commented, holding up the paper. "I mean, he must have so much untapped knowledge down here."

"There's more in Lustraya," Poppi said, walking over to me and taking the paper from my hand. "He and the scholar Treysen have a blast in their workshop there. In my early days at the mountain, I could hear the rocks rattle with them setting off their experiments. It was . . . a time."

Treysen. That name sounded familiar . . . Nic. That was her brother. My stomach soured as I thought of my former handmaid. Last time I knew anything, she was laid up in the infirmary in the mountain with three deep gashes to her chest. She should be dead, but there was something keeping her alive.

Now that I have been exposed to the knowledge that I have, it could be magic. Or her iron will to not leave her brother kept her from taking her last breath.

"He must be a special kid for Viper to bring him into his fold," I stated.

"He is one of our most gifted minds. Damien is protective over him."

That seemed to be something Damien was fond of doing. He was a lot of things, but I couldn't deny his big heart and the way he cared for the people around him. He was a devoted King, if even to a fault.

"What are you two doing?"

We spun around to find Viper standing in the threshold, arms crossed and a coy expression.

"She was snooping," Poppi said quickly, putting the blame on me.

I shot her a glare but said nothing to defend myself because, yes, I was snooping, and I didn't care.

"Find anything interesting?" Viper asked, stepping forward.

"Not really," I replied, leaning against the desk now. "But you should know that I tested my magic this morning and there were some . . . effects."

"She almost killed herself. I had to perform a sacrifice," Poppi said plainly.

"Whose side are you on?" I practically yelled at her.

"And how did it go?" Viper asked calmly, quizzically. "What did you feel, smell, hear?"

"I can feel it," I said without hesitating. "It's there, I can feel it even now. It's like if there was a bucket attached to the rope; all I have to do is pull the rope and I have the magic. A tingling feeling flows through me, but it slips away.

"I tried to grab the 'rope' several times this morning and it kept falling away until I grabbed it and pulled. That's when everything went wrong. I felt the magic begin to consume me and I couldn't make it stop. I wasn't in control any longer and the magic wanted to destroy everything."

"She nearly decimated a whole hollow," Poppi added. "She was drawing purely from source."

"How was that any different from you though?" I asked, turning on her. "When you summoned the storm, were you not drawing from the same place?"

"I went past my limits, yes. But that is why I had the candles. I was using them as a conduit. The fire helps ground and provide for me to be able to wield the air." She took a pause before mumbling. "You would know that if you had actually listened, taken Viper's advice and read first."

"I like to learn things physically first. I can read in between training."

"You two argue like little children. It's amazing you can get anything done; nevertheless, being some of the best warriors this continent has to offer," Viper reprimanded. "But Poppi is right, you can't just pull straight from source. Or maybe you can . . ." He stopped mid-thought and grabbed his notebook to jot something down.

"There is much still to be rediscovered about magic, Dani. But in the future, I would caution you to find a conduit or anchor to help you pull from. I'm glad you're okay. In the meantime, however, I do believe the three of us are needed elsewhere."

Right. Clara's preparation and training.

"Viper, before you go, should we all discuss just how much information we want to reveal to the Guard?" I asked.

"All of it. All that you know."

That was the last thing I expected to hear from him. "All of it?"

He nodded in agreement.

"But why? Wouldn't that make us entirely vulnerable to Imeria?"

"We have nothing left to lose, Dani," Viper replied. "Lustraya is on the brink of collapse. The Fae could be at the walls by dawn. Damien is a few days away, and Imeria needs to be prepared. Besides, those guards have missed your leadership. I don't think you realize the impact you had on them."

I felt the tattoo on my back slither. I had missed the Guard, even though we had only been together a few days before I left. They were good men and women. Strong. Capable. There was no one else I would rather ride into battle with.

"Okay," I responded and turned to Poppi. "Can I count on you to have my back in there, minus the attitude?"

She rolled her eyes. "For now."

29

ARRIVAL

We met the Serpentine Guard in the north tower, in the room where we had devised the plan to smoke out the traitors at the ball. The old memories hit me hard as Poppi and I stood at the front of the room where Samir once stood.

I hope he and Ary were okay, wherever they were.

The members of the Serpentine Guard slowly filled the room, Mads and Harrison coming in last behind them all. I looked around the room once more for a pair of eyes that would not be there. Where was he?

Poppi nudged my arm with her elbow and tilted her head slightly to the room as my indication to get started. Right. Time was not on our side here.

"Hello everyone," I said as confidently as I could muster in this moment. Do they hate me for leaving them? Believe me a traitor to my oath? "It's great to see you all again. I wish it was under better circumstances, but the Fates seem to have their own way of wanting things done these days."

There were a few chuckles from around the room, but most remained stoic and focused with their hands clasped behind their backs or arms crossed over their chests.

"I know these are unusual circumstances and you're probably wondering why you're here, so I am going to get straight to the point for everyone's benefit." I took a deep breath. "Lustraya is at war with an enemy long since thought myth. They are cunning, fast, cruel, and on their way here. Right this very moment. They threaten to upset a delicate balance and tear this continent to shreds. To decimate the humans. They are called the Fae."

Scoffs of disbelief skittered around the room, along with a few snickers, but mostly just denial came from those assembled. When neither Poppi or I faltered in our steadfast seriousness and Mads nor Harrison shot down the notion, the room began to sober.

"You can't be serious?" someone asked from the back. "Fae? As in from the stories we heard as kids?"

I nodded in confirmation. "I know it seems outrageous, but it is true. Poppi here has seen them with her own eyes; has fought them. They stole her brother away and murdered her parents as well as their village. This is not a fight that has happened overnight. They have slowly been etching their way into Lustraya for almost a decade and now they are coming here."

"So, you brought them here then," Aria accused me. I remembered her; she was once part of my team here. She no longer looked at me with confidence but instead with mangled distrust.

"There are a few reasons why they could be moving into Imeria, but the point of the matter is that they are coming. And Poppi and I are here to help you get ready to defend your home."

"You said Lustraya was at war for almost a decade," another shot out. "Why would we need to take advice from you all? Sounds like you haven't been doing a good job at keeping them away."

A few laughs rocked through the room and when I turned to look at Poppi for something to say, she was gone. I blinked quickly, hoping it was a trick of the light but the spot next to me remained empty.

"I suggest you watch your tongue, or I'll cut it out for you," I heard her hiss from somewhere in the crowd of guards.

I whipped my head around, spotting her short haircut just behind the man who had spoken. She had her hand cupped around his mouth and knife to the side of his neck. He looked surprised she had come up on him so swiftly.

Poppi released him slowly and backed away into the shadows. Seconds later, she was back at my side, knife still in hand.

"The Fae," she said in a calm rage. "Are patient. They will wait you out till they see your soft spot and strike. Imeria has shown their soft spot, just like Lustraya did many years ago. We have asked your Queen to aid us in our fight because it is no longer just Lustraya's.

"Princess Daniella is not someone to be mocked. You all know her, fought with her, competed with her. She has shown immense courage and strength the last year and you will show her respect."

I saw pride gleam in Mads and Harrisons eyes as Poppi stared intently at everyone gathered. Viper, for all his placidness, even puffed his chest slightly.

"The way I placed a knife to your throat is slower than what any Fae would do," Poppi continued, pointing with the tip of the blade to the man for effect. "Your Queen says that you all are her best. We are here to show you how to fight against someone who will always be quicker and one move ahead. Is that something you all are capable of doing?"

Grunts of agreement chorused around, and I steeled my shoulders back, my lungs breathing out a sigh of relief.

"Then let us take to the Ring and get started," I announced.

In less than an hour, all of the Serpentine Guard had arrived at the Ring and were heavily embedded in the exercises that Poppi and I had given them.

Metal clashed and clinked together, shouts and grunts accompanying the fray. We paired everyone into groups of three or four with instructions to disarm only one person as fast as they could. Should be easy, right?

For most, yes. They tried, and within one minute of defense were disarmed without hesitation. It wasn't supposed to be easy, and that was the point.

"You will need to learn to use both a sword and dagger in the fight; two swords together if your arms can handle it," Poppi called across the Ring. "They will try to hit you fast and swift; the quicker they take you out, the better for them."

"Watch your right," I called to Aria as I circled around her group. "You leave it open to vulnerability." She shot me a glare, throwing her shield and sword down.

"Let's see you do it then."

The commotion around us halted as several other members of the Guard heard her challenge.

"Okay."

Whether she expected push back or reprimand, I didn't know, but she looked surprised when I drew my sword from my back and stooped to pick hers up.

"Choose," I instructed to her. She hesitated for a moment before saying, "Kammeron, Ilias, and her—Poppi."

I found Poppi across the circle and her eyes lit up with delight. She had been waiting for another moment where she could put me on my ass, and here it was.

"So be it," I said, mirroring Poppi's own wicked grin. I spun my swords in my hands, waiting for them to assemble.

"Don't pull your punches," I told them. "I like a good challenge."

I heard the shuffle of a foot and flicked my sword up above my head, catching Kammeron's strike and tossing it aside.

"That's all you got?"

Ilias spurred into motion next, sending a volley of swings my way that I was able to parry. Kammeron joined in with him, the two of them charging me with swift and stiff cuts.

They were excellent swordsman; their ability to keep light on their feet and swing with power a true testament to their training. Any other day I would be proud, but today I had to prove a point.

If there was anything I learned with my time in Lustraya, it was that being agile and precise was better than being stronger. That's what today's lesson was about. So, I kept my feet moving, my blades turning and cutting as they tried to box me in near the wall.

It was a smart plan; one I would do myself if I could. But all the while I was fighting the men, I kept one eye on Poppi and knew what she saw as they continued to push me to the wall: opportunity.

If I knew Poppi, she would walk to the edge and out of my sightline before jumping onto the ledge and attacking from above. It's what I would do too.

But the second lesson here had to also be 'expect the unexpected' and as I watched Poppi move further to the side, I knew I had guessed right.

Kammeron lunged forward, his sword narrowly missing my ear; Ilias slashing through on my left. I had less than a minute before Poppi reentered the fight and when Kammeron banked right once more, I sent a fist flying into his ribs, leaving me just a wide enough opening to roll onto and off his back as he bent forward.

I heard the swish of Poppi's dagger fly past me and land in the mud just as my feet did. They landed in the same spot.

"Nice try," I goaded her.

"Who says I was trying?"

"I think you all have made your point," a deep, gruff voice said behind me. It had been weeks since I had heard that voice and based off the wide-eyed look and bow Poppi was giving now, I knew it was Damien.

I turned to find the King standing at the edge of the Ring; Colonel Baylon Anders and Lord Callen Hornborn with him. His eyes glinted with mischief and pride, and I quickly lowered myself into a curtsey as he cut across the space.

The rest of the Serpentine Guard stood back with chests out and swords down as the King entered the Ring.

I held my curtsey until I felt a finger place itself under my chin and lift it. His eyes met mine and he smiled softly.

"Glad to see you've managed to keep yourself in one piece."

"If you ask that same question to Poppi, I'm sure she'll give you a different answer."

He chuckled. "Stand, my dear, and come with me. There is much we have to discuss."

I did as he asked, rising from my curtsey and sheathing my sword. I planted the other one into the ground for someone else to use, shouting back to the Serpentine Guard, "Keep going. You have your plans."

In a rare display of affection and unity, Damien held his hand out for me which I took.

We had never done anything remotely like this in Lustraya, but we were in front of Imerians now, and they needed to know that even though we may be a kingdom on the verge of collapse, we were united.

I felt the stares of everyone on our backs, the weight growing heavier with each step until we finally made it back up the steps and toward the palace.

"It's nice to see you again, Your Highness," Callen said as he followed behind me and Damien.

"You as well, my Lord," I said back. "I hope the trip down here went smoothly."

Anders grunted. I see there would be lots for us to talk about, indeed.

We turned a corner, Damien taking us in the direction of the War Room. How did he know where it was? That was when Aeddan appeared in front of us.

"Right this way, Your Majesty," he looked to me, then to Damien and I's joined hands before adding, "Your Highness."

If I didn't know Aeddan, I would think he was just another arrogant Imerian soldier, one who was biting back disdain for its neighboring kingdom. But I did know Aeddan and I knew that look.

He was caught off guard, hurt. I knew it by the way a muscle in his jaw ticked ever so slightly.

As much as I wanted to release our hands, I didn't. As much as I wanted to run to Aeddan and reassure him it wasn't what it looked like, I couldn't nor would I.

This was my life now, and he needed to see the show with his own eyes. A few stolen moments and an eternity of longing was not going to change that for either of us.

Damien gave my hand a gentle squeeze as we approached the War Room. "Are you okay?" he whispered lowly to me.

"Yes," I lied. "Just happy you're here."

I could see that he didn't believe me, but he took the answer for what it was and stepped forward into the room.

Clara was waiting with Armas and Luscette already seated at the table, a few more of her advisers in attendance for this meeting.

"Damien," she announced. "So good of you to finally meet up with us. Come." She waved us over, her hand showing us to the seats left open for our court.

"I trust you had a decent journey?" she asked.

"About as decent as one can imagine during these times."

We sat down as one, Damien's form towering over mine and the others. How had I never noticed just how large he was? Almost like a bear.

"Clara," he said. "You know I am not one to play by court manners and politics, so I am just going to ask bluntly if you have changed your mind?"

Clara huffed out a laugh, shaking her head like she expected nothing less from the king. General Armas did everything in his power not to roll his eyes at the King's bluntness.

"I expect nothing less from you, Damien," she replied. "And to answer your question: yes. We have reconsidered."

A gasp crept from my lips, my mouth dropping into a small O. A thousand questions swirled in my head, but none of them I would ask, especially as I watched how Damien remained unfazed by her confession.

"There's a stipulation in there . . . ." he accused lightly. Clara nodded.

"We agree to give you one legion of our soldiers to go north with you, but . . ." My stomach dropped. "They are only to be used as back-up and go no further than twenty miles in either direction of our border."

"For fuck's sake . . ." Damien ground out.

"Watch it, Damien," Clara said cooly. "Or I send you nothing at all."

"Twenty miles inland? That helps us in no way!"

"That is not my problem to solve," she pressed. "We have our own troubles on this side, thanks to you. Should my own people need the protection, I want my soldiers close to help defend."

Damien rubbed a hand down his face. "Clara, please, this isn't a game. This is a real threat and they are coming."

"Not for a week," Armas stated as he stood from his seat. "Our scouts have it on good authority that the Fae have remained near the Lustrayan woods just on the opposite end of our border. If they tried to move inland here it would take them five to seven days at best and worst."

"You're an idiot if you believe that," Anders said, standing as well. "The Fae could be here in the next two days if they wish it. If they are moving that slow, it's for a specific purpose. They're onto you. They are smart and if they know you're tracking them, then they will purposely lead you astray, you fool."

"That's enough," Damien grumbled to his Colonel. "But he is right," he said, louder for everyone this time. "The Fae are cunning and strategic. They will wait you out for as long as they think they must, waiting for when you get lazy or comfortable. That's when they will strike."

"And how certain of this are you?" one of Clara's advisers asked.

Damien unbuttoned his cuff and rolled up his sleeve to reveal a long and jagged scar running up the length of his forearm. "I speak from experience."

"So, you have seen one of them, then?" Luscette asked with curiosity.

"Seen. Fought. Killed. War is just a game to them, Clara. And it's coming to your doors."

For the first time in a long time, I could see a flash of fear pass over Clara. For the first time since I had been back, she looked like she believed us now.

"You get one legion," she repeated. "But you may use them as you wish."

Damien's shoulders relaxed a bit as she amended her previous offer.

"Thank you," he said but I could tell he was still not pleased.

Lustraya burned as we sat here, and the walls were creeping in on Imeria. How much longer did we have till we all were decimated?

Damien looked at me then back to Clara, his eyes lost in thought. I knew that look. That was the look he gave me when he wanted to tell me about the Fae the first time and didn't. It's the look he gives anyone when he wants to dismiss the room for a private audience. I knew what he was going to ask for the moment before he said it.

"There is more," he said, and I let my head fall against my chest. "But I would like to speak to you without extra ears."

He looked to the court that surrounded her; Callen and Anders taking the cue they knew so well and standing from their seats. They and I all knew what Damien would most likely tell Clara about: magic. It was time for the truth to be set free if that's what we wanted to remain to be.

I stood up as well, giving Damien a soft smile and knowing look. He kissed my knuckles in thanks, our performance for the Imerian court working, as the three of us left the War Room as a unit. I could hear the creak of the chairs being pushed back and the shuffle of feet behind us as Clara's court followed suit.

The doors opened and closed, and then I was left out in the hallway with Anders and Callen.

"That seemed to go well," Callen mused.

"If by well, you mean I hope that this palace remains in one piece by the time they're finished speaking, then yes. I hope it does go well," Anders said.

"Gentleman," I interjected to their squabbling. "It's been nice to see you again but if you'll excuse me, I think I'm going to retire for the rest of the day."

"Of course, Your Highness," Callen said with a bow.

I curtsied back stiffly before leaving them to stand there and wait for Damien.

The room had become stuffy; the day dragging on in a slow trudge with anticipation for the arrival of our doom. I needed to relax and gather my thoughts.

Hopefully, Poppi was having a better go of the day now that she could fight the people who set her teeth on edge. How did it all come to this? Just months ago, I would have never believed that this was why Damien needed a princess; needed someone to use as a pawn for the ravages of war.

I pushed the door to my room open, feeling relief as I stepped through it and closed it behind me. I rested my head there for a minute. Then two.

I prepared the last six years of my life for this very scenario and now that it was here, I couldn't help but wonder if it was all going to be worth it. The fighting. The loss of life. The chance that we could lose everything we had spent centuries building.

I walked away from the bedroom doors and to the plush couch by the fireplace. I curled myself up on it and allowed myself to feel everything that I had been repressing since being back. Fear clawed its way through my body. We had two to seven days and then we were at war

My head began to pound. I couldn't think, couldn't breathe. I felt like the walls were beginning to close in on me. The weight of duty and responsibility clung too close, and if I wasn't careful, it would drown me.

The hammering of a fist on my door echoed from the front of my room.

"Go away!" I called to the person. They answered with another round of aggressive knocking.

"Poppi, if that's you, I'm going to kill you!" I shouted, still not leaving my spot on the couch.

But it wasn't Poppi who was at my door. It was Aeddan and he burst through like a crazed animal. I sat up straight at the sound of the intrusion, my feet hitting the ground a moment later, my body poised for an attack. When I saw Aeddan stomp through the threshold and slam the door shut, I allowed myself to relax.

"Aeddan, please. I do not have it in me to fight with you right now," I said, pinching the bridge of my nose.

"Good. Then you're going to listen."

"Excuse me?" I snapped, moving around the couch and to him. He marched forward and I met him head on with equal fervor. "Aeddan, if this is about the other night . . ."

"Shut up," he demanded, stopping a foot away from me. "You need to get away from this. From all this. Tonight, tomorrow. I don't care but you need to go."

"I'm not going anywhere, Aeddan. How dare you think you could make me?"

"This isn't a game, Daniella. You have to leave. You need to get as far away from this kingdom as you can before the Fae arrive."

"I'm getting really, *really* tired of people telling me what to do," I ground out in a low voice. I was seething. How dare he come in here and try to boss me around like I was some kind of child?

"Maybe it's because we know what's best for you and we are trying to protect you. Lustraya cannot loose both its King and Princess. You need to go."

"You're right, I'm a fucking princess! And I do know what's good for me, because what's good for me is that the people and kingdom I care about are safe!" I shouted at him. "I don't need anyone's permission to do *anything!*"

His chest heaved as he took another step closer, closing the space between us and cupping my face in his hands.

"And before you were the people's princess," he breathed. "You were mine. You're still my Princess." His eyes blazed with longing, fear, and another emotion I would not let myself admit was there.

"Dani," his voiced quivered as he said my name and I felt the walls around my heart crack. "Dani, I cannot bear to lose you. The thought of you being on that battlefield destroys me because what if I'm not close enough to have your back? What if they take you? I can't. I can't keep losing you again. Definitely not like that."

His thumbs played circles on my cheeks, the touch soft as his words cut like knives.

"Aeddan, please. Please stop making this so hard," I said, pulling his hands from my face. "I can't keep having this argument with you," I whispered, running a hand through his short locks and then over his jaw. I traced the edge of it with my thumb before following the lines of his shoulder to his arm, my hand cresting over his shirt till his heart was beneath my palm.

"My heart breaks every time I see you and can do nothing about it. You are my everything, Aeddan. There is nothing in this world that I wouldn't do for you. No human or Fae I wouldn't kill to make sure that you were safe, and that smile I adore so much stayed on your face."

He wrapped his hand over mine, tipping my chin up to look him in the eyes.

"You are the very air I breathe, Daniella Castille. When I am not with you, my soul wanders the planes of this world searching for you, until it is reunited with yours. And it will find you in every lifetime. I am yours."

"And you are mine."

Tears slid from the corners of my eyes as he held me. There was no greater pain in my life than knowing I had this wonderful man, and I could not be with him. There would never be another for me. It will always be him.

He dipped his head down to brush his lips against mine. My breath caught at the contact, my body going molten as he pressed his lips down onto mine.

It was sweet and soft. A test of will. A test of courage.

"Please . . ." he begged. "Please stay as far away as you can from this mess." His lips brushed mine as he spoke, his words an echo of a hurting heart.

And in that moment, I realized that there would never be another moment like this between us. That in a matter of days we could be dead on a battlefield, and all of this distance would be for nothing. So, I did the most reckless thing I had ever done in my life; I reached my lips back to his and kissed him back, harder and deeper.

I clutched his hand like the lifeline it was as my other hand slid to the nape of his neck and pulled him in tighter.

Aeddan groaned at my brashness, his hands sliding down my torso and to my back, clutching me like I was clutching him.

Our kissing increased in ferocity, our lips parting and tongues clashing in beautiful harmony. I pulled away only long enough to catch my breath before his lips were on mine again. My heart was bursting from my chest; the poor thing unable to hold back any longer.

I broke the kiss off again, my hands holding the sides of his face and stroking his cheek with a loving touch.

"Is everything okay?" he asked softly.

I smiled at him in a way I knew I never would anyone else. I reached a hand down to grab his in mine. I tugged it gently, urging him to follow me over to where the fireplace roared and the couches welcomed us with blankets and pillows.

"Dani, what are you . . ."

I dropped his hand when I had us in the center of the carpet and took a small step back. He watched my motions carefully, wondering what I was going to do next.

Silently, I bent down and undid the laces of my boots. I kicked them off and tossed them to the side, my eyes never leaving Aeddan's. I watched as he stared confused and then realization hit him. His eyes turned hungry. Desperate.

I untucked the shirt from my pants next; Aeddan swallowing hard as the skin of my midriff was exposed. I pulled the shirt over my head entirely, my bandaged chest the only thing keeping me from baring myself to him. I took that off too.

Aeddan clenched his jaw, his hands making fists like he was fighting for control of his body. Still, I kept on. I quietly removed my pants and undergarments, tossing them to the pile of clothes that had now accumulated to the side.

On shaky feet, I walked slowly to Aeddan, letting him get his fill of watching my body move toward him. I felt powerful and more alive in this moment than any other in my life. With my eyes still trained on his, I rest my hands on his hips, fisting the fabric and pulling until it was hanging loose.

"Dani . . ."

"Arms up."

He did as I asked, the tension in his upper body forcing his muscles to flex. I tossed his shirt over to where I left mine and I did what I had longed to do: I placed my hands to his bare chest and kissed the skin where his heart beat softly.

Aeddan groaned, the sound spurring me to kiss his chest again. I created a line of small kisses up to his neck and then his jaw, stopping the trail just as I was ready to kiss his lips again.

"There will never be anyone else in this world for me. You have my heart and my soul already. Now I want you to have my body."

His hands grabbed my bare waist, his fingertips digging into the flesh.

"Dani, if we . . ."

"I know," I breathed. "There's no going back for me either."

In one swift motion, he scooped me up and crashed his lips to mine, his kisses coming desperate and hurried as he took me down to the carpet.

I moaned as his lips found the hollow of my throat, kissing and sucking on the tender flesh with delight. He trailed down further, sending sparks cascading over my body, and when his mouth caught my nipple and flicked it with his tongue, I nearly cried in ecstasy.

"Aeddan," I breathed as he kissed and sucked, nipping the sensitive bud until I was arching into his chest. He paid the same amount of attention to the other one, his free hand kneading my chest.

"Perfect . . ." he whispered against my skin. "Absolutely." Kiss. "Fucking." Another kiss. "Perfect."

He kissed me tenderly down to my navel, his hands moving to my knees and pushing them open, so I was bared completely to him.

"You're fucking gorgeous, Dani." He slunk down to his stomach, pressing another tender kiss to the top of my sex. I bucked my hips against him at the sensation. "When you come, Princess, I want it to be with my name on your lips. Do you understand me?"

Yes. Gods, yes, did I understand. My entire body was alight now, every cell craving his touch.

He smacked my pussy, eliciting a tiny scream from me. "I said, do you understand me?"

"Yes," I whimpered.

"Good girl."

He wasted no time as his tongue licked me clean up my entrance, my body going molten as he dove his tongue deep into me.

The restraint he held onto before was gone as he fucked me with his tongue, sucking and kissing like a man starved in the desert for water. My hands plunged into his hair, gripping onto him desperately. He met my demand by sliding a finger into me and curling it till he hit my sweet spot over and over again.

"Gods!" I cried, as he inserted a second finger, his tongue swooping over the sensitive bud at my apex.

"Fuck," I whimpered. "Aeddan, I'm going to come . . ."

He thrust his fingers harder and deeper till I was right on the verge of combustion and then he . . . stopped. What?

I sat up, quickly looking down to him.

"Aeddan, I was just about to—"

He pressed a finger to my lips, a wicked grin on his face.

"I said you would call my name when you came." He stood up, his hands undoing the laces of his pants. From here, I could see the length of him stretching against the fabric. "But I didn't tell you when you could."

He was big, bigger than I anticipated. I swallowed hard as he removed his articles of clothing and he sprung free. My mouth watered at the sight of him.

"That's right, Princess," he said, going back down to his knees. "Look all you want because this is all yours."

He hovered his body over mine, placing a kiss to my lips. And then another each time he lowered his body closer to mine until we were chest to chest. His hand reached between us, lining his cock up with my entrance.

"I'll go slow," he purred in my ear. "Just let me know if I hurt you."

I wiggled my hips forward, urging him closer. Aeddan let out a husky laugh. "Always the impatient one, my Princess."

I was going to say something sassy back, but my words were cut off as he slid the tip of himself in. My breathing hitched, my hands flying to his shoulders as I clutched onto him.

He pulled out slightly, sliding back in with a small thrust. I moaned at the sensation, my leg wrapping around his waist to urge him in more.

He obliged my request; his thrusts coming in faster and deeper.

More. I needed more.

"Aeddan, please . . ." I begged.

"I don't want to hurt you."

"I don't care." I met his gaze with my own. "I need you. All of you. Right now. Please."

Never have I ever begged for something so much in my life and not felt like a coward. But this was Aeddan. He was my heart, and I wanted to brand that on my body forever.

He kissed me again as he pulled out to the tip and slammed back into me fully. I cried out in pain and pleasure, my body singing at his touch.

He continued his thrusting at a punishable pace, our bodies going slick with sweat.

"Gods, Dani. You feel so good," he groaned, which only made me want him more.

My body craved him and responded to his touch in ways I never knew existed. Stars burst behind my eyes as I felt tension build in my abdomen, a tingling sensation shooting down my spine.

"Aeddan . . ." I breathed. "Aeddan . . ."

I clung to him as he thrust harder and faster into me, my orgasm threatening to tear me apart from the inside out.

"Aeddan!"

He grabbed my face and kissed me harshly. "That's a good girl. Now, look at me, Dani."

I did what I was told and gazed into his eyes. "I want you to look at me when I come in you. When you come on me."

There was something so primal in his words, so dangerous and reckless that I couldn't resist his demands. He fucked me harder and deeper until I felt his cock twitch and he grunted; my body spasming as my orgasm rocked through me.

I called his name like a prayer, repeating it over and over as wave after wave of pleasure coursed through me.

"That's it, Dani. Come for me. I got you, Princess. I got you . . . Fuck."

He slammed into me once more to the hilt, holding himself there as he spilled himself into me.

"Fucking hell," he groaned as he brought his lips to mine in a string of sweet and soft kisses. "There will never be another for me."

I pushed his sweaty hair from his face, smiling sweetly up at him.

"Never."

He gave me a final kiss before sliding out of me and onto his back, pulling me into his chest in one motion. I breathed in the scent of him—cinnamon and leather. I wanted it imprinted on me forever.

We laid curled there for a long time until I felt the rise and fall of his chest deepen and soft snoring filled the room. I smiled to myself as I pushed up on my elbow to look at him.

It was the most peaceful I had ever seen him. He looked almost boyish with the way his face softened and his hair curled around his forehead.

Aeddan. My Aeddan.

I reached up and dragged a blanket from the couch and over our bodies, snuggling us in. I was too drunk on euphoria to care about anything else in this moment. Right now, all that mattered was that Aeddan was here in my arms, and I wasn't ever letting go.

30

TOO LITTLE, TOO LATE

A blonde haired, blue-eyed little girl ran across a field of flowers, her brother following close behind holding a frog. "Just touch it!" he hollered as she screamed.

Behind them watched their mother, a woman of dark hair and tanned skin from working in the sun's hottest days. She laughed as she watched her children laugh and play. The boy tossed the frog back to the earth and continued his chase of his sister.

They were twins, identical in face but could not be more different when it came to their personalities. He was wild and free while she liked to know before she jumped. They were the perfect replicas of their parents.

Their father came up the road just then, smiling and shouting at them that he was back. He was a professor, and a damn good one. People came from all over the kingdom to hear his expertise. He was kind, generous, and fiercely protective of the family he had been given.

"Good afternoon, my love," he said, planting a kiss to the mother's cheek.

"Welcome home, my love," she said, placing a kiss to his lips.

They were madly in love and near inseparable. They had been through hell and came out on top. They had everything they ever wanted.

That's when the clouds turned grey and black, and thunder and lightning cracked across the flower fields.

The children screamed.

"Mama! Papa!" they shouted as they ran home to their cottage. "Help us!"

"My babies!" cried the mother. She stepped forward to go after her children, but her foot got stuck. She looked down to see a stream of red. She turned her head, following its path, and that's when she screamed. And screamed.

For her love laid in the cold, dead grass; eyes glassy and body like stone.

"Save me, Mama! Save me!"

The woman was too stunned to move, too stunned to think.

"Dani," the father gasped, blood dripping in a trail from his mouth. "I-I . . ."

The woman screamed as her heart cleaved itself into a million pieces. Aeddan . . . her Aeddan.

"Dani . . ." he murmured one last time as the thunder boomed in the distance.

She heard her name echo in her head with each stroke of sound from the storm until she was gasping for breath and holding her ears. She wanted to make it stop . . . make it stop . . . make it stop.

That's when my eyes flew open and I found myself with shallow, rapid breathing.

It was a dream. It was all a dream. Or a beautiful nightmare.

But the loud noises and the call of her name were real, and soon Poppi was bursting into her room, breathing as if she had sprinted her way here.

"Dani, you need to get up," she commanded. "Get dressed because they're here . . . oh, my gods."

Poppi had stormed through the room and around the couches to find me laying on the floor bundled in a blanket with Aeddan.

Hurt and betrayal marred her features as she took in the sight before her. Her mouth dropped in surprise, her eyebrows scrunching together.

"How could you?" she whispered, shaking her head with disgust before turning and stomping back out the door.

"Poppi," I called after her. "Poppi, come back!"

I threw the blanket off me and reached for Aeddan's shirt on the ground to cover up with. I was nearly to the door when two more figures graced its entryway.

Maddox and Harrison were dressed in their battle blacks; metal shoulder pads and breast plates emblazoned with the Serpent of Imeria and swords ready for battle.

"What's going on?" Maddox asked as he took in my appearance. His eyes traversed down my bare legs and then roamed to the still made bed. Finally, they settled on the couch and the person who was standing there in nothing but his pants.

"Holy shit," Harrison breathed.

"You fucking idiots," Maddox chided.

The men pushed further into the room, slamming the door behind them.

"Are you two actually insane?" Maddox asked in bewilderment. "Seriously. For once, did either of you think this through?"

"Calm down, Televerre," Aeddan said sternly. The scent of cinnamon and leather washing over me as I felt Aeddan come stand behind me. I wanted to melt into his chest, feel his arms wrap around me as he told me everything was going to be okay.

Instead, I wrapped my arms around my middle, holding myself together as guilt and shame hung over me like a cloud.

"Do you even realize the implications of what you have done?" Maddox pressed on. "Damien is here. Do you think he is going to take it well when he finds out you fucked his future Queen?"

"Don't be so crass," I said sullenly.

I looked to my friend. He was angry, but I could tell behind it all that he wouldn't be for long. It wasn't too long ago he was urging Aeddan and I together. Not long ago that Aeddan confessed his feelings about me to him and Harrison.

Maybe that's why they looked so shocked and stunned. Because maybe this was too little, too late.

"We never meant for anyone to find out," I tried again. "We just . . ."

"We know," Harrison said, with a surprisingly gentle tone. "We know."

Silence hung thick in the air as we all grappled to compose ourselves.

"Why are you here?" Aeddan finally asked.

Maddox switched to soldier mode. "The Fae are here. Their ships have been spotted just off the horizon and they're approaching fast. At this speed, they'll be here before nightfall."

My breathing ceased. The Fae. They were here. Already? No. It wasn't possible.

But wasn't it? Afterall, the last few days of my life here have been filled with nothing but the impossible.

"Clara is summoning all Serpentine Guard members to the War Room," Harrison chimed in. "Dani, I think it best you find Poppi and meet us there."

"Right. Yes. Of course." I needed to snap out of this trance. The Fae were here which meant we had very limited time to form the ranks and secure the palace. We had so much to do, and I needed to speak to Poppi.

Harrison put a hand to Mads' shoulder. "We'll leave you two." Harrison pulled Maddox back out the door, the latter looking none too pleased with the situation and the former . . . well, he paused with the door half-closed.

"I wish it could be different for you both," he said sympathetically before the door clicked back in place.

"Oh my gods." I turned, my head falling into Aeddan's chest as his arms wrapped around me.

"It's okay," he murmured against my hair. "It's okay. I've got you."

"Aeddan, what have we done?"

I looked up into his beautiful face, the flashes of him lying dead in the flower field flashing through my mind. My heart clenched with worry and fear.

"We can deal with the consequences later," he stated, kissing me on the head. "Right now. We have a battle to win."

He was right, and I shook my head in agreement because forming words was too much work.

We separated unwillingly; Aeddan finding the rest of his clothes as I stripped off his shirt. I stood there stark naked and watched as he dressed quickly and efficiently. He would have to run to the north tower to suit up before heading back to the War Room; our time together coming to a grinding halt.

He watched me watching him, and when he stood back up and walked over to me, I couldn't help but feel the pangs of loss. This could very well be the last time I ever see him.

"Come here," he murmured as he grabbed my face and placed his forehead against mine. "I know what you're thinking, Princess. And this isn't the end. It's just the beginning. I need you to hold on, okay?"

He lowered his lips and kissed me tenderly. I wrapped my arms around him, pulling him in close one more time. My whole life I made myself into a hardened warrior, someone who didn't let emotions cloud her judgment or get in the way of the things she wanted. But as I kissed Aeddan, I realized how wrong I had been to not let a feeling like this into my life.

It gave me a reason to fight. A reason to believe. And I would stop at nothing now to make sure the man in front of me made it out of this mess alive.

"I'll see you soon," he said before placing one last kiss and walking to the door. He turned with a hand on the handle to look at me one last time. "Beautiful."

Then he was out the door and running into the hands of danger.

I scoured the palace for any sign of Poppi. The archives, the parlor, several different rooms, the great hall, even the Ring. And still, no sight of my friend.

The look of devastation on her face as she saw me lying next to Aeddan will forever be seared in my brain. She would tell Damien what she saw; that I was sure of. The question was when she would reveal it.

Poppi was calculated enough to strike when the opportunity best suited her. One thing she didn't know is how it would also affect Aeddan. The Serpentine Guard was quietly known but not well understood. The oath the bound warriors swore was to forsake all others but the Queen under the punishment of death. If Poppi told Damien about what she saw, Aeddan and I would be reunited all right, but beyond the veil.

A group of soldiers ran past me, their footfalls heading out to the Ring. Vantage point wise, the cliffs offered a great view of the water and were within reasonable distance of the docks. Admiral Luscette would have at least a dozen boats from her fleet heading out to meet the Fae at this point. Or at least I hoped.

I turned the last corner, the door to the War Room coming into view. If Poppi wasn't here at this point, then she had bolted from the palace, and that would officially be a problem for later.

I threw the door open to find the room bursting with men and women battle ready. Papers had been strewn around, voices carried as people shouted at one another over the best course of action.

But my gaze went straight to the man at Clara's left. He no longer resembled the peaceful and sweet man I fell asleep next to last night. No. Now lines were etched on his forehead, his mouth pressed into a firm, hard line as he negotiated with Armas about where they wanted to station their people.

It took everything in me to peel my eyes from his form, and I was only able to do that because there, standing on Clara's right, was Damien. And next to him, Poppi.

If looks could kill, I would be on the floor right now based off the level of hatred Poppi leveled at me. Damien and Clara halted their conversation, turning to me in unison.

"We thought you'd never make it," Damien said as I approached his side.

"Apologies, Your Majesty," I said. "It took a moment for me to locate my leathers."

It was the truth, after all. I spent too much time digging through chests and armoires to find my old leathers. Luckily, they still fit and were a solid black. No serpent emblem in sight. If I placed a silver cape over the shoulders it would look as if the uniform had come from Lustraya itself.

Damien bent down to kiss my cheek, something he had never done. I stifled my shock as he pulled away, hoping no one thought my behavior odd, but Damien felt my body go rigid and frowned before turning his attention back to the task at hand.

"You're here now, and that's all that matters," he assured me. "Come, I need your assistance."

Aeddan watched our interaction closely, his nostrils flaring with distaste at the display Damien and I were giving the rest of the court.

"I need you to head up a unit here." He pointed to the top of one of the hills separating the palace from the city proper. "We will need to set up archers and have the rest of the foot soldiers ready as backup."

"Backup?"

He sighed. "Daniella . . ."

"Damien."

We launched into a stare off, neither one of us willing to compromise the issue at hand. Damien knew I would want to be on the front lines of any skirmish. Instead he was intentionally setting me up as far away from the action as possible.

"For once, will you please just listen?"

I ground my teeth and narrowed my eyes venomously at him but remained silent. I would not embarrass him nor myself in front of this large crowd of people. We needed to be a united front if we wanted to succeed in this face-off with the Fae.

"You will be stationed here," he said once more, pointing to the hill. "Greyborne will be here with a small unit from Lustraya and one from Imeria." His finger moved to the foothills just below. "Poppi will be on the opposite side with a legion of Imerians; Halle at the front lines."

"I told you we don't need you there," Clara said, exasperated. "My warriors are more than capable of defending their own ground. We need you at the high points. Here, here, and here."

"We're wasting time, woman," he spat. "The Fae grow closer as we argue. You don't know how they fight. We do. Letting just one of our soldiers be there to help guide could mean the difference in countless lives being lost."

"Don't act all high and mighty, you ignorant—"

"Enough," I found myself saying. "Damien is right. There is a time to argue and it isn't now. We need to mobilize as many soldiers as we can. Dispersing is a sound strategy, Clara. In the spirit of cooperation, I will take my unit to the hilltop and provide archer support. The rest go on horseback to guide those on foot. By now, I hope we have some ships already out in the water to begin the first phase of attack."

"That's right," General Armas said. "Luscette has taken fourteen ships out and we await their signal. With any luck, the Fae see our numbers and turn around."

I scoffed. "They would never back down from a fight. This is going to be their favorite challenge yet." I turned to the room. "Now is not a time to let bias and bad blood spoil our unity. We have one goal and one common enemy, and that is to protect these walls and these people. If anyone has a problem with that, they can meet me on the battlefield."

No one so much as moved a muscle as I finished my rant. Good. They needed a firm hand.

"Kristian," I called, looking for his familiar face. He appeared next to me, having been resting against the far wall, waiting for orders. "You and me to the stables. We have a lot of ground to cover."

"After you, Your Highness," he said with a wink. Gods, I missed him. And Gunnar, wherever he was.

In the middle of the table I spotted Viper, his wickedly keen eyes observing everything that was happening at our end. The corner of his mouth tipped up slightly and it sent a shiver down my back. That kind of approval could mean so many things to Viper, and I dare not guess which one it was.

"Let's go," I said to Kristian, turning our backs.

"Wait," Clara called. "Wait," she repeated. I turned to face her as she walked to the back corner of the room. She picked up a long black leather sheath, a sword with a blue sapphire inlaid at the top of the hilt, the metal workings twisting and weaving like the waves of the sea.

I let out a small gasp as she walked back to me and set the sword in my hands.

"I almost forgot," she said, so no one else could hear her. "This belongs to you."

I gripped the sword firmly, looking at my mother with wonder. I thought I lost this the night of the ball, but here it was as if it and I had never been parted. I pulled the sword out, careful as to not hit Clara with it.

The metal gleamed in the firelight, the etchings on the edge of the blade catching and dancing in its glow.

"Samir found it and had it polished before he left," she touched my cheek. "He would be proud to see the woman you've become in his absence. Now go. We haven't got much time."

I nodded, forcing the lump in my throat down as I strapped the sword to my back and grabbed Kristian. Behind us, the room exploded in conversation again.

"That was . . ." Kristian began. "Intense."

"That's my mother for you."

He looked down to me and grinned. "I missed you, Dani."

"I missed you too," I said back with equal sincerity. "Now let's go kick some Fae ass."

31

SAVIOR

Everywhere we turned, guards and soldiers took up their battle stations. Even outside in the stables, the horses were saddled with their own forms of armor. I reached for my mare, their coat shiny and stance strong. They had been well cared for since I'd been here.

We brought them out of the stables and into the fray, each of us attaching our shields to the sides, and a bow and arrow at our backs.

"Where are our units?" I asked Kristian.

Given the state of my morning wake-up call, I didn't exactly get all the details I needed before going into the strategy meeting.

"They should be just at the edge of the palace gates waiting for us," he said. "We ride together but once we get to the bottom of the hills we'll have to separate."

"Of course."

"Anything I should be made aware of when it comes to these Imerians?"

I chuckled. "Not really. They're about as stubborn willed and headstrong as the rest of us. Though, they might just ignore you if you speak. They'll follow direction, but it will be a quiet ride."

"Sounds good to me," he replied as he dug his heel into his horse's side. "As long as they don't get us killed."

We spurred the horses into action, galloping away from the palace as fast as we could. I took the chance to peak over my shoulder and out to the cliffs. I thought that I would barely be able to glimpse the approaching Fae, but wrong I was.

Though faint, I could see the white sails of over a dozen ships streaming forward to the cliffs. Kristian followed my gaze and I could see the swift shift of panic in his eyes.

"The closer they get, the more the chance of them bottoming out on the rocks increases. If the gods will it, the tide will be going out by the time they get here. It will slow them down."

Kristian nodded, unconvinced, but like the rest of us, he shoved that fear deep down and locked his gaze forward again; our priority being getting settled in our stations.

It was a short ride, and soon we were coming up on the blended units of Imerians and Lustrayans, neither of which looked happy about being put in the proximity of the other.

We pulled against our reigns, sending clops of dirt flying and our horses whining our arrival. Dozens of soldiers turned their heads in our direction, the others too far away to notice what was happening.

"Soldiers," I yelled over the buzzing of conversation. I waited till there was silence before continuing. "For those of you who may not know me, I am Princess Daniella of Lustraya and this is Lieutenant Greybourne of Amir. We are here to lead you to your battlegrounds. Archers!" Several heads perked up. "You're with me. Ground men, you're with Kristian."

As if working as one mind, Kristian navigated away from me, his men and women following him. I stayed where I was, my archers shuffling through the crowd and to me. I counted fifty of them and felt that pit in my stomach open.

Only fifty archers against an entire fleet of Fae. By the old gods, I prayed they were the best shots in the whole continent. I watched as they formed ranks without hesitation, the black and silver armor of the two kingdoms melding together in a curtain of chaos.

"We must hurry to the top of that hill." I pointed out in the distance. "From there, you will spread out and wait for my signal. Your target is the Fae. They will be coming from the coast, so keep your eyes peeled for your flanks.

"They are fast, agile and can hear from across the fields. Any word you say, they will know. So, unless it's important, I suggest keeping it to yourself if you don't want them knowing your location. Any questions?" When none of them moved, I took it as my sign to turn my horse to the front and set it into a trot.

The trek to the hill was agonizingly slow and I did my best to not let my impatience show. Kristian and his soldiers followed closely behind us. He had a hundred men at his disposal; all of which I hoped made it to see another day.

When the road forked, I went high as Kristian stayed low. I waved my band of archers on, checking to make sure Kristian didn't need anything before we parted. He looked at me with sorrowful eyes.

"If this goes badly—" he started to say before I cut him off.

"This is not a goodbye, Kristian. We will live to see tomorrow."

"If this goes badly," he stated again. "Then I want you to know it has been an honor getting to know you and fighting by your side. You are the princess that Lustraya has been waiting for."

His words struck me deep and it filled me with pride for the kingdom that I now called my home. He turned his horse and raced after his soldiers, leaving me no choice but to do the same. As I rode up the hill, I realized that we had something that the Fae would never have—hope.

They were a people filled with greed and hate. And while the humans had their downfalls, we at least had the courage to stand up and fight back against their evil.

# # #

The afternoon sun began its descent, and as we stood upon the hilltop and watched the Fae ships grow closer, I could begin to feel their anticipation creep in. Many of them hopped foot to foot anxiously; most of them double and triple checked their bow strings and their arrows for any deformities.

For anyone who ever talked about the glories of battle, they made damn sure to leave out the part where it was incredibly boring. Not that I was eager for there to be dead bodies littering the grass between here and the palace. It was more of the patience needed to keep myself and my unit from acting out.

The sails of the Fae came closer, and when I saw a man atop a horse come to the peak of the cliff top, I knew the time had come.

I could tell from the glint of the metal of the helmet that it was Armas and the man next to him had to be Anders. At least I hoped it was. There is no telling if plans had changed since Kristian and I departed from the palace.

The shadows of men crossed the field; hundreds of soldiers coming to take their place to hold the line against the looming threat. The sound of cannon fire began to fill the air as the Fae met the Imerian armada head on.

"Ready your bows!" I shouted. "Form your lines!"

The archers hurriedly secured their quivers to their backs and brought their bows into place at their sides. They did as they were told and moved into two formations, one line going high while the other went low.

"You do not release an arrow until I tell you to! You stay low to the grass and wait. Our best advantage is that they don't see us coming from the air. Let those on the ground take the attention. If something happens, you hold these lines. You do not stop firing until your quiver is empty and once it is, you keep fighting.

"The Fae do not expect us to be capable and willing to fight; to die. They will wreak havoc upon this world if we do not stop them. It is up to us to give them pause, to make them retreat. We can win this, but only if you believe it is possible. Are you all with me?"

I waited for them to shout in agreement, but as the trained and smart soldiers they were, they didn't. Good. Their tight set jaws and determined faces were all I needed as confirmation.

"Let's give them hell."

Cannon fire continued until the first Fae ship reached the harbor. A second one followed right after and it brought me immense relief to see it crash on the rocks just as I hoped it would.

The ship bottomed out, the hull cracking and splitting. The shouts of the Fae rang out as their boat failed them. But even so, they poured out from it and into the water; their powerful bodies working through the water and to the shore like it was nothing at all.

I felt the magic in me stir, felt it coil itself tight.

I wonder if Poppi and Viper could feel their magic like I could? Was theirs protesting this fight too or was it just mine?

I watched the two men from the top of the cliff backtrack down and to the waiting lines on the field. They turned their horses away to opposite sides, each of them sending warning of the impending fight.

I saw the front lines form their shield walls, watched as the soldiers all held their swords a bit higher and tighter. My own archers squirmed from their positions, the anticipation growing on us all.

"Steady," I reminded them. "Stay steady."

More ships reached the coastline, more row boats pouring from them after the disaster of the first few boats getting too close to the shore.

And then, it began.

The first group of Fae made their appearance, their tall and lithe bodies coming up from the cliff's hillside in swift, easy strides. My magic snapped its jaws.

More followed until nearly two hundred Fae were charging to the waiting human army. Armas raised his sword high and mighty, Anders right behind him with the wailing of a battle cry.

The front line was the first to move, the shield wall taking the brunt of the Fae impact. Spears reached through the wall and out, slicing and tearing at the Fae's skin as they attempted to leap over and through.

But the wall held, and soon the second wave of the human army began to move; Armas and Anders at the helm. They swooped in from the sides, the men forming a crescent around the Fae; the maneuver a way to try and limit their mobility and catch them off guard. The more that went down now, the better.

"Hold!" I called again as I saw one of my archers twitch with the need to shoot.

More Fae crawled up the hill as another line of humans entered the fray. Maybe it was the magic or just experience, but I could smell the blood beginning to cover the soil; both human and Fae.

More of the bodies below us crashed and fell. From my point, I couldn't tell who was fairing worse. All I knew is that soon the last of the human line ran into battle and phase one of our attack strategy was over.

"Archers! To your feet!"

They stood immediately, their feet finding their ground and arms raising to pull arrows into bow strings.

"Ready!"

They notched their arrows. Below us, I heard Kristian give the call, and he and his men were off and running to the Fae who had broken free and were heading this way.

I watched my friend descend into the chaos and though my heart ached to see him run toward danger, the soldier in me snapped into place harder. He could only come back alive if we did our job and do it we would.

"Aim!" I held my arm in the air, waiting for the precise moment when the Fae would enter our strike zone.

Come on, come on, come on . . .

They were close, so close. I could see the top of Kristian's helmet first and then I saw the Fae.

"Fire!"

Arrows of silver, blue, purple, and black soared through the air; a faint whistling accompanying them as they met their marks. Fae after Fae dropped to the ground; the ones left standing looking around for the culprit.

"Again!" Once more, they notched their arrows and drew them back. "Fire!"

The second volley hit home once more just as more human soldiers came onto the battlefield. Poppi and I had only enough time to teach the Serpentine Guard how to attack and avoid their speed, which was how I was able to pick them out so easily on the field. Where they moved, bodies dropped. Where they weren't, carnage lay in wake.

Arrow after arrow, my archers launched. The Fae were onto us and now able to dive away from their oncoming attack. I drew my sword from my back, feeling the strength of Samir wrap itself around me.

I would not stay on this hilltop a coward.

I looked to the man beside me, a first lieutenant for Lustraya.

"I'm going down there," I announced. "Keep them firing until you can no longer and then run for cover. If the Fae get to you, you will die. And we need archers. So do not fail me."

He nodded once, bowing to me with, "Yes, Your Highness."

I paid no more mind to what happened next as I turned my horse around and flew down the hillside to the battlefield.

My blood roared in my veins, my horse carrying me fast on the wind. If I made it out of this alive, there were going to be many people angry with me and I didn't care. I knew what I could do, what I had to do.

We moved closer to the field, and soon the smell of gore and hatred filled my nostrils. I raised my sword in front of me and struck the first Fae I could, lobbing his head right off his shoulders and to the ground. He had been making his way to the archers.

Arrows soared above me; the lieutenant doing the job I had given him beautifully.

Another Fae swooped for me, and I managed to get a slash to her abdomen. She dropped to her knees as the blood left her.

On and on I moved, working my way through the outskirts and into the craziest part of the battle.

Shouting overwhelmed my ears; the ferocity of metal on metal ringing louder than any bell. My horse stayed steady underneath me as we stormed through, taking down as many foes as possible.

"That a girl, that a—fuck!"

The horse bucked and shot to the side, launching me from the saddle as she did. We both hit the sodden ground with a thunk and a splash. My head spun, my ears ringing as I lifted my head to see what happened. Empty eyes met mine as the horse laid there lifeless.

She was dead.

And I was caught in the middle of the battlefield with three Fae charging toward me. I didn't have time to mourn the creature as I stood on shaky legs and reached for my sword. They were on me seconds later, their steel reaching out to meet mine.

Our dance began, and Poppi was right about their swiftness. They moved like a light breeze and as sharp as a blade. They cut and spun around me, leaving me very little time to roll out and under their advancements.

I managed to land a cut to the face of one while sending a dagger into the thigh of another. The man screamed just before I sent the end of my sword sliding through the skin of his neck. He screamed no longer.

More bodies fell and as I searched around for an extra weapon, I watched in horror as Maddox limped backward from his advancing attacker. My heart stopped. Time stopped.

The Fae pulled back his sword and sent it careening for Mads' head.

"Nooooo!" I screamed so loud and intensely that I didn't realize I was doing it until I was. It was the mountain pass all over again, and instead of Nic, it was Mads.

No, no, no, no. Not him. Not today.

I pushed the scream further, taking a step with it as my palms reached forward and to the side.

"Noooo!" I screeched, sending wave after wave in the direction of the Fae.

Maddox fell backward as the Fae grabbed its ears. Seconds later, his head was rolling from his shoulder as Poppi walked forward to help Mads to his feet.

"About fucking time!" she called, before taking on another Fae in front of her.

Magic. The scream was magic, and it was alive and buzzing through my veins now. It felt good, like everything that was meant to be was at my fingertips. When I felt the magic stir earlier, I was scared. The thought to use it in battle had crossed my mind but after the disaster of the hollow, I was terrified to touch it again.

"You need a conduit. Something to anchor the magic. Keep the balance . . ."

The balance. There needed to be a balance.

I stared down at my hands and knew what I had to do. It was crazy and stupid. It would probably get me killed, but it was worth a shot.

I placed my hands to the ground, my knees sinking into the muck and ruin. I pulled on the tether that ground me to my magic, but instead of yanking on it, I coaxed it like I would do a lover.

Help me, I said to it. *Help me right this wrong.*

I felt the magic run to my hands and through my arms. I felt it seize my entire being again and for a moment I panicked. I would lose control after this. Was I ready?

The ground rumbled under me in reply. Yes. Yes, I was ready.

I gave myself over to it: to the power, the feeling, and the unknown. Let it guide me into what I wanted it to do. I closed my eyes and pictured tree roots growing out long and strong to reach up and grab Fae and pull them down. I pictured lightning cracking across the sky and striking our enemies down where they stood. I pictured the ground cracking open and swallowing those who sought to harm anyone and everyone I cared for.

And then the magic surged deep and true.

Roots sprouted, thunder rumbled, and the ground shook. My vision clouded over in a blue haze as I gave myself over to the magic; letting the dead bodies that littered the field be the payment for saving those that lived. Their sacrifice now aiding me in my cause.

I roared out and lightning cracked. I didn't know what or who I was. I couldn't see if what I had asked was coming to fruition but by the screams that followed, I knew it was.

Still the ground rumbled, and I roared once more, digging my hands deep into the ground until it was up to my wrists. I was one with the magic now. I would become it.

"Dani!" Someone called but I didn't know who. It could be so many people. "Dani, stop!"

The magic pulsed harder until it was ripping the air from my lungs; my body going weak as the magic got stronger. It was consuming me now, taking everything that I was giving it.

"Dani, let go! Let go of the magic! You're going to die!"

It was Poppi. My friend, my enemy, my mirror. I listened for her voice once more, clawing my way through my body and back to the light.

Lightning cracked in the sky again.

"Dani, you have to stop! Reel the magic back in!"

But that's not what it wanted. It wanted full release from the home it had been buried in. I felt her grab my face and pull it down from where it faced the sky.

"Princess, let go."

That soft voice wasn't Poppi though, it was Aeddan. He was alive, and he was touching me.

"Let go, Dani. You've saved us. Now let it go."

But I couldn't. I was too deep.

"Come back to me, Princess."

I heard the love in his voice, felt his forehead touch mine as he whispered the same words once more to me. Aeddan. I had to come back for him. I couldn't leave him. Not now, not ever.

I thrashed against the tether once more, but it only got tighter.

Please, I begged the magic. *Let me go back to him. Let me go.*

There was a small moment of restraint, and I used the opening to kick myself back to the surface of my being. I pushed and pushed like I was coming up from the depths of the sea with no air.

"That's it. Come home," he praised, his touch becoming my anchor to reality.

Home. Home was Aeddan. Home was Imeria and Lustraya. Home was where I learned to fight and love. I kicked to the surface and breathed in deeply, collapsing into the arms of the man who turned my world on its axis.

I coughed and sputtered, the noise raspy and choked.

"What the hell was that?" Armas asked with what sounded like fear. "She almost took out our right flank!"

Aeddan cradled my head to his chest, pulling me close and out from the trench I had dug myself into.

I looked around to see Damien, Anders, Poppi, Harrison, and Mads forming a circle around where Aeddan and I crouched on the ground. I couldn't form the words to explain myself even if I wanted to.

All of them exchanged looks of bewilderment and confusion, except Poppi and Damien, the latter telling the group, "She's a practitioner."

"A what?" Armas asked incredulously.

"Daniella is a practitioner," he said again, turning his full attention to the general. "One history has been waiting for."

Armas was right to look scared at Damien's admission. I don't know what damage my magic just did, but I know what I felt. It was complete and total power, and I wanted more—needed more. The magic in me swirled around gleefully at the thought.

"I tried to tell you, General. The tides have shifted, and the time is now." Damien looked down to me with hope and admiration; two things I did not deserve. My friends all followed suit, their love marring their fear of me. "She will be our salvation."

The word hung heavy around me, the precipice for such a thing too great to comprehend at a moment like this.

"No," Armas said defiantly, his jaw locking. "She will be the reason for our annihilation."

To be continued

ACKNOWLEDGEMENTS

Wow! Hello everyone and welcome back! Can you believe we have made it to book two already? Seriously, what another crazy adventure this is all becoming and there is so much I want to say, but I'll do it quickly.

Firstly, I want to thank you as a reader. You have no idea how much one person, one voice, or one social media post can influence how this book reaches people. No matter if you are family, friend, or you found *The Kingdom Accords* and *Rise of the Fallen* through the internet, I am forever grateful that you took the time out of your day to read my words.

To my lovely developmental editor Z at Blue Couch Edits, your attention to detail helped make this story what it was. You're the best! To Aspen, I am so glad we could collaborate again. See you in the next one!

To my friends and family (y'all know who you are!) who keep me sane and humble, happy hour is on me when this drops and expect more voice notes than ever before when I start working on book three. I love each and every one of you something fierce.

Thank you for reading!

Wanting to stay in the loop? Come find me on social media and sign up for my newsletter where I give all the updates and behind the scenes!

Instagram: laurenaguiar.author

Threads: laurenaguiar.author

TikTok: laurenaguiarauthor

Website: laurenaguiarauthor.com

(Are we sensing a theme here?)

About the Author

Lauren is just another millennial trying to get it together. After a lot of soul searching, she realized that her true passion in this life was storytelling and decided to honor her inner child's dream and write *The Kingdom Accords* series. With more writing soon to come follow her on social media for any and all updates to come!

9 798994 568705